To Lucia Macro, for making this happen,

And to Joyce Mulvaney,
for being there to celebrate. . .
Cheers!

And to Morgan and Brody and Mark, with love.

With gratitude to Nick
at LOST AND FOUND
at Grand Central Terminal!

WENDY CORSI STAUB

LIVE TO TELL

AVON

An Imprint of HarperCollinsPublishers

AVON BOOKS
An Imprint of HarperCollins*Publishers*
10 East 53rd Street
New York, New York 10022-5299

Copyright © 2010 by Wendy Corsi Staub
Excerpt from *Scared to Death* copyright © 2011
by Wendy Corsi Staub
ISBN-13: 978-1-61664-250-1

First Avon Books paperback printing: March 2010

Avon Trademark Reg. U.S. Pat. Off. and in Other Countries, Marca Registrada, Hecho en U.S.A.
HarperCollins® is a registered trademark of HarperCollins Publishers.

Printed in the U.S.A.

Prologue

New York City

He lunges across Sixth Avenue mid-block and against the light, leaving in his wake squealing brakes, honking horns, angry curses through car windows.

No need to look over his shoulder; he knows they're back there, closing in on him.

Darting up the east side of Sixth, he blows through an obstacle course of office workers on smoke breaks, tourists walking four abreast, businessmen lined up at street food carts. Ignoring the indignant shouts of jostled pedestrians, he searches the urban landscape as he runs. July heat radiates in waves from concrete and asphalt. Sweat soaks his T-shirt.

Just ahead, across Fortieth Street, he spots the subway entrance. For a split second, he considers diving down the stairs. If a train happens to be just pulling in, he can hop on and lose them—at least for the time being.

If there's no train, he'll be trapped like a rat in a hole—unless he hoofs it through the dark tunnel and risks being electrocuted by the third rail or flattened by an oncoming express.

No thanks.

Nothing can happen to him. Not now. Not when the plan is about to come to fruition.

Not when sweet victory is so close he can taste it like sugar.

He races past the subway, his thoughts careening through various scenarios of how the next few minutes of his life might play out. They all end the same way: he's apprehended. Incarcerated.

Even if he could possibly hide in midtown Manhattan in broad daylight with the cops hot on his trail, it makes no sense to try. The NYPD aren't the only ones looking for him.

At least if he's arrested, he'll be safe—for now.

But first, he has to stash the file where no one can possibly stumble across it—and where he himself will easily be able to retrieve it and resume his plan. When he's free.

Where? Come on, think. Think!

If only he had time to open a safe deposit box somewhere.

If only he could bury it like treasure, entrust it to a stranger for safekeeping, throw it into an envelope addressed to a trusted friend in a far-off place . . .

Before all this, he had a circle of confidants.

Now, he trusts no one other than Mike.

He tried to call his old friend yesterday, since he has a vested interest in this thing.

He did leave a message: "Mike, it's me. Dude, I was right. It's bigger than I thought. I'll be in touch."

Now that he's had time to think things through, though, he's glad he didn't reach Mike. Better not to drag him into this dangerous game.

He bounds across Fortieth and up the wide concrete steps into Bryant Park, zigzagging northeast past dog walkers and the carousel; past stroller-pushing nannies and office workers eating lunch out of clear plastic deli containers.

Approaching the crowded outdoor dining patio of the Bryant Park Café, he spots a commotion beside the entrance. A young wife tries to soothe the screaming baby propped against her shoulder as her agitated husband argues loudly with the hostess about a reservation. The baby's stroller is abandoned in his path, a fuzzy pink stuffed animal lying on the ground beside it.

Seeing it, he's struck by an idea—one that's either so far out there that it'll never work, or so far out there that it *has* to work.

There's no time to sit around considering the odds.

Rather than leap over the stuffed animal, he scoops it up as he passes, hoping bystanders are too busy watching the argument at the hostess stand to notice. He doesn't bother to look back, and nobody calls out after him as he cannonballs down the wide concrete steps on the north side of the park.

Emerging onto West Forty-second Street, he hurtles eastward, passing the main branch of the library. He scoots across Fifth Avenue amid hordes of pedestrians in the crosswalk, then across East Forty-second against the red "Don't Walk" sign. With the stuffed animal tucked under his right arm, high against his chest like a football, he sprints the remaining block and a half to Grand Central Terminal.

No one—not even the national guardsmen on patrol in this post–9/11 era—gives him a second glance as he races at full speed from the Vanderbilt entrance toward the cavernous main concourse. Otherwise-civilized people zip pell-mell through here all the time. The MTA conducts its Metro North commuter line on a precise schedule; a few seconds' delay might mean waiting an hour to catch the next train to the northern suburbs.

It's been a while, yet he knows the layout of the vast rail station very well. Knows the location of the ticket counters and subway ramps, the arched whispering gallery near the Oyster Bar, the upper and lower level tracks, the stationmaster's office, the food court, the lost and found . . .

The lost and found.

Looking furtively over his shoulder, he spots a blue uniform at the far end of the corridor. Changing direction, he veers toward the steep bank of escalators leading to the subway station below Grand Central, slowing his pace just enough to be sure the cop has time to spot him. Then he skirts down the left side of the escalator with the harried walkers, past the lineup of riders holding the rubber rail along the right.

At the bottom, he hops the turnstile. Predictably, those behind him protest loudly. He races through the familiar network of corridors to an exit and a set of stairs leading up to Grand Central Terminal again, closer to Lexington Avenue. Again, he runs toward the main concourse, emerging at last beneath the domed pale blue ceiling with its celestial markings.

He takes the stairs beneath the balcony back down to the lower level, and then ducks into a doorway leading to an empty track.

Panting, huddled in the shadows against the wall, he turns the stuffed animal over and over, looking for the most unobtrusive spot.

There.

With his index finger, he probes at a seam in the synthetic fur. The toy is well made; it takes a few moments before the stitching gives way. He creates a small tear just wide enough.

Then he takes the memory stick from his wallet and shoves it into the hole until it disappears into the stuffing.

Swiftly examining the toy, he convinces himself no one could possibly discover the gap in the seam unless he was looking for it.

He tucks the animal under his arm again and scurries back out into the station and down a short corridor to the lost and found.

"Can I help you, sir?" asks the middle-aged woman at the service window, looking up from sorting through a labeled bin marked "February: Mittens and Gloves."

Winded, he holds up the stuffed animal. "I just found this."

She reaches for a pen. "Where? On a train?"

"No . . . on the floor."

"Where on the floor?"

"By the clock," he improvises.

She doesn't ask which clock. In this terminal, "the clock" means the antique timepiece with four luminescent opal faces that sits atop the information booth, a meeting spot for thousands of New Yorkers every day.

"All right—" She reaches for a form. "If you can fill this out and—"

"Sorry," he cuts in, "but if I don't catch the 4:39, my wife is going to kill me."

"It's only—"

He's already out the door.

He takes the stairs back up to the main concourse two at a time. Nearby, at the base of the escalators leading up to the MetLife building, a transit cop scans the crowd while speaking into a radio.

A moment later, the cop spots him, and he knows it's over.

For now.

CHAPTER ONE

Glenhaven Park, New York

MOMMY, HEEEEELLLLLLLLLLPPPPP!!!!!!!!!!!!!!!"
Startled by her daughter's scream, Lauren Walsh
drops the apple she was about to peel and bolts from the
kitchen, taking the paring knife with her, just in case.

Sadie is in the living room—in one piece, thank God,
and sitting on the couch in front of the television, right
where Lauren left her about two minutes ago. Tears
stream down her face.

"What's wrong, sweetie? What happened?"

"Fred! Fred's gone!"

She immediately grasps the situation, seeing the contents of Sadie's little Vera Bradley tote dumped on the
couch beside her: a sticker album and stickers, a couple
of Mardi Gras necklaces, a feather boa, and the pack
of Juicy Fruit Lauren bought her at Hudson News right
before they got on the train.

So there's no intruder to fight off with a paring knife.
She loosens her grasp on the handle, the notion of using
it as a weapon suddenly seeming laughable.

Almost laughable, anyway.

Lauren has never been the kind of woman who checked the closets and under the bed. She spent dauntless years on her own, single in the city, before she met Nick.

But this is different. Living alone with a preschooler in a sprawling Victorian while the older kids are gone at sleepaway camp and their dad is—well, *gone*—has bred a certain degree of paranoia, no doubt about it.

"Mommy, find Fred!" Sadie's cherubic face is stricken, her green eyes filled with tears.

Before Nick moved out last winter, Fred was just another stuffed animal on Sadie's shelf. Someone brought it to the hospital back when Sadie was born, with a Mylar "It's a Girl" balloon tied to its wrist.

When Nick left, all three of the kids developed strange new habits. Ryan took to biting his nails. Lucy pulled out her eyelashes. Poor little Sadie, already a notoriously fussy eater, now lives on white bread, peanut butter, and the occasional sliced apple. She also regressed to thumb sucking and pants wetting, and started dragging the pink plush rabbit, newly christened Fred, everywhere she went.

Which wasn't much of anywhere until recently, because Lauren couldn't bring herself to leave the house most days. She felt as if the whole town was talking about her husband leaving her for another woman.

Probably because they really were talking about it. In a tiny suburban hamlet like Glenhaven Park, the gossip mill runs as efficiently as the commuter train line.

"Mommy."

"It's okay, Sadie. Where's Chauncey? Maybe he took Fred." God knows their border collie has been known to steal a fuzzy slipper or two—which is why he hasn't been allowed upstairs in the bedrooms in years.

"No, Fred wasn't in my bag. He didn't come into the house with me."

"Okay, so he's probably in the car."

"Go look! Please!"

Lauren is already headed for the kitchen to exchange the paring knife for her keys, biting her tongue. It's probably not good parenting to say, "I told you so" to a four-year-old.

But she *did* tell Sadie not to bring Fred with them to the city today. And when she insisted, Lauren wanted to carry the stuffed rabbit herself, worried Sadie would lose it.

Sadie protested so vehemently that it was simply easier to give in. More bad parenting.

And the fact that Lauren's about to serve apple slices with a side of peanut butter for dinner doesn't exactly cancel it out. But why bother cooking for two—one finicky preschooler and one mom who lost her appetite, along with a lot of other things, in the divorce drama.

The screen door squeaks as Lauren steps out the back door into the hot glare of late afternoon sun. The neighborhood at this hour is so still she can hear the bumblebees lazing in the coneflowers beside the small service porch.

She could cut some of the purple and white blooms and bring them inside.

But again, why bother? It's just her and Sadie.

Why bother . . . why bother . . .

So goes the depressing refrain.

There was a time when she didn't consider cooking or gardening a bother at all.

She remembers wandering around the yard with pruning shears on summer days as Ryan and Lucy romped on the wooden play set. She'd fill the house with a hodge-podge of colorful flowers arranged in Depression-era tinted glass Ball jars discovered on a cobwebby shelf in the basement. Then she'd feed and bathe the kids early, letting them stay up just long enough to greet Nick off the commuter train. He'd tell her about his day as they shared a bottle of wine over a home-cooked dinner for two, something decadent and cooked in butter or smothered in melted cheese.

That was before Nick became overly health conscious—which, surprise, surprise, was not long before he left.

But she doesn't want to think about that.

Nor does she necessarily want to think about the good old days, but she can't seem to help herself. It was on one of those hot summer nights, Lauren recalls, that Sadie the Oops Baby was conceived, after an unhealthy, fattening romantic dinner laced with cabernet and Van Morrison.

The pregnancy put on hold their plans to remodel the house. They were going to expand the kitchen, add a mudroom, replace the back stoop with a deck—something that wouldn't clash with the Queen Anne style. Nick was a big believer in preservation of architectural integrity.

Only when it came to marital integrity did he run into trouble.

They never did get around to remodeling.

Now they never will.

Lauren gazes up at the house—two stories, plus a large attic beneath the steep, gabled roof.

The clapboard façade, fish-scale shingles, and gingerbread trim are done in period shades of ochre and brick red. The classic Victorian design—tall, shuttered bay windows, a cupola, and a spindled, wraparound porch—charmed her the first time she laid eyes on it, years ago.

Painted Lady Potential, proclaimed the ad in the *Sunday Times* real estate section.

She kept reading. It got better.

Four-bedroom, two-bath fixer-upper in family neigh-borhood. Eat-in kitchen, large, level yard, detached garage. Walk to shops, train, schools.

It was located, the Realtor told her when she called about the ad, on Elm Street in Glenhaven Park. Elm Street—evocative of leafy, small-town charm. Elm Street—where families live happily ever after.

Sight unseen, Lauren was sold.

Nick was not. "*Nightmare on Elm Street,*" he told Lauren. "Ever see that movie?"

She hadn't. But lately, she's been feeling as though she lived it.

How did she end up alone in the house of their dreams?

She'll never forget the day she and Nick first set foot inside, looked at each other, and nodded. They knew. They knew this house would become home.

It—like the fact that they'd found each other, fallen in love, gotten married—seemed too good to be true.

They marveled at the china doorknobs, gaslight fix-tures, cast-iron radiators, chair rails, and pocket doors; high ceilings with crown molding; the ornate wooden staircase in the entrance hall. There were even a couple of hidden compartments where the nineteenth-century owners had stashed their valuables.

Yes, the place needed work. So what? They were young and had a lifetime ahead of them.

Now Lauren wonders, as she often has for the past few months, whether she'll have to sell the house. Some days, she wants to list it as soon as possible. Others, she's certain she can't bear to let go.

What's the old saying?

If something seems too good to be true, it probably is.

She takes a deep breath, inhaling the green scent of freshly mown grass. The lawn service guys must have been here today while she and Sadie were in the city. The flowerbeds have been freshly weeded and the boxwood hedge has been shorn into a precision horizontal border.

The yard looks a lot tidier than it did in summers past, when she handled the gardening and Nick mowed. But when they moved up here from the city, they never wanted that manicured landscape style. They never wanted to become one of those suburban Westchester families that relied on others to maintain the yard, the house, and the pets, even the kids.

Yeah, and look at us now.

First came the weekly cleaning service Lauren's friends insisted on hiring for her right after she had Sadie. By the time the two-month gift certificate expired, colic was in full swing, and Lauren was relieved to let someone else continue to clean the toilets and do the laundry.

She kept the cleaning service.

By the time Sadie was toddling, her older siblings' traveling sports teams kept the whole family on the go. Chauncey was left behind so often that Lauren was forced to hire a dog-walking service. Sure, she occasionally misses those early morning or dusk strolls with Chauncey—but not enough to go back to doing it daily.

She kept the dog walkers, too.

Nick hired the lawn service last March, just in time for the spring thaw, as he put it—ironic, because it was also just in time for the killing frost that ended their marriage.

Yes, she had seen it coming. For a few months before it happened, anyway. That didn't make it any easier for her to bear.

And the kids—Lauren hates Nick for their pain; hates

herself, perhaps, even more. She was the one who'd gone to great lengths to maintain the happy family myth, such great lengths that the separation blindsided all three of them.

Nick had wanted to tell Ryan and Lucy last fall that they were seeing a marriage counselor. But Lauren was afraid they'd start piecing things together, suspecting the affair. Or that they'd ask pointed questions that would demand the ugly truth or whitewashed lies.

Nick was probably right—though she wouldn't admit that to him. They should have given the kids a heads-up when things first started to unravel.

He was right, too, that sending Ryan and Lucy away to camp for eight weeks was the healthiest thing for everyone.

When he suggested it back around Easter, Lauren— who for years had frowned upon parents who shipped their kids hundreds of miles to spend summers in the woods among strangers—had taken a good, hard look at what their own household had become. She was forced to recognize that her older children would be better off elsewhere while she picked up the pieces.

Still, she didn't give in to Nick about camp without a fight. God forbid she make anything easy on him in the blur of angry, bitter days after he left. She wanted only to make him suffer.

In the end, though, Ryan and Lucy went to camp.

They were homesick at first—so homesick Lauren was tempted, whenever she opened the mailbox to another woe-is-me letter, to drive up there and bring them both home. Now that it's almost August, though, it's clear from their letters that Ryan and Lucy are having a blast in the Adirondacks.

Lauren has only Sadie to worry about for the time

being, while she figures out how to move on after two decades of marriage.

She has yet to come up with a long-term plan. It's hard enough to keep her voice from breaking as she reads bedtime stories in an empty house, to fix edible meals for two—and to keep tabs on Sadie's toys.

Find Fred.

She walks down the back porch steps, past fat bumblebees lazing in the flowers, and crosses over to the Volvo parked on the driveway.

Please let Fred be in the backseat . . .

Please let Fred be in the backseat . . .

Fred is *not* in the backseat.

A lot of other crap is: crumpled straw wrappers, a dog-eared coloring book and two melted crayons, a nearly empty tube of Coppertone KIDS, a couple of fossilized Happy Meal fries, and one of Sadie's long-missing mittens whose partner Lauren finally threw away in May.

Lauren carries it all back into the house and dumps it into the kitchen garbage before returning, empty-handed, to the living room.

Sadie, tearstained and sucking her thumb, looks up expectantly.

"Sweetie, you must have dropped him, somewhere in the city. I couldn't find—"

Cut off by a deafening wail, Lauren helplessly sinks onto the couch. "Oh, Sadie, come here." She gathers her daughter into her arms, stroking her downy hair—not as blond this summer as it has been in years past.

Is it because she's growing up?

Or because she's been stuck hibernating with a shell-shocked mother who's barely been able to drag herself out of bed and face the light of day . . .

Riddled with guilt, Lauren says, "I'm sorry, baby."
About so much more than the lost toy.

"I want Fred! I love him! Please," Sadie begs. "I need
him back."

I know how you feel.

In silence, Lauren swallows the ache in her own throat
and fishes a crumpled tissue from the back pocket of
khaki shorts that last August felt a size too small. Now
they're a few sizes too big, cinched at the waist with her
fourteen-year-old's belt.

The Devastation Diet. Maybe she should write a book.

Lauren wipes her daughter's tears, then, surreptitiously,
her own. "Come on, calm down. It's going to be okay."

"I want Fred!"

Lauren sighs. "So do I."

I want a lot of other things, too.

*Looks like we're both going to have to suck it up, baby
girl.*

"Please, Mommy, please . . . where is he? Where?
Where?"

"Shh, let me think."

Mentally retracing their steps, Lauren is sure the
stuffed animal was with them in the cab from her sister
Alyssa's apartment to Grand Central, because it almost
fell out of Sadie's bag when they climbed out on Lexington. She remembers carrying both Sadie and the bag
across the crowded sidewalk, through the wooden doors,
along the Graybar passageway. She set Sadie down and
gave the bag back to her when they stopped to buy a *New
York Post* and some gum at Hudson News.

"You must have dropped Fred at the station or on the
train. Next time we go to the city we can check lost and
found," Lauren promises.

That's not going to cut it: Sadie opens her mouth and wails.

Now what?

Lauren closes her eyes and lifts her face toward the ceiling.

Where the hell is Fred?

Never mind that, where the hell is Nick?

Why does he get to start a new life and leave Lauren here alone to handle the fallout from the old? Lost toys, lost souls . . . none of it seems to be his problem anymore. No, he's moved on to a two-bedroom condo down in White Plains—furnished with "really cool stuff," according to Lucy. Complete with a "gi-mongous, kick-butt flat-screen," according to Ryan. On a high floor, "close to God and the moon," according to Sadie.

"Good for Daddy," Lauren says whenever the kids tell her stuff like that. She tries hard to keep sarcasm from lacing her words because you're not supposed to speak negatively about your ex to the children. That's got to be right up there with letting them have their way, saying *Why bother?* and *I told you so*, and giving them apples for dinner.

Then again, as far as Lauren's concerned, any bad parenting on her part is vastly outdone by the ultimate worst parenting on Nick's. Walking out on three kids pretty much takes the prize, right?

Sadie sobs on.

Lauren's eyes snap open.

"You know what? Daddy will get Fred for you."

That's right. Let Daddy deal with something for a change.

Poor Sadie cries harder—probably because she's already figured out that Daddy is hardly the most reliable guy in the world.

But it's time for him to step up.

Lauren grabs her cell phone.

Nick's is still the first number on her speed dial—only because she has no idea how to change it. Ryan had to program the phone for her when she got it, and it seems wrong to ask a twelve-year-old boy to bump his father's number to the bottom of the list—or, for that matter, delete it altogether.

At least from the speed dial. Several times, carrying her phone in her back pocket, she's apparently accidentally bumped the keypad, calling him without realizing the line was open.

"Pocket dialing," Lucy and Ryan call the phenomenon. They think it's hilarious that Nick, in the middle of a client luncheon, once got to hear tone-deaf Lauren driving along and singing at the top of her lungs the way she does when she's alone in the car—or thinks she is. Nick was amused by it, too, back when they were married.

Now that he's gone, though, pocket dialing is no laughing matter. She really doesn't want him privy to what she says or does when she assumes she's out of his earshot.

Today, Lauren dials his number the traditional way, and the line rings repeatedly. Just when she thinks the call is going into voice mail, Nick picks up.

"Hey, what's up?"

He's answered her calls that way for as long as he's had caller ID: *Hey, what's up?*

She used to think it was sweetly intimate. Now it seems cold and impersonal. Go figure. Maybe that's because he used to pick up on the first ring. Now it's the fifth, undoubtedly giving him time to roll his eyes and inform whoever happens to be in the vicinity of his window office in the Chrysler building that it's the ex, calling with some unreasonable request.

This time, he would be absolutely correct about that.

She holds the phone away from her for a moment, toward Sadie, still sobbing beside her. "Do you hear that, Nick?"

"What is it?"

"It's our daughter."

"What's the matter with her?"

"She's crying because she's lost Fred."

Lauren waits for Nick to ask who Fred is.

When he does, she hates herself for asking, in return, "How can you not know?"

Of course he doesn't know. He doesn't live here. Then again, even when he did, he never paid much attention to the kids' little quirks.

To be fair, a lot of men don't. Even her perfect brother-in-law, Ben, is an occasionally imperfect dad, according to her sister.

But Lauren isn't in the mood to be fair right now. Not with an inconsolable child on her hands and yet another lonely night stretching endlessly ahead.

"Fred is Sadie's favorite stuffed animal," she succinctly informs Nick as she carries the phone to the kitchen. "She takes Fred everywhere."

"Oh. Well, did you check the compartment in her room?" He's referring to a small nook concealed by a secret panel in Sadie's closet. A while back, Lauren had followed her nose and discovered her youngest was stashing uneaten meat and vegetables there, tired of being nagged about her fussy eating habits.

"She lost Fred in the city, not at home." Lauren picks up the paring knife again.

"What were you doing in the city?"

"Having lunch with my sister. Nick . . ." She pauses, and then swallows the next two words she was about to say.

Can you—

No, that's too wishy-washy. If she phrases it as a question, he's free to say no.

"I need you," she says instead, "to stop by the lost and found at Grand Central and pick up Fred, then bring him over here when you get home tonight."

"How do you know it's at Grand Central?"

Leave it to Nick to depersonalize Fred.

"I don't, for sure. But we were in the city when she lost him." Emphasis on the *him.*

"You were in the city today and you didn't bring Sadie to see me?"

"We were busy. I'm sure you were, too."

"Not too busy to take five minutes out for my daughter. My office is right across the street from Grand Central. You could have told me you were going to be there."

She could have. But then she'd have had to see him. And today was supposed to be an escape, not a miserable reminder of her estranged husband.

"I know where your office is," she says curtly. "Listen, you need to go check the lost and found, and if Fred's not there, then . . . I don't know, look around the station."

"*Look around?*" he echoes incredulously. "How would I ever be able to—"

"You need to do this, Nick, because, believe me, Sadie will never be able to function without Fred."

There's a pause on the other end of the line.

Lauren begins slicing the white flesh of the apple with rhythmic little jabs of the knife.

"Sadie won't be able to *function?*" Nick finally echoes in her ear. "Don't you think that's a little dramatic?"

"Hell, yes, it's dramatic. She's four, Nick. Think about it. First you left, then Ryan and Lucy did, and now Fred's gone . . ."

*And that means I'm all she's got . . . and I'm over-
whelmed, so step up, dammit!*

"I've got a client meeting. I doubt lost and found will
even be open by the time it's over."

"Then go check before the meeting."

"I'm in the middle of a workday."

"You're not too busy to take five minutes out for your
daughter. And anyway, you're right across the street from
Grand Central," she reminds him pointedly.

He sighs. "Okay. I'll go check when I have a chance.
What am I looking for, exactly?"

"A pink stuffed rabbit."

"Got it. A pink stuffed rabbit that answers to Fred."
He snickers.

There was a time when Lauren might have cracked a
smile. But now her face feels as brittle as the rest of her.
"Call me when you find him."

"You mean *if* I find him."

Him. Good. Small triumph.

"If he's not in the lost and found, then check the floor
on the entrance off Lex, and check Hudson News."

"Which Hudson News?"

"The one just off the main concourse."

"There are about a hundred Hudson News stands off
the main concourse."

"A hundred? Don't you think that's a little dramatic?"
Touché, Nick.

He sighs. "I suppose you want me to check them all."

"Only if Fred's not in the lost and found," Lauren tells
him, and hangs up.

It's been over fourteen years since Jeremy vanished, yet
every moment of the horrific aftermath remains fresh in
Elsa Cavalon's mind.

She relives the nightmare daily: realizing her son was missing, searching the house, calling Brett at work, calling 911, calling Jeremy's name through the streets of the neighborhood until she was hoarse.

"It doesn't go away."

Elsa didn't make the statement, but she might as well have.

"No," she agrees with Joan, her latest therapist, seated in a chair opposite her. "It doesn't go away."

She isn't sure what they were talking about, exactly— her mind tends to wander during her sessions. No. Not just then. Her mind wanders always, no matter where she is, to the past, and Jeremy.

It doesn't go away . . .

The pain? The regret? The guilt?

No matter. None of it goes away.

"You constantly go over every detail in your mind, looking for clues," she tells Joan. "Even after all these years, you think there might be something you missed."

Joan nods.

"You wonder what really happened that day. You wonder what's going to happen today—whether a police officer is going to show up at your door and tell you they found him. But not him. His—"

Her voice breaks. She can't say it.

His remains.

Chin in hand, Joan sits silently waiting, the way therapists so often do, for Elsa to regain her composure.

Intimately familiar with the process, she's been through more than her share of shrinks since her son disappeared.

The first, when they were still in Boston, was Dr. Hyland. She was the one who told Elsa that she had only two options.

"You can either curl up and die, Elsa, or you can go on living."

Elsa didn't care much for Dr. Hyland.

There were others. They move a lot because of Brett's job as a nautical engineer, and he insists that wherever they land, she get herself right into therapy.

In Virginia Beach, she saw grandfatherly Dr. Saunders; in San Diego, a tattooed woman named Hedy; in Tampa, the effete John Robert—pronounced *Jean Rob´ere*, though he wasn't French.

Here in coastal Connecticut, it's serious, bespectacled Joan.

None of the trained professionals can give Elsa the answers, or the forgiveness, she so desperately needs. None of them can convince her that what happened to her son wasn't her own fault, on some level.

They merely help to keep her going, reminding her of the possibility, however slight, that Jeremy himself—or the truth about what happened to him—might someday surface. That wisp of hope keeps her alive.

Hope, and the medication she's been on since her suicide attempt years ago, not long after she lost Jeremy. Antidepressants, they're called. As if swallowing a pill could magically erase one's bleak state of mind and make the world right again.

It can't. But swallowing enough pills could make it all go away—or so she decided one morning just before they moved to Virginia Beach. She had made the choice between Dr. Hyland's options at last. She had chosen to curl up and die.

Brett found her, though—just in time.

In the hospital, he stayed by her bedside for days on end, as though he was afraid she was going to try it again.

She didn't. She saw the ravaged look in his eyes. She couldn't do that to him. He couldn't bear to lose her, too.

So she was released from the hospital, and she started taking medication.

Back then, it was all Elsa could manage just to get out of bed in the mornings, numbly moving through her waking hours doing what is necessary to stay alive: namely, eating and breathing. Not much more than that, most days.

In her early twenties, Elsa had been a runway model, and she'd kept her looks over the years.

But after the tragedy, her dark hair—always kept sleek and chic—grew long and straggly. Her face, preternaturally bare of makeup, became gaunt; her figure dangerously skeletal.

For a while, she honestly thought she was going to die, even if not by her own hand.

Brett and all those therapists were right, though, about her needing to find a new purpose. When she did, she slowly came back. Not back to life. But back.

Dr. Hyland was wrong. There are other options. You can curl up and die, or you can go on living . . . or you can, as Elsa has, settle on something in between.

Every night when Nick Walsh walks into Grand Central Terminal at rush hour, he has a single objective: getting right back out again, on a northbound train, as quickly as possible.

More than ninety-nine percent of the time, that's exactly what happens. But once in a while, things go wrong. A car gets struck at a suburban crossing, a tree falls across the tracks, there's flooding in the Bronx, a power failure, ice . . .

You never know when you're going to be stuck here for a while, waiting for service to resume, or forced to rely on a bus or car service with tens of thousands of other stranded commuters.

That's why, on nights like this, when everything is moving like clockwork, you don't hang around and thus increase the odds for something to go wrong.

There's a 6:22 leaving in ten minutes from track twenty-nine, but by the time Nick detours down to lost and found on the lower level, grabs Sadie's lost toy, and makes it onto the train, there likely won't be any seats left. He'll have to wait twenty-three minutes for the next one, and by the time he's walked to his building, taken his car from the garage, and driven up to the house in Glenhaven Park and back, it'll be well past nine o'clock.

Well, if things go well in the lost and found, maybe he can still make the 6:22. Better to stand around on a moving train than in the station, right?

Having lied to Lauren earlier about having a late day meeting, he just hopes karma won't come back to bite him in the ass.

But it just slipped out. He couldn't help it. He was irritated that she'd been in the neighborhood with Sadie, hadn't bothered to tell him, then had the nerve to call him up and start ordering him around. She seemed to assume he had nothing better to do in the middle of a workday than go on a scavenger hunt to retrieve something that shouldn't have been lost in the first place.

Aren't you being a little hard on Lauren? asks an annoying little voice in the part of his brain reserved for postmarital guilt.

Maybe. But not nearly as hard as she is on me.

When he reaches the small lost and found office, several people are there ahead of him. One, a blond teenage girl about Lucy's age, is standing at the service window, scrolling on a hot pink iPod, accompanied by an equally blond friend who's busily texting into her phone. Behind them, a middle-aged businessman impatiently checks both his BlackBerry and his watch.

Taking his place in line, Nick thinks back to what the world was like in the good old days before everyone was plugged in; tries to recall whether people actually interacted with one another in public places.

At forty-five, he's plenty old enough to remember the pretechnology era, but he's never given it much thought. It all must have been terribly inconvenient and inefficient—communication, entertainment . . .

Then again, if you don't know what you're missing, you can't miss it, right?

Nick thinks of his marriage.

Right. Absolutely right. All those years spent stagnating in suburbia, thinking he was content, and he had no clue.

Then he met Beth.

Well—not exactly. He *knew* Beth. Casually. He'd seen her around town, and on the commuter train. But she didn't travel in the same circles. Her kids are older than his; in fact, Beth is a few years older than he is . . . not that she looks it.

He never really *knew* her, though, until that snowy December night a year and a half ago, when they found themselves sharing a double seat on the late local home after their respective corporate holiday parties.

Glenhaven Park is almost at the end of the line. By the time they reached their stop, the rail car was all but empty. They were both tipsy. Flirting shamelessly.

He'd been too distracted to call Lauren to come pick him up. Beth had her car; she drove him home. It was snowing. Springsteen was on the car radio, singing "Santa Claus Is Coming to Town," and it reminded him of college, and snowy nights after bars in cars with girls.

He didn't kiss Beth good night when she dropped him off, but he wanted to. Damn, he wanted to. Out of the blue, he, Nick Walsh, husband and father of three, wanted to kiss a woman who wasn't his wife.

And suddenly he, Nick Walsh—who had been estranged from his own mother for decades because she'd left his father for another man—got it.

What are you supposed to do when you meet the right person—and realize you're married to the wrong one? Suffer on indefinitely? Or seize a chance at happiness?

That night, for the first time in years, he considered reaching out to his mother. He'd lost track of her—hadn't even bothered to find her and let her know when his father passed away a few years earlier—but if you really want to locate someone in this day and age, you probably can.

He climbed into bed beside Lauren, sound asleep in flannel pajamas, and he thought about his mother, and then he thought about Beth.

It was the first time he ever wondered what he might be missing. And so, Beth later told him, did she.

And now I know.

Good old pretech days forgotten, Nick checks his BlackBerry.

There's a text message.

He smiles.

Did you find Sadie's toy? Are you on the train yet?

"Not yet," he texts back to Beth, and "I wish."

A woman behind him emits a phlegmy cough. Hoping

she covered her mouth, though it doesn't sound like it, Nick looks up to check the progress at the counter.

"This is it," the teenage girl decisively informs the very patient middle-aged woman behind the counter. Then the girl turns to her friend and adds, less decisively, "Don't you think, Miranda?"

"Huh?" Her friend looks up from her phone.

"Like, don't you think this is my iPod?"

"Check the playlists."

"Yeah, but everyone, like, has the same playlists as me, you know?"

"I don't have the same ones as you."

"Yeah, but you're a freak."

Miranda sticks out her tongue. "Brat."

The businessman makes the impatient sound Nick was just about to make, sparing Nick a couple of dirty looks from the two blondes. Behind him, the woman coughs again.

"So what's the consensus, ladies?" asks the lost and found woman.

The one who isn't Miranda shrugs. "I guess it's mine."

"Great." She hands over a form. "You'll need to fill this out, and I'll need to make a photocopy of your ID."

Photocopies? Paperwork? No way is Nick going to make the 6:22. Unless the paperwork is only for valuables?

Apparently not. The businessman, it turns out, left a five-dollar folding umbrella on a New Haven local the other morning. It takes him forever to figure out which of the couple dozen black folding umbrellas in the "July: Umbrellas" bin belongs to him, and when at last he does, he, too, has to fill out a claim form.

Finally he's on his way, and it's Nick's turn.

It's 6:20.

"My daughter lost her stuffed animal in the station," he tells the woman, admiring the patience in her chocolate-colored eyes. If he had to work here and deal with people all day, he'd want to kill them or himself.

"When did she lose it?"

Good question.

"Recently." He'd assume today, considering that Lauren told him Sadie couldn't live without it—*if* his ex-wife didn't have an annoying habit of turning even minor household issues into urgent crises.

"Recently as in this week? This month?"

He nods. For all he knows, the toy has been missing for a month, but . . .

"She lost it in the station?"

"Yes."

"Do you know where, exactly?"

Nick quells the urge to challenge her exceeding patience and remind her that if he knew where, exactly, he most likely wouldn't be here.

"I have no idea. She was with my wife. Ex-wife," he amends hastily . . . and is rewarded with, not a dirty look, but not exactly a pleasant one.

"Do you know what the toy looks like?"

"It's pink," he tells her, "and it answers to Fred, and if I don't get it back to Sadie, then, believe me, life as we know it is over."

She smiles, God love her.

"You have kids," he guesses.

"You bet. Hang on a second."

She turns to peruse the shelf behind her, and returns to the counter with a large blue bin marked "July: Misc."

"It's pink, you said? Is it a pink flamingo?" She pulls one out.

"No. Not a flamingo."

The woman behind him hacks away like she has tuberculosis.

Repulsed, he tries to remember what Lauren said about Fred. Was he a cat? A duck? Whoever heard of a pink duck?

"Is it a dog?" She shows him one. "It's the only other pink toy in here."

He nods vigorously. "Yup, that's Fred."

"You sure? Because it's been here for a week."

"Positive," he lies. "That's when she lost it. About a week ago."

Maybe not, but it's pink, and it's furry, and there are no other pink toys, and the woman behind him is coughing up God only knows what, and he's desperate to get out of here. If it's not Fred, Sadie will probably never know the difference.

"I just need your driver's license so that I can make a copy, and I need you to fill out this claim form." The woman slides a clipboard across the counter.

"You actually keep a record of every single thing people lose and find around here?"

She smiles and nods. "Every single one."

"Do you have a feeling, one way or another?" The therapist's voice intrudes on Elsa's melancholy thoughts.

She looks up to see Joan watching her.

"A feeling about what?" she asks.

"About whether Jeremy is alive?"

Or dead.

Ever tactful, Joan doesn't complete the question.

The wisp of hope drifts, as it does from time to time, like a helium balloon whose string was swept beyond her grasp by a cold, cruel wind.

"What do you think, Elsa?"

In this particular moment, she doesn't *think*. She *knows*.

A mother knows.

There's no mistaking the aching emptiness; the sense that you will never again cradle your sweet child in your arms.

"He's dead," she says resolutely.

CHAPTER TWO

D o you want white or red? I brought both." Holding a paper bag from the wine store, Trilby McCall follows Lauren to the kitchen, her heeled sandals tapping across the hardwoods.

"Is the white chilled?"

"Yep."

"Definitely white then. Maybe that'll cool us off."

Lauren steps around comatose Chauncey on the floor in front of the fridge, pushes her sweat-dampened hair back from her forehead, and looks up to make sure the paddle fan is still turning. It is, but does little to stir the sultry night air.

"It feels good in here, actually," Trilby comments. Her long, dark ponytail has plenty of bounce and she looks cool and crisp in a linen top and capris, making Lauren wish she'd changed out of her dated, pleated, too-big khaki shorts.

"Are you kidding? It's a thousand degrees."

"Well, Bob keeps our AC cranked so high I need mittens at home."

Air-conditioning—yet another thing Lauren and Nick didn't want when they moved here. Too sterile. They both enjoyed fresh air through screens, falling asleep to the hum of crickets or the loamy smell of rain.

Toward the end, though—last summer—Nick looked into installing ductwork for a central cooling system. Gnats were getting in through the screens, he said, and the house felt too damp with all the humidity, and it wasn't good for the allergies he claimed to have developed . . .

Yeah, right. Looking back, it's pretty clear that Nick was allergic to one thing only: marriage.

"What are Bob and the kids doing tonight?" she asks Trilby.

"Right now?" Trilby checks her watch. "Either arguing about bedtime, or snooping around in the cupboards for some kind of crap to eat because all we had for dinner was salad."

"I can top that. All we had for dinner was apples dipped in peanut butter. And that was hours ago."

It's almost eight-thirty now. When Trilby called earlier wanting to stop by tonight, Lauren almost told her no. She's tired, and Sadie is weepy and needy, and Nick has yet to call back about Fred. She'd been planning on tucking her daughter into bed—hopefully Sadie's own bed, with Fred on the pillow beside her—then collapsing in front of some mindless television show.

But it's always hard for Lauren to say no to Trilby. In fact, it's always been hard for her to say no to anyone. But she's learning.

"There's nothing like divorce to help you discover your inner bitch," Trilby likes to say, and she's right. Lately, Lauren has gone from feeling defeated and depleted to feeling like she's not going to let anyone push her around. Particularly Nick.

"Hey, there, how's it going?" Trilby leans over Sadie,

who's hunched over a coloring book, scribbling a Disney princess a moody shade of dark gray.

"Bad."

Trilby shoots a questioning look at Lauren over Sadie's blond hair.

Lauren shakes her head.

A fellow mom, Trilby nods that she gets the message: *Don't ask.*

"I like your princess, Sadie. Even if she is a little . . . drab." She watches Sadie hunt through the crayon box. "How about some pink? Or yellow, maybe?"

"No."

"Who is that, Mulan?"

Sadie nods grimly and exchanges her gray crayon for a brown one.

"You know, nobody ever colors princesses in my house." Trilby straightens and removes the bottle of white wine from the bag. "Our coloring books just have trucks. Or Spider-Man."

Sadie looks up with guarded interest.

"Do you think Dylan and Justin would like a Mulan coloring book?" Trilby asks.

The barest hint of a smile. "No."

"Yeah. I don't think so, either. Oh well."

Lauren grins at her friend. The mother of two sons, Trilby is often wistful about Sadie's—and Lucy's—girly trappings. She frequently comments on what they're wearing, right down to sparkly nail polish, and she reveled in Lucy's tiara stage years ago. In fact, she took to wearing one, too, whenever she came over, so they could be princesses together.

Lucy. The thought of her older daughter brings a pang. Lauren misses her, and Ryan, too.

And Nick? Do you miss him?

Yes—she misses the old familiar Nick, anyway. The one who was comfortable and steadfast and sweet. The Nick who had grown up in a broken home and was determined to make his own marriage last forever.

Not New Nick, the midlife crisis stranger, who tossed aside his wife like a used tissue.

"Did you call that guy I told you about?" Trilby asks.

"What guy?"

Trilby tilts her head meaningfully in Sadie's direction.

Oh. The child psychiatrist. Lauren had asked Trilby for a recommendation, thinking it might be a good idea for Sadie to talk to a professional. Trilby's own kids are completely well-adjusted, but she's plugged into the network of moms who rely on child-rearing experts for everything from kiddie yoga to sex education.

"I haven't called him yet," Lauren tells Trilby, "but I will."

"Don't wait too long. You know everyone around here goes away in August—even doctors."

"I know." Making a mental note to call first thing tomorrow, Lauren moves a pile of unopened mail—including a letter from her husband's divorce attorney—from one end of the counter to another. She'll get to that later, too. Much later. Ugh.

"Hey, how was lunch with your sister today? Was it good to get out?" Trilby opens one of the glass-paned top cupboards and takes out two wineglasses. She knows her way around Lauren's kitchen as well as Nick ever did.

"It was pretty good, actually. Sadie hung around with the baby and the nanny while Alyssa and I went out to a sushi place."

"Grown-up food in the city. Lucky you. I ate two bites of Dylan's corn dog at the pool snack bar for lunch. And about twelve Popsicles."

Sounds good to Lauren, who can just imagine what Nick would have to say about corn dogs and Popsicles for lunch. The man who used to order—and hoard—his own personal boxes of Thin Mints from the Girl Scout down the street is now adverse to pretty much anything that's not natural or organic or whatever his new healthy standards require.

"Did you see anyone interesting?" Lauren asks Trilby.

"At the pool? What do you think?"

"You never know."

"Right. I suppose our neighbors Bill and Hillary could pop over to do a few laps, or Martha Stewart could show up to work the snack bar."

"That's not what I meant."

"I know it's not." Trilby hoists her butt onto the counter as Lauren opens a drawer to look for the wine opener. She casts a cautious glance in Sadie's direction before saying, "I didn't see her there."

Lauren nods, fishing out the corkscrew she and Nick used to use every Friday for an at-home date night when the kids were young. That, too, fell away.

She might be past wishing Nick hadn't left—she doesn't want him back now—but that doesn't stop her from wondering how this happened to them; when, exactly, it all went wrong.

Was it when, out of nowhere, she found herself pregnant a third time? When Nick was struggling not to lose his job as most of his department was laid off in a corporate restructuring? When his father died? When he met Beth?

What a midlife crisis cliché, all of it.

"Beth hasn't been around the pool for a few days now," Trilby comments. "Maybe she got a new job."

Beth had, according to Trilby, been laid off for a few months now—a fact Nick neglected to mention to Lauren and possibly to the kids—not that they'd be likely to tell her. They don't like to bring up their father's girlfriend in her presence.

"Or maybe," Trilby goes on, "she's away on vacation."

"I doubt that."

"Why?"

"Because *he*"—no names in front of Sadie—"isn't off until the middle of August. He told me he's going to Martha's Vineyard then."

"With *her* and her kids?"

"He didn't say. But I doubt he's going alone. And he's not only *not* taking his own kids, but this means he won't be around the whole week after they get out of camp."

"Why then?"

"He said that's the only week the house was available."

Trilby shakes her head, catches Lauren's eye, and mouths the word "bastard."

Happily remarried now, Trilby went through a bitter divorce of her own a decade ago. She gets what Lauren's dealing with—most of it, anyway: the isolation and desolation, the other woman lurking in the wings, the anguish of giving up dreams, accepting a new, unwanted lifestyle, dividing up a household.

But Trilby and her first husband didn't have children together. She escaped the constant heartache on their behalf, the burden of solo parenting, the lonely weekends and holidays without her kids, the custody upheaval—although Lauren realizes she's yet to experience the worst of that.

Until June when they left for camp, her children were supposed to spend Wednesday nights and every other weekend with Nick. But he was consistently late for weeknight visits, stuck at the office—or so he claimed. And on weekends, Ryan and Lucy were so involved with sports and parties and extracurricular events that those encounters, too, became sporadic. Meanwhile, Lauren wasn't any more thrilled about sending Sadie off alone for the weekend than, she suspects, Nick was to take her on.

He didn't press her on any of it. Maybe he will, once the divorce is final. But for the summer, he seems content to pop in to see Sadie just often enough to disrupt the household.

Lauren opens the bottle of wine, pours some into the glasses, and hands one to Trilby. At the table, Sadie swaps her brown crayon for black and scribbles some more.

"Before I forget, I'm heading up the Junior League tag sale in September, and we're going to be looking for donations in a few weeks. So if you have anything around here that you want to get rid of . . ."

"I have plenty that I want to get rid of," she tells Trilby, "but I can't imagine anyone actually paying for any of it."

"You'd be surprised at what people buy. Last year, some woman offered me a dollar for the roll of tape I was using to put up signs."

"Seriously?"

"Seriously. So . . . cheers." Trilby clinks her glass against Lauren's. "What should we drink to?"

Beyond the screen above the sink, Lauren sees a car pulling into the driveway. Nick. Thank goodness.

"To Fred," she declares, and Sadie's head snaps up at the mention.

Trilby doesn't ask who Fred is. She knows.

A car door slams outside, and Chauncey launches into a barking fit from the next room.

"We lost Fred in the city earlier," Lauren whispers to

Trilby, and then tells Sadie, "Sweetie, I think Daddy's here."

"Does he have Fred?"

He must, or he wouldn't be here, right?

"Go find out."

Sadie starts to race toward the back door, then remembers and changes direction, scurrying toward the front. Nick always makes a formal entrance now that he's moved out. Sometimes he even rings the bell. But only if the door is locked. Which it is.

The old-fashioned doorbell pierces the air.

"Go ahead and open the door for Daddy, Sadie," Lauren calls. "Make sure Chauncey doesn't get out, though."

"Nick doesn't have the keys anymore?" Trilby asks in a low voice.

"He does, but he doesn't use them. Maybe he thinks I've changed the locks."

"You haven't?"

"No. Should I?"

"Hell, yes." Trilby takes a big swallow of wine. "Can we hide in here or do we have to go say hello to the SOB?"

"*You* don't." Lauren sets down her glass and resists the urge to pat her hair. She hasn't touched a brush or seen a mirror since she visited the ladies' room at the sushi restaurant. At that point, her long, russet-colored hair was looking decent, but that was, what? Eight hours ago? Right about now, it probably has all the vitality of dead leaves.

"Wait." Trilby stops her with a hand on her shoulder and tucks an errant clump of hair back from Lauren's face, behind her ear. "There. That's better. Want some lipstick?"

"What am I, thirteen with a crush? I couldn't care less what I look like. It's Nick, remember?"

"Wrong attitude. You need to look great to him, of all people. Make him kick himself every time he sees you."

"How about if I just kick him every time I see him?"

Lauren leaves Trilby snorting into her wine and heads for the front hall.

"All right, how about a few more in the living room with the skyline and sunset framed in the window behind you," the staff photographer suggests, collapsing his tripod, "and then we'll call it a night."

Congressman Garvey Quinn looks questioningly at his wife, who shakes her blond head wearily. Like their two teenage daughters, Marin is accustomed to the PR machine that accompanies a campaign. But it's far more intense now that Garvey's set his sights on a gubernatorial nomination, with still greater aspirations beyond that. Marin's clearly had her fill of the spotlight already, and the primary is still almost two months away.

"Can't we call it a night right now?" sixteen-year-old Caroline protests. "I've got stuff to do."

"Like what? Go on Facebook and write snotty stuff about your so-called friends?"

Caroline's wide-set black eyes—identical to her father's—glare at her younger sister Annie, who merely smiles with satisfaction.

"I do not write snotty stuff on Facebook."

"Yes you do, and you're going to lose Dad a bunch of votes that way," Annie retorts with a toss of her blond hair.

"My friends aren't old enough to vote yet."

"Well, their parents are, and they won't vote for Dad when they figure out what a CB you are."

"Oh my God, are you for real? I am *so* not a CB."

"What," Marin Quinn asks her daughters, "is a CB?"

Garvey takes it upon himself to answer: "Cyber bully."

He's been reading up on the topic of Internet safety, among countless others, in preparation for the upcoming primaries. He intends to arm himself with everything there is to know about every potential issue facing the people of New York State—a daunting task, to say the least.

"I'm not a cyber bully, Dad."

"Of course you're not," he tells Caroline, and shoots Annie a warning glance when she opens her mouth again.

"I told Sharon I don't want the two of you on Facebook all summer." Marin shakes her head. "That's how you talked me into hiring a summer nanny in the first place, Garvey. To keep the girls occupied while you and I are campaigning."

Yes, though it hadn't exactly been his idea; it had come from his campaign staff. Specifically, Beverly. Her cousin Sharon—whom she described as a "delightful, all-American blonde"—had just gotten out of college in the Midwest and wanted to move to New York.

Garvey was agreeable. He didn't want the girls at loose ends all summer long. He convinced his daughters that it would be like having a big-sister-slash-cruise-director—someone who would plan fun outings and keep an eye on them.

Marin—who prided herself on being a hands-on mom—was reluctant, but eventually gave in, realizing her place would be on the campaign trail in the months ahead.

And so Sharon was hired.

What Beverly had failed to mention was that her

cousin hadn't graduated; she had flunked out of college—community college. Within five minutes of meeting Sharon, Garvey concluded she was the kind of girl who gave stunning blondes their dim-witted reputation.

In the month she had been working for the Quinns, Marin had grown increasingly frustrated; sweet-natured Annie had taken to calling Sharon "the Bubblehead" behind her back; and just yesterday, Caroline had said, "Daddy, can we please get rid of her? She's useless."

That did it. Garvey will have to get rid of her. Beverly won't be pleased, but too bad. His daughters' needs come first.

"Mr. Quinn? We're losing light," the photographer nudges from the next room.

"Come on, girls. Just a few more pictures." Garvey puts a hand on both their shoulders and leads them out of the kitchen, where they just staged yet another happy family scene for the camera.

The takeout containers are buried in the trash; though Garvey's pretty sure the photographer couldn't care less that the "homemade" potatoes in the rarely used six-hundred-dollar skillet actually came from Dean & Deluca. Or that neither Marin nor Caroline eats red meat and their perfectly grilled steaks will be fed to the dog or the maid.

It looked good for the cameras, and that's what counts.

Garvey can just see the caption: *The wholesome, all-American Quinns whip up a wholesome, all-American meal together after a long day on the campaign trail.*

Well, Garvey was on the campaign trail, anyway. He lunched with the local chapter of the League of Women Voters, then stopped in to visit a couple of disabled veterans before hurrying home to the East Side apartment for the photo shoot. All in a day's work.

He'll be glad when the primary is over and the nomination is secure. After a term as a conservative Republican congressman from New York City—a notoriously rare breed—this is the opportunity he's been waiting for all his life. According to the latest polls, the governor's mansion could very likely be in his future.

Barry Leonard, his campaign manager, keeps telling him that he has nothing to worry about; that it would take a serious screw-up between now and September for Garvey to lose the GOP nomination—or the election after that.

If Barry Leonard had any idea . . .

But he doesn't, Garvey reminds himself. *Not yet, anyway.*

And if all goes according to plan, the one person who does will be silenced long before November.

Seeing Nick down on one knee in the foyer, hugging Sadie against his chest, Lauren is struck by a ferocious wave of regret. It's all she can do not to stop dead in her tracks to take in the tender father-daughter reunion.

Even now that all is said and done, there's no doubt that Nick loves the kids.

I'm the one he doesn't love.

No mistaking that. Not when he looks up, sees her, and his dark eyes harden immediately.

"Hi, Lauren."

"Hi, Nick."

Chauncey, wagging his tail beside Nick, barks his approval.

That's right. Your master's home, Lauren tells the dog silently, *but don't get too attached.*

"Did you bring Fred?" Sadie asks, eagerly eyeing the shopping bag in his hand.

"I brought Fred." He hands over the bag.

With a squeal, she grabs it. "Thank you, Daddy! Wait, I made you a picture!" She races toward the kitchen as Nick gives Chauncey an obligatory pat before getting back to his feet.

A full head taller than Lauren, he's always had a fairly solid build and had developed a bit of a paunch over the last year or two. It's gone now though, Lauren notices. Something tells her his own weight loss, unlike hers, has little to do with grieving their marriage. No, these days, he's all about vanity and a new lease on life.

"So where was Fred?" she asks. "In the lost and found?"

Nick nods. "Do you know how many stuffed animals kids lose in Grand Central Station?"

"I don't know, a lot?" she asks disinterestedly, wondering if she's supposed to regret asking him to go out of his way to look for Fred.

"Do you know how many of them are pink? That place was a nightmare." He shakes his head wearily. *Woe is me.*

She'd love to inform him that having to sort through a bunch of lost toys is hardly the worst thing that could happen to a person. Not by a long shot. But before she can speak, Sadie cries out in the kitchen.

"Lauren? Problem here," Trilby calls urgently.

Lauren hurries in that direction, trailed by Nick and Chauncey, too.

Sadie stands in the middle of the kitchen holding the empty shopping bag and crying, pointing at something. Lauren sees the pink stuffed toy that was obviously hurtled across the room in dismay. Even from here, she can tell it isn't Fred.

Chauncey goes over to sniff the toy with interest.

"What's wrong, honey?" Nick appears genuinely bewildered.

"*That's . . . not . . . Fre-ed*," Sadie sobs.

"It's not?"

"No," Lauren says succinctly. "It's not."

There's a long pause.

"I thought it was."

"Really? Because that's a dog. Fred is a rabbit. I told you that. Remember?"

"You told me Fred was a dog, Lauren."

"Why would I do that when he's a rabbit?" she bites out through clenched teeth, barely containing a tide of fury.

Conscious of Trilby taking in the scene, Lauren isn't sure whether to wish her friend weren't here, or be glad she is. Without her presence, the floodgates would surely burst.

Nick tries to hug Sadie, who stiffens and weeps inconsolably.

Resisting the urge to shove him out of the way, Lauren kneels at her daughter's side, brushing her hair back from her face. "You need to go back to Grand Central and find Fred for her," she tells Nick over Sadie's head.

"*Now?*"

"Now would be good. Five minutes ago would be even better."

"You're insane if you think I'm going all the way back to Manhattan for a toy. I'm sorry Sadie, sweetie, but Daddy will look tomorrow, and if Fred isn't there, Daddy will get you a new Fred."

Kind of like Daddy got himself a new me, Lauren thinks grimly.

Judging by the look on Trilby's face, she's reading the thought loud and clear.

Fed up, Lauren gets to her feet and faces Nick.

Over Sadie's wailing, she tells him, "Just go. I'll handle it."

Some hopeful, delusional, *idiotic* part of her expects him to protest. To sweep Sadie into his arms—and maybe herself, as well—and apologize for being such a jerk. To promise them both that he'll move heaven and earth to find Fred. To tell them that everything is going to be okay.

Old Familiar Nick would have done that.

Midlife Crisis Stranger Nick just looks at her for a moment, and then he does just as she asked.

He goes.

CHAPTER THREE

More than three weeks later, Lauren dangles her feet in the town pool, frowning behind her sunglasses. She hates the muggy heat, hates the lazy quiet, hates that she practically has the place all to herself.

In the old days, those were the very reasons late August was her favorite time to visit the recreation complex adjacent to the town park. Most local families go on vacation during this two-week window between summer camp and Labor Day. So at this time of year, even on hot, sunny days, there's no need to get here precisely at noon when it opens to ensure availability of chairs and umbrellas, no wait for the lap lanes, no line at the snack bar.

Nice, right?

Not today.

Today, Lauren finds the pool depressingly lonely.

At least she can be sure that she's not going to run into the Other Woman, who has reportedly spent a good part of her summer here, sunning and swimming.

She's currently in an expensive rented beach house on Martha's Vineyard with Nick, having conveniently shipped her own two college-age kids off to Europe with her ex-husband. That detail was provided by Trilby, who is far more plugged into the local gossip than Lauren is. Or cares to be.

When it comes to details about Beth, Lauren can't decide whether she wants to know or not. The details might be painful, but ignorance is far from bliss.

In the deep end, a trio of adolescent boys, including Ryan, practice their dives.

Watching her son bounce somewhat recklessly off the high board, Lauren tells herself there's no need to worry. He'll be fine. Of course he will.

When you've lived through a nightmare, there's nothing left to fear.

True, the end of her marriage wasn't the absolute worst that could happen . . . but it was pretty damned close.

Ryan splashes safely into the pool.

Relieved, Lauren waves as he emerges and climbs up the ladder. Either he doesn't see her, or he purposely ignores her.

She'll bet on the latter. Ryan made it clear when they arrived that he isn't thrilled she's here. His friends were all dropped off by parents who have better things to do on a summer Friday afternoon. Probably pack for—or unpack from—their fabulous family vacations.

Trilby, too, has abandoned Glenhaven Park, having gone down the Jersey Shore with her family.

I really need to make some new friends.

The women with whom Lauren socialized before Nick left were part of their circle as a couple—mostly the parents of Lucy and Ryan's friends.

Now that she's emerging from her cocoon, she has no desire to rebuild those fractured friendships. Maybe she should make an effort to reach out to the moms of children Sadie's age, something she never bothered—or needed—to do before.

They're all so much younger, though; many of them still on their first child, or nursing newborns, or pregnant. Those days are long behind Lauren.

That doesn't mean you can't find something in common with them, she reminds herself.

Anyway, Sadie could use some friends, too, after a summer hanging around in the house with just miserable mom for company.

She looks around. A smattering of stay-at-home moms lounge in the adjacent grassy shade. There's a cliquish air about them; Lauren can't imagine going over and introducing herself.

Another cluster of young, chatting mothers stand waist-deep in the water, keeping watchful eyes on babies napping in shady strollers and toddlers and preschoolers splashing in the shallow stairwell.

If Sadie were here, Lauren might attempt to mingle. But Lucy, bored with the pool scene, took her little sister over to the playground—after asking if Lauren would pay her for "babysitting."

"Mom?"

She looks up to see Ryan, dripping wet, standing over her. He's growing up; he's starting to look more and more like his father, she thinks, with a twinge of both affection and pain.

"Where's your towel?" she asks him automatically.

"Dunno. Can I have money for the snack bar?"

"Please?"

He flashes a brief, rare grin. "Please?"

"There are a couple of dollars in the pocket of my bag on the chair over there." She points to the spot she staked out earlier, when it was beneath the shade of a tree. Now it's in full sun. Time to move.

"Can I have ten?"

"*Dollars?*"

"Please."

"You don't need ten dollars for a bag of chips or an ice cream, Ry."

"I'm getting a burger and fries."

"But you ate lunch an hour ago."

Ryan shrugs. "I'm hungry again."

He's been ravenous day and night since he got back from camp. All that fresh air, or maybe all the growing he did in the eight weeks he was gone. She'd sent away a little boy and gotten back a man. He's going to need his father now more than ever.

"Mom . . . money?"

"My wallet is locked in the glove compartment," she tells Ryan. "The car keys are in my bag. Go get the keys, get the money, put the wallet back in the glove compartment, and make sure no one sees you do that."

He rolls his eyes.

"I'm serious, Ry."

"Where are we, Mom, the South Bronx? Do you really think I'm going to get mugged *here*?"

"You never know. Bad things happen everywhere. And make sure you lock the car again. Okay?"

He's already heading toward her bag on the chair.

"Ry! You need to reapply your sunscreen."

"After I eat."

"Make sure you lock the car!"

"I heard you! Geez! I said okay!"

Watching her son take her keys and stalk off toward the parking lot, Lauren makes vigorous circles in the water with her bare foot.

Damn Nick. He left for the Vineyard the day after the kids got home, seeing them only briefly in between. He did send them a few text messages after he left—a form of communication both Ryan and Lucy relish. Lauren isn't big on thumb typing, but Nick started getting into it right around the time he began his affair. Lauren suspects that it was Beth, and not his teenage kids, who prompted him to jump on the technology bandwagon.

Poor Ryan. He's been hoping his father will have time to take him on an overnight fishing trip before the summer's over—a longtime summer father-son tradition. But Lauren doubts that's going to happen. Next weekend is hers, and she's planning to take all three kids to Rye Playland, another summer tradition.

All too soon after that, it will be Labor Day; back to schedules and routines. Lauren might actually be looking forward to that. She isn't sure.

Why don't I ever know what I want anymore?

"Here."

She looks up to see Ryan standing over her again, holding out her keys. His fingernails are, she notices, bitten down to stubs.

"Did you lock the car?"

"You only told me to five times."

"So did you?"

"Yes! Okay? Yes!"

"Don't speak to me in that tone. Did you find a ten?"

"I found a twenty."

"You don't need—"

"I know, but you didn't have a ten."

"Bring me the change, okay?"

"Okay!" he says, as if he thinks she's told him that five times, too. He looks over toward the snack bar. His friends are already at a picnic table, eating.

"Mom—your keys."

"Put them back in my bag, Ry."

He huffs over, drops them in. She opens her mouth to

tell him to push them down inside so they won't fall out, but he's already dashing toward the snack bar.

The camp didn't just send her back a man, she notes, climbing out of the pool; they sent her back a mercurial, derisive man, very much like . . .

No. That's not fair.

Just because Ryan looks like Nick—that doesn't mean he's picked up on the way Nick treats her these days and is following suit. It's just his age.

Regardless of his new moodiness, Lauren reminds herself, sitting on her chair and toweling off, Ryan isn't Nick.

Her gaze falls on a nearby mom who is kneeling on a blanket, doling out Goldfish crackers and juice boxes to several look-alike children.

Watching her, sensing her contentment, Lauren feels as though she knows her—knows her life, anyway.

You're married, and your husband works in the city, she guesses. *You're living happily ever after here in suburbia—or at least you think you are.*

I was you. I had your life. I took it for granted, just the way you are.

There's still a tiny part of her that would give anything to have those days back again, blinders and all.

There's another part of her, though, that would never go back, not even if she could have known what was coming. No, especially not knowing what was coming.

Two summers ago, after her father-in-law died of cancer, she and Nick had discussed that very topic in the car on the way home from the funeral in Baltimore.

Would you rather die a slow death and have the chance to say good-bye, or would you prefer to die in an accident and never know what hit you?

Nick took the latter option. She couldn't understand it. Not back then.

"One minute you're here, the next you're not?" she shuddered. "I'd rather know what was coming, even if it was horrible, so that I could prepare myself and the kids."

"You mean if you were the one who was going to die, or if I were?"

"If I were. *Or* if you were. Either way, I'd rather know."

"Not me. Either way, I think it's better not to know," Nick told her. "That way, you get to go about your daily life, same as always, until the very last second."

Oh, the irony.

Nick, after all, was the one who got to know—probably a mere few months after that conversation—that their marriage was doomed.

Lauren was the one who got to go about her daily life, same as always, until the very last second.

She grasped, the moment she found out about Beth, that her own life as she knew it was over. Just like that. Just like being hit by a truck.

Yes, she forced Nick through the motions—counseling, talking, dating, sex—but she really had no illusions about saving their marriage. Maybe she was trying to make it harder on him.

Or maybe she was just trying to do it her way, after all. Trying to buy time, to prepare to say good-bye.

Across the grass, the young mom packs away the extra Goldfish crackers and juice boxes, probably looking ahead to more of the same tomorrow. Probably thinking about heading home, and getting the kids cleaned up, and making dinner in time for her husband to get off the train from the city.

Probably never dreaming that one night, he might get off that train with another woman and want to kiss her.

Lauren wishes she'd never pressed Nick for the gritty details of his relationship with Beth. At the time, she'd thought hearing them would make it easier to hate him—and thus, easier to let go.

She was probably right about both of those things, but now she carries the added burden of all those memories that aren't even her own. Every time she glimpses Beth from afar, she imagines her in Nick's arms during one of their countless intimate moments stolen while Lauren was shuttling the kids to tournaments or away with her sister on a spa weekend Nick gave her for Mother's Day.

"You need a break," he'd told Lauren on that sunny May day over a year ago. "Go to Red Door with Alyssa. The kids and I will hold down the fort here."

Bastard.

And now he's off on a permanent vacation while she holds down the fort forever.

Lauren forces herself to lean back in her chair, tilt her face to the sun, and close her eyes.

In a perfect world, Nick would get what's coming to him.

But the world is far from perfect, and he's most likely lounging on an Atlantic beach somewhere at this very moment, without a care in the world.

"Next!"

Byron Gregson steps forward, glad there's no one in line behind him. The fewer witnesses, the better.

"Hi. I'm looking for my daughter's toy. She dropped it here in the station when we were here a few weeks ago—I can tell you the exact day."

"Can you now." The woman behind the counter doesn't seem particularly impressed. "All I need to know is the month."

"July. It was a pink—"

"Toy. Right. July. Be right back."

Byron watches her step away. So far, so good.

For three weeks, he's been waiting for this opportunity. Three weeks spent in a hellhole prison cell for mugging a tourist over by Penn Station, stealing the guy's wallet.

Even now, despite everything else that's happened to him—despite everything else he's *done*—he's incredulous that he, Byron Gregson, is a common street thief.

The other stuff—it kind of goes with the territory when you work in this field.

But pickpocketing?

Desperate to get out of town, he had few options—and all of them demanded cash. He didn't dare use his ATM card or a credit card—he couldn't risk a trail.

So he did what he had to do: ran up behind some old guy and grabbed the wallet he'd foolishly tucked into the back pocket of his baggy Wranglers.

Never in a million years would he have imagined that the guy's wife—a puffy, florid-faced woman in a track suit—would fight back, grabbing on to him and screaming bloody murder.

He wrenched himself from her clutches and shoved her. Hard. Again, he had to. All that commotion—it was the last thing he needed.

Naturally, a couple of cops spotted him and gave chase.

All those blocks in the hot Manhattan sun, knowing he wasn't going to make it, knowing he needed to come up with a perfect, brilliant plan . . .

And I did.

Naturally, he couldn't make bail. As he told the court-appointed lawyer, if he'd had access to money, he wouldn't have robbed the poor schmuck in the first place.

"How does someone like you wind up robbing innocent people on the street?"

"Hard times," he said with a shrug.

The lawyer shrugged, too. Plenty of people were out
of work. The papers were full of dire headlines about
former middle-class people who were now homeless,
white-collar executives working in factories, even a
former executive turned bank robber. A reporter-turned-
thief? No big deal, in the grand scheme of things.

He'd done the crime; he'd done the time—gladly. Far
preferable to the potential sentencing for extortion.

Now it's time to pick up where he left off.

"Here we go." The clerk is back, plunking a big plastic tub on the counter between them. It's marked "July:
Misc." "Have at it."

Peering in, his heart pounding in anticipation, Byron
sees that it's about half-full.

He pokes around, trying to act as casual as any dad
might if his daughter lost a regular old toy.

But he doesn't have a daughter—and this wasn't a
regular toy—and, Jesus, where is it?

"It was pink," he tells the woman, as panic rapidly
begins to set in.

How can it not be here?

"Maybe you lost it somewhere else."

"No, I . . . I know it was here, and I know someone
turned it into the lost and found, because . . . I had a
friend come down and check, right after we lost it, and
she saw it here."

"Why didn't she pick it up for you?"

"I . . . wanted to do it myself." That makes no sense,
of course. But he can barely think straight.

Could someone have seen what he'd done that day?

No. Absolutely no way.

He'd been careful.

"Maybe someone else took it by mistake?" the woman suggests. "That could happen."

His head snaps up. "You just hand things out to anyone who wants them?"

"No, we don't just *hand* them out," she retorts, suddenly a lot less friendly. "We take down the contact information for every single person who comes in here—and they all have to specifically identify whatever it is that they lost."

"I'm sorry." He shifts gears, and it takes every ounce of self-control for him to muster a calm smile. "I don't mean to get all worked up, but my daughter will freak out if I come home empty-handed because she thinks Mrs. Slappydoodle is here."

Mrs. Slappydoodle? Give me a break.

But the woman is smiling, softening.

"You know how kids are," he adds for good measure.

"I sure do."

"Do you have yourself?"

"Four. And grandkids."

"What! How can you possibly have grandkids at your age?"

She all but pats her hair.

"My baby girl is thinking she's going to be tucked in tonight with Mrs. Snapdoodle."

Snapdoodle?

Was that it?

Snappydoodle? Slappydoodle?

Slappydoodle. Right.

Oops.

"You know . . ." The lost and found woman looks thoughtful. "I do remember a dad who came in here one night awhile back, looking for some toy his daughter had lost in the station—just like you. He was in a real hurry, talking about his ex-wife . . . anyway, I could tell he had no clue what he was even looking for, other than that it was a pink stuffed toy."

"Really."

"Now, that doesn't mean—"

"Did he take a pink stuffed toy with him?" he cuts in anxiously.

She nods, and her gaze flicks past his shoulder. A quick sidewise glance tells him someone else is waiting to be helped. Fine. Byron will make this quick, and be on his way . . . to God knows where. At this point, does it really matter? He'd travel across the world to get his hands on that file again: his ticket to financial freedom. But with any luck, he'll just be a subway ride away from whoever snatched his file out from under him.

No unsuspecting stranger—or kid—would ever stumble across the memory stick concealed in the stuffing. No way. The file is still safe—for the time being.

"Listen, if you can just check the records and give me the contact information, I'd really appreciate it," he tells his friend behind the counter.

"That, I can't do."

His heart sinks. "Please?" He offers her the charming smile that has wheedled plenty of forbidden information from reluctant sources over the years.

"Sorry," she says firmly, "not allowed to hand out information like that."

"Are you kidding me?"

"I'm dead serious." And she looks it now.

"All I really need is his name."

"No."

"Come on. Please." Gone is the pretense of nonchalance. He's begging, and she knows it, and she couldn't care less, shaking her head.

"Check back with us," she advises. "If that other dad got the wrong toy, you can be sure his ex-wife and his daughter are going to let him know about it." She gives a maddening chuckle. "He'll be back."

"But he hasn't brought it back yet, and it's been weeks, you said."

She shrugs.

"You've got to be kidding me."

"Dead serious," she repeats.

Forgetting the seasoned reporter charm, he snaps, "Since you refuse to give me his name, the least you—"

"I refuse to because I can't."

"Well, the least you can do is call him for me and ask him if he has my daughter's toy."

Her eyes have hardened. "No," she says simply.

"You can't? Or you won't?"

She shrugs.

This is ridiculous. Should he ask for a supervisor?

No. If he learned anything in all those years as an investigative journalist, it's to know when to persist and when to quit—for the time being, anyway.

"Now if you'll please just . . ." She tilts her head, indicating for him to step aside.

He spins on his heel, fists clenched at his side in fury, nearly crashing into the person behind him, who stands holding an open newspaper.

"Sorry," he mutters as he brushes past, thoughts already careening ahead toward his next move.

CHAPTER FOUR

O kay, Daddy, we'll see you then . . . I love you, too . . . Here's Ry."

Watching Lucy hand the receiver over to her brother, Lauren notes that for all the growing up her oldest daughter did over the summer, she hasn't reverted to calling Nick "Dad."

It's been years since she started fifth grade and informed her parents that she would no longer be referring to them as "Daddy" and "Mommy." She went back to "Daddy" last spring, when Nick left.

Lauren isn't quite sure what to make of it, and she hasn't commented on it.

" 'S'up, Dad?" Ryan heads out of the kitchen with the phone.

That Nick actually called the house—instead of texting the kids' cells—was somewhat surprising. Lucy jumped on the phone when she recognized his number on the caller ID, and Ryan hovered beside her waiting for his turn.

"Make sure you let Sadie talk to Dad before you hang up," Lauren calls after Ryan.

No reply.

No surprise.

She isn't in the mood to go chasing after him. Anyway, if Ryan doesn't put Sadie on the phone with Nick, she'll probably never know the difference. It's not as though their youngest child has asked for her father much lately—or, for that matter, for her pink stuffed bunny. But Lauren suspects they both weigh heavily on Sadie's mind.

"I'm starved." Lucy snags a grape tomato from the salad Lauren's throwing together. "When's dinner?"

"Soon. Did you remember to pick up the mail for the Hilberts and the Levines?" The next-door neighbors on either side of them are vacationing together in the Outer Banks this week.

"And the O'Neals. Yes."

"The O'Neals went with them?" They're the across-the-street neighbors.

"No, they're in California. We're, like, the only ones left on the block this week. Can we go someplace good next summer, Mom?"

"Like . . . camp?"

"I was thinking Europe. I've never been there."

"Welcome to the club."

"That's so sad. Everyone should visit Europe before they turn twenty-one."

"Yeah? Who told you that?" Glancing at her daughter, Lauren knows right away.

Beth.

"Never mind," she tells Lucy, who shrugs and steals another tomato as Chauncey trots into the kitchen. "Can you please feed the dog?"

Lucy opens a cupboard and finds a can of Alpo. "You know, Mom, it's crazy for you to pay someone to walk him every day when you can pay me instead."

"I'm not the one who does the paying, your father does," Lauren reminds her. "And you weren't here all summer, and you won't be here when school starts, so . . ."

"But I'm here now."

"So are Ingrid and Ted." Chauncey's regular walkers, a middle-aged woman and a college-age man, work for Dog Days, the local service Nick hired. Until he decides it's no longer necessary, she might as well keep them around to make her life easier.

The same goes for Magic Maids, the cleaning service. Now that Lucy and Ryan are home, Tuesday—the regular cleaning day—can't come soon enough.

"Here you go, boy."

As Lucy puts a bowl of dog food on the floor in front of an appreciative Chauncey, Lauren admires her daughter's effortless beauty. Lucy is blessed with a trim athletic build, big green eyes, and a flawless complexion that's seen a little too much sun this summer for Lauren's peace of mind—though she secretly acknowledges that the glow is becoming. Lucy's perpetual ponytail has been replaced, over the summer, by a new style. Damp and freshly shampooed, it falls straight and silky past her shoulders.

Any second now, she's probably going to come home with her first boyfriend.

And I'll have to handle that on my own, too.

But Lauren will have to worry about it when the time comes. What matters now is that Lucy is all right—faring better, perhaps, than anyone. She's no longer pulling out her eyelashes. Nick was right about one thing: the time away from home obviously did their older daughter a world of good.

As for their youngest child . . . Sadie did see the child psychiatrist, Dr. Rogel, once. Lauren can't tell whether it helped or not. For the first half hour, Sadie spoke to the doctor alone, behind closed doors.

"But you said I'm not s'posed to talk to strangers," she protested when the doctor summoned her in.

"It's okay. I'm right here. And Dr. Rogel's not a stranger. *I* know him."

"But *I* don't."

"You can talk to him. That's why we're here."

Miraculously, once she got over her shyness, Sadie actually did open up to Dr. Rogel. She talked a lot about Fred, her missing toy rabbit.

When Dr. Rogel met with Lauren after the session, he asked if Fred was real. Apparently, he thought Fred might be some kind of psychological metaphor for Nick.

When he found out Fred was real and had, indeed, gone missing, Dr. Rogel nodded knowingly.

"It's very common for children of divorce to become excessively attached to, and even hypervigilant about, their belongings."

Lauren was so stuck on the phrase "children of divorce" that she didn't think to ask any follow-up questions.

Children of divorce.

It's surreal, even now, to hear Lucy, Ryan, and Sadie described that way.

Children of divorce? Her kids? How did this happen?

She should probably schedule a return visit to Dr. Rogel for Sadie before school starts. Maybe for all three of them. It's expensive, and insurance doesn't cover it, but Nick told her to do whatever she thought was necessary.

Dr. Rogel did mention that he'd be going on vacation in August. But maybe he's back by now—or hasn't left yet. And he said another doctor would be covering his patients in his absence.

I'll call and make an appointment for Sadie, Lauren decides. *She needs it.*

Hell, maybe I need a shrink, too.

"So . . . how's your father?" she asks Lucy, reaching for an avocado that's been ripening on the windowsill.

"Good. He said there's no cell service out at the house he's renting, so he can only call us when he's in the town."

"I thought he's been texting you."

"He did, a few times—he must have been in town."

"Mmm hmm."

Lucy looks hard at her. *"What?"*

"Nothing."

"Don't you believe that?"

"Believe what? I didn't even say anything."

"You said 'mmm hmm,' like you think Daddy made it up about the cell service and not being able to get in touch with us more."

"I don't think that, sweetie."

Okay, that's a lie. And judging by the flash of misgiving in Lucy's eyes, maybe she doesn't believe Nick, either.

"What else did Daddy have to say?"

"Well, I told him we got our fall schedules for school in the mail yesterday."

"Oh, that's right." Lauren has been meaning to take a look at them, but they seem to have gotten lost in the household shuffle.

"When I told Daddy I have Mr. Trompin for HR, he said—"

"Wait, what's HR?"

"Homeroom."

"Oh. Right." Lauren wonders why that would be relevant to Nick, but doesn't necessarily want to admit she doesn't know. She must have missed something.

Why does she keep missing things? She needs to do a better job of staying on top of the mail, and the kids—

"Daddy said to tell Mr. Trompin he says hi and that he misses playing basketball with him."

Oh—that explains it. Mr. Trompin is obviously one of the guys Nick used to shoot hoops with over at the park on Sunday mornings.

"Oh, and Daddy's coming home tomorrow," Lucy adds.

Lauren looks up. "What time?"

"He didn't say. It doesn't matter; we're not seeing him until the next day. He's picking us up for brunch."

Sunday. Clearly, he's going to miss half of his officially scheduled weekend visitation with the kids. Not that anyone other than Lauren seems to mind.

Well, she doesn't *mind*, exactly. Now that Lucy and Ryan are home from camp, breathing a little life back into the house, she's hardly anxious to spend an entire weekend alone here. Still . . .

You'd think Nick would want to rush back from the beach to be with them, after so much time apart. You'd think, too, that he'd at least check with Lauren to make sure he's not screwing up her Saturday plans.

He would be if she had any.

Does he assume that she doesn't?

Lauren thrusts the knife's blade into the avocado.

Maybe she should actually make some plans, just to prove a point.

When Nick resurfaces, he's going to get an earful from her—or maybe from her attorney. Yes, let no-nonsense Emerson Snyder—who'd come highly recommended by Trilby, who used him for her own divorce—straighten out Nick.

After all, you don't just ignore court orders—and that's what the custody agreement is . . . isn't it?

Oh geez, who knows?

Lauren wishes she hadn't been too distracted by her wounded heart to pay more attention to the legal arrangements. Maybe she'd have a leg to stand on now had she pressed Nick to stick to the visitation schedule from the beginning. But no, she'd gone along with his lackadaisical approach, happy to spare the kids that whole back-and-forth routine—and, all right, happy to have them all to herself.

"You don't actually expect us to eat that, do you?"

Lauren follows Lucy's gaze to the spongy brown spots on the overripe avocado.

"No, I don't expect you to eat that." She steps on the pedal of the trash can and chucks the whole thing. "Maybe we should go out to dinner. What do you think?"

"Because of a rotten avocado?"

Lauren shrugs. "Just because."

"Really? We never go out to dinner anymore—I mean, not with you." As soon as the last words leave her mouth, Lucy looks as though she wishes she could take them back.

Of course the kids eat out whenever they're with Nick. Nick is the one with the job—and the one who can't cook.

Lauren, who *can* cook—and in fact was marinating chicken breasts to go with the salad—suddenly doesn't feel like it tonight. There's not a breath of breeze at the open window, and the kitchen must be a hundred degrees. An air-conditioned restaurant—and a meal someone else cooks and cleans up after—couldn't be more appealing.

"We'll go down to Mardino's," she decides, reaching for Saran wrap to cover the half-made salad. "Can you go help Sadie get her sandals on while I clean this up?"

"Sadie's still in her bathing suit. She's watching *The Wizard of Oz* on TV."

"What?"

Wait a minute—that's right. When they got back from the pool, Lauren had told Sadie to go wait for her in the living room and watch television and she'd bring her some dry clothes.

And then I got busy in the kitchen, and I forgot. Terrific.

Lauren's first instinct is to beat herself up over it—and to tell Lucy to forget about the dinner they can't really afford when there's perfectly good chicken in the fridge.

But everyone needs to treat themselves sometimes, right?

Right.

And sitting around in a wet swimsuit has never killed anyone, has it?

Neither—as far as she knows—has a divorce.

"If you'll clean up the salad scraps," she tells Lucy, "I'll go find something for Sadie to wear."

Her daughter eyes the cutting board, littered with vegetable peels, onionskins, and celery strings. "Okay, but we really should compost this stuff, Mom. We all have to do our part to save the planet, you know?"

Yeah, well, we'll worry about the planet tomorrow, Lauren wants to tell her. *Tonight, let's just focus on saving ourselves.*

She can hear Ryan, still on the phone with Nick, as she leaves the kitchen.

"Yeah, and Mom let me have a couple of guys over to watch the Yankees–Red Sox last night," he's saying, "and she made us those brownies I love . . . yeah, with the chocolate chunks . . . I know they aren't, but they're good . . . Yeah, well, whatever. I have to go, Dad. Wait, here, talk to Sadie first."

Maybe, Lauren thinks with a faint smile as she unfastens the doggy gate at the foot of the stairway and heads up to Sadie's room for her clothes, the tide is turning at last.

Smiling so hard his face hurts, Garvey Quinn wishes the old lady would release her death grip on his hand. But she's been grasping it for what feels like five or ten minutes, going on and on about her health problems and her family's health problems and her neighbors' health problems, and how she suspects there's a secret toxic waste dump somewhere around here.

Garvey isn't so sure she's wrong. This industrial western New York town is maybe an hour's drive from the notorious Love Canal, and look what happened there.

"Even my cousin's dog has cancer now," the woman informs him with more anger than sorrow.

"I'm sorry to hear that, Barbara Ann."

He sees a glint of pleasure in her weathered face as she registers that he remembers her name. Yes, and he only heard it once, when she first came up to him, introduced herself, grabbed his hand, and refused to let go.

Barbara Ann. Of course he remembers. In the grand scheme of things, remembering names is one of the simplest tasks on his daily agenda. He has all kinds of little tricks for doing so.

Barbara Ann—that's an easy one.

Ba-ba-ba . . . ba-ba-bara Ann.

Garvey was a Beach Boys fan back in his college days, when all his friends were listening to so-called alternative music. Image-conscious even way back then. Typical conservative Quinn behavior.

"Nobody's listening to me!" Barbara Ann rails. "I talked to my doctor and I wrote to the mayor. I even called *Eyewitness News.* You know what?"

"No, what?"

"I got to talk to an assistant reporter, and she said she'd send someone down to check things out, and do you know what?"

"No, what?" he asks again.

"She never did."

"Is that right."

She vigorously nods her scarf-covered, chemo-ravaged head. "Nobody ever does what they say they're going to do. And that's the biggest problem with the world these days."

"I couldn't agree with you more."

Garvey studiously keeps his gaze fastened on her lash-less eyes beneath a brow-less forehead, fighting the urge to look beyond her toward the closed businesses lining Main Street. Amid plate-glass windows covered with brown paper and "For Lease" signs, all that remains open are an OTB, a rent-to-own center, a tanning salon, and a chicken wing joint.

There are plenty of problems in Barbara Ann's world these days. Of that, Garvey Quinn is certain.

But there are problems in his own world as well—including a potential crisis that churns his stomach if he allows himself to consider it.

"That's why we need you to win this nomination." Barbara Ann squeezes his hand harder. "You have good old-fashioned values and you stand behind your word. You care about the people. You care about our health. Really, that's what caught my eye when I was reading about your campaign. Your interest in health care issues."

Ah, health care.

Yes, he's interested.

"You and I are cut from the same cloth. I may have cancer, but I'm a churchgoing woman, Congressman. I don't believe stem cell research is the answer and I'm glad you don't, either."

Garvey shakes his head thoughtfully. "Let's just hope things go our way in the primaries next month, Barbara Ann."

"They will if I have anything to say about it."

"Thank you. I appreciate the support."

"You're welcome. And if there's anything you can do to get the press or the government to look into what's going on here . . ."

He nods. "I'll see what I can do."

"Good." She sighs heavily. "I'm just so afraid I won't live to tell what I know about that chemical waste dump."

Her words strike a chord with him.

Somewhere, someone is probably hoping that you won't, Barbara Ann.

But who knows if that's true in her case?

Just because it's true in his own . . .

He needs to get his hands on that file before the truth comes out and ruins him.

"It was very good to meet you, Barbara Ann," he says, with practiced patience, as if he has all the time in the world for her. For anything.

"You too, Congressman." At last, she loosens her grip on his hand. "And thank you. God will bless you for what you do."

Let's hope so, he thinks grimly.

But at this point, Garvey Quinn needs more than blessings.

"One more stop," a campaign assistant tells him as they stride toward the waiting black sedan. "On the way, we need to go over the speech for—"

"Would you give me a minute, please?" BlackBerry in hand, Garvey scrolls through his new text messages.

The first is from Caroline.

Daddy. I miss u. When r u coming home?

He smiles briefly, then scrolls past it and one from Annie, not bothering to read that just yet.

Ah, there it is.

All good. Expect news tonight.

With a crisp nod of satisfaction, Garvey deletes the text, then tucks his BlackBerry back into his pocket.

Tonight.

He just hopes it's not too late to keep the file from falling into the wrong hands and jeopardizing everything he's ever worked for, wants . . . *deserves.*

"That reminds me—the lawn needs cutting," Elsa tells Brett across the table for two at the Bayview Chowder House. They meet here every Friday night: same time, same table, same servers, same crowd, same menu, same wardrobe, even: a polo shirt and chinos for him, a summer dress for Elsa.

Funny that a woman who once considered herself an adventurer could take such comfort in predictability.

Brett looks up inquisitively from the crab claw he was about to tackle. "We were talking about whether we'll get home in time to catch the beginning of the Yankees–Red Sox game. How does that remind you that the lawn needs cutting?"

She backtracks through her thought process—which, as usual, was partly on the conversation, and partly on Jeremy, who is perpetually alive in the back of her mind.

Now isn't a good time to bring up their lost son.

Is there ever a good time?

Not as far as Brett is concerned. It isn't that he doesn't care. It's just that he doesn't like to dwell on their tragic past—not, she suspects, as much for his own peace of mind as for Elsa's. Ever protective of her, Brett treads warily around the topic of Jeremy, and only when forced.

"I don't know what made me think of it," she tells her husband with a shrug. "It just popped into my head."

Brett shrugs, too. "I'll get to it over the weekend."

She nods, but she doubts he will. Mowing the lawn isn't his thing—part of the reason he wasn't crazy about buying a house when they moved back to Connecticut.

Until now, they've always lived in rentals. Someone else took care of the maintenance, inside and out.

Brett is ready to put down roots here, but not literally. He wants nothing to do with yard or garden tending at this stage in their lives.

But Elsa really, really wanted a house. A real house— not a condo or an apartment.

She wasn't sure why, at the time. But Joan, the new therapist, has since helped her figure it out.

"Somewhere in the back of your mind, Elsa, do you feel the need to maintain your lifestyle the same as it was when Jeremy lived with you? Just in case?"

She could only nod.

"Yet you've said you have a strong feeling that your son is gone forever."

"I . . . I guess I just can't let myself completely give up hope. Even if there's one chance in a billion that I'm wrong, that he's alive and might find his way back to us again . . ."

"But if that were the case, Elsa, you must be aware that

Jeremy's no longer a little boy," Joan pointed out gently. "He's old enough to live on his own. He wouldn't need to have a room in your house, or a yard to play in . . ."

Elsa nodded. She got it. Really, she did.

But a mother doesn't give up, no matter what she senses in her heart.

So now they own a circa 1950 ranch with a perpetually overgrown lawn. It's less than a mile from the golf course—a huge selling point for Brett, whose handsome face is ruddy, tonight, from playing eighteen holes before meeting her here for dinner.

Ordinarily, he'd have waited until Saturday morning to hit the links, but it's supposed to rain tomorrow. And God forbid he begin a summer weekend without golf.

There had been a time, Elsa recalls, when he'd wanted Jeremy to learn, too. Brett used to fantasize about the father-son rounds they'd play in years to come. He even signed him up for junior lessons at the club when Jeremy was old enough, with encouragement from Elsa and whatever doctor they were seeing at the time.

It seemed like such a good idea to everyone, until . . .

Remembering the incident that had put an end to that venture, Elsa toys with her fork, poking at the wedge of salmon on her plate.

I should have known that wouldn't work out. Maybe I did know. But it was so nice to see Brett enthusiastic about spending time with Jeremy . . .

Across the table, her husband crushes a crab knuckle with a crustacean mallet.

Jeremy . . . the golf club . . . those horrible screams . . .

Elsa sets down her fork, her stomach churning with the memory.

"What's wrong?" Brett asks, but she can't bear to meet his eyes.

He remembers that day, too, she knows, though they haven't spoken of it since Jeremy disappeared.

The last straw, Brett had said at the time. But of course, it wasn't.

"Elsa?"

She forces herself to look up. "The . . . the salmon. It's overcooked, I think."

"Send it back."

"No, that's all right."

"Want some of this crab?"

"No, thanks," she says, and tries not to wince as he brings down the mallet with another sickening crunch.

"Long walks on the beach."

Nick glances up at Beth, who stands by the king-size bed holding a pair of flip-flops. "What?"

"Long walks on the beach," she repeats, a smile playing at her lips as she tucks the flip-flops into her open suitcase. "That's what people say in all those personal ads—people who are looking for love."

"Oh. Right."

But he's not following her train of thought.

A moment ago, they were surveying the pile of dirty laundry on the floor and discussing whether to throw a couple of loads into the washer, or just pack their bags with dirty clothes for the trip home tomorrow.

Now, out of nowhere, Beth has shifted to walks on the beach and personal ads. She has a habit of doing that—jumping from one topic to another—and he has a devil of a time keeping up.

With Lauren, Nick always pretty much knew what she was talking about—sometimes, even what she was going to say before she said it—and why. After all those years together, you learn to read a person.

That's not necessarily a good thing. Or a bad thing.

It is what it is, as Beth would say. She's fond of little catchphrases like that.

"I just think it's interesting"—she stoops to pick up a damp beach towel—"that some people go to such lengths to find the perfect partner, and other people who are perfect for each other just kind of stumble across each other. Like we did. Is this yours, or did it come with the house?"

He blinks.

Oh, the towel.

He peers at it. "I'm not sure. Just leave it here."

She nods agreeably and tosses it aside.

Lauren would have asked him how he could not be sure whether something belongs to him, and how he could so carelessly discard something that might be his without at least taking a closer look.

But then, Lauren would know whether the towel was his or not, because she always keeps—*kept*—track of things like that.

Not just household items, but his clothes, too. With his wife—*ex-wife*—around, he never would have managed to show up at a beach house for a week with only one pair of swim trunks because he had no idea what he'd done with the others and didn't have time to hunt them down. Lauren would have packed his bag along with hers and the kids', a few days in advance, the way she always did when they were going somewhere.

Sometimes, he misses that.

Misses *her.*

Sometimes.

But there's Beth, self-assured and sexy in a short, flirty coral-colored sundress and a beaded ankle bracelet, bare skin golden brown from their week at the beach, blond hair long and loose. Even her feet are pretty—tanned, toenails polished to match the dress.

He can't help but compare her to Lauren, the sunscreen queen, who freaked out a few years ago when the doctor removed a tiny precancerous speck from her shoulder. It wasn't even the dangerous kind of skin cancer, but she's doused herself and the kids in sunblock ever since.

"We can take another long walk on the beach tonight," Beth tells him, "and maybe one more in the morning, before the ferry."

"That would have to be pretty early. We're a long way from the dock and we're on the 6:30 ferry."

Beth sighs. "I don't want to go back to the real world. I don't want to get back out there with my résumé. Nobody's even thinking about hiring until September."

She was, until she got laid off last spring, a graphic designer at a prominent fashion magazine. That drew him to her—the blend of corporate and creative. She would ride the train in suits and heels that were sexy yet businesslike, not easy to pull off. He noticed her long before they ever met; admired her looks in a detached, married-man sort of way. It never occurred to him that he could have her, that he even wanted her. Not until that restless, magical December night, when out of nowhere, forbidden need came roaring to the surface.

Had he even realized, before then, that he was frustrated or unsatisfied by his life?

Does it matter?

Once he understood that he wanted Beth, could have her—*had* to have her—there was no turning back.

Now, he puts his arms around her from behind and buries his face in her neck. She smells like shampoo and soap and suntan lotion. Not the protective, dermatologist-recommended, triple-digit-SPF kind. No, she smells like coconut oil, a scent that evokes the tropics and bikinis and wanton sex.

"I don't want to go back, either."

"So let's stay."

"Another night?" Nick lifts his head in surprise. "*Can you?*"

If she can, he can maybe call in sick to work. No, wait, they have to vacate the rental house for someone else. But maybe there's an inn, or—

"Not another night. Forever. Let's just run away."

He laughs and goes back to nuzzling her neck. "I thought you were serious."

"I was, for a split second." She sighs and turns to face him. "Why does life have to be so complicated? Why couldn't we have met twenty years ago, when we were free?"

"We're free now," he reminds her. "Your divorce is final, and mine will be—"

"We're not really free. We have to deal with exes, and kids, and finances . . ."

"At our age, who doesn't?"

But her ex is remarried and left her well-off, her kids are in college, and anyway, Beth isn't Nick's age—she's older.

So much for the theory that men only leave their wives for younger women.

"Reality does bite, doesn't it?" Beth shakes her head. "It's a nice fantasy, though. Running away together."

It's what his mother had done—just took off with another man.

He never imagined in a million years that he'd be able to forgive her for that, but maybe he has, now. Maybe he'll find her and tell her.

Maybe not.

After all, he's done just fine without her, all these years. Was probably better off. His father did a great job raising him. His mother had never been the maternal type.

"Where would we go?" he asks Beth.

"I don't know . . . the South Pacific?"

"Or Europe. Tuscany. Think of the views. And the food—organic, fresh . . ."

"I've never been, have you?"

"To Tuscany? No. How about Morocco?"

"That's not in Europe," she points out.

"No, but I've always wanted to see it."

"Rio."

"Hawaii," he counters.

"Some deserted island in the Caribbean? Or we could just stay here. Forever."

"That," he agrees, "would be amazing."

"Let's do it."

Seeing the serious expression in her brown eyes, he says, "Wait—you're serious?"

"No. But let's pretend I am, just for tonight. Let's talk about all the things we'd do if we never had to go back."

"Deal." He pulls her closer. "Maybe we can even *do* one of the things we'd do a whole lot more if we never had to go back."

She laughs silkily. "Is that a proposition?"

"Hell, yes." Grinning as she reaches up to untie the halter of her sundress, Nick decides that life is just about perfect.

CHAPTER
FIVE

Jay-Rod, his teammates called him, back when he was playing third base for his high school team on Long Island. Of course, Jason Thomas Rodriguez is no relation to the Yankees' A-Rod, but no harm in letting people assume so. Not that many people did—unless he managed to mention it.

Like many a teenage athlete, he'd always dreamed of playing in the majors. And like the vast majority of them, he didn't even come close. Flubbed a minor league tryout after graduation, and that was that. Jay-Rod gave way to Jason again—just another screwed-up kid from a lower-middle-class broken home.

Dream over.

Nightmare begins.

For a few years, he got himself into and out of trouble, onto and off of the streets. Drugs, petty crime. Then he met Irena, fell in love, cleaned up his act.

He found an affordable studio apartment in Queens, landed a job in Manhattan—custodial work at Grand Central Terminal, but still.

Now he goes by JT, having distanced himself from both the disappointed athlete and the street thug he'd once been. These days, he lives his life on the up and up—most of the time.

With a twinge of guilt, he pats his pocket to make sure the folded piece of paper is still there.

What he did wasn't really *wrong*, though. In fact, it was actually kind of heroic. He imagines himself telling Irena about it when he sees her. She has a soft spot for little kids. Wait till she hears how he helped a total stranger get his dying daughter's favorite toy back from whoever snagged it from the lost and found.

Heroics aside, no one in his right mind would have turned down the offer to make such easy money. Especially since JT had been told he'd be paid a token amount for his efforts to find the toy even if he failed.

But he hadn't. It had taken all of two minutes for JT to let himself into the closed lost and found office and find the record of the person who had mistakenly claimed the damned thing.

Mission accomplished, easy breezy. The ultra-organized lost and found photocopies the driver's license of everyone who claims lost property, attaching it to the original claim form and filing away a hard copy just ripe for the taking.

Now all JT has to do is go over to the pub, hand over the photocopy, and collect his money.

Exiting the terminal on the west side, he's hit with a blast of muggy August air laced with the faint stench of stagnant gutter water from a late day thunderstorm. A few stray commuters hurry along Vanderbilt Avenue, but midtown is relatively quiet at this hour.

Passing a hand-in-hand couple, JT thinks wistfully of Irena, who's probably in bed by now. Her breakfast shift at an Astoria Boulevard diner begins at four.

Someday, they'll be able to see more of each other.

Someday, when Irena has graduated from Queensborough Community College and no longer has to work two jobs just to pay her tuition. Someday, when she's his wife.

His pulse quickens at the thought of the diamond ring he's been saving up to buy. With his next paycheck and the extra cash he's about to pocket, they'll be engaged by Labor Day.

He crosses the narrow avenue and walks up two blocks, toward the pub. Turning west, he sees that the sidewalk between here and Madison becomes a plywood-framed tunnel, protection from the construction zone on an overhead skyscraper.

Yeah. Like some flimsy strips of wood will keep pedestrians safe from a falling crane or steel beam. Things drop from the sky all the time here—construction equipment, air-conditioning units, suicides—but native New Yorkers take that sort of thing in stride.

His footsteps echoing through the deserted wooden walkway, JT notes that the overhead bulbs meant to light the area are burned out. Figures.

He wipes a trickle of sweat from his brow, thinking that a cold beer would go down easily right about now. Maybe this guy he's meeting at the pub will buy him one, in addition to paying him for his efforts.

If not, maybe I'll just treat myself.

"Excuse me?"

JT glances over his shoulder to see a beefy-looking stranger coming up through the shadows behind him. After he looks around to see that there's no one else in the walkway, JT's street smarts kick in. He takes a wary step backward. "Yeah?"

"I'm supposed to give you this in exchange for some information." The guy flashes a fistful of green.

"But—"

"Yeah, I know, my brother was supposed to meet you over at the pub . . ."

Brother? Momentarily confused, JT thinks of the guy he met earlier. He was on the short side, wiry, balding.

This one is built like a bull. A bull with a hand that's now fanning a bunch of hundred-dollar bills—a lot more than JT was supposed to be paid. His eyes widen.

"But," the bull continues, "he couldn't make it. Had to rush over to the hospital."

Oh geez. JT wonders if the brother's kid is going to live long enough to see her favorite toy.

"So he sent me to close the deal for him."

Close the deal?

JT laughs nervously. This guy makes it sound almost like they're doing something shady here.

Which you are, he reminds himself. But in the grand scheme of things, considering his own past, this isn't so bad. He's not hurting anyone—he's helping.

"Did you get the information for my brother?"

JT nods, again checking the street, making sure there's no one around to see the exchange and mistake it for a drug deal or something.

Coast is clear.

He reaches into his pocket and pulls out the piece of paper.

The guy unfolds it and looks at the photocopied driver's license while JT looks at all those hundred-dollar bills, almost within his reach. Yeah, he'll definitely go get himself a cold one after this. Maybe a couple, to celebrate the unexpected windfall.

Giving a satisfied nod, the guy folds the paper again and tucks it into his pocket. When his hand emerges, it isn't empty.

Too late, JT spots the pistol. Before he can react, he feels its hard nose probing point-blank against his chest . . .

And then he feels nothing at all.

Lauren wipes a trickle of sweat from her forehead as she carries a glass of ice water into the living room. She stepped out of a tepid shower less than ten minutes ago and she's wearing only a thin baby doll nightgown, but it's impossible to cool off tonight.

Exhausted, she sinks onto the living room couch, directly in front of the rotating floor fan. The blades stir the sticky air but don't cool it, and there's not a breath of breeze through the screen at the open window.

Chauncey, lying on the rug, opens one eye to look at her, then closes it again as though he doesn't have the energy for anything more strenuous.

That's why they call this the dog days of August, Lauren decides, and yawns.

She should probably just go up to bed.

But that would feel, in some strange way, like giving up. In bed before nine o'clock on a Friday night?

No way. She isn't giving in yet, no matter how tired she is.

Anyway, the house is cooler downstairs.

Yeah—maybe ninety-five degrees compared to ninety-six upstairs.

This is stupid. When she was married, she had no qualms about turning in early. Nothing to prove, not even to herself.

It isn't just the thought of her ex-husband living it up on an island tonight with his new girlfriend while Lauren sits here drinking tap water and sweating . . .

Come on—yes it is. It is just that, and you know it.

Thank God this summer is almost over. It's time she exited the pity party and reclaimed her life.

Last year at this time, she was wistfully thinking about all the home improvement projects she could do if she just had a couple of kid-free days. Nothing major, but over the years, she taught herself how to paint and wallpaper and slipcover . . .

She's no longer in the mood to do any of that. Why bother when they might end up selling the house? The only smart thing to do would be to pare down their possessions in anticipation of a move—and Trilby's reminded her several times that she needs tag sale donations.

Tomorrow, she decides. *A rainy Saturday is perfect for cleaning out drawers and closets.*

Lauren sets the dripping water glass on a coaster and picks up a magazine. The pages feel damp—all the paper in the house feels damp at this time of year. She leafs past an article about weight loss, an interview with a country singer, a list of clever household hints, most of which seem to involve baking soda.

Bored, she exchanges the magazine for the remote and turns on the television, wondering if there's anything on worth watching.

Then again, even if there is, she's not sure she possesses the patience or stamina tonight to be enlightened, or educated, or even entertained. Maybe she should just turn off the TV and read a good—

"Mommy!"

Lauren sighs. Not again.

There had been a time when she'd have leaped to her feet at the sound of Sadie shouting from upstairs long after she'd been tucked into bed. A time when Chauncey, too, would have come alert at the sound, no matter how hot it was.

Those days are over. Now it's routine for Lauren to be regularly summoned to Sadie's bedside for everything from a knock-knock joke to a mosquito bite that needs maternal scratching.

"Mommy!"

Chauncey doesn't even bother to open one eye.

"I'm down here, sweetie," she calls back and adds— for what feels like the hundredth time tonight—"Go to sleep!"

Aiming the remote, she clicks through a couple of channels. There must be something . . .

"Mommy!"

Some nights are worse than others. On a good night, Lauren has to climb the stairs to Sadie's room only a couple of times. On a bad one, it can be a dozen or more.

This has been a bad one.

She closes her eyes wearily and calls, "What's the matter now, Sadie?"

"I need you!"

Yes. She does. She needs me.

Sadie's just a little tiny girl, afraid of the dark and the bogeyman and, tonight, of lions and tigers and bears and the Wicked Witch of the West.

The Wizard of Oz scared the living daylights out of poor Sadie.

She needs to watch more age-appropriate television.

No, she needs to watch less television, period.

She needs her mommy.

Her daddy, too.

This is *so* not fair.

She tosses the remote aside, steps over Chauncey, opens the doggy gate, and heads up the stairs.

* * *

The small pub off Vanderbilt Avenue is conveniently located within spitting distance of Grand Central Terminal's west entrance. Earlier, the bar was jammed with commuters. But happy hour is long over, and the crowd has thinned considerably, leaving Byron Gregson with a clear view of the entrance from his barstool perch.

He checks his watch, then looks again at the door. Still no sign of the man Byron knows only as JT, who said he'd be here twenty minutes ago, with or without the information.

If he brings what Byron asked for, JT will be rewarded well for his efforts.

Even if he doesn't, Byron promised to give him a token tip—his way of ensuring that he won't needlessly spend an entire night sitting here nursing ridiculously expensive draft beer, waiting for someone who can't deliver and has no incentive to show up.

But maybe the tip wasn't incentive enough. Again, he looks at his watch.

"Another Guinness?" the bartender asks, swirling his rag across the polished wooden surface of the bar, close to Byron's nearly empty mug.

Again, he checks the door.

"Sure," he tells the bartender with resignation. "Another Guinness."

"It's hard to believe New York is out there somewhere," Nick comments, sitting beside Beth on the sand and gazing out at the western sky, where the water remains tinged with faint pink traces of a spectacular sunset.

"Maybe it's not out there."

"What?"

"Maybe something happened to the rest of the world since we've been here, and all that's left is this island."

Nick looks at her. "What about our kids?"

"You're right. Bad fantasy." Even in the twilight, her eyes remain masked behind oversize Chanel shades. "But you have to admit, it's hard to think about the city right now—hot, steamy, smelly. Cabs honking and construction noise and all those people rushing around, sweating in their business clothes, when . . . I mean, look at us."

Yes. Look at them. Barefoot and tanned, wearing just bathing suits, lounging on a remote beach on the island's easternmost tip. Look at them, a world away from the city and from judgmental small-town eyes.

Beth sighs and leans back, elbows propped in the sand. "Oh well. You know what they say. Everything has its price."

"You got that right." Nick lowers his sunglasses again and admires her flat stomach from behind the lenses.

Lauren never wore a bikini, but if she had, she wouldn't look like this.

Okay, that's not fair. Lauren looked—looks—pretty damned good. Even after Sadie. In fact, the last few times he's seen her, he's noticed how thin she's become.

But she doesn't look glamorous-thin, the way Beth does. No, Lauren looks more like she's wasting away.

Nick himself is at least partially to blame for that, he supposes.

But who wants to spend the last night of a glorious vacation on a guilt trip?

Not me.

"So what do you think? Should we go into the water?" he asks Beth.

"In a couple of minutes. I kind of like sitting here watching the sun set."

"So do I, but we can see it from the water, too."

"You do know that dusk is prime feeding time for sharks."

"I do." He grins. "But I'll take my chances. I just don't feel like I might die tonight."

For some reason, a conversation he once had with Lauren flashes into Nick's head. He seems to recall that it, too, took place at the tail end of a vacation—it must have, because he remembers that they were in the car, stuck in traffic on the thruway.

No . . . the Jersey Turnpike.

Would you rather die a slow death and have the chance to say good-bye, or would you prefer to die in an accident and never know what hit you?

Wait—they weren't on their way back from vacation.

They were coming from Baltimore. His father's funeral. One of their last trips together, before he met Beth.

Would you rather die a slow death . . .

No. No way. Nick, who for six months had watched pancreatic cancer ravage the man he loved so dearly, was adamant that it would be better to never know what hit you.

Not Lauren. She was all for long good-byes, she said.

And that's what happened to our marriage.

He realizes it now.

I let it die a slow death, even though it felt wrong.

Even though I knew on the night I wanted to kiss Beth in the car that I would leave her.

He'd been so tempted to tell Lauren, early on, that it was over. Even when she insisted on trying, insisted on therapy.

He shouldn't have gone.

But I did it for her.

I did it her way, not mine.

He should explain that to Lauren, the next chance he gets. Maybe he will.

Only he suspects she won't choose to see the selflessness in his final act. His wife—*ex*-wife—who has always been so fair, is anything but fair to him these days.

He supposes there's a part of him that doesn't blame her.

But there's a part of him that does. A part of him that wishes she could just wish him well and move on, the way he has. Not everything is meant to last forever.

Hell, *nothing* is meant to last forever, right?

As if to punctuate the point, Beth asks, "So you're assuming that if you were going to die tonight, you'd know it?"

"I think maybe I'd sense it, on some level."

"Really?"

He lifts the sunglasses again and looks at her. "Sure. I guess. Why?"

"I don't know . . . it's kind of morbid, don't you think?"

"You're the one who brought up dying. And sharks."

"Yeah." She's silent for a minute. "What would you do if you *did* feel like you might die tonight? Or . . . soon?"

"For one thing, I wouldn't go swimming at dusk. And for another . . ." He slides a hand over her bare thigh.

"Oh Lord, you want to do that *every* night."

"True. Maybe that's what's going to kill me. You have to admit that there are worse ways to go than having a heart attack while you're having sex. In fact—if I got to choose the way it had to end, that would be it."

"Good. I really hope that works out for you. Meanwhile . . . this is a public beach, so . . ." She brushes his hand off her thigh.

"Party pooper."

He stands up and brushes the sand off the backs of his legs, then stretches a hand out to her. "Come on. Let's go for that swim. Next best thing to a cold shower."

Beth shakes her head. "No, thanks."

"Why not?"

"I don't know . . . maybe I'm not feeling as lucky as you are." Her mouth grins, but Nick still can't see her eyes—and something tells him they're not smiling.

Down at the opposite end of the hall, Lauren can see that Sadie's bedroom door is ajar and the bedside lamp is on. That's how her youngest child gets herself through the long nights since Nick moved out. At least Sadie has managed to sleep in her own bed again now that Ryan and Lucy are back—when she manages to sleep at all.

Lauren passes both Lucy's and Ryan's rooms. All is silent behind their closed doors, but she's sure they're both awake—plugged into headphones, no doubt.

Back when they were an intact family, it bothered Lauren when the two older kids would retreat into their own little electronic worlds, unable to hear her and unwilling to interact.

But as she and Nick battled to the bitter end of their marriage, she found herself relieved the kids could insulate themselves from the blistering words hurtled back and forth by their parents. Behind closed doors, plugged into their iPods, Lucy and Ryan could escape.

Little Sadie, however, could not.

Poor baby.

Lauren finds her sitting up in bed, hair tousled, knees huddled against her chest, face flushed.

"What's the matter, Sadie? Are you too hot?" Lauren

is already crossing to the box fan in the window, making sure it's on the highest setting.

"No. Not really."

"Do you need some more water?" she asks Sadie. There's a half-full glass on the nightstand beside Sadie's lineup of Barbies, though, and it's still floating with ice cubes.

"No."

"Want me to take you to the bathroom?"

Sadie shakes her head, looking distressed.

"Did you have a nightmare?"

"No."

"Are you still afraid of lions and tigers and bears? Because I told you—"

"No!"

"What is it, then?" Lauren asks gently, crossing the pink carpet to her daughter's bed.

"Fred."

"Fred?" That catches her off guard. The first few Fred-less nights were brutal, but it's been a while since Sadie's brought up her missing toy.

"Daddy said he's going to look for Fred when he gets back from his vacation, and he's coming back tomorrow."

"That's good, but, sweetie . . . Daddy might not find him."

"He promised he'd try."

To his credit, Nick didn't promise that he *would*.

Still—he'd damned well better get himself over to the Grand Central lost and found again on Monday.

Meanwhile . . .

"You know, that guy looks pretty lonely over there," Lauren comments, pointing at Sadie's dresser across the room.

On top sits the wrong stuffed animal—the pink dog Nick claimed from the lost and found. Lauren had carried it up to Sadie's room the morning after she tossed it across the kitchen, hoping it might grow on her in Fred's probably permanent absence. Here it's sat, apparently untouched and unnoticed.

"I don't like him."

"Maybe you would," Lauren suggests, starting toward the dresser, "if you got to know him."

"No." Sadie shakes her head vehemently. "I don't want him! I want Daddy!"

Lauren stops in her tracks.

"I mean, Fred," Sadie hastily amends. "I want Fred."

"I know what you mean, baby."

Swept by a familiar, heart-sinking sensation, Lauren returns to the bed. She moves Sadie's oversize Dora the Explorer pillow out of the way and sits down, and begins stroking her daughter's hair. "It's not easy to lose someone you love, is it?"

"Daddy says he'll find Fred."

"Daddy will try. But he might not be able to."

"He said he would."

Lauren nods. "I know. He'll try."

I hope.

After all, Nick doesn't have that great a track record when it comes to keeping promises.

Vows.

Lauren probably shouldn't expect so little of him as a father. He does love the kids—of that, she's certain.

Still . . .

He loved her, too, and look what he did to their storybook marriage.

Nothing Nick could possibly do would surprise me anymore.

* * *

Stepping out of the pub, Byron is caught off guard as much by the darkness as by the moist wave of heat that greets him. He'd completely lost touch with the world outside while he was in there nursing beer after beer and waiting for some loser who didn't even bother to show up.

It's getting late—and he has a feeling this is going to be one of those nights. Relentlessly hot and steamy all the way through.

He thinks longingly of his air-conditioned apartment across the river in Jersey. But a good night's sleep isn't worth the risk. He doesn't dare go back there now. The place has to be under surveillance.

He'll return to the Lower East Side dive his friend Mina rents. No AC, to be sure, but there's a creaky old window fan.

Mina gave him the key once, a long time ago, so that he could water her pot plants while she was away for a week.

"You have potted plants?" he'd asked her, thinking it odd that a woman like Mina had a green thumb.

She shook her head slyly. "*Pot* plants."

Right.

Mina's not away now, but—to put it delicately—she works nights. She'll have no idea he's crashed at her place in her absence, and if she does happen to come home before dawn, well . . . he'll just have to tell her what's going on.

Not in detail, of course. He'll just say he needs a place to crash for a night or two, until . . .

Until who knows when?

Byron hesitates on the street, trying to decide whether to head over to Times Square to take the A or E train downtown, or to Grand Central to take the Lexington Avenue line.

Grand Central.

Maybe he'll run into JT and shake him up a little. He'd been so sure the kid was going to come through for him. The least he could have done was put in an appearance to collect his kill fee and tell Byron he couldn't get what he needed.

That's hard to believe.

Freakin' kid has keys to the whole damned station, the way he described it.

Rounding the corner onto Madison, Byron sees that the next cross street is blocked off. Cops on walkie-talkies, and big blue police barricades.

A movie shoot?

Nope. Glancing down the block, over by the plywood construction tunnel, he sees an ambulance, yellow crime scene tape, and a crowd of onlookers.

Early in his career, Byron was a beat reporter. He recognizes the signs.

Somebody's dead.

There was a mugging, or a cab jumped the curb and hit a pedestrian, or maybe a crane dropped from the construction site overhead.

All in a day's work for the press, and the cops, and the jaded New Yorkers who stand by, watching.

No skin off Byron's nose, either. He can just as easily access Grand Central from the next block.

Again, his thoughts turn to JT and the failed attempt to get his hands on the name of whoever has that stupid toy in his possession.

Now what?

Now . . . who knows?

Maybe he had one too many beers to care right now.

I'll just get a good night's sleep and worry about it tomorrow.

Byron Gregson walks on toward Grand Central, never thinking to look over his shoulder.

Not here.

Not on the subway.

And not on the deserted block of Ludlow Street where his luck runs out at last.

Left alone again in her room, Sadie listens to her mother's footsteps retreating down the hall and tries hard to keep the hot tears in her eyes from spilling over.

Big girls don't cry.

That's what Lucy told her today at the playground, when she fell. Lucy had been pushing her on the swing, but then she started talking to some boy, and she stopped pushing, and Sadie tried to make the swing go again by pumping her dangling legs, and she slipped off and fell into the wood chips.

"You'll be okay," Lucy told her, and she hugged her.

Lately, people are always telling Sadie that she'll be okay. Her sister, her brother, her parents . . .

But she doesn't believe any of them.

Why should she? They all leave her. Everyone but Mommy.

Mommy promised her all summer that Lucy and Ryan would come home soon, and they finally did.

But she didn't say that about Daddy. Sadie knows that he's never coming home again. Not to this house. Not to her.

And Fred—Fred is gone, too.

Sadie's gaze falls on the stupid pink dog on the dresser across the room, sitting there between her My Little Pony lamp and her Tinker Bell music box. His black eyes are looking right back at her, like he's trying to tell her something.

Something like, *See? I belong here.*

"I don't want you," she reminds him, and turns away, wiping her eyes on the sheet.

Lucy was wrong.

Big girls do cry.

CHAPTER
SIX

Standing on the wooden deck off the master bedroom, Nick stares at the eastern horizon, where the first streaks of light are beginning to appear.

He hasn't slept at all, and he isn't sure why.

Exhausted by his evening ocean swim and a rigorous bout of lovemaking, he had expected to drift right off to sleep. Beth had, snuggled against him, their limbs entangled in each other and the sheet. A warm sea breeze from the open window stirred strands of her hair to tickle his bare chest, but he didn't want to move and disturb her.

No, he wanted to stay just like that, arms wrapped around Beth, her head against his heart, forever.

But eventually she rolled away. Nick was left restlessly listening to the distant waves, wishing they could soothe him to sleep as they had every other night of this vacation.

It didn't happen, and now it's much too late. The alarm clock will go off any time now, and it will be time for him and Beth to go back to the real world.

His kids are the only thing Nick misses about that—but not as much, he guiltily admits to himself, as he'd expected to. They no longer need him the way they used to. Lucy and Ryan because they're older and more self-sufficient, and Sadie because . . .

Well, he's not sure why, exactly. All he knows is that he can't quite connect with his youngest child. It's always been that way.

Maybe he didn't take enough time to bond with her as a newborn, too caught up in his career.

Maybe, unlike his own father, he's just not the paternal type. Maybe he's more like his mother.

All he knows for sure is that he couldn't help but favor the older kids—albeit unfairly—because their lives were more interesting. Faced with the choice of spending his precious weekend afternoons changing diapers or on the soccer field sidelines, he'd chosen the latter.

Of course Lauren, who was home with the baby 24–7, tended to complain about that.

"You're the one who used to pray for rainouts," he reminded her. "Now you want to go to the games?"

"Lucy and Ryan want me there."

"They want me there, too."

"But I have to get out of the house," she said. "You're out all the time."

"Working," he pointed out, and off they went on one of those maddening, can't-win arguments.

Now Sadie, who hasn't even been to kindergarten yet, is seeing a shrink. He could tell by the way Lauren discussed the situation that she probably blames that on him, too. Maybe it is his fault. But not entirely.

He supposes, looking back, that they could have just brought Sadie along to the autumn soccer and lacrosse matches, to the basketball court in winter, to Little League and girls' softball games in spring.

But Sadie caught enough colds as it was, and the weather was often raw, and Lauren was overprotective, in Nick's opinion.

Plus, it was such a hassle to lug the necessary gear—diaper bag, stroller, port-a-playpen—across the fields . . .

Excuses, excuses.

The truth is, Sadie arrived just when Nick was hitting his stride—as a corporate executive, as a husband, as a father, as a homeowner. Having a baby in the house again cramped his style and threw off the family rhythm. Not long after they found themselves with another mouth to feed, the economy began to tank. It was all Nick could do to hang on to his job as the axe fell all around him. Then his father got sick, was declared terminal, died.

How, he wondered back in those grim days, had his life become such a shambles?

"It was like falling off the carousel horse just as the brass ring was within my grasp," is how he described it to Beth, not long after they met.

"Maybe not."

"What do you mean?"

"Maybe I'm the brass ring," she said with a sly grin.

She was. Having Beth in his world revitalized him in ways he'd never dreamed possible. But even she can't erase the baggage, the endless distractions, the responsibilities that will follow him for years to come.

There's only one way to escape.

Well, two, if you count death.

The alternative, while infinitely more appealing, is hardly a viable choice.

Is it?

No, he tells himself firmly. *You can't run off with your mistress. You're going back to the real world, and that's that.*

Nick takes one last, wistful look at the seascape before heading inside.

"Morning, Daddy."

Startled by his daughter's voice, Garvey looks up to see Caroline standing in the doorway of his den—not just awake at this early hour, but fully dressed in khaki shorts and a pale green polo.

He aims the TiVo remote at the television and presses the pause button, freezing the preternaturally cheerful morning news anchor in a gums-baring smile.

"Good morning, sunshine. Is the building on fire?"

Most teenagers, Garvey knows, would respond with a clueless "huh?" or just a blank stare.

Not Caroline Quinn.

"Pardon me?"

"I just can't imagine that you'd be out of bed before seven on a Saturday morning for anything less than a full-scale emergency evacuation."

His beautiful daughter rewards him with a chuckle and tosses her long black hair. "Actually, we're evacuating to the Hamptons—did you forget?"

He frowns. "Where's your mother?"

"Right here." Marin appears behind Caroline, wearing a crisp white linen dress and a straw hat. Snow White and Rose Red, Garvey finds himself thinking, as he often does when his wife and daughter stand together. Marin a fair, blue-eyed blonde looking ten years younger than she is, and Caroline a striking brunette who appears—well, if not a full decade older than her years, then at least twenty-one.

Caroline's rapid maturation scares him.

A lot of things about Caroline scare him.

Back in July when he fired Sharon, the summer

nanny, he had fully intended to replace her. Caroline had convinced him that she and Annie would be fine for the remainder of the summer.

"I'm sixteen, Daddy," Caroline had said. "I'm perfectly capable of looking after myself and Annie for a few weeks. Right, Annie?"

"She's more capable than the Bubblehead," was Annie's assessment.

True.

But Garvey worries. If anything were to happen . . .

And now his wife is taking the girls out to the beach?

Much too dangerous.

Rip currents, sharks, Caroline in a skimpy bikini . . .

And I can't be there to keep an eye on her.

"What's this about the Hamptons?" he asks Marin.

"I told you yesterday—Heather Cottington invited us out for the weekend, and the girls and I are going."

"I wasn't even here yesterday."

"What else is new?"

"Why are you going to the beach? The weather is lousy."

"It's supposed to clear up by this afternoon."

"Here in the city. You'll be way out east. The rain is moving that way."

"Then we'll be at the beach in the rain," she replies impatiently. "What do you want from me?"

He looks at Caroline.

"Daddy, please? I've been looking forward to this."

"Don't worry, Car, we're going," Marin assures her. "Please go tell Annie that the car will be here in five minutes and make sure she's ready. Her asthma has been bothering her this morning, so make sure she did the nebulizer like I told her."

Their daughter sighs heavily, but doesn't protest. Ordinarily, she might, but Garvey can tell by her expression that she's not thrilled to witness the tension between him and Marin.

Caroline plants a kiss on his cheek. "See you, Daddy. Have a good weekend."

"You too, angel. And be careful." He waits until his daughter has left the room, then turns to Marin. "Since when do you and the girls take off without at least telling me?"

"I told you about it on the phone when I called to ask you what you wanted me to do about that charity auction."

Oh. Maybe she did.

He remembers that call. It came in on the heels of the one about Byron Gregson sniffing around the Grand Central Terminal lost and found. Needless to say, Garvey had been a little preoccupied when he was talking to his wife.

"When will you be back?" he asks Marin.

"Monday afternoon. Why?"

"*Why?*" he echoes incredulously.

"Why does it matter? You won't even be here."

"Yes, I will. I'm scheduled to be in the city all weekend."

"But not *here*. And none of your appearances in the next few days involve us—not that I'm complaining," she adds, seeing him open his mouth to remind her that it was her choice to take a break from the campaign whirlwind.

"I'm free tomorrow until mid-afternoon."

"Then come out and meet us."

He shakes his head. She just doesn't get it.

"Why the beach?"

For that matter, why Heather Cottington? Marin's longtime friend—a vocal Manhattan Democrat—is hardly one of his favorite people.

"Summer is almost over, and the girls want to enjoy what's left of it, and so do I."

"We have our own beach house. You can—"

"It's not exactly our own."

True. It belongs to the family—*his* family. On any given weekend, Garvey's New England–based siblings, nieces, and nephews can be found at the sprawling island residence.

Marin shakes her head. She's never been very fond of his sisters, but she tolerates them—and vice versa, Garvey suspects.

"Anyway," she continues, "Nantucket is too out of the way."

"You can fly there in less time than you can drive to Long Island at this time of year, with traffic."

"There's no traffic at this hour."

He raises a dubious brow. They both know the Long Island Expressway is impossible on summer weekends.

"Even if there is traffic, none of the girls' friends go to Nantucket," she reminds him. "They go to the Hamptons. And so do our friends. Mine, anyway."

Ah, yes. Separate friends.

Increasingly separate lives.

This isn't how it was supposed to be. Not for him and Marin. They were going to break the pattern established by his parents, his grandparents, and perhaps every Quinn ancestor dating back to the *Mayflower*.

When they met, Garvey desperately wanted to avoid the brand of brittle relationship he'd seen among couples in his own family. Head over heels in love with Marin, governed by his passion and naïve young heart, he truly believed their marriage would be—*could* be—different.

He'd been wrong.

It wouldn't be.

Couldn't be.

Not after what happened to them.

Somehow, the traumas that had seemed to irrevocably bind them early in their relationship resulted in the very obsession that ultimately drove him away—emotionally, in any case. Physically, too, as often as he could manage to flee the domestic scene while maintaining his political Family Man persona.

His campaign now is based on that wholesome, old-fashioned image: loving father, loyal husband.

His marriage was supposed to be based on trust.

But you don't dare burden the woman you love with secrets as dark as his. A mistress is nothing in the grand scheme of things. Garvey has kept the truth from Marin for her own sake as well as for his.

He'll tell her only if, by some horrible twist of fate, the truth does manage to come out somehow—despite his desperate maneuvering to keep it hidden. But it won't matter what he says to Marin then, because she'll leave him anyway.

She might be willing to follow him to the governor's mansion, but he's pretty damned sure she won't be willing to visit him in prison after what he did. And that's where he'll be—for the rest of his life, most likely—if he doesn't get his hands on that file.

"Mrs. Quinn? The car is here," the maid announces from the doorway.

"Thank you." Marin looks at Garvey. "We have to go."

He shrugs.

She turns away.

Then, for some reason—nostalgia? guilt?—he hears himself say, "I'll miss you."

Slowly, she turns back.

"I know I'm busy, but . . . it's not like I don't need you and the girls, Marin. You know that, right? You know that I'm doing this for all of us. For our future."

Are you? her blue eyes ask.

He nods, as if that can possibly reassure her.

If only there was something he could do or say to convince her that he only wants what's best for her—for their daughters—for all of them. That's all he's ever wanted. If he didn't care so much—if he wasn't so fiercely devoted to his family—he wouldn't have done what he did years ago.

Love.

I did it for love.

But who could possibly ever understand that?

Marin?

No.

"I wish you weren't going away now that I'm finally home again."

"I wish you were coming with us."

Touché.

Wishes are useless, anyway.

"Maybe . . ." Marin is still looking at him, her expression softening. "If you can slip away from the fundraiser tonight, you can always meet us out east for a late dinner."

"I'm the guest of honor. How can I slip away?"

In the pause that follows, the connection evaporates. Just like that.

"It was just a thought. See you, Garvey."

She leaves without kissing him good-bye.

He settles back in his leather wingback chair again and aims the remote at the television. Fast-forwarding through the local news, he can easily tell at a glance

which segments he missed. There's one about juror se-
lection in a celebrated trial, which doesn't concern him,
and one about yet another MTA fare hike, which does—
though not at this particular moment.

Ah . . . that might be it. Seeing a familiar dead-body-
outline graphic in the panel behind the anchor, Garvey
stops fast-forwarding, backs up a few frames, and presses
play.

"Police this morning are investigating a murder on the
Lower East Side," the anchorwoman announces.

The news desk gives way to a handsome, square-jawed
reporter standing beneath an umbrella. Behind him is a
graffiti-covered brick building. "The body of a man was
discovered on the sidewalk here shortly after nine last
night. He had been shot once in the back of the head.
Robbery is not a suspected motive as the victim was
carrying cash. He did not, however, have a wallet or any
identification."

Garvey leans forward, rubbing his chin, pleased.

"The victim is described as Caucasian, in his thir-
ties or early forties, with short dark hair and a medium
build," the reporter goes on. "Authorities are asking
anyone with information to please contact the Crime
Stoppers hotline at 1–800–555–TIPS. For CBS–2 News,
I'm John Metaxas, reporting live from Ludlow Street."

"Whoa . . . what are you guys doing?"

Lauren looks up from the Van Morrison CD case in
her hand to see Ryan climbing over the gate at the foot
of the stairs. He's barefoot, wearing only a pair of jersey
knit shorts, and has a serious case of bed head.

"Morning, Ry." She glances at the digital clock on the
cable box. "I mean, good afternoon."

He smiles or winces, she can't tell which. "I was tired."

"I know. It's fine to sleep in, especially on such a dreary day."

"What are you doing?" he repeats.

"We're cleaning," Lucy informs her brother from her perch on the floor beside the built-in bookcase.

"Are the maids coming today?"

"We don't just clean before the maids come!" Lauren protests.

"We don't?"

"Mom, we kind of do," Lucy tells her.

Okay, point taken. They *do* tend to spend Monday nights running around straightening the house in advance of the Magic Maids' Tuesday morning arrival.

"So, like, did a bomb go off in here or what?" Ryan asks.

Lauren follows his gaze to the piles of books, CDs, and DVDs scattered over the floor, along with a couple of throw pillows she never liked and a table lamp no one ever bothers to turn on.

"We're going through the whole house and getting rid of stuff," she tells her son. "So if there's anything you know you don't want . . ."

"Or anything you might want to keep," Lucy adds slyly, "like your baseball cards . . ."

"*What?* You can't throw away my—"

"She's just kidding, Ry," Lauren assures him.

"Yeah, we're not really throwing anything away. We're giving it to Trilby for some tag sale she's having. I bet someone would pay a dollar for a crate of baseball cards."

"Shut up, Lucy."

"We don't say *shut up* around here," Lauren admonishes her son.

"We do when someone is threatening to sell someone else's stuff."

"Can't you take a joke?" Lucy shakes her head.

For once, Ryan ignores her. "Can I have some breakfast, Mom?"

"Help yourself. Lucky Charms or Frosted Flakes."

He doesn't bother to reply, just steps around Lauren and shuffles off to the kitchen. Cold cereal isn't what he had in mind, she knows. Saturday mornings have always meant pancakes with chocolate chips mixed into the batter, and lots of melted butter on the griddle. But the tradition fell by the wayside over the summer.

"Hey, Ry?" Lauren calls after him. "If you want pancakes, I'll make some in a little while."

"Can you make them now?"

Lauren hesitates. She's up to her eyeballs in household clutter, and Sadie will be safely occupied with TV for at least another twenty minutes. She's up in Lauren's bedroom, probably engrossed in some hideously inappropriate cartoon filled with dialogue like *Blast, you've foiled my plan to take over the world!*

"I'll make them later," Lauren calls back to Ryan, feeling like the world's worst mother.

"Never mind." In the kitchen, he bangs a cupboard door.

"Here's another Tom Clancy book," Lucy announces.

Lauren looks over to see her holding up a hardcover she just plucked from the bookshelf.

"What should I do with it, Mom?"

"Put it into Dad's box."

"Okay, but I really don't think he's going to want all this stuff. He doesn't have a lot of room in his apartment."

"Then he can get rid of it himself. I'm not going to throw away his things."

"That's pretty nice of you." Lucy gives an admiring nod, obviously convinced her mother is ex-wife of the year. "Most wives—I mean, ex-wives—probably would just dump everything in the garbage."

Yes, Lauren among them. But those books weigh a ton. Let Nick lug them all out of here next time he comes to get the kids. Let him sort through them and the memories they'll bring. Every novel Lucy pulls from the shelf reminds Lauren of their newlywed apartment or past vacations or cozy afternoons spent in this very room when Lucy and Ryan were little, listening to CDs and reading.

"Did Daddy ever actually read all these?" Lucy asks, tossing another book onto a growing stack.

"Sure."

"I can't picture him actually sitting down and reading a novel."

"He used to do that all the time."

"Really?" Lucy takes another book from the shelf—this one a Robert Ludlum espionage thriller. "Maybe I'll read one of them and then I can talk about it with Dad. This one looks good."

"You don't usually like to read books like that," she tells Lucy, her heart going out to her daughter, trying so hard to relate to a man who's making no effort—that Lauren can see, anyway—to relate to her.

"It looks adventurous and I, you know, like adventure."

"Okay, sweetie. That's fine."

Lauren looks at the CD in her hand and the pile on the floor, tempted to chuck the whole heap. When was the last time anyone even used the stereo? The kids have their iPods, and every song here would probably just remind Lauren of the good old days. Who needs that?

"Mom?"

"Hmm?" She looks up to find Lucy watching her.

"You're doing great."

"What do you mean?"

"Everything. Being alone. Being sad about Dad. Being stuck with us all the time. I think you're doing great."

Lauren's eyes well up and an enormous lump rises in her throat. Her instinct is to protest, but what message would that send to a daughter who's looking at her with pride? Lucy needs a strong female role model. *And you're all she's got*, Lauren reminds herself, *so buck up.*

"Thanks, Lucy. I really needed to hear that. You're doing great, too. All of you."

"*I* am, I guess. But Ryan's not, and—"

"What's wrong with Ryan?"

"He's so nasty. He's always in a bad mood."

"He's thirteen."

"Not yet."

"Almost. Trust me, you were the same way."

Lucy gives her an I-don't-think-so shrug. "What about Sadie? She cries a lot. About everything. And she freaks if she thinks anyone's touched her stuff."

"She's four." Even as the words come out, Lauren cringes inside.

She's four. He's twelve.

The kids' ages aren't the only reason they're troubled. This is not just some developmental stage they're going to grow out of. They'll carry broken-home baggage for the rest of their lives. There's nothing any of them—not the kids, and not Lauren herself—can do about it.

"Whatever." Lucy goes back to the books.

Lauren looks down and realizes she's still holding the

Van Morrison CD. With a grim, decisive nod, she tosses it into the box with other relics for Trilby's sale.

"That's not my concern," Garvey hisses into the phone, pacing the length of the wide hallway leading from his study to the master bedroom.

"But—"

"Just do what needs to be done. And this time, do it yourself."

"But do you realize what that—"

"Yes. I realize it. We have no choice. I don't want anyone else involved this time. No professionals."

As in hit men. It was fine the first time. The second, even. But now . . .

"Get it done. And make sure there's no mess left behind. Do you understand?"

"I understand."

"Good. Call me when you have the file."

He jabs a finger against the end button, abruptly disconnecting the call.

Hell. This has gone from bad to worse.

But he has no choice. He tried to go about it the honorable way—with minimal collateral damage, as they say—but that didn't work.

What if this doesn't work, either?

Don't think about that. It'll work.

He paces down the hall again, jaw set, past a row of framed family portraits.

He can hear Shirley, the maid, vacuuming at the far end of the apartment. No way could she have heard a word he'd just said—not that he'd uttered anything incriminating, even if she had been listening.

He's so close.

So close to losing his grasp on the situation . . .

So close, too, to obtaining his goal and securing his future.

One more obstacle . . . an obstacle that is, unfortunately, human.

Luckily, compartmentalization is a dominant family trait, and one that's served Garvey well.

Where would he be if he allowed himself to sweat the small stuff?

As Garvey learned once before, a long, long time ago, one obstacle—human or not—is insignificant, indeed, in the grand scheme of things. You do what you have to do in order to remove it, you make sure no one will ever be the wiser, you move on . . . and, whatever you do, you never, ever look back.

can't take your call right now, but if you'll leave your name and number, I'll get back to you as soon as I can."

Hearing the outgoing message—yet again—on his father's cell phone, Ryan wonders whether it's time to leave another message.

He left one earlier, both on this number and on Dad's home number. Same message, pretty much: "Dad, it's me . . . Ryan. I was just wondering if you were back yet. Can you call me when you get this?"

Apparently, he hasn't gotten it yet, two hours later. Or maybe he has, but hasn't had a chance to call back yet. Ryan found himself dialing repeatedly all afternoon, hoping his father will happen to pick up, hanging up whenever the voice mail does. Not wanting his father to find a bunch of missed calls from Ryan's cell phone number alone, he tried a few times from the house phone, too. Let Dad think one of his sisters is calling, too, or Mom, even. Otherwise, Dad might suspect just how needy Ryan's feeling right now, and feel bad about being away for so long.

There have been plenty of times when Ryan isn't opposed to instilling some paternal guilt, but now isn't one of them. He wants his father to see him as a grown-up—man-to-man. Maybe that'll make him more likely to want to take Ryan on their annual fishing trip this summer.

Last night, he promised Ryan they'd talk about it.

Well, he didn't promise, exactly.

He said, "We'll see. I can't even think about it till I get home and see what's what, Ryan."

That wasn't exactly promising. But Dad hadn't said no, either.

"Who's on the phone?"

Ryan looks up to see his older sister standing in the doorway of his room, wearing her usual annoying expression, as though she just caught him doing something wrong.

He tosses the cordless receiver onto his bed, telling Lucy, "You can't just barge in here!"

"I didn't barge in. I'm not even in." She motions at her polished toenails, carefully positioned on the hallway side of the threshold. "Anyway, your door was open."

Yeah, because it's too hot up here to have the doors closed. Not because he wants company.

The weather outside is gray and gloomy, but still muggy. Ryan's bedroom, tucked beneath the gabled roof, is sweltering.

"Who were you talking to just now?"

"No one."

They both look down at the cell phone in his hand.

"Okay. So you were just talking to yourself like a crazy person?" She shrugs. "Whatevs."

"Nobody says whatevs anymore."

"I do," replies Lucy, who, in her new, postcamp, who-cares-if-anyone-thinks-I'm-cool confidence, somehow manages to actually *be* cool.

Not that Ryan would ever tell her that.

However, a couple of his friends did say it yesterday at the pool. In fact, they didn't just say that Lucy's cool, but that she's also very hot.

Which, if Ryan really thought about it, is pretty disgusting, so he's trying very hard not to. But he did allow himself to notice, in passing, that his sister has transformed into a semi-cool person over the summer. And he's not the only one.

Lucy's been hanging around with Josh Zimmer at the pool since they got home. He's in her grade, but he's not the kind of guy who ever would have paid attention to Lucy before.

Things change.

Ryan hates that. Hates change. Why can't life go back to the way it used to be?

"Mom said to tell you that the weather's supposed to start clearing up and she'll drop us at the pool in a little while if you want to go," Lucy informs him.

"Maybe." He nibbles the ragged edge of his thumbnail and wonders if any of his friends will be around. Probably not. Just about everyone is away. His friend Ian will be home tomorrow, though. He texted earlier to see if Ryan wants to hang out.

"Can't, dude," Ryan replied. "I'm seeing my dad."

"That sucks," was Ian's response.

"Yeah," Ryan texted back automatically—then wondered if he really did agree.

He misses Dad, yeah. And he'd give anything to be able to go away fishing with him, just the two of them. But it's not like he can't wait to spend a gorgeous summer Sunday in some boring restaurant with his sisters. Dad doesn't seem to have a lot to say to any of them when he takes them out to eat, and spends a lot of time checking his BlackBerry.

Probably because of that lady, Beth. She calls and texts and e-mails Dad. A lot.

Ryan knows she's his father's girlfriend, but Dad hasn't actually come out and said it. Mom hasn't, either. But last spring when Ryan was at the snack bar putting ketchup on a couple of hot dogs before a Little League game, he overheard two of his teammates' mothers talking about some guy having an affair and dumping his wife—dumping his whole family, pretty much.

At first, he didn't realize they were talking about his own parents. The moment he figured it out, he knew he was going to throw up. He dumped the hot dogs into the garbage and ran to the bathroom. Then he asked the coach to let him sit on the bench that game because he was sick, and the team lost.

"So are you going to get rid of anything?"

Startled by his sister's question, Ryan looks up to see her surveying the piles of stuff around his room: books, school projects from last spring, a million comic books, a million baseball caps, fishing equipment, sports equipment, clean and dirty laundry . . .

He wishes, not for the first time, that his bedroom door had a lock on it. But none of the rooms in this house lock, other than the upstairs bathroom—which Ryan wishes didn't have a lock on it, because Lucy is always in there for hours and there's nothing he can do about it.

"Mom said we have to clean out our rooms for the tag sale, too," she tells him.

"What's a tag sale?"

Ryan sees Sadie in the hallway, listening in, as usual. There's no privacy around this house. None.

"It's where people give away stuff they don't want anymore," Lucy explains. "Did you see all those boxes Mom and I filled up downstairs?"

"Yeah."

"Those are for the tag sale."

"Do I have to give something away?" Sadie asks, looking worried.

"Well, now that you're a big girl, there are probably some toys you've outgrown, and some clothes, too, so—"

Sadie bursts into tears so abruptly that Ryan finds himself actually feeling sorry for her—which he rarely does, because it's not easy to be the only guy in a house full of women, including a little crybaby sister who's always making a scene.

"You don't have to give away your toys, Sades," he assures her.

Lucy nods vigorously. "Just the ones you don't play with anymore. Like that My Little Pony set you got for—"

"I play with that!" Sadie wails. "I play with everything!"

"*What* is going on up there?" Mom's voice calls from the foot of the stairs.

Great. Just great.

Sadie bellows, "Lucy and Ryan said I have to give away my toys!"

"I did not!" Ryan protests. "I said you didn't!"

"Mom, I was just saying that Sadie can get rid of the stuff she's too big to play with," Lucy calls, and Sadie cries harder.

"I play with all my toys!"

"Will you all please just get out of my room?" Ryan goes over and kicks the door closed in his sisters' faces.

God, he hates his life.

Brett sighs behind his newspaper, and Elsa, seated in the opposite chair, looks up from her book. "What's wrong?"

"I can't believe I'm just sitting around on a Saturday afternoon. I had so many things I wanted to do today"—he lowers the paper to look at her—"and if it weren't raining out there, I'd be rushing from one thing to the next."

"Like mowing the lawn?"

"And playing golf, and getting the car washed, and watching the Yankees–Red Sox . . ."

The televised game is in an indefinite rain delay. Every ten minutes or so, Brett reaches for the remote to turn on the TV in hopes that it might have started, but the field remains covered with a tarp, the announcers making idle on-air chatter.

"Maybe we can go to a movie or something," Elsa suggests. "Want to check the paper and see if anything good is playing over at the Cineplex?"

"Already did. Nothing. But there was something interesting here." He leafs back through the pages, folds the paper open to an article, and hands it across to her.

"What am I looking at?"

"The article about the new upscale condo community they're building over by the golf course."

"What about it?"

"It's going to be gorgeous. Every unit will have a fireplace and a deck with a view."

"Of the golf course?"

"No, of the sound!"

"Very nice," she agrees, handing the paper back.

"Maybe we should go look at a model."

"Why? We already have a house. With a private backyard," she adds. She'll take privacy over a cookie-cutter condo deck and a sound view any day.

"We can't even keep up with the yard work," Brett protests.

Speak for yourself, she wants to say. He's the one who isn't doing his part—which merely consists of mowing the lawn. Meanwhile, Elsa has her work cut out for her, thanks to the avid gardener who formerly owned the house.

The landscape is loaded with shrubs and perennials, and when the Cavalons moved in, the borders and beds desperately needed tending.

Brett suggested that they hire someone to tend to it, but Elsa wanted to do it herself. She didn't really know why it mattered so much to her, or even what she was doing. But eventually, she got the hang of pruning and staking and dividing—even planting flowers in the barren raised beds out front.

"Someone else would do the work in a condo," Brett points out now. "Worry-free."

"I don't want to live on top of other people, though. I like privacy."

"It's a mature adult community, Elsa. It's not like there will be a million kids running around, or loud parties at all hours."

No kids running around.

She considers that.

"If we were to move to an adult community," she says slowly, "then I guess it would mean we weren't considering another child at some point."

Brett's eyebrows shoot up and he removes his reading glasses abruptly, leaning forward to stare at her. "I didn't know we were still considering it."

"We never really ruled it out."

"But it's been years, Elsa. I didn't know it was still an option."

She shrugs. "I didn't know it wasn't."

They look at each other.

What are you doing? she asks herself, scarcely able to

believe she raised this topic after all those years of trying to avoid it. It just came out, as if catapulted from some deep, dark region of her psyche.

After Jeremy was lost to them, Brett wanted another child. He brought it up a lot at first, and then just occasionally, over the years.

Elsa couldn't bear the thought of it. Another child—a replacement.

No. It was out of the question. Besides, she wasn't exactly stable in the aftermath of their loss. How could she take care of a child when it was all she could do to get out of bed in the morning?

It's been a long time now since Brett raised the subject.

And now here she is, bringing it up again out of nowhere.

"Do you want to look into it?"

Seeing the spark of interest in his eyes, she automatically says, "No, it's not that . . ."

But maybe it is.

Oh hell. She doesn't know where any of this is coming from, or what she wants.

"I mean," she elaborates, watching him warily, "not yet, anyway. I just—"

"Not yet? But when? We're not getting any younger, Elsa."

"I know. But—"

"If this is something you want, then we need to talk about it."

"I didn't say it was something I *want*. Only . . . it's not something I want to rule out by moving into a retirement community."

"It's not a retirement community, it's an adult—"

"I get it. Adults only. No kids. If we moved into a place like that, we'd be closing the door for good."

"And you want to leave it open."

"Maybe. I don't know."

She can't handle the way he's looking at her, suddenly so full of hope. Not the kind of hope she's kept alive all these years—hope for Jeremy. But hope that she can finally accept that he isn't coming home, and move on.

No. That's one door she can't bear to close.

Elsa looks away, out the window. "Look, the sun is starting to come out. Maybe your game is on again."

"It's not being played here. It's in Boston."

Boston.

Where they lost Jeremy.

"I've been thinking," she tells Brett abruptly, "about calling Mike Fantoni, setting up a meeting."

His eyes narrow. "Why?"

"Because we're back in New England, and he's right in Boston, and—"

"Elsa."

"What?"

"Don't do that to yourself. Why pour salt on an unhealed wound?"

She doesn't reply. That's exactly what it would feel like to see Mike again. Pure agony. And yet . . .

"Look, don't you think Mike would have called if he had something?" Brett asks. "It's not like we've been out of touch with him. He always knows where to find us."

Of course he does. Always has. Of course he would have called.

"You're right," she tells Brett. "Forget it."

He looks at her for a long time, then out the window where the sun is, indeed, making a halfhearted effort to banish the gloom.

Brett reaches for the remote. "Let's see if that rain

delay is over. Like you said, Boston isn't that far away."

No, Elsa muses. *Not that far away at all.*

Standing in the middle of her room, Sadie surveys the pile of belongings she just gathered from her bookshelves and toy chest.

There must be something here that she doesn't want to keep.

Candy Land? The box is ripped at every corner, and the yellow piece and some of the cards are missing.

No.

She puts it back on the shelf.

The plastic grocery cart set, complete with pretend produce items?

The cart lost a wheel, and Sadie doesn't even like vegetables.

No.

Into the toy chest go the cart and its cargo.

One by one, she considers several dolls, a few more games, and a little suitcase filled with dress-up clothes.

Now the floor is empty, the shelves and chest are full again, and Sadie wants to cry. What is she going to do? She can't find even one toy she's willing to part with, and Lucy said—

The moment she spots the pink stuffed dog on top of her dresser, she knows she's off the hook.

There's something she doesn't want. Stupid dog. How could anyone mistake it for Fred?

Sadie climbs onto a chair and plucks it down. The chair teeters and she grabs the edge of the dresser to keep from falling.

If she fell and got hurt, it would be the stupid dog's fault. And Daddy's, too.

Scowling, Sadie climbs off the chair and takes one last glance at the dog, just to make sure. Its black button eyes seem to stare sadly at her, and she looks away quickly.

She doesn't want it. Why would she?

She carries it out into the hall and down to the landing. In the foyer below, she can see a row of boxes Mommy and Lucy have spent the day filling with stuff for the tag sale.

The front door is propped open. She slips down a few more stairs and sees that her mother is out on the porch, stacking a box on top of a couple of others.

Sadie doesn't feel like talking to her about the pink dog again.

Moving quickly, she goes all the way down and opens the doggy gate. She looks at the nearest box—one Mommy marked with a marker in big black letters. Sadie doesn't know what they spell, but she recognizes the ABCs: F-R-A-G-I-L-E.

Sadie hurriedly stuffs the pink dog into the box.

As soon as she does it, she feels bad.

Why? It's just a stupid toy.

Sadie shoves the top of the box closed. She can still see a clump of pink fur in the crack between the flaps.

She reaches out to push it deeper into the box, but instead, her fingers wrap around a fuzzy pink paw.

Maybe . . .

The phone rings, startling her.

Sadie hurriedly drops the paw and runs back up the stairs, leaving the gate open and the pink dog behind.

Lauren spent most of the day wishing the sun would come out, but now that it has, its rays stream through the living room's bay windows to cast a greenhouse effect she definitely could do without.

She wipes a trickle of sweat from her cheek with her shoulder as she hangs up the phone at last, hoping it won't ring again for a while.

She just spent a half hour on a pair of back-to-back calls—one from her mother, the other from her sister. Lauren figures the two of them probably talked to each other first and decided they were worried about her.

"I wish you'd come up and visit," said her mother, who still lives in the small upstate hometown Lauren gladly left behind years ago.

"I wish you'd come down," Lauren replied, knowing that was unlikely. Her parents rarely make the two-hundred-mile trip now that her father has had a couple of heart surgeries. Mom's license is expired at this point; she relies on Dad to cart her everywhere she needs to go. Totally dependent on her husband. She always has been.

I swore I would never let myself become like her, and I'm not. Good thing.

Lauren found herself promising her mother she'd visit soon.

Then she found herself promising Alyssa she'd come into the city tomorrow afternoon for brunch while Nick has the kids.

She really doesn't want to do either of those things, though.

Maybe I'm not as independent as I think. What happened to learning how to say no? Embracing my postdivorce inner bitch?

God, she misses Trilby. She's always good for a swift kick in the pants, reminding Lauren not to let anyone push her around.

Then again, who knows? Maybe deep down, Lauren really does need a hometown visit. Maybe it would be nice to be miles and miles away, back in a simpler place where her private business isn't churning the local gossip mill. And it would certainly be nice to let her nurturing parents take care of her and the kids for a while. So nice not to be in charge, for a change, of the household . . .

With a grunt, she hoists yet another heavy box of castoffs into her aching arms and hauls it out to the front porch to await transport to the church basement for the tag sale.

Returning to the hall, she notices that the doggy gate is ajar. Closing it, she wonders if she should just get rid of the gate. Chauncey knows he's not allowed upstairs, and he's never once snuck past it when it's open.

She picks up another carton of discarded relics from the dining room. She marked the box "FRAGILE" due to a couple of mismatched teacups and saucers, but nothing else is breakable: stray silverware, fancy candlesticks, elegant linens that are never used because you have to iron them, and who has time to iron a tablecloth if you're cooking the kind of dinner that would be served *on* a tablecloth?

After wearily depositing the box on the front porch with the others, she surveys the stack. Maybe she should cover it with a tarp or something, as much to protect the cardboard from the rain as to fend off potential thieves.

Then again, the boxes are filled with things she doesn't want in the first place—and this is Glenhaven Park. Half the people in town don't even bother to lock their doors at night or when they're not home.

Lauren was among them, until Nick left. Now, she locks the door at night. She'd lock it during the day, too, when the house is empty—if she could trust Lucy and Ryan not to keep losing their house keys.

As she told Ryan, bad things happen everywhere.

Inside, the phone rings once again.

Lauren sighs and goes in to see who it is. If her mother appears again on the caller ID, or even Alyssa, she'll let it go straight into voice mail, not in the mood for any more chitchat this afternoon.

But the number belongs to Nick's cell. Good. Maybe he's back and wanting to see the kids tonight after all.

"Hello?"

Nothing.

The call must have been lost. He's probably in the car and drove out of tower range, or maybe he's still on the ferry.

Then she hears something on the other end of the line—a rustling sound.

"Hello? Nick?"

Heavy breathing—gasping, really—reaches her ears, and then a low moan. She recognizes it instantly as Nick's voice. He used to gasp and moan like that when he was about to—

Lauren hangs up abruptly, horrified.

Obviously, Nick is in bed with his girlfriend. He must have rolled over on his phone, pocket dialing her.

Lovely. Just what she needs—an audio bite to go with the visions of Nick and Beth in each other's arms.

Footsteps bound down the stairs. "Mom? Was that Dad?"

Uh-oh. Ryan.

"I heard it ring," he goes on, "but I was in the bathroom."

Maybe she should lie, say that it was a wrong number or something. But Ryan would be able to check the caller ID . . . or maybe he already has.

"It was Dad," she tells him. "He just wanted to let us know that he, uh, made it home safely."

"But I wanted to talk to him!" Ryan is already reaching for the phone.

"Wait, Ry . . . I could use a hand with these boxes."

"Later." He's dialing. "I need to talk to Dad."

Lauren watches helplessly as Ryan listens to Nick's phone ringing, then going into voice mail.

"Dad, it's me again . . . Mom says you're home. I really need to talk to you, so . . . call me."

He hangs up, avoiding Lauren's gaze, and redials. Nick's other number rings into voice mail as well. This time, Ryan doesn't leave a message—just hangs up.

"Guess he's busy," he tells Lauren.

"Guess so," she replies, hating Nick more than ever before.

Expertly knotting his black bow tie, Garvey eyes himself in the mirror. To look at him, standing here in a tuxedo, outwardly calm and collected, no one would ever imagine his inner turmoil.

By now, he expected to have received a reassuring all-clear. That has yet to come. For all he knows, the so-called human obstacle still exists and might just be preparing to get the better of him.

Satisfied that his bow tie is straight, he strides out of the bedroom and down the hall. As he passes the series of family photographs, his gaze falls on one of his paternal grandmother, and it stops him in his tracks.

What would Eleanor Harding Quinn think of his situation?

She wouldn't have wasted time questioning how he'd managed to get himself into it, that's for sure. She didn't care much for details, had little patience for explanations of any sort. If she were alive, and knew what was going on, she'd advise Garvey to do whatever he can to extract himself from the situation with his reputation—and future—intact.

Don't worry, he silently assures his grandmother. *I always know what to do—thanks to you.*

A sturdy, handsome woman, Garvey's grandmother looks so like him. But where he prides himself on maintaining his cool, Eleanor Harding Quinn had a rip-roaring temper and rarely—if ever—smiled. She wears her no-nonsense expression even in photographs.

There were whispers about her within the family circle—mostly about whether she was mentally stable, as far as Garvey could tell. His father steered clear of her at all costs, but then, he was equally distant from his own children. To his credit, he never kept them from seeing his mother; in fact, he sent a willing Garvey to visit her every summer at Greymeadow, the family's sprawling gray-shingled country house amid acres of woods and meadows in the Hudson Valley.

Grandmother Quinn was the one who believed in him, assuring him that he was destined for even greater things than his illustrious family had already achieved.

"You're a Quinn. You can make anything happen, Garvey," she told him when, as a child, he dared to confess that he wanted to become president one day. "Just be prepared to give it your all."

He certainly has.

Now, with everything he's worked for hanging in the balance, he remembers something else his grandmother once told him.

They were at the country estate one June weekend, and his grandmother was surveying a flowerbed that had been planted by the gardeners in her absence.

"I told them no red," she noted, her black eyes dangerously displeased behind her wire-rimmed glasses. "See how the red clashes with the pink and purple? Do you see that, Garvey?"

Garvey nodded, more interested in the gate mounted to huge pillars alongside the long, winding driveway. The massive iron gate had been made in France, fancy grill-work etched with the word "GREYMEADOW."

Garvey always wondered what it would be like to shed all decorum, jump on that gate, and swing on it. He spent his entire childhood speculating about it, and never did find out.

When his grandmother—in pearls and silk stockings—dropped down on her hands and knees beside the flowerbed, however, he forgot all about the gate. He watched in fascination as she clawed at the soil with her manicured, diamond-bedecked fingers. She tore out one red petunia plant after another, ripping them into shreds and tossing them aside—she even tore a dangling earth-worm in half and tossed it aside.

"There," she said, when the plants had been deci-mated, their remains in an untidy heap.

"Why didn't you just ask the gardeners to fix it?"

"Because sometimes, the only way to get something done right is to do it yourself." She brushed her hands against each other, and crumbles of soil fell away. Her fingers were stained red from the blossoms. "You do what has to be done, and then you wash your hands and you move on. Don't you ever forget that, Garvey."

He never did. He frequently reminds himself that Grandmother Quinn wasn't afraid to get her hands dirty when necessary—and that he shouldn't be, either.

And he never has.

But garden soil is one thing.

Human blood is quite another.

Shaking his head, Garvey heads out the door.

can't take your call right now, but if you'll leave your name and—"

"Where do you think Daddy is?" Lucy asks yet again, as Lauren hangs up on Nick's voice mail yet again without leaving a message.

She's already left three on his cell and a couple more on his home phone. Ryan texted and e-mailed him as well, about an hour ago—when Nick was almost an hour late.

Now it's been two hours with no word, and Lauren is growing concerned, though she's not letting on to the kids.

In response to Lucy's question, she simply shrugs and says, "I'm sure he's on his way."

But she isn't sure at all.

She hasn't heard from Nick since yesterday's unfortunate pocket-dial call—which, of course, she didn't share with the kids.

When he failed to return Ryan's call last night, she privately thought it was possible that Nick might have since realized what had happened earlier. Maybe he'd been so embarrassed that Lauren had overheard his intimate moments with his girlfriend that he didn't want to call back and risk an uncomfortable confrontation.

Not that Lauren would ever bring it up. *Ever.* She's done her best to forget it, in fact.

Anyway, Nick could have just dialed Ryan's cell to talk to him directly. She's surprised he didn't.

With a pang, Lauren looks at her three children, sitting around the kitchen table dressed for brunch with their father. Ryan has on a polo instead of a T-shirt; Lucy's wearing a too-skimpy—in Lauren's opinion—skirt and top, and Sadie's in a pink ruffled sundress with a dozen strands of beads around her neck.

They're such great kids. How can Nick bear to be away from them? How can he ignore them?

Maybe he isn't. Maybe something's wrong.

"I'm worried about Daddy." Lucy echoes her thoughts. "What if—"

"You know, I should have talked to him myself when he called Friday night and made these plans with you guys." Lauren shakes her head. "I bet he meant next Sunday. He's probably still on vacation."

Ryan's head snaps up. "You said he called yesterday to say he was home."

"Oh, right. I forgot about that." She shouldn't have lied. But she was trying to protect Ryan—and, perhaps, to protect Nick as well. Big mistake.

"Anyway, Mom, he definitely meant this Sunday," Lucy insists.

"Maybe you misunderstood."

"No. I make plans with people all the time. Trust me, I didn't screw it up."

"Well, Dad did." Ryan, who has been mostly silent, scowls. "He totally blew us off."

"Maybe he's on his way and he's stuck in traffic or ran out of gas or something," Lauren suggests.

"He would have called." Lucy clutches the Robert Ludlum book she started reading last night. She was planning to show it to her father.

"Maybe he forgot his cell phone," Lauren tells her, "or the battery's dead."

"Why are you making excuses for him, Mom?"

I'm not. I'm protecting the three of you from disappointment.

"Do you want more Goldfish crackers, Sadie?" she asks, picking up the bag.

Her youngest nods and slides her plastic bowl toward Lauren, who refills it for the third time. Poor little thing has been starved.

So is Lauren. She looks at the stove clock. Right about now, she should be sipping a Bloody Mary in an upscale Manhattan bistro. When she called Alyssa earlier to say she'd be late, her sister moved the reservation ahead an hour. "I'm just glad you're not calling to cancel," she told Lauren. "I had a feeling you might."

No. Lauren is actually looking forward to her outing in the city. She's exchanged her usual shorts and flip-flops for a little black dress she found in the back of her closet last night. She'd worn it years ago, for someone's wedding, but a couple of kids later, had been unable to squeeze into it again.

It fits now, though. It's even a little baggy. But at least it's presentable.

While she was browsing through her closet, she found countless outfits that are suitable for the tag sale. She'll get back to filling boxes later, or tomorrow. It was cathartic.

"Can I call Ian?" Ryan interrupts her thoughts.

"Mom already said no," Lucy reminds her brother. "Why don't you stop asking?"

He shoots her a glare and turns back to Lauren. "Mom, this is so stupid. We're sitting here wasting a beautiful day and Dad's not even going to show up."

He has a point. The sun is shining in a brilliant blue sky, and the heat wave has broken—for now, anyway. The temperature is in the low eighties and a refreshing breeze stirs the white ruffled curtains at the windows.

"Anyway, how do you know Dad's not going to show up?"

"I just do, okay?" Ryan tells his sister.

"No, you don't."

The phone rings, putting an abrupt end to the bickering.

"Daddy!" Sadie exclaims, as Lucy answers it with an anticipatory "Hello?"

Lauren sees her face fall immediately.

"Oh, hi, Aunt Alyssa. Yeah, she's right here. Hold on." Lucy glumly hands the phone to Lauren.

She lifts it to her ear. "Hi."

"Why aren't you on a train?"

"We're still waiting for Nick, so . . ."

"Where the hell is he?"

"I've been wondering the same thing."

"I'll change the reservation again. Do you think two-thirty is safe?"

"No, just go ahead without me. Even if he shows up now, there's no way I can catch a train in time to meet you."

"Three?"

"No, seriously, Lys, forget it for today."

"This is so unfair of him to do to you, Lauren."

Never mind me . . . what about the kids?

She hangs up, unsettled.

"I want to do something with my friends, Mom," Ryan says promptly. "Please? I haven't seen Ian all summer and—"

"Okay, okay. Go ahead and call him."

Ryan makes a beeline out of the room.

"Thanks, Mom," Lauren calls after him.

"Thanks, Mom," he calls back, footsteps pounding up the stairs.

"Why did you let him go?" Lucy asks, turning on Lauren.

"Because he's right. He hasn't seen Ian all summer, and it's a beautiful day."

"But what if Daddy shows up and Ryan's not here?"

"We'll deal with that when it happens."

If it happens.

Where on earth are you, Nick? Are you okay?

"Hey, Mom! I need a ride to Ian's," Ryan calls from the top of the stairs.

It's Lucy who responds, clearly exasperated. "How about asking and saying *please*?"

"You're not Mom!"

"I am," Lauren calls, "and how about saying *please*?"

She can just see Ryan rolling his eyes before offering a perfunctory "Please?"

"Okay." Lauren turns to her daughters. "Come on, we'll all go. We can drop off Ryan at Ian's and go to the mall to buy some back-to-school clothes."

"Yes!" Lucy fist-pumps the air as Sadie looks up from her Goldfish crackers, stricken.

"I don't want to go."

"Sure you do. We can shop together," Lucy tells her little sister. "Won't that be fun? I'll help you pick out some new big girl shoes for school."

"I don't want new shoes."

"Come on, Sadie, everyone needs new shoes for kindergarten. And nice new dresses, and—"

"But what about Daddy?"

"Daddy couldn't come today, sweetie," Lauren tells her gently. "But Lucy and I want to take you shopping."

Sadie looks down, saying nothing.

Lounging beneath an umbrella, his toes buried in hot sand, Garvey watches Caroline paddle back into the breakers on her surfboard.

"That's far enough," he calls, but his daughter can't possibly hear him over the pounding waves.

Marin, in a chair beside him, looks up from her book. "She's careful. Don't worry."

Don't worry.

Yeah, right.

Worrying about Caroline comes as naturally as breathing for Garvey. You don't live through the horror of almost losing a child without becoming hypervigilant.

Garvey sits forward in his canvas chair, shielding his eyes with his hand.

"Did you come out here just so you could keep an eye on her?" Marin asks.

"No," he replies truthfully. "But now that I'm here . . ."

"I'm just glad you are." His wife reaches over and squeezes his hand. "That was the best surprise ever."

She's referring to last night, when he showed up, unannounced, at the Cottingtons' big, gray-shingled beach house. Still wearing his black tuxedo, carrying a hastily packed overnight bag, he arrived close to midnight. The girls were asleep, but Marin and Heather Cottington were sitting on the deck polishing off a bottle of pinot grigio.

Garvey suspected it wasn't their first when Marin swayed to her feet and threw her arms around him.

"What are you doing here?" she kept asking.

Providing myself with an alibi.

Imagine if he had told her the truth. All of it, right then and there.

He would never do it, of course . . . but he can't stop thinking about how Marin would react if she knew. A part of him wonders if she might not just understand what happened all those years ago, and why he would go to such great lengths to see that it stays buried.

She is, after all, his wife . . .

And the mother of his children.

Ah—the great irony in that. Marin's maternal role is the one reason she might be able to forgive him—and the one reason she might not.

That's why he's never told her. He never will.

And should anything not have gone as planned yesterday—should there be any kind of mess, despite his instructions—he'll be in the clear.

Such a shame that anyone had to die.

But really, just look at all the lives that will be saved in the grand scheme of things. Yes, when Garvey takes office, health care will be at the top of his agenda. That will more than compensate for this weekend's unfortunate casualties.

I just have to focus on the greater good.

I have to do whatever it takes to make this go away.

"I just wish you could stay." Marin is still holding on to his hand.

"So do I."

The morning flew by—breakfast, church, and now this sun-soaked respite before he hits the road.

He looks at his watch, then glances up at the Cottingtons' house above the dunes. Heather's up there preparing a lunch he's told her repeatedly he can't stay to eat. He has to get back to Manhattan for a late afternoon rally, a photo op, and a dinner.

"Ten minutes," he tells Marin, "and then I've got to go."

"Are you sure you can't wait until Annie gets back?" Their younger daughter went off with Chelsea Cottington to visit a friend down the beach.

Garvey shakes his head. "I have to be back for the—"

"Excuse me," a voice cuts in, and a shadow falls over Garvey's outstretched legs.

He looks up to see a woman standing there. She's wearing a gauzy white cover-up that whips around her in the sea breeze, and a large sun hat she's holding to her head with a tanned hand. Her face is almost completely concealed by a pair of movie star sunglasses.

"You're Garvey Quinn, aren't you?"

With an inward sigh and a campaign smile, he tells her, "Yes, I am."

"I knew it!" She gestures at a pair of chairs a few yards away, where her companion, clad in boardshorts, sits watching them. "I told my boyfriend that was you, but he didn't think so."

"Well, if you made a bet, you won."

She laughs delightedly—then goes on to tell him, in excruciating detail, about the proposed housing development that will infringe upon her wooded backyard in Nassau County. Garvey listens dutifully and gives her all the appropriate feedback, ever conscious of the ticking clock, Marin's impatience, and his baby girl out in the Atlantic trying to catch a wave.

At last, the woman makes her way back to her boyfriend.

Marin sighs. "It never ends."

"You know that it—"

"I know, I know. It goes with the territory. Sometimes it's exhausting."

"Sometimes?"

She squeezes his hand. "I just wonder if it's worth it."

"It will be." He looks at his watch. "I have to go."

"I know you do."

He can't see her eyes behind the sunglasses, but her mouth is taut.

"I'll see you and the girls back in the city tomorrow. Don't forget, we have that dinner at—"

"I won't forget, Garvey."

"Tell the girls—"

"I will."

He stands and checks to see if Caroline is anywhere near shore so that he can wave her over for a hug.

No.

Casting a gaze out at the water, he doesn't see her there, either.

For a moment, his heart stands still.

Then her head pops up amid the breakers.

Garvey watches her for a few more seconds, until he's satisfied that she's okay. Then he reluctantly turns his back, forces himself to walk away.

Over the years, he's found comfort in the familiar Bible verse he learned years ago, in Sunday school: "Fathers shall not be put to death for their children, nor children put to death for their fathers; each is to die for his own sin."

Now that his past is closing in, Garvey can't help but wonder . . .

What about a child who would not be alive at all, but for her father's sins?

* * *

Shopping with the girls, Lauren almost managed to put Nick's absence out of her head.

Almost.

Every so often, she stepped away from the girls to surreptitiously check her cell phone, just to make sure she hadn't somehow missed a return call from him. She hadn't.

Now, arriving back home in the late afternoon, she side-steps a barking, tail-wagging Chauncey and goes straight to the phone to check the voice mail and caller ID log.

No Nick.

He obviously got confused about the day, or forgot, or . . . something.

Fear threads its way through her once again. Nick might be forgetful—and, okay, a jerk—but he should have called to check in by now.

Lauren listens impatiently to a message from her mother, wanting to pick a date for the visit, and one from a boy named Josh, looking for Lucy.

"Daddy didn't call?"

She looks up to see Lucy behind her, paper shopping bags in hand and an expectant expression on her face.

"Sweetie, I'm sure everything's okay. Oh, and some-one named Josh called looking for you."

"Really?" Lucy perks right up at that. "What did he say?"

"To call him back."

"Great! I'll do it upstairs."

Lauren should probably ask her who Josh is, and why she's so happy to hear from him, but isn't it obvious? Lucy likes Josh. Josh—hopefully—likes Lucy. And any-thing that gets her mind off her disappointment in Nick is probably a healthy thing.

"Why don't you go put your new clothes on hangers before they get wrinkled? And here, maybe you can help Sadie do the same thing with her dresses." Lauren offers Lucy the bags from Gymboree and Gap Kids.

Sadie didn't want to shop for new clothes; she didn't want to try anything on; she didn't even want to carry the bags into the house.

Now, however, she grabs at the purchases. "I can put them away myself."

"But you can't reach the hangers," Lucy points out. "Let me help you."

"No, I can do it!"

"Fine." Lucy disappears with a shrug.

Lauren sighs, not in the mood for a tantrum. "Sadie—"

"I don't want anyone in my room!"

"Why not?"

"I just don't."

"Sadie—"

"No!"

Pick your battles, Lauren reminds herself. She looks her youngest child in the eye, both admiring and dismayed at the spark of determination she sees there.

"Okay, sweetie, you're right. You're a big girl. Go ahead and hang up your own clothes."

Sadie takes the bag from her and marches out of the room.

Frowning, Lauren watches her go. She doesn't look back.

Concern over Sadie gives way to renewed concern that something might have happened to Nick. Lauren picks up the phone again and dials his cell phone, hoping to hear a "Hey, what's up?"

Instead, she's greeted by the usual recorded greeting.

This time she opts to leave a message. She hasn't in a few hours.

"Nick, it's me again. The kids are upset that you didn't show today. They're worried, and I . . . so am I. Please call me back, okay? *Please*. As soon as you get this."

"I don't understand why you let Garvey get away with so much, Marin." Heather Cottington pokes at her salad with a polished silver fork. "You really need to let him know that it's unacceptable to come sailing in here out of the blue, and then sail right back out again."

"Unacceptable to you?"

"Of course not. You know my door is always open for houseguests. Lord knows I have the room." Heather waves her empty fork toward the house, silhouetted against a twilight sky.

From this perch on the wooden deck amid the dunes, the home looks even grander than it is. Light spills from windows on all three levels. Marin's girls are inside, along with Heather's three teenagers and a large group of friends.

"I just think it's hard on you and the kids when he comes and goes like this," Heather goes on.

She should talk. Her own husband, Ron, isn't here. He's away on one of his many golf weekends.

But Marin isn't about to bring that up. What does it matter? They're not talking about Heather's marriage. They're talking about hers.

Why? Why does Heather have to bring this up again? Didn't they have this same discussion earlier today, over a lunch that Heather kept saying she prepared just for Garvey—who, she knew all along, couldn't stay to eat it?

It makes Heather feel better to criticize other people's marriages, given the state of her own.

Or maybe she has a point, Marin admits reluctantly—
but only to herself.

Aloud, she says, "We're used to Garvey coming and
going on the spur of the moment."

"I think that's sad."

"It isn't. Not to us. And it goes with the territory."

Ignoring her friend's dubious expression, Marin sips
from her lime-infused Perrier, glad she opted not to join
Heather in another bottle of wine tonight. Last night,
they overdid it—Marin did, anyway. She woke up queasy
this morning and it lasted, along with a headache, all
afternoon.

Heather, who drank twice as much wine as Marin, appeared no worse for wear—which speaks volumes about
her tolerance level. She's the embodiment of the 4Bs—
Marin's private nickname for a certain type of woman:
blond, bejeweled, boozy, and bone-thin.

Women like that populate her social circle back in
Manhattan. Marin supposes that she herself fits the bill
on a good—or bad—day, depending on how one looks
at it.

Funny, because she never wanted to become one of
those women.

But you aren't.

She might have the physical trademarks, but she's different.

You just keep telling yourself that.

But it's true! Marin is much kinder, and softer, and she
lacks the overbearing sense of self-entitlement . . .

*If you're so different deep down inside, then why do
you spend so much time with women like that?*

Because they're there.

It's that simple. She doesn't meet a vast assortment of
women in her everyday life. Neighbors, private school

moms, charity volunteers, political wives—they're all of a certain ilk. 4B ilk.

Like she just told Heather—it goes with the territory.

"It's campaign season," Marin points out. "After the primary, and the election—"

"Garvey will be governor of New York State. Don't think for one minute that your lives will settle down."

"Sure they will. We'll be living in Albany, remember?" she can't resist pointing out, and waits for Heather to wrinkle her surgically perfect nose.

It doesn't take long. "Don't remind yourself. Or at least don't remind me."

Really, the snob factor is astounding—even to Marin, who's been party to it for years now.

You'd think she'd just told Heather they'd be moving into a cardboard box on the Bowery instead of the New York State governor's mansion.

Wait—do people even still live in cardboard boxes on the Bowery? Or has that neighborhood, too, been transformed, like so many Marin frequented in her brief bohemian past?

"I just think Garvey takes you and the girls for granted," Heather informs her.

"He loves us more than anything," Marin replies, shaking her head. Maybe she should have had wine tonight. She's feeling more tightly wound by the second—in direct contrast to Heather, who dismissively waves a bare, salon-tanned arm.

"Nobody said Garvey doesn't love you . . . but is that enough?"

"What do you mean?"

"I saw the look on your face when he said he had to head back early today. You were disappointed. And the girls were, too."

"Garvey is an excellent father and husband, Heather."

"I'm not a constituent, Marin. I'm your friend. You don't have to feed me the party line. He's already got my vote."

Marin can't help but laugh at that. "Heather, you co-chaired a Planned Parenthood fund-raiser. Garvey will have the right-to-life endorsement. I don't believe for a minute that you're going to vote for him."

"Okay, okay, but he doesn't need me. Thanks to the Spitzer fiasco, plenty of people are going to go for the family values ticket."

"Let's hope so."

"Mom?"

She looks up to see someone standing on the stairs leading from the house.

For a split second, Marin isn't sure whether it was even one of her own daughters' voices, or which daughter it is. But only for a split second.

"What's wrong, Annie?"

"You can't believe how snotty Caroline is being."

I bet I can, Marin thinks wearily. No surprise. Caroline has always been spoiled. It's her own fault, as well as Garvey's.

"What's going on, Annie?"

As she listens to the latest account of Caroline's misdeeds, she finds herself wishing Garvey were here to handle it for a change.

But the reality is, that wouldn't necessarily help. Caroline is a true Daddy's girl. And Annie—well, it's not that Garvey is blatantly unfair to her.

But he treats her differently. There's no denying it.

Perhaps the girls aren't even aware of it, but Marin is.

Would things be different, she often wonders, if Annie had been born under different circumstances? Would Garvey love her more? Treat her more fairly?

Looking at her younger daughter, who looks so like Marin and nothing like a Quinn, Marin wishes he could find it in his heart to forgive her for something that isn't her fault. Something she doesn't even know she did.

But she didn't *do* anything. It's not about what she did. It's what she *is*.

No.

It's about what she *isn't*.

The saving grace is that Annie herself doesn't know the truth. They agreed never to tell her. What would be the point? It all worked out in the end, thanks to Garvey.

Who can blame him for the way he indulges Caroline?

Who can blame him for the flicker of regret Marin sees on his face every time he looks at Annie?

Who, indeed?

"I'll take care of it," Marin assures Annie, rising from the table and putting an arm around her youngest child's shoulder.

I'll take care of you. *No matter what.*

It's a promise she made to Annie before she was even conceived—fiercely, fervently, perhaps suspecting the bitter disappointments that lay ahead.

But Garvey didn't, try as she might to warn him.

He really believed everything was going to be okay.

And wasn't it, in the end?

Didn't he make it so?

Garvey Quinn is nothing if not a good father. No one would argue that.

Ryan had really been looking forward to seeing Ian today. They hung out at his house all afternoon, watching a movie in the home theater, playing tennis on the private court, swimming in the backyard pool, then soaking in the hot tub.

Staying for dinner had seemed like a great idea when Ian's mother invited him, but now Ryan isn't so sure.

"How are your parents, Ryan?" Ian's mom asks, pretty much the second they all sit down at the big teak table on the patio.

The way she says it—as if Mom and Dad are still a single unit—bothers him.

"They're good," he replies, and cuts into the enormous slab of beef on his plate. Medium rare, just the way he likes it, served alongside grilled jumbo shrimp, baked potatoes with sour cream, corn on the cob . . .

Heaven.

"So your dad is living in the city now?"

"Uh . . . no." He puts the piece of steak into his mouth so she won't expect him to elaborate. She's the kind of mother who's fussy about manners, and everyone knows it's impolite to talk with your mouth full.

"No? Where is he living?"

Maybe he shouldn't have talked Mom into letting him stay to eat. Not that he'd had to do as much begging as he'd expected. When he called, he could tell by the clattering pots and pans that Mom was in the kitchen, but she told him she wasn't cooking—she was cleaning, obviously still caught up in her clutter-removal frenzy.

Ryan wasn't crazy about the idea of going home to be put to work. Besides, Mrs. Wasserman said they had plenty of steak and shrimp.

That's the kind of house Ian lives in, with both his parents and a little brother who never seems to bother anyone. A huge brick house in Glenhaven Crossing, one of the newer developments on the edge of town. A house where there's steak and shrimp for dinner on a regular old night—*extra* steak and shrimp for unexpected guests like Ryan.

But at least the Kraft macaroni and cheese Mom said she'd throw together for dinner back at home wouldn't be served up with nosy questions.

Ryan chews, swallows. "He's living in White Plains."

"White Plains? Really? Hmm, did I know that?"

Something tells Ryan she did.

"Does he live all by himself, then?"

"Yeah." *Who else would he be living with?* Ryan wants to ask.

But he's afraid he knows the answer, and he definitely doesn't want to get into all that. He hurriedly pops another piece of meat into his mouth.

"Do you see him often?"

Ryan chews helplessly. This time, Ian answers for him.

"Ry was supposed to see him today, but his dad bailed."

"Bailed? What do you mean, bailed?"

Thanks a lot, Ian.

"It means he didn't show up. Right, Ry?"

Ryan shrugs, even though his mouth is no longer full. What is there to say to that, besides *Shut up, Ian*?

That wouldn't really be fair. After all, Ian's right.

Still, Ian doesn't like to talk to his mother about his own life. Why does he have to talk to her about Ryan's?

"Do you mean something came up at the last minute?" Mrs. Wasserman addresses Ryan directly.

"Janet, let him eat," Mr. Wasserman protests.

"He's eating. We're all eating. Ethan, that's enough salt on the corn." She grabs the shaker out of Ian's brother's hand. "I hope your father at least called to tell you he wasn't coming, Ryan."

When someone asks you a question they have no business asking, it's okay to lie, right?

"Yeah," Ryan tells Mrs. Wasserman. "He called."

He shoots a look at Ian, in case he feels like contradicting that.

"He was probably too tired from his trip to hang with you today," Ian comments.

"What trip is that?"

"My dad went to the beach for a few days."

"That's nice. Where did he go?"

"I'm not sure," Ryan lies.

"Was it Martha's Vineyard?"

So Mrs. Wasserman already knew that? Then why did she bother to ask?

Probably because she knows Dad was away with his girlfriend.

I bet the whole town knows. And I bet she was hoping I'd spill the dirt. As if.

"I'm not sure," Ryan reiterates.

"Hmm."

At last, Mrs. Wasserman takes a bite of her own meal.

Ryan breathes a silent sigh of relief. He's known Ian's mom since he was, like, five. He liked her well enough until last spring—specifically, until Mom and Dad separated.

"I haven't seen your mother all summer. Has she been away?"

Ryan shakes his head, vigorously sawing at a hunk of beef.

Mrs. Wasserman sits with her fork poised, waiting for him to say something more.

He doesn't.

After a moment, she asks, "So she's been here in town all summer?"

"Pretty much."

"I wonder why I haven't seen her."

"Janet," Mr. Wasserman says.

"Yes?"

"Let him eat."

"I'm just making dinner conversation."

"It sounds like an interrogation."

"I'm concerned about Lauren. I haven't seen her since the—" She breaks off.

Funny that a person who has so much to say apparently doesn't want to utter the word "separation."

"Why don't you just give her a call if you want to know how she is?"

Ian's dad, whom Ryan has always considered a quiet, nerdy kind of guy, just became his new hero.

"I'll have to do that. Ryan, honey, I don't mean to bother you. I'm just concerned. I know what it's like. I came from a broken home, too."

Ethan looks up with interest. "How did your house break, Mommy?"

"No, it didn't break, it was . . ."

"Broken," Ian supplies, a mischievous gleam in his eye.

"How?" Ethan persists.

"It means my parents were divorced. Like Ryan's. And I remember how very hard it was on me. Ryan, I want you to know that if you ever need someone to talk to, I'm here."

Yeah, sure. Ryan tries to imagine himself baring his soul to his new pal, Mrs. Wasserman.

Uh, I don't think so, dude.

"I mean it, Ryan. If you ever feel like you want to confide in someone who's been in your shoes . . ."

"Thanks," he murmurs.

She looks pleased. "Good. Does anyone want some more shrimp?"

Ryan shakes his head, having lost his appetite and wishing he was anywhere other than here—even back at his so-called broken home.

When Garvey's cell phone rings in the midst of a dicey cocktail hour conversation about campaign finance, he's relieved.

"I'm sorry, gentlemen, I'm expecting a call and this might be it." He reaches into his pocket and checks the number.

This is definitely it.

He hurriedly excuses himself from the group of businessmen and ducks through the nearest archway leading out of the hotel ballroom.

"Is it done?" he asks into the phone as he strides toward an isolated corner, keeping his voice low.

"Yes."

"No mess this time, right? You made sure?"

"No mess."

"And you have the file."

The telltale silence on the other end of the line answers the question—which wasn't really a question, dammit, because it never occurred to him that they could possibly come this far and fail.

It's all Garvey can do not to cry out in sheer frustration and rage.

But there are eyes on him, of course. Plenty of security at these dinners, and press, too—not to mention hundreds of people wanting to shake his hand.

"I think I know where it is, though."

"You *think*?"

"I—"

"Perhaps we should discuss this in person," he suggests into the phone, keeping his expression as neutral as if he were having a mundane chat with his wife or a campaign adviser.

"Wouldn't that be too risky?"

"Hell, yes," he mutters through clenched teeth. "But it's riskier to let this drag on and on."

If you want something done right . . .

But he doesn't dare do this himself. All he can do is provide explicit instructions, and make it absolutely clear what's at stake here.

"Where do you want to meet?"

"The usual place."

"And the usual time?"

"Yes."

He hangs up without a good-bye, pastes a cheerful smile on his face, and makes his way back to the ballroom full of supporters.

It's been a year since Lauren bothered to open the secret cubby in the kitchen—which ostensibly means that anything stored inside can safely be tossed away.

She's been moving from closet to cupboard for a few hours now, doing her best to forget that Nick has yet to get in touch with her. Then again, maybe he's called Ryan's cell phone by now. Ryan's still over at Ian's, but any second now he should be calling for a ride. When he does, Lauren is sure, he'll mention that his father called and is just fine.

On her hands and knees, she empties the narrow space, which, like the hidden cupboard upstairs in Sadie's closet, is concealed by a decorative panel and lacks a knob. The two shelves are mainly lined with a collection of old florist vases left over from the days when she had a husband who sent her flowers.

The vases might have outlasted the husband—not to mention the flowers—but it's definitely time to get rid of them, Lauren decides.

Suddenly, Chauncey, asleep on the floor nearby, stirs to life. His ears prick up as if listening for something.

Sure enough, Lauren hears footsteps on the driveway outside the open windows.

Barking, the dog barrels toward the back door, prepared to either greet or attack the newcomer, as needed.

"It's okay, boy, shh," Lauren tells him.

She gets to her feet and turns to see a figure standing on the other side of the screen door. For a split second, relieved, she thinks it's Nick.

Then she remembers that Nick usually comes to the front now. She flips on the outdoor light. Ryan.

"How did you get home?" She nudges Chauncey out of the way with her knee and unlatches the door.

"I walked."

"All the way from Glenhaven Crossing? Why? I was going to pick you up!"

Ryan shrugs and reaches for the handle.

"Careful—don't let anything in with you." She eyes the moths flitting around the overhead bulb. "Why didn't you call me for a ride?"

"You know . . .'cause I knew you were busy."

"Ryan, it's dark out and you're twelve years old. You don't go walking around town by yourself at night."

"I was fine."

"You were lucky. Remember what I told you—bad things happen everywhere, all the time."

Why does that phrase keep popping into her head?

This time, it sparks renewed trepidation. She hasn't heard from Nick yet.

"Mom, I'm fine," Ryan tells her.

"Yes, and thank God for that." Lauren can just imagine what Janet Wasserman thinks about a single mother who can't be bothered to pick up her child. Then again . . . "I'm surprised Ian's mother let you go off alone, Ry."

"Um, she didn't really know. I just kind of . . . left."

"Did you have a fight with Ian or something?"

"Nope. Can we not talk about this right now? You kind of sound like Mrs. Wasserman."

"Oh, God help me."

Ryan snorts.

"Sorry. That just slipped out. Forget I said that. You know I like Ian's mother a lot."

"Yeah, Mom, sure you do."

"I do," Lauren protests—not very convincingly, it seems, because Ryan shakes his head.

The boys have been friends since kindergarten, and Lauren was friendly enough with Janet Wasserman over the years, though never particularly close. Swapping playdates, chipping in for classmates' birthday gifts, arranging rides to and from school activities . . . those were the kinds of things she was comfortable discussing with Janet.

Not personal lives, though. Janet has long held a well-deserved reputation as a busybody. Harmless, but a busybody nonetheless.

"Come on, Mom," Ryan says, "she's not your friend."

"No," Lauren admits. "Not lately. Maybe I once would have considered her a friend, though."

"Why did you lose all your friends when you and Dad split up?"

Startled by the question, she's about to deny Ryan's

assumption. But why? He's not blind, or stupid. He knows a circle of women no longer surrounds her—that Trilby is all she has left.

"I'm not sure why, exactly, Ry. I guess when you go through hard times, you find out who your true friends are."

She watches him digest that and prays it's not a lesson he'll have to learn the hard way.

"Do you want to make new friends?" he asks.

"Sure. But it's not easy." Not wanting him to feel sorry for her, she changes the subject—sort of. "So did Mrs. Wasserman ask you a lot of questions?"

"Pretty much."

"About what?"

"You know . . . stuff."

"Me and Dad?"

Ryan looks uncomfortable, and Lauren decides there's no such thing as a harmless busybody.

"What did she want to know?"

"Everything."

"What did you tell her?"

"Nothing."

"Oh, Ry . . ." Lauren loops her arms around her son's shoulders. He's almost as tall as she is. Someday soon, he'll be taller. But he's still her little boy.

Ryan was always so easygoing, so nurturing, so sweet. So . . .

On my side.

Not that he's chosen sides in the divorce—they've been careful not to drag the kids into it. Of Lauren's three children, though, it's her son who has always made her feel like half of a two-man team that sticks together, win or lose. Always.

Years ago, when Ryan was just a toddler, she stubbed

154   WENDY CORSI STAUB

her toe. She remembers hopping around in pain, trying not to curse in front of the kids. Ryan disappeared into the next room and came back with a box of SpongeBob Band-Aids and the boo-boo bunny ice pack from the freezer.

"I fix you up, Mommy," he said, and gently kissed her toe.

She cried.

She cried again when she repeated the story to Nick that night.

"I feel like he thinks he has to be the little man of the house when you're not home," she told him. "Lucy, she's in her own world. It's not that she doesn't care—it's more that she doesn't notice. But Ryan looks out for me."

"That's good. When you're old and decrepit, he can come take you out in your wheelchair to the early-bird special," was Nick's glib response.

"Really? Where will you be?" she asked indignantly.

"Dead and gone, I'm sure."

He was kidding around, but even at the time, she was sobered by the thought of being widowed, even in the far-off future. It was inconceivable that Nick might die and leave her alone one day—even though women statistically tend to outlive their husbands, and he was almost eight years older than Lauren in the first place.

She didn't like to think about it, though. They had a whole lifetime ahead of them.

Till death do us part.

Nick, apparently, heard it wrong.

Nick heard *Till Beth do us part.*

Damn him, she thinks automatically, as always—then feels guilty, remembering that she's spent the last few hours worrying about his well-being.

"Has Dad called your cell phone, Ryan?"

"No. Why?"

"I just thought you might have heard from him."

"You mean you haven't?"

Seeing the worry in her son's eyes, Lauren wishes she hadn't brought it up. Time to change the subject. "So listen, Ry, I'm sorry you had to deal with Mrs. Wasserman."

"I didn't. I just ignored her."

"Good. You have to be polite, okay? But you don't have to tell her anything that isn't her business."

"Don't worry. I won't."

"At least you ate well, right? Steak and shrimp? Was it good?"

"It was okay. Got any leftover macaroni and cheese?"

Lauren smiles. "In the fridge."

She goes back to filling a carton with the old florist vases, and Ryan puts the macaroni and cheese into the microwave.

"Is someone coming to pick up all this stuff for the tag sale?" he asks, eyeing the boxes and clutter on the floor.

"No, I have to get it over to the church basement tomorrow morning."

"By yourself?"

"I guess so."

"I'll help you," Ryan tells her, and for the moment, he really is her little boy again. Sweet Ryan, always there to help her; always on her side.

"Can we do it early, though, Mom? I told the guys I'd meet them at the pool when it opens."

Her little boy, with his own life to lead.

"Early," she agrees. "And I'll drop you at the pool afterward."

Then she remembers . . . Beth will be back in town this week; she might be there.

Should she warn Ryan that he might run into her?

No. No way. He doesn't have reason to avoid her—not like Lauren does.

Or does she?

Maybe it's time to stop rearranging her life for fear of crossing paths with Beth—or with the local gossips.

Yes, let them talk.

Let Beth feel guilty when she sees Lauren—if she has it in her.

If she doesn't, well, that's life.

Lauren squirms inside, thinking again of yesterday's phone call from Nick, so obviously in the throes of love-making . . .

Or was he?

Of course he was, she tells herself. She's heard him make those noises countless times. Gasping . . . moaning . . .

Then again—those sounds aren't merely associated with passion. She supposes that a person in trouble—Nick in trouble—might sound the same way.

What if he'd had some kind of accident and was calling for help?

It happens. People drive their cars off the road and are trapped, injured, with their cell phones.

But if that were the case, she'd have been notified by now . . .

Unless he hasn't been found.

"Mom, do you think five minutes is long enough?" Ryan asks, and she looks up to see him peering at the microwave.

"Five minutes? One minute would have been good, two, tops!" Lauren forgets, for the time being, about Nick as she hurries to help her son.

* * *

Looking up as Garvey exits the elevator in his running clothes, the doorman puts aside his *New York Post* and steps out from behind the desk. "Morning, Congressman."

"How are you, Henry?"

"Fine," he replies, though Garvey figures it's a lie. Henry's in the middle of a nasty divorce. "You?"

"Fine." Far from it, but just as Garvey doesn't want to hear the sordid details of the doorman's business, he isn't about to spill his own.

"Glad to hear it. Looks like it's going to be another hot one today."

"You know it. That's why I always like to get in my exercise before the sun comes up."

"I know you do. Have a good run." Henry holds the door open for him.

"See you in a bit."

Garvey jogs off down the block, still lit by streetlights. Behind him, he assumes the sky is just beginning to brighten, but he's heading west toward Fifth Avenue and Central Park.

He waves as he passes Eddie, the Korean grocer, arranging cellophane-wrapped gladiolus bouquets on the sidewalk display.

"Good morning, good morning," Eddie calls, same as always.

Rounding the corner, Garvey spots a pair of familiar deliverymen wheeling box-laden hand trucks from their van to a store. They, too, greet him as he passes.

He smiles—at them, and to himself. Yes, there's something to be said for establishing a good, solid routine.

Garvey crosses Fifth, enters the park, and runs along the stone-lined transverse road and through the arched tunnel. He takes East Drive north, alongside the reser-

voir. There's little automobile traffic at this time of morning, but there are plenty of joggers, along with bikers and
Rollerbladers, most of whom whiz past.

He runs a steady pace, keeping his eyes peeled on the
path ahead.

There.

On a bench, a helmeted figure in a bulky T-shirt and
black leggings adjusts a pair of blades. From here, it's
impossible to tell whether it's a male or a female—but
Garvey knows.

As he passes, the figure rises from the bench and falls
into pace near him—not right alongside, so that they
appear to be together, but close enough to carry on a
conversation and not be overheard. There's no one in the
immediate vicinity, and these days, most people work out
wearing iPod earphones anyway.

"Tell me what happened yesterday," he commands in
a low voice.

As he listens to the disturbing tale, he can feel his jaw
clenching in fury. They follow the road in its westward
turn, following the curve of the reservoir. His tightened
fists pump at his sides in rhythm with a heart that isn't
racing from exercise alone.

"Is that it?"

"That's what happened. Yes."

"So where is it, then?"

"I told you, I'm not a hundred percent sure, but—"

"Why don't you take a wild guess," he bites out.

"He has a kid. Three, but there's a little girl, and—"

"Where?" Garvey asks impatiently, glancing at the
skyline behind him. The sun is coming up.

"Westchester. Glenhaven Park. Do you know where it
is? It's only about twenty minutes from—"

"I know where it is. Go."

"There are kids involved."

"Do you think I don't know that?"

"But you can't expect me to—"

"You'll do whatever you have to do. You don't even *have* kids, for God's sake."

"That doesn't mean it doesn't make me sick to think of—"

"Oh really? Then you've certainly changed your tune in the last fourteen years, haven't you?"

Garvey's question is met with silence. He's always known how to hit low and dirty, right where it hurts most.

"Listen to me. You have no choice. You're in this as deeply as I am now. You have to do whatever it takes to find that file. Do you understand me?"

"Whatever it takes."

Garvey nods.

Conversation over.

With a burst of anger-fueled adrenaline, he sprints away, heading toward the still-darkened western sky like a nocturnal creature trying to outrun the dawn.

CHAPTER
NINE

Perched on the front steps with her second cup of coffee, Lauren watches a monarch butterfly fluttering around a hydrangea bloom on the shrub beside the porch and wonders what to do about Nick.

Something is wrong. She's sure of it. He should have called last night; certainly by now.

Lauren left one last message on both Nick's phones before she went to bed, telling herself that she'd take action in the morning.

It's morning. What are you going to do?

Nothing yet. Ryan is up, getting ready to help her with the boxes and then meet his friends. He asked about Nick again, first thing, and Lauren didn't want to worry him. She assured him that his father must have gotten the Sunday brunch date wrong, that he'd probably made other plans, that he'd undoubtedly resurfaced too late last night to call.

Ryan seemed satisfied with that.

I wish I were.

When she gets back, while the girls are still asleep, she'll do something about the Nick situation.

Like . . . ?

Like call the police . . .

And tell them what? That your husband went away with another woman and hasn't come back yet, or called—other than to let you in on a little heavy-breathing episode?

She can just imagine a seasoned cop's reaction to that bit of news—particularly a local cop, who'd quite possibly already be privy to the sordid details of Lauren's marital problems.

Yet Saturday's wordless call from Nick isn't a detail she'd be able to leave out if she calls to report him missing, given her theory that he might have had some kind of accident.

Frustrated, she watches the butterfly move on to a clump of pink and purple verbena beside the porch rail. A breeze stirs the flowers. Lauren shivers—not entirely from the chill in the air, though it's definitely there.

Just yesterday, it was summertime.

This morning, the first hint of autumn is palpable.

The maple and oak leaves remain lush and green; the perennials are at the height of their bloom. The neighborhood still languishes in that lazy, half-deserted August aura.

Yet the air isn't quite as humid today. It feels cooler. And the dappled morning sunlight seems to fall through the trees at a longer angle, casting shadows where there were none just a few days ago.

Or maybe it's just her imagination. Paranoia about Nick, making the world suddenly seem like a threatening place.

As if to punctuate the thought, Lauren suddenly sees, out of the corner of her eye, a stranger coming up the street—a shaggy-haired guy wearing a baseball cap, shorts, a T-shirt.

Not wanting to be caught watching him—and not quite sure why—she turns to glance at the stack of boxes waiting on the porch behind her.

As soon as Ryan gets out of the shower, the two of them are going to load the car and transport the boxes out of here.

This is your last chance to change your mind about any of that stuff, she reminds herself.

But what would she possibly want to retrieve now? The ugly curtains she and Nick bought on clearance for the downstairs bath years ago and never bothered to hang? The double-rings-etched silver frame that once held the wedding portrait now stashed in the bottom of her dresser drawer? The Van Morrison CD?

Really, she doesn't want any of it . . . but suddenly, the idea of parting with it brings a pang of regret.

It's because of Nick. Because she's worried about him. Not because she's genuinely nostalgic about all the household belongings packed inside, never to be seen again.

I'm wondering if I'm ever going to see Nick again. That's the problem.

"Mrs. Walsh?"

She looks up, startled, sloshing coffee over the rim of the cup.

The stranger in the baseball cap is now standing at the foot of the steps. From here she can see that he's college-age, with a scruffy goatee and a tattoo on his right bicep.

"Sorry . . . I didn't mean to scare you."

"It's okay."

"Sorry," he says again, watching her wipe her coffee-spattered hand on her denim shorts. "I'm here to walk your dog?"

Is he asking her, or telling her?

"Your regular dog walkers are on vacation this week," he explains.

That makes sense, she supposes. Who *isn't* on vacation this week?

"So you work for Dog Days?"

"Yeah. My name is John."

"Hi, John. You can call me Lauren."

"Because Mrs. Walsh is your mother-in-law, right?"

"Excuse me?"

"Women always say that. 'Don't call me Mrs.—that's my mother-in-law.'"

How about *Don't call me Mrs.—my husband traded me in for another woman.*

Or *I've never even met my mother-in-law because her son stopped speaking to her when she left his father for someone else. And yeah, I guess it does run in the family.*

"I'll get Chauncey." Lauren turns toward the door and jumps, once again startled to find someone standing right behind her.

Oh. It's just Ryan this time, his hair damp and spiky from his shower.

"Geez, Ry, you scared me!"

"Sorry—I'm ready to go, Mom."

"Can you just grab the dog?" She wipes her hand, once again wet with coffee, on her shorts. "This is John. He's here to walk him."

Ryan and John size each other up, then exchange the customary guy greeting.

"Hey."

"Hey."

"How come you don't have a bunch of other dogs with you?" Ryan asks.

"A lot of people are on vacation. I guess they board them. So your dog gets me all to himself today."

"Actually, Chauncey loves to hang with the other dogs, but . . . whatever."

"Ry, are the girls still sleeping?" Lauren asks as he starts into the house—and she immediately regrets the question.

"I guess," comes the reply.

What is she thinking, letting this stranger know that she has two daughters asleep in the house?

Uneasy, she glances at John. He doesn't even seem to be listening.

"Wow, that sucks," he says, focused on the porch railing.

Lauren follows his gaze to see that the butterfly has become ensnared in a spiderweb. Watching it struggle to free itself, she thinks again of Nick, trapped in his car, helpless, calling her . . .

The police. I need to call them, tell them everything, no matter what they think of me.

Ryan reappears quickly with a frisky Chauncey. John pats the dog's head and is rewarded with a trusting lick on the hand. He fastens the leather leash to Chauncey's collar. "Okay, fella, let's go."

Ryan picks up the nearest box. "Ready, Mom?"

Lauren hesitates. "We need to wait until John gets back with Chauncey."

"What? But you said we could do this fast so I can go meet the guys."

"I know, but—"

"Half the time no one's even around when the dog walker comes," Ryan points out. "They just come and go. What's the big deal?"

"I can put the dog back in the house," John assures

her, as Chauncey strains at the leash, ready to get moving. "Someone's home, right?"

"Yes, but . . ."

My innocent daughters are home, asleep, and you're a stranger, and I'm feeling paranoid this morning and I don't trust you.

"They gave me your key," John tells her, "so you can lock the door and everything."

They gave him her key? They just hand out keys to anyone?

Well, not just *anyone*. Surely the agency screens even its short-term employees.

Lauren thinks back, trying to remember whether anyone has ever pinch-hit for the regular walkers before. Not recently.

Possibly last summer, though. She never paid much attention to who was coming and going, accompanied by a posse of barking dogs.

After all, back then, she wasn't living in the house alone. And before Nick gave her reason to avoid being seen around town in public, she didn't spend much time at home on summer days.

"Mom, come *on.*"

"Go put that in the car, Ryan. I'm going to wake up Lucy."

"Yeah, good luck with that," Ryan mutters, passing her with the box.

Lucy isn't exactly known around here for bouncing cheerfully out of bed in the morning.

John is already headed for the sidewalk with Chauncey.

As she steps into the house, Lauren can't help but look back over her shoulder at the helpless butterfly caught in the spider's web.

* * *

Sitting on the window seat in her bedroom, Sadie watches Mommy and Ryan load the last of the boxes into the back of the car.

There goes all the stuff Mom says they don't need or want anymore.

Sadie wipes a tear from her eye, wishing she didn't care about anything in the boxes. But she does. She can't help it. She can't help but feel like it's a part of Daddy and now it's leaving, just like he did.

Maybe Mommy feels the same way. She keeps looking around like she's nervous about something, and she doesn't seem to want to go.

Ryan does, though. Even from here, Sadie can see that he's antsy to get moving. And he keeps shaking his head at whatever Mommy is telling him.

Sadie wishes she could hear what they're saying. Her window is open, but someone is mowing a neighboring lawn and the noise drowns out their voices. For all she knows, they're talking about how they're going to make her give away all her toys and clothes.

Finally, Mommy backs out of the driveway.

As soon as the car is safely out of sight, Sadie gets up and goes over to her toy box.

She pulls out the length of fishing line she stole from Ryan's tackle box yesterday while he was at Ian's. He doesn't like anyone in his room while he's gone—in fact, that's why she got the idea.

Last winter, when Ryan thought someone was stealing his Archie comics, he secretly taped a strand of fishing line across the doorway to his room so that he'd be able to tell if anyone went in there while he was gone.

No one did . . . until cleaning day.

It turned out the maid service had a new lady who kept

finding the comics on the floor and dumping them into the trash. Mommy and Daddy said that was what Ryan got for being careless.

Sadie never leaves her things around the way Ryan does. Lucy, too, and even Mommy sometimes. But Sadie knows where everything is.

Everything except Fred.

She wipes away another tear.

Daddy said he'd get Fred back for her. She really wants—*needs*—to believe that.

Meanwhile, it will be easier for her to keep track of the rest of her belongings, in case anything else goes missing.

She opens the desk drawer where she keeps her art supplies and takes out a roll of Scotch tape.

It takes her a few minutes to rig the fishing line across the doorway at shoulder height for herself—and leg height for everyone else in the house.

There.

It's impossible to see the fishing line unless you're looking for it . . . and no one will.

Sadie looks around her room, memorizing exactly where everything is—which doesn't take long, because everything is right where it should be. Then she ducks under the fishing line and walks across the hall to Lucy's room.

The door is open. Sadie overheard Mommy telling Lucy to get up a few minutes ago, before she went down to load up the car with Ryan.

"I'm up, I'm up," Lucy assured Mommy. She even went down the hall to the bathroom, as if to prove the point before Mommy, satisfied, went back downstairs.

Now, however, Lucy is back in bed, lying on her back, eyes closed. There's a hardcover book lying open on her bed.

"Lucy?"

No reply.

"Lucy?" Sadie repeats. "Why do you think Daddy didn't come yesterday?"

Her sister doesn't say anything.

She must be sleeping.

Sadie turns away.

"I don't know, Sades."

Startled, she looks back at her sister.

Now Lucy's eyes are wide open—and her expression tells Sadie that her big sister is even more worried about Daddy than she is.

Stepping from her car onto the sunlit parking lot at Tide-water Animal Rescue, Elsa inhales the briny breeze off the nearby Long Island Sound.

Remember to appreciate the tiniest pleasures, Joan told her before she left the therapist's office after her last appointment.

Tiny pleasures. Yes. Sunshine, salt air . . . puppies.

A trucker found a newborn mixed-breed litter yesterday, abandoned in a plastic laundry basket left along I–95. According to an e-mail Elsa received early this morning from Karyn, the director of the privately funded shelter, only three of the puppies had made it through the night.

Hurrying across the pavement toward the low, cedar-shingled building, she hopes the trio is still hanging in there.

She opens the door to an encouraging sign: Karyn seated at her desk, bottle-feeding a tiny bundle of black fur.

"Morning, Elsa," she says softly—which is completely out of character for a vivacious motor mouth like Karyn. Obviously, she's trying not to jar the puppy.

"Good morning. Who do you have there?"

"This is Zuko."

"Zuko?"

Karyn nods enthusiastically. She gives a temporary name to every animal, believing an identity is important even for the shelter's transient residents. A major film buff, she tends to choose characters or elements from her favorite movies, based on her perception of the creature's temperament or appearance.

"Remember John Travolta in *Grease*? Black hair, black leather, very cool . . . Danny Zuko."

Elsa grins. It could be worse. Much. Just last week, they took in a Rottweiler Karyn dubbed Hannibal—as in Lecter—whose owner mercifully surfaced a few days later to reclaim him.

Elsa peers into the cardboard box on the floor beneath a strategically placed warming bulb. Curled together on a blanket are two more puppies. Unlike their brother, they have russet-colored fur.

"I suppose these are the Pink Ladies?"

Karyn shakes her brunette curls. "Close. The runt is Frenchy, but the other one's a male—his name is Greased Lightning."

"Why?"

"You'll see when you pick him up. Listen, why don't you grab yourself some coffee and then update the Web site with the puppies? I took some pictures of them earlier—they're in the digital camera by the computer."

Elsa heads over to the coffeepot in a kitchenette alcove, then settles herself in front of the computer with a steaming cup.

Of all the tasks that come along with her shelter volunteer work, this is her least favorite. Every time she logs onto the site's pet adoption page—with its tagline *Won't*

You Provide One of These Lost Souls with a Loving Home?—she's reminded of Jeremy.

Karyn doesn't know about him, though. When Elsa met her, and Karyn asked whether she had any children, she said no. It's not the whole truth, but it spares her having to answer additional questions that are even more painful.

She uploads the photo of the puppies, then writes the copy to go along with it.

Somewhere out there, someone has a loving home and a heartful of longing . . .

Just as Elsa once did.

I still do.

If Jeremy were to come home now . . .

Eyes flooded with tears, Elsa checks to make sure Karyn hasn't noticed. No, she's over by the cardboard box, trying to get a grip on a squirming reddish puppy—Greased Lightning, no doubt.

She hastily wipes away the tears and does her best to focus on the copywriting until Karyn interrupts her.

"Hey, want to trade places? This little guy needs his bottle and some serious cuddling—and I'm pretty much cuddled out."

With an eager nod, Elsa goes over to the most comfortable guest chair in the office, settles into it, and holds out her arms.

"Careful—he's a little escape artist. I'll go grab the bottle. Got him?"

"Got him," she assures Karyn, holding the writhing puppy close and nuzzling his soft fur with her cheek. Within moments, he settles his warm little body against her.

Karyn returns with the bottle, her brown eyes widening in surprise behind her wire-rimmed glasses. "Wow. What'd you do to him?"

She shrugs. "I'm not sure."

"Well, you've definitely got the touch. Too bad you never had kids—you'd be a great mom."

The moment the words are out of her mouth, Karyn looks as if she wants to take them back. "Sorry," she tells Elsa, "I know that's personal. I mean, maybe you didn't want kids, or maybe you couldn't have them—oh God, why do I always say the wrong thing?"

"It's okay." Not really, but . . . poor Karyn. *And poor me.* "You're right. It *is* too bad. And maybe I would have been a great mom . . ."

But I wasn't.

If Jeremy were here, you could ask him. He'd probably be glad to tell you about all the mistakes I made.

But Jeremy isn't here.

Jeremy doesn't know that Elsa can see many things more clearly now—things she would have done differently, given the chance.

And if she's right—and he isn't coming back—then she'll never be able to tell him how sorry she is for failing him.

Glenhaven Episcopal Church, a classic white clapboard structure with a steeple and stained glass windows, sits on the tree-shaded green in the heart of town.

When Ryan and Lucy were little, Lauren brought them to a series of music classes in the basement recreation room. She hasn't set foot in here since, but it's changed little, if at all, over the years. Same damp smell, same dim fluorescent lighting, same wooden stage framed by worn maroon velvet curtains and filled with folding chairs and tables that are taken out as needed.

They're not needed today—and if they were, there wouldn't be space to set them up. The rec room is jam-packed with castoffs for the upcoming tag sale. Not just boxes of knickknacks and bags of clothing, but furniture, too. Nice furniture.

As Ryan returns to the car for their last box, Lauren runs her fingers along the polished surface of an Art Deco–style dressing table with a rounded mirror.

"If you're interested in that, you'd better get here early on sale day."

Lauren turns to see the woman who introduced herself as Alana from the Junior League. She's either stiff or shy—Lauren couldn't tell which at first, but—noting her arch smile—she's now leaning toward stiff.

She's noticed that Alana keeps peeking into the boxes Lauren and Ryan have brought in, taking stock of what's inside. She isn't exactly wrinkling her nose, but she's not looking tempted to put aside anything for herself, either.

"Oh, I'm not interested in this." Lauren hastily removes her hand from the dressing table. "I'm here to get rid of things, not accumulate more."

"Well, there really are some great pieces here. Furniture, and clothing, too."

Was that a hint? Is she taking in Lauren's coffee-stained shorts and faded Gap T-shirt and thinking she'd do better in some other mom's hand-me-downs?

"I'll be back with clothes, too, before the week is out," Lauren informs her. "My kids are growing like weeds, so I've got to go through their closets."

Imagine—Alana doesn't look thrilled by the prospect of wardrobe donations from the Walsh family.

Thankfully, Ryan appears, lugging the final box.

"Is that it?" Lauren asks.

"That's it." He plunks it down, hard—with the distinct sound of breaking glass. "Oops."

Alana shakes her hair-sprayed head. "I certainly hope that wasn't anything valuable."

What, she thinks there might be vintage Haviland Limoges amid the wreckage?

Dismayed, Ryan looks at Lauren.

"It's okay, sweetie. Accidents happen." She reaches for the box and notes that it's the one she marked "FRAG-ILE." Of course it is.

But who cares about a couple of old teacups?

"What are you doing?" Alana asks as she lifts it.

"We'll take this one home and get rid of whatever's broken, then bring the rest back."

"That's not necessary. I can take care of it."

"Oh, I wouldn't want you to cut yourself," she tells Alana—just as her cell phone rings in her back pocket.

Nick?

She hurriedly plunks the box down—more breaking glass—so that she can answer it, dimly aware of Alana's incredulous expression.

It isn't Nick. The call is from home.

"Mom, it's me."

"Is everything okay?" she asks Lucy as her thoughts fly to the unfamiliar dog walker. What if—?

"No," Lucy replies. "Have you talked to Daddy today?"

With another twinge of foreboding, she tells her daughter that she hasn't. Conscious of Ryan's concerned gaze—and Alana's curious one—Lauren adds, "I'm sure he'll call. Don't worry."

"I can't help it. I sent him a bunch of texts and he never answered any of them. I just tried to call him at home and on his cell phone and at work, too, because Sadie was worried, and I got his voice mail, too. He should be there by now, Mom, it's after nine o'clock."

"Maybe he's out of cell phone range and he can't get messages."

Silence. Lucy isn't buying that. She knows something is wrong. Not oops-crossed-wires wrong.

Seriously wrong.

"Listen, I'm going to drop Ryan off and then I'll be home. We'll figure things out when I get there, okay?"

"Okay," Lucy says in a small voice.

Hanging up, Lauren sees that Alana is now holding the box marked "FRAGILE."

Lauren no longer gives a damn whether she cuts herself or not. She can keep the box, and everything in it.

"Come on, Ryan." She fishes her keys from her pocket. "I know you have to meet your friends."

"Maybe I should just come home with you instead, in case . . . I mean Dad . . . we don't know where he is, and—"

"Dad's fine," she assures Ryan—and Alana, in case she was thinking about telling her Junior League friends that the philandering Nick Walsh is now MIA.

"Are you sure?"

"Yes."

Nick *has* to be fine. *Please, please, please let him be fine*.

If only it were possible to make something happen simply by telling yourself over and over that it will—that it *has* to.

But no one knows better than Lauren that that's impossible. If it weren't, Nick would still be here with her and the kids, instead of . . .

God only knows where, she thinks bleakly.

CHAPTER
TEN

Back when she and Nick were still married, Lauren spoke often to his assistant, Georgia. If she couldn't reach him in his office or on his cell, she had no qualms about calling Georgia directly and asking her to track him down.

Things are different now.

She's had no contact with Georgia since Nick moved out. She often wonders what—if anything—he's told his colleagues about the situation. Do they even realize he's no longer living at home? Maybe not—she doubts he bothered to change his address in the personnel files. He gets very little corporate mail, but what there is still comes here to the house.

Now, as she dials Georgia's number with both her daughters looking on from their seats at the kitchen table, she rehearses her words carefully. The moment she hears the assistant's familiar voice on the line, though, she forgets what she was going to say.

"This is Georgia."

"Georgia, this is . . ." *No, not Nick's wife.* " . . . Lauren Walsh."

"Lauren!"

Funny, what one can read into one word spoken over a telephone line.

She knows about the split, Lauren realizes. *And she's nervous.*

"How have you been? And the kids? How are the kids? They must be getting so big."

"Yes . . . listen, Georgia, I need . . . is Nick in today?"

There's a pause.

Lauren's heart sinks.

It's a simple yes-or-no question. Rather, it would be, on any given weekday. Nick should be there.

"Actually—I'm not quite sure he's in yet," Georgia tells her.

"Yet? I mean, it's almost ten-thirty. That's not like Nick. Did he have an early meeting or something?"

"Um . . . can I put you on hold for a few minutes, Lauren?"

"Sure."

Canned music fills the line.

Lauren looks at the girls, sitting there in front of their untouched bowls of soggy cereal, and offers a bright, fake smile.

"Is she going to get Daddy?" Lucy asks hopefully.

"I think so."

Please, please, please let that be the case.

"Eat your breakfast, girls."

Sadie pushes her cereal away. "It's mushy."

"I'll pour you a fresh bowl."

Sadie shakes her head vehemently. Watching Lucy put an arm around her little sister's shoulders and give her a squeeze, Lauren fights a wave of apprehension.

"Lauren?" Georgia is back on the line.

"Yes?"

"I'm going to transfer you to HR."

Homeroom? is Lauren's first thought, living, as she does, in her own little suburban mom world, far from corporate America. *What the heck is Georgia talking a—*

Oh.

HR. Human resources.

That makes about as much sense as homeroom, though. Maybe they routinely transfer all the nosy ex-wives to HR.

"Thanks, Georgia."

"Sure. Good luck."

Good luck?

Does Georgia, too, suspect that Nick is in some kind of trouble? Does she know something Lauren doesn't?

Lauren realizes, with an odd burst of relief, that "good luck" is the kind of thing you say to a spurned woman calling around looking for her ex-husband.

The coffee she drank earlier burns in her stomach as she waits on hold again. She busies herself unloading the dishwasher, not wanting the girls to see her face. Chauncey comes sniffing around the clean dishes and she nudges him away with her shin.

When she arrived home ten minutes ago, she'd been glad to see that the dog had been walked and returned to the house without incident. Now the replacement dog walker is the least of her concerns.

"Mrs. Walsh?" an unfamiliar voice asks over the phone.

"Yes?"

"This is Marcia Kramer. Georgia Ames said you needed to speak to me."

"No, I actually . . . I needed to speak to my husb— ex-husband. I'm not sure why she transferred me to you."

"She did say that Nick was expected this morning but isn't in yet."

"So he *is* back from vacation, then?"

"He's due back today, yes. But we haven't heard from him and he's apparently running late."

"I see."

In the awkward moment of silence that follows, Lauren's thoughts race through various reasons Nick might not have returned her calls or shown up for work this morning. All are grim.

"I can get a message to him when he arrives, if you'd like?"

"Thank you. If you could just have him call home— me—the kids." She hates that she's stammering, hates that Georgia put her in the position of having to talk to a stranger about her ex-husband's whereabouts, hates that Nick is missing, and—because it's always there, even now, amid the worry—hates that he left her.

She hangs up the phone and turns to see the girls' expectant faces.

"Daddy's not at work yet," she tells them.

"Can you call Beth?"

Under ordinary circumstances, Lauren might have snapped at Lucy's suggestion. Now, she actually considers it—albeit only briefly. "I don't think that's a good idea. Anyway, I don't even have her number."

"I do. It's programmed into my cell."

That gives Lauren pause. She doesn't particularly want to imagine her daughter cozily chatting on the phone with Nick's mistress.

"Dad gave it to me," Lucy explains, "in case I ever need him and can't get ahold of him."

"You can always get ahold of me."

"Mom! I know that. He meant on weekends when we're at his house, or whatever."

"Why wouldn't you be able to get ahold of him when you're at his house?"

"You know . . . if he has to go out for a little while."

Lauren stares. "Dad goes out without you when you're at his house?"

"Sometimes. You go out when we're at your house, too."

"Oh, Lucy, come on. This isn't *my* house. It's *our* house. And Dad is supposed to be spending that weekend time with you, not . . ."

Her. Beth. The other woman.

Why, though, is she surprised?

For the first time in a long time, she allows herself to consider that Nick might actually be missing of his own accord. That he might have carelessly gone off someplace with no regard for the kids.

Maybe she won't call the cops after all. Not just yet. And she definitely won't call Beth.

"So do you want it, Mom?"

"What?"

"Beth's number."

It's not Lucy's fault Nick has a girlfriend whose number is in Lucy's phone.

This is so not the life Lauren had envisioned . . . for any of them.

It's been a long time since she cried over her failed marriage, but suddenly, she can feel hot tears in her eyes. She turns away quickly.

"No, I don't think I need Beth's number. But thank you."

"Maybe we should go check Daddy's apartment. I have the key."

"No," Lauren repeats. "Come on, girls. Let's go."

"To look for Daddy?" Sadie asks.

"No. To the pool." *Because I can't put these children through another second of sitting around here worrying. If something horrible happened, they'll all know soon enough, right?*

"We're going to the pool?" Lucy is incredulous.

"Yes, it's a gorgeous day and I don't want to waste it sitting inside."

"But . . . what about Dad?"

"Dad can get ahold of us on my cell phone, or yours." Lauren hastily wipes her eyes and turns back to Lucy. "Go on up and get your bathing suits on, girls, and then we'll go. Okay?"

"Sure. Come on, Sadie," Lucy says, so agreeably that Lauren knows she's seen the tears. She quickly bends over to finish unloading the dishwasher, surreptitiously wiping them away on the sleeve of her T-shirt. A fresh flood quickly replaces them, and she gives in, crying as she puts away cups and plates and silverware.

Oh, Nick. What have you done? Where have you gone? And what am I supposed to do about it?

The task completed, tears streaming down her face, Lauren stands staring bleakly out the window, absently watching dappled shadows moving over the grass as the breeze stirs the surrounding foliage.

Gradually, she becomes aware of a different kind of shadow. More solid. Long. It almost looks like a human silhouette, cast in a sunny patch of lawn.

A chill creeps over Lauren as she leans toward the screen, peering out at the strange shadow. Is the blur from her tears creating an optical illusion?

Or is someone really there?

Even as she wonders, she has the distinct sensation that she's being watched.

She presses the heels of her palms into her watery eyes, then looks again.

The shadow is gone.

Did she see me?

For a moment there, it seemed as though Lauren Walsh had indeed realized she had a backyard visitor. But then she rubbed her eyes, and that split second was enough time to slip farther back among the leafy boughs at the edge of the yard. From here, it's still possible to see the figure framed in the window—but impossible to be seen.

Lauren looks out again, seemingly scanning the landscape. Then she nods, as if she's quite satisfied that there's nothing—no one—out here.

Ha. You couldn't be more wrong, Lauren Walsh.

On the other side of the flimsy window screen, the woman seems poised, thoughtful, seemingly unaware that she's being watched. Then she turns and disappears from view.

Just as well.

Watching Lauren Walsh, alone in her kitchen and crying, has been quite a disquieting experience.

Not as visually disquieting, by any means, as anything that occurred over the weekend—but disquieting just the same.

Why was she crying?

She was just on the phone asking about her ex-husband. Her voice came through the screen loud and clear.

Does she suspect the truth about him? Maybe. Maybe she just didn't want to let on in front of the kids.

Besides—there were no witnesses; there is no easy evidence.

She'll never know—not for sure, anyway.

Poor woman. But what's the difference, really? He

already left her. She'd be alone either way. Alone with her children in this creepy old house in the middle of nowhere.

Well, not as middle-of-nowhere as Greymeadow . . . but it's hard to believe that this rinky-dink town is less than an hour's drive from Manhattan.

In some ways, this would be a hell of a lot easier to do in the city. More anonymity. No one gives you a second glance.

Here, one must make an effort to blend into the suburban landscape so as not to raise suspicion.

On the other hand, back in Manhattan, people are naturally wary. They're quick to retreat, slow to trust. Being invited into the home of someone you've just met would be next to impossible. Breaking in would mean getting past deadbolts, alarms, doormen, even window bars.

Here in Glenhaven Park, it's almost laughably simple—if one were inclined to look for the humor in a deadly serious matter such as this.

But this, of course, is no joke.

This is life or death.

"What are you doing home?"

They say it in unison, Marin and Garvey, staring at each other in surprise across the threshold of the master bedroom. Dressed in a suit and tie and carrying a briefcase, he was about to walk out; wearing a beach dress and sandals and carrying a straw bag, she was about to walk in.

For a moment, they just look at each other.

Then Marin stands on her tiptoes and gives him a perfunctory kiss on the cheek. He puts an arm around her—also perfunctory. It's not like they haven't seen each other in ages.

"Aren't you supposed to be at a groundbreaking for a hospital in Yorktown?" she asks.

"Yonkers. And not until noon." And he was so unsettled by the missing file that he canceled this morning's breakfast meeting with his advisers—but of course he doesn't mention that to Marin.

"Where are you going now?"

"To my office to go over some paperwork. I thought you were staying out at the beach until later today."

"We were planning to, but it really cooled off overnight, and anyway, poor Caroline—"

"*What?*" Garvey's heart lurches. "What's wrong with her?"

"Relax. She got a lot of sun yesterday, and I didn't want her out in it today."

"Are you sure that's all?"

Their eyes lock for a long moment.

"Yes," Marin tells him, "I'm sure."

But Garvey isn't. Every time Caroline so much as winces, or complains of the slightest ache, he's swept by a familiar dread.

There's no reason to think his elder daughter won't live a long and healthy life—that's what Garvey was told years ago, by a trusted physician.

But can you ever be sure?

Of course not.

Any one of us could be struck down by lightning at any time, Garvey reminds himself. *Or be hit by a bus, or . . .*

Or gunned down in a random mugging on the street.

Like Byron Gregson.

"Where is she?" he asks Marin abruptly.

"In her room. But seriously, Garvey, she's fine."

He's already striding down the hall, needing to see for himself.

Caroline's bedroom door is closed. He sets his brief-case on the floor and knocks.

No reply.

His breath catches in his throat as he knocks again.

"Annie, I told you, leave me the hell alone!"

Relieved to hear her voice—foul language and all—he pushes the door open. "It's not Annie."

"Oh—hi, Daddy." She's lying on her stomach on her bed in front of an open fashion magazine, bare legs bent behind her, feet swinging back and forth. Her face is flushed pink.

"Mom said you're sick."

"*What?* I'm not sick. Why does she have to freak over every little thing?"

"You know how she is." Garvey shrugs and rests the back of his hand against his daughter's forehead. "You feel warm."

"Duh—that's because I have a sunburn. But hey, guess what? I learned the pop-up."

"What's the pop-up?"

"It's this move where you get up on your feet on the board in one quick motion. I thought you used to surf."

"I did."

Summer on Nantucket—a lifetime ago. The Beach Boys playing in his head as he tried to catch a wave in frigid water, wanting to impress a teenage Marin watching from the sand . . .

"Were you any good at it?"

Garvey grins and shakes his head. "Not very. Are you?"

Caroline nods. "We should go together sometime, Daddy. Wouldn't that be fun?"

"Absolutely." He pats her tousled dark hair. "Are you sure you're feeling okay?"

"I'm fine. Why are you always worrying about how I'm feeling?"

Garvey toys with the fringe on a throw pillow. "Because you're my little girl. I'm supposed to worry about you."

"You don't worry about Annie."

"Sure I do."

"Not like you worry about me. Is it because I was sick when I was little?"

He nods, not wanting to discuss it with her. Caroline knows very little about her childhood illness. She was too young to remember, and has never asked many questions. Garvey and Marin decided long ago that there's no need to burden her with the details. All she knows is that she was in the hospital, had surgery, got better.

But maybe those days of Caroline's willing oblivion are coming to an end, because she asks, "Daddy? What did I have, exactly?"

He feigns confusion. "What do you mean?"

"When I was sick. Was it cancer?"

"No, nothing like that." *Something far rarer, and much more lethal.*

"Can I get it back again?"

"Absolutely not."

"But was it—"

"I've got to go get some work done now, okay? You get some rest."

Garvey plants a kiss on Caroline's cheek and leaves the room, closing the door again behind him.

Passing the gallery of family photos in the hallway, he glances, as always, at his favorite, a prominently displayed black and white father-daughter portrait.

The sitting with a well-known photographer was an appropriate—and bittersweet—Father's Day gift from

Marin. Garvey knew only too well what she was thinking. Neither of them ever said it aloud, though.

The photo was taken years ago, but every detail of the day is as vividly etched in Garvey's mind as the precious image is captured on film.

He remembers Marin, six months' pregnant with Annie, huffing and puffing up the four flights of stairs to the Tribeca studio. It was on the top floor—exposed brick, barren floor space, skylights.

He remembers how the sunlight spilled over Caroline's silky hair as she sat for hours on his lap, so still—so very still.

"What a serene little girl she is," the photographer commented, and Garvey forced a smile.

The smile appeared in the portrait, as well—a sweet, tender smile directed at his little girl, whose head was tilted against his chest, dark eyes solemnly looking up at her daddy.

"She looks just like you," the photographer said, several times. He even grinned at Marin and asked, "Are you sure she's yours?"

"No," Marin quipped in return, patting her rounded belly, "but I'm pretty sure this one is."

Garvey was sorry when the session was over that day. He would have been quite content to sit there forever with his daughter safely held in his arms.

I still would, he thinks, and forces himself to turn away from the picture.

He can't believe, after all these years, that the past is coming back to haunt him in a way that he never imagined.

That some lowbrow reporter with spectacular luck and a sketchy plan actually thought he could get away with blackmailing one of the most powerful men in New

York should have been laughable. Yet somehow, instead of a joke, Byron Gregson turned into Garvey's worst nightmare—even posthumously.

But it'll be over soon, he assures himself.

For all he knows, the mission to Glenhaven Park has already been accomplished. Really, there's no reason to think that it won't be.

He hopes that this time, there will be no bloodshed.

But sometimes, it simply can't be avoided.

And sometimes, if you want something done right . . .

Garvey sighs, shaking his head, praying it won't come to that.

CHAPTER ELEVEN

Higher!" Sadie calls, pumping her bare little legs as the swing arcs into the air.

Lauren steps back a bit, positioning her hands as it pendulums back toward her.

They've been at it for a good ten minutes now, and her arms are getting tired. She can smell the chlorine from her swim wafting from her skin. She wouldn't mind jumping back into the water. Funny, because earlier, she was chilly in the pool and couldn't wait to get out.

But it's warm here in the open field with the sun high overhead.

And her nerves are on edge.

Even a vigorous swim didn't ease the tension gnawing away at her. Tension because of Nick—and because, back at the house earlier, she could have sworn someone was lurking in the backyard.

She knows what she saw—for a split second, anyway. She knows what she felt—a pair of eyes on her.

Yet who's to say whether her own mind conjured both the shadow—a trick of the light?—and the sensation? Would it be that surprising, under the circumstances?

It might be more surprising to find that someone had actually been out there.

Imagine—a garden-variety Peeping Tom in Glen-haven Park. Ludicrous.

About as ludicrous as it is for her to be here with the kids, like it's just an ordinary summer's day. But she's got to keep them busy, at least, until she knows more about Nick.

She's almost found herself wishing Beth would show up. If she does, Lauren has every intention of putting her pride aside and questioning her about Nick's whereabouts.

That she isn't here doesn't bode well.

"Higher, Mommy!"

She gives the swing another push and Sadie giggles, soaring toward the clear blue sky once again.

"I can't wait until he's that age."

Lauren turns to see a man strapping a chubby, bald baby into one of the harness swings on the adjacent bar.

"Higher!" Sadie screeches, descending again.

"Sometimes I wish she were *that* age," Lauren replies, indicating her daughter and then the baby.

"Really? How come?"

"Mommy! Higher!" Sadie demands. "Higher!"

"Guess." Lauren smiles wryly, and the dad laughs.

The dad? How do you know he's a dad?

She sneaks a sidewise look at him. Baggy khaki cargo shorts, five o'clock shadow, a bit of a gut, baseball cap, boat shoes without socks—yep. He's a dad, taking the week off from a corporate job, no doubt.

Then again, he might be an uncle. Or a manny. Trilby says lots of local women are hiring male sitters for their sons.

"I'd get a manny for my boys if Bob weren't such a jealous type," she once told Lauren.

"Bob probably wouldn't be a jealous type if you weren't such a flirt," Lauren returned with a grin.

"True. Can you imagine having a strapping young manny around the house?"

Lauren couldn't imagine it, no.

She sneaks another peek at the guy pushing the baby on the swing. He's not exactly strapping—nor particularly young. Early forties, she'd guess.

He sees her looking. "So you're saying I should be glad my son can't talk, is that it?"

His son. So she was right the first time. He *is* a dad.

"Enjoy it while it lasts," she advises, appreciating the momentary distraction of casual conversation. "Once they start talking, they don't stop—unless they're thirteen, and you need information from them. Then it's like they took the vow of silence and will be shot if they speak."

"What kind of information do you need?"

"Is the party going to be chaperoned? Who drank the rest of the milk and put the empty carton back into the fridge? You know—that sort of thing."

He laughs. "I don't need that kind of information yet. But I do need to know other things."

"Like what?"

"Like, is something hurting you or are you just screaming for the hell of it?"

"Oh, right. I remember those days. Trust me, after three kids, I know the answer is usually B, I'm just screaming for the hell of it."

He laughs again. Wow, she's on a roll.

"So you have three kids?"

She nods and indicates Sadie. "She's my youngest."

"He's my only."

"One is good. One is outnumbered."

"Not exactly."

Hmm. A single dad?

"You know," he goes on, looking around, "I kind of expected this playground and the pool to be more of a happening place."

"It usually is, but it's August. The town is empty right now—everyone's on vacation. Are you new here?"

He nods. "We just moved into a house over on Castle Lane."

"Really? That's the next street over from me. I'm on Elm."

"You know the three-story stone house on the corner of Castle and Second?"

She nods, impressed. "The one with the portico? That's an amazing house." A mansion, really. Interesting, because this guy doesn't strike her as fabulously wealthy.

"It's an architectural masterpiece," he agrees. "Our place is four doors down on the opposite side."

"Really? Then you must be right in my backyard."

"What does your house look like?"

"A dark yellow Queen Anne."

"I think I've seen it through the trees out back. I'm in the dumpy white Cape with the puke green shutters."

She laughs.

"Ah, finally."

"Finally what?"

"You're laughing. You seemed so serious, like you've got the weight of the world on your shoulders."

If only he knew.

"I was hoping to make you laugh—even if it is at my poor little house."

"Actually, I haven't even seen your house. I mean, I never go down that street, believe it or not."

"Oh, come on, the neighborhood's not *that* bad."

"No, I just don't have any reason to—it's a dead end."

"Cul-de-sac, the Realtor called it."

"Yeah—I guess 'dead end' lacks a certain charm."

"So does 'rundown wreck'—that's probably why she listed our house as a 'fixer-upper.'"

"Hey, we have one of those, too."

"Well, I hope your husband is handier than I am."

Nick. The mere thought of him sucks the fun right out of the conversation.

"He's not handy. I mean, I don't know how handy you are, but he isn't handy at all."

And he isn't my husband anymore, either.

And he seems to have fallen off the face of the earth over the weekend, and I have no idea what to do about it, or where I even fit into the picture, other than as the mother of three very upset children.

Suddenly uncomfortable, she rakes a hand through her hair, still damp and stiff as broom bristles, thanks to the chlorinated water.

"Luceeeee . . . look at meeee!" Sadie trills from the swing, and Lauren follows her gaze to see her older daughter racing up the hill from the pool. She's on her phone.

No—her phone is pink.

Patting her pocket, Lauren realizes her own phone is missing. In her distraction, she must have left it up at the pool—and now Lucy has it.

Nick must have called at last.

Madison Avenue in the East Sixties is a sea of yellow taxicabs and black Town Cars. The sidewalks are crowded, and Marin and Annie have successfully lost themselves in the throng, their faces mostly concealed by oversize sunglasses. There will be no photos in tomorrow's *Post* or *Daily News* captioned *Wife and daughter of gubernatorial hopeful Garvey Quinn spotted overspending and overeating.*

"Too bad Caroline has to miss out," Annie comments, licking the double-scoop ice cream cone she's holding in one hand and swinging a Barneys shopping bag in the other.

She means it, Marin realizes, hearing the wistful note in her younger daughter's voice. Annie adores her big sister—and Caroline treats her like crap.

Always has.

Maybe, somewhere deep down inside, Caroline harbors resentment toward her sister based on a truth she's never even been told. In essence, she does know what happened to her—but not the whole story. Is it possible that she senses it?

She was a toddler when Annie was born. She could very likely have picked up on the emotional roller coaster surrounding Marin's pregnancy and her sister's birth—the shroud of secrecy, the bitter disappointment.

She might even have some memory of her own ordeal in the months that followed—and subconsciously hold Annie to blame.

Just as Garvey does.

He'll deny it to his dying day, but Marin doesn't buy it for one moment.

She saw the look on his face when the lab results came back. She knew, even before he said it, that he didn't want her to carry the pregnancy to term.

And she knew that this time, she was going to stand up to him. It was their baby, but her body. She made the final decision, without her husband's support.

Caroline's own resentment of her sister might very well have nothing to do with her own latent memories or instincts. Maybe she's simply picked up on her father's feelings and mirrors them.

She is, after all, Daddy's girl.

Annie is not.

But I love her enough to make up for her father—and her sister, too, for that matter, Marin thinks fiercely.

"Oh, Mom, look!" Annie stops walking and points at the plate-glass window of a pet shop. "Isn't he beautiful?"

The purebred puppy stares back at them with soulful eyes.

"He is," Marin agrees.

"Can we get him?"

"Annie, you know you're allergic."

That's been a sore spot in the Quinn household for years—mostly with Caroline and Garvey. Both of them often talk about how they would love to have a dog. Garvey, Marin suspects, because the dog would complete the wholesome family image. Caroline, meanwhile, has always claimed to be an avid animal lover—probably because she knows her sister's allergies mean no pets allowed.

"I could get shots," Annie tells Marin. "Dr. Federman said so. Then the fur wouldn't bother me as much."

"But he didn't say that if you got shots, you wouldn't suffer at all. It's not worth it, Annie."

"I really want a puppy, Mom. Please? Look how cute and cuddly he is."

"Sorry, Annie. Come on, let's go see if we can find those jeans you wanted."

"I'd rather have a puppy," she says good-naturedly, and Marin smiles, shaking her head.

"Meanie. Dad would say yes."

What is there to say to that?

Dad must love you more, then.

Or *Dad doesn't care that your allergies would make you miserable.*

Or maybe just "I'm sorry, Annie."

For a lot of things. Things I hope you never, ever have to find out about.

"Mom—" Lucy thrusts Lauren's cell phone at her. "I was near your chair and I heard it ringing so I answered it."

"Is it Daddy?"

She shakes her head. Her green eyes are frightened.

"Lucy—here, watch Sadie." Lauren takes the phone and moves away from the playground with it, not wanting the girls—or the dad—to overhear.

Bad things happen everywhere . . . even here.

Lauren's heart is pounding as she answers the phone with a strangled-sounding "Hello?"

"Mrs. Walsh?"

"Yes."

"This is Marcia Kramer again. From—"

"Yes, from Nick's office. I know. Have you heard from him?"

"I'm sorry, we haven't."

Lauren's heart sinks.

It's better than bad news . . . but it definitely isn't good.

"Some of his colleagues are concerned," Marcia Kramer goes on. "They say this isn't like him. No one has been able to track him down at home or on his cell phone. I was wondering—"

She breaks off, clears her throat.

"I hate to ask, but . . ."

Again, Marcia seems unable to bring herself to the point.

Feeling sick inside, Lauren has a good idea what it might be. She sinks onto a bench and turns her back to the playground, clutching the phone hard against her ear.

"Would it be possible for you to put us in touch with Nick's—*friend*?"

There it is.

She knew it.

Some small part of her—an immature, wounded, vindictive part of her—is tempted to feign innocence—or at least cluelessness. *Nick has a lot of friends*, she might say. *I have no idea which one you mean.*

But this is serious. Nick is missing.

"Beth," she tells Marcia. "That's her name."

"And she's Nick's—"

"Girlfriend. Yes. Beth." Lauren rarely says the name out loud. It doesn't sit well on her tongue, sounds odd to her ears, even now.

Beth.

I hate her, she thinks churlishly—ridiculously, under the circumstances. But the small, immature part of her seems to have taken over suddenly, smothering rationality. *I don't want to call Beth looking for Nick and I don't want Marcia Kramer or Georgia to call Beth looking for Nick and I sure as hell don't want Lucy to call Beth. Ever. For any reason.*

"I understand she was traveling with him on the trip."

For God's sake, Marcia Kramer, Lauren wants to scream, *don't you understand how excruciating this is for my family?*

"Yes," she hears herself say, almost sedately. She looks over at the playground. Lucy is pushing Sadie on the swing, but watching Lauren. She can sense her daughter's trepidation from here.

The dad and baby are gone, she notices. Just as well.

Tears fill her eyes as she looks at her daughters. Hers . . . and Nick's.

They need to find out where their father is.

Chances are, Beth will know. She might even be with him at this very moment.

"Have you heard from—Beth—at all today?" Marcia wants to know.

"I haven't heard from Beth *ever.*"

"So you don't have her phone number?"

"My daughter does," she says, resigned. "I'll get it."

Elsa wearily eyes the raised flowerbeds that run along the front of the house. They desperately need watering—if it's not too late. Most of the plants have shriveled or keeled over entirely.

Why did she have to go and plant all those impatiens back in May, when she and Brett first moved in?

Because the nice, knowledgeable man at the nursery told you that impatiens love shade, remember?

"We've got plenty of that," Elsa assured him. The new house is perched beneath a canopy of towering tree limbs, casting the entire yard in shadow most of the day. The beds themselves are sheltered by an overhang—which wouldn't be a problem if impatiens didn't happen to love water as much as they do shade. The weekend's rain didn't do them a bit of good.

As Elsa unwinds the garden hose, she hears movement in the yard next door.

"Hi there," a female voice calls, and she reluctantly looks up.

"Hi."

Her neighbor, a breezy, middle-aged divorcee named Meg, waves across the low boxwood hedge.

"Nice day for gardening," Meg observes.

"Yes, it is."

"Not a nice day for working inside, but that's where I'm off to."

Elsa knows that Meg is a part-time cashier at Macy's over at the mall, and that being on her feet for hours aggravates her bunions. She mainly works there because of the employee discount, which helps her to keep her three teenagers in clothes and shoes. But her paycheck barely covers her bills, and her louse of an ex-husband is frequently late with his support payments.

Elsa knows all of this—and much, much more—because Meg loves to chat across the hedge whenever she happens to catch Elsa in the yard.

She's a likable woman, and would probably be a good friend—if Elsa wanted, or needed, a friend.

She used to have many. As a child, as a young fashion model in New York, as half of a married couple . . .

Now all those people have faded away.

No they haven't. They've been pushed away.

You *pushed them away.*

But it had to happen.

Friends share their lives—past and present—with each other.

Elsa has no intention of revealing her personal tragedy across the hedge, or across a lunch table, or anywhere else friends meet.

It makes for a lonely existence, but this—like everything else that's happened to her—is Elsa's lot.

With a wave, Meg gets into her car and drives off.

Elsa looks again at the limp impatiens bed. They're just flowers. Summer is waning. Who cares?

I do. I don't know why, but I care.
Feeling oddly bereft, she turns on the sprinkler.

On the driveway back at home, Lauren gets out of the car lugging the straw beach bag, heavy with wet pool towels.

"Lucy, can you hang these out on the line?" she asks her daughter, who's helping her little sister out of the backseat. "And Sadie, you need to go straight upstairs and change out of your wet bathing suit."

For once, nobody protests.

Good. That should give Lauren a few minutes alone to check the voice mail and make sure there aren't any disturbing messages from—or about—Nick.

She hands the beach bag to Lucy and heads toward the house with Sadie trailing along behind her. There's not a cloud in the sky and the sun is still shining, but it's not as warm as it seemed earlier, on the playground. Again, Lauren notes that a fall chill seems to be in the air today.

Or maybe the chill has nothing to do with the weather.

Where are you, Nick? What's happened to you?

Lauren unlocks the back door and opens it cautiously, expecting Chauncey to make a dash for it as usual.

He doesn't.

"Chauncey?" Lauren opens the door all the way and listens for his jangling collar and welcoming bark.

Silence.

"Chauncey!" As she crosses the kitchen, she remembers John, the new dog walker, and wonders, fleetingly, whether he ever brought Chauncey back.

Wait a minute—yes, he did. She remembers being relieved about that when she got back from the church this morning—before she spoke to Georgia, and Marcia, and found out that—

"There he is, Mommy!"

For a split second, she thinks Sadie is talking about Nick. Then she spins around and sees her daughter pointing to Chauncey, sprawled out in a sunny patch of rug in the next room, sound asleep.

"Is he okay?" Sadie asks anxiously.

Lauren takes a few steps closer. The dog is snoring. "He's fine. He's just taking a nice little catnap."

"Don't you mean dognap?"

"Well, dognap is something different." It's what she'd thought, for a moment, John had done to Chauncey.

Talk about paranoid . . .

Why would anyone want to steal a big old mutt?

Sadie goes closer to Chauncey and leans over him, her elbows resting on her knees. "Are you okay, boy? Why are you so tired?"

"Maybe the new dog walker exercised him more than he's used to, honey."

"But he always gets up to see us when we come home."

That's true, and the thought gives Lauren pause.

Chauncey is getting old. Maybe he's getting sick, too.

Please, no. The kids won't be able to take it. Not anytime soon.

That thought reminds her of her more immediate concern.

Lauren turns back toward the phone, saying, "Sadie, please go up and get on some dry clothes, okay?"

Sadie hesitates, still looking at Chauncey. "Are you sure he's all right?"

"Positive. Now go. Your lips are turning blue."

Lauren waits until her daughter is safely out of earshot.

Then she picks up the receiver and hears the beeping dial tone that indicates a message is waiting.

But it's from Rosa, one of the managers at Magic Maids.

"Hello, Mrs. Lauren, we have three ladies for you this week and they will see you tomorrow at around ten."

Every week, without fail, she calls to confirm the standing appointment and let Lauren know how many cleaners she's sending. It varies from two to four, and the staff turns over constantly. Lauren always leaves a few dollars for each cleaner as a tip, for which they thank her so profusely she wishes she could afford to leave more.

She erases the message and hangs up the phone.

Okay—so, no message from Nick.

No message *about* Nick.

Should she leave another one *for* Nick?

What's the use? If he's checking his phone, he knows she and the kids are worried about him.

If he's not checking his phone . . .

Why would he not check his phone?

Again, Lauren forces frightening thoughts from her head. Turning away from the phone, she finds herself looking again at Chauncey. It really is unlike him not to stir when someone comes home.

Frowning, Lauren stares at him . . . then turns abruptly away.

Pulling open a drawer, she finds the dog-eared address book where she keeps all the contact info for everyone involved in the Walsh household, from her OB-GYN to the trash collection service.

The kids tease her about not using an electronic organizer to store it all, but she's glad she didn't listen. It takes her about two seconds to flip to the Ds and locate the number for Dog Days . . .

But a full minute, at least, to bring herself to dial it.

Is there really any need to check up on John? He did the job he was supposed to do, and he was perfectly pleasant about it.

Yes, but Chauncey is acting strange, and Nick is missing, and this morning she thought she saw someone lurking in the shadows . . .

Yes, because you're losing your mind.

And even if you're not—what makes you think John has anything to do with any of those things . . . especially Nick?

Then again . . . the guy shows up here out of the blue, a stranger with her house keys, at the same time her ex-husband disappears . . .

Not that he disappeared from this house, or even lives here anymore . . .

But he's gone and John's around and Chauncey's out of it and there was a shadow in the yard and it's all either oddly coincidental . . .

Or ominous.

Call. You have nothing to lose.

Mind made up, Lauren dials the number. She can't remember ever having called it before. Nick has always dealt with the service.

"Hello, Dog Days, Jeannie speaking, can I help you?"

"Hi, Jeannie. My name is Lauren Walsh and I'm over on Elm Street in Glenhaven Park."

"Chauncey's mom!"

Lauren hesitates. She's not one of those overly enthusiastic dog people who signs Chauncey's name to their family Christmas card, but now is not the time to quibble about the validity of canine offspring.

"Er . . . right. Chauncey's mom," she agrees. "Our

regular dog walkers seem to be away and we had someone new—"

"John. I hope everything is going all right with
him?"

Relieved that at least he's officially employed there,
she says, "Everything is going fine, but I just wanted to
. . . you know . . . confirm that he works for you. I was
a little taken aback to have a total stranger show up with
my house keys, so . . ."

"I'm sorry . . . didn't you get the notification?"

"Excuse me?"

"We always send an e-mail to let you know when there
will be a change of staff, to make sure it's okay with the
homeowner. We sent it out last week to the address we
have on file . . ."

Which would be Nick's. And he either didn't get it, or
neglected to tell Lauren.

"If you didn't receive it, Mrs. Walsh, I'm so sorry . . ."

"You know what? My husband must have gotten the
e-mail, and forgot to mention it." No need to tell Jeannie
of Dog Days about the divorce, or that she won't be sign-
ing Nick's name, either, on the family Christmas card.

Lauren hangs up the phone and looks again at
Chauncey.

Maybe she should go over and give him a poke—just
to make sure he's okay.

Nah—let sleeping dogs lie.

She can see him breathing from here. He's fine. Just
tired.

Who isn't? she thinks with a yawn—just before a
bloodcurdling "Mom!" pierces the air.

The photo albums were among the first items Elsa unpacked
when they moved into the house. They always are.

There are no built-in living room bookshelves here, like there were in Tampa, so Elsa made a home for the row of albums on the raised brick fireplace hearth beside her favorite chair.

Every day, she brews herself a cup of strong tea and she sits down to leaf through the pages. Some might view the ritual as self-torture. Others, as therapeutic.

For Elsa, it is both. She looks at the pictures daily because she has to. Because she can't—won't—let go.

Sometimes, she makes her way through the whole stack of albums, losing herself in the memories. Other days, she flips through only a few pages before she's had enough. Sometimes, she goes through the photos chronologically; other times, randomly.

Today, it's random.

Jeremy in his new room, Jeremy at the carnival with a helium balloon, Jeremy on the first day of school, Jeremy with Elsa . . .

Your son looks just like you, people used to say, and she would smile. It was true. Jeremy, with his black hair and eyes, was the spitting image of Elsa.

He's smiling in many of the early photographs—yet his eyes betray a hint of desolation, even then. Why didn't Elsa notice that in person? Why can she only see it in retrospect, captured on film? Why now, when it's too late to help him?

But you did try to help him. You just couldn't figure out how. You didn't get the chance.

Frustrated, she puts the album aside and carries her half-full mug into the kitchen. After pouring the lukewarm tea down the drain, she carefully rinses every trace from the white porcelain basin. The protective glaze has worn away, leaving the surface porous; vulnerable to stains, cracks, scratches.

Lost in thought, Elsa runs the tap for a long time, absently watching the water engulf imperfections that can never be washed away.

Water. Uh-oh.

Abruptly, she turns off the faucet, slips her bare feet into a pair of sandals, and steps outside.

The forgotten sprinkler rotates with a rhythmic pattering, drenching a wide swath of the front walkway. Elsa waits for it to pass, then darts over to the spigot. She turns the valve and the spray becomes a trailing dribble, then a steady drip into the flowerbed.

Even from a few yards away, she can see the results of the prolonged drenching, but she steps closer, just to be sure.

Yes.

The plants that were seemingly wilted beyond salvation have miraculously sprung back to life.

For a long time, Elsa stands staring at the rejuvenated garden, wondering whether it just might be a sign.

Her mind made up, she goes inside.

It's time to call Mike Fantoni.

As she walks down the hall toward her room, Sadie shivers in her wet bathing suit.

Maybe she shouldn't have insisted on going into the water one last time after the swings.

Mommy was anxious to leave the pool, but Sadie wasn't ready yet. It wasn't that she was having so much fun—just that she dreaded going back home.

"Can I stay here with Ryan?" she asked her mother.

"No. He's with his friends."

Sadie turned to her sister. "Will you stay with me?"

"No, I want to go, too." Lucy didn't even bother to look at her. She seemed more obsessed with her phone today than usual, checking it every two seconds.

"Why don't you want to leave, Sadie?" Mommy asked.

"Because I want to go back into the pool," she lied. "Pleeeeeeease."

Mommy let her. Only for ten minutes. It was freezing cold and it wasn't even fun. Sadie didn't know any of the other kids her age. They were all playing together on one end of the wide steps as she splashed around, shivering, on the other.

But she figured anything was better than going home.

Now that she's here, though, it's not so bad. Not upstairs, anyway.

But the downstairs looks different now without all the stuff Mom gave away. Sadie isn't comfortable there.

And Mommy said yesterday that she was going to clean out the bedrooms next.

Not my room. No way, José.

That's what Daddy used to say whenever he was in a good mood, a long time ago.

No way, José.

Sadie hasn't heard him say that in a long time.

The second floor is drafty. All the bedroom doors are open for the cross breeze, and the ceiling fans are on.

As Sadie approaches her bedroom door, she reminds herself that she needs to duck under the fishing line from now on.

She's about to, when she stops short at the threshold.

The fishing line no longer stretches across the doorway.

How can that be?

She made sure it was in place before they left earlier. She was the last one down the stairs; Mommy and Lucy were already waiting for her by the back door.

That can only mean one thing.

Someone was in the house—in her room—while they were gone.

"Mom!"

For a moment, Lauren can't tell which of her daughters is calling for her—or where the voice is coming from.

Lucy, she realizes. She's still outside in the yard.

"Mom!"

Lauren hurries to the back door, wondering if Lucy stepped on a bee or something.

But there's nothing gingerly about her daughter's barefoot dash across the grass toward the house—and she's waving her phone in her outstretched hand.

Lauren immediately prepares herself for the worst—until she sees Lucy's expression.

It's not bad news, because her daughter is grinning broadly, her face etched in relief.

"Guess what? I just heard from Daddy!" she announces exuberantly. "He's totally fine!"

CHAPTER TWELVE

At dawn on Tuesday morning, Marin awakens in an empty bed with a splitting headache.

That Garvey isn't here isn't unusual. He frequently goes for an early morning run.

That she didn't stir when he left is most definitely unusual.

Marin attributes it—and the fact that her head is pounding—to her own foolishness the day and night before. The chocolate ice cream cone on the street was the only thing she'd ingested all day—followed by a champagne toast to her husband and two glasses of red wine at last night's fund-raiser dinner—a meal she didn't even get a chance to eat.

That part wasn't her fault. She had ordered the vegetarian entree. There was a mix-up in the kitchen, and she was served beef instead. By the time they brought her a new plate, the head table had been summoned for a photo op, and she was whisked off on an empty stomach.

Flashbulbs, people, endless small talk, smiling until her face hurt . . .

All in the line of wifely duty.

After the fund-raiser, Garvey was off to another event. She collapsed into bed beside an empty pillow, wondering, in a wine-induced melancholy, if marrying him had been the worst mistake of her life.

No. Not the worst mistake.

She knows what that was. She's been paying for it every day for more than twenty years now.

Twenty-one years, five months, and three days. She could figure out the hours, too, if the prospect of turning her head to the nightstand to check the digital clock wasn't so excruciating.

She should probably get up. She has a million things to do today—as she does every day—and she never allows herself to linger in bed.

But maybe just for a few more minutes . . .

Marin closes her eyes and wills herself back to sleep, but sleep refuses to come. Instead, she finds herself looking back—something she rarely allows. If you keep moving, stay busy enough, there's no time to lie around and wonder what might have been, if only . . .

Everyone in Marin's world had wanted her to marry Garvey. She's well aware that few—if any—of the Quinns were rooting for Garvey to marry her.

True, she had gone to all the right schools, worn all the right clothes, traveled in the same circles as Garvey. That they met in the first place really wasn't surprising. That they made it down the aisle surprised everyone—except the two of them.

They were crazy about each other. They had everything in common—well, everything that mattered. Or so Marin believed, at first.

She, too, had been raised in the Back Bay—though not in a four-story brick townhouse that had been in the family for generations. Her entrepreneurial parents were as wealthy as—if not wealthier than—the Quinns. But nouveau riche didn't cut it in Garvey's world.

Perhaps her biggest sin, as far as Garvey's famously conservative family—and, at first, even Garvey himself—were concerned: Marin didn't go to church.

In addition to his law degree, Garvey had obtained a master in theological studies from Harvard Divinity. He spoke seven languages, including Hindi, Arabic, Latin, and Hebrew. But he didn't speak Marin's.

"I don't believe in atheism," Garvey informed her early in their courtship—but not early enough to nip their romance in the bud. It was already too late for that.

"Well, I don't believe in God," she shot back.

"How can you not?"

Marin shrugged. "I wasn't raised with religion."

She could tell it was a deal breaker right then.

Sure enough, he soon made a halfhearted attempt to stop seeing her. That lasted about twenty-four miserable hours.

Then they were back in each other's arms, and to hell with the rest of the world.

Had Marin known Garvey all her life, she might have recognized that she was his brief—and only—rebellion. It was fueled, she later realized, by the most meaningful loss of his life: the recent death of his grandmother, Eleanor Harding Quinn.

Marin has never quite been able to grasp her husband's complicated relationship with his grandmother, whose formidable influence far overshadowed even that of his own parents. As far as Marin can tell, the relationship was built on a foundation of mutual respect rather than genuine affection.

No one other than Garvey seemed to miss the family

matriarch. If anything, there was almost an air of relief that she was gone. Once, when her name came up at a family gathering, one of the more distant cousins intimated that Eleanor had suffered from some kind of mental illness. But the subject was dropped immediately, and when Marin asked Garvey about it, he replied that it was the cousin, and not his grandmother, who was crazy.

Marin wasn't surprised. She knew how much Garvey's grandmother meant to him. Eleanor wanted for Garvey what he wanted for himself. Her death—unexpected, from pneumonia—brought her grandson either profound grief or perhaps, Marin suspects, subconscious relief, a fleeting reprieve.

In any case, Garvey temporarily lost sight of his goals. Maybe he needed to blow off some steam after all those years spent living up to his grandmother's ideal. Maybe he wanted to fall in love. Or maybe he needed to. Maybe it was just part of the master plan.

Every great man needs a loyal woman by his side, he told Marin—so frequently that she sometimes felt as though he'd been keeping a checklist of all the elements necessary to get him to where he wanted to be.

Family Pedigree: the Quinn bloodline went back to the *Mayflower*. Check.

Ivy League Education: Harvard Divinity and Harvard Law, like his father and grandfather before him. Check.

Trust Fund: kicked in when he turned twenty-one. Check.

Loyal Woman: enter Marin. Check.

"How would you like to be first lady one day?" he asked her not long before he proposed, and she knew he was dead serious.

"I'd love it," she told him. But she didn't really mean it. What she really meant was, *I love you.*

Nothing else mattered back then.

His parents had no choice but to go along with the engagement. It was either that or disown their only son.

Their June wedding date was set well over a year in advance, to be one of the biggest social events of the season.

Then, the September before it was to take place, Marin found herself pregnant.

She dreaded telling Garvey. She kept telling herself that he would understand and support the decision she had already made—and that everything would work out for the best.

She was dead wrong.

Running along the reservoir in the predawn gloom, Garvey is alone today. Yesterday's meeting was a risk—slight, but a risk just the same.

Two days in a row would be foolhardy. He doesn't even like to risk phone calls—though he received two yesterday.

Both times he saw the familiar number pop up in the caller ID, he sensed it wasn't going to be good news—and he was right.

This is going to take more time than he expected. More time, and a helluva lot more money. But there's no choice. Now is not the time to get sloppy.

"Tread carefully," was his curt advice. "Do you understand me? I don't want any red flags going up over there just now. It's too soon after the others."

"Don't worry. I've been watching them. I already have a plan. All I need to do is borrow—"

"Don't tell me what you need to do! Just do it."

The less he knows, the better. That's what he thought at the time, anyway.

Now, however, he wonders.

Borrow . . .

Borrow what? Borrow from whom?

"Borrow" implies that someone else will be involved. And that's out of the question. Surely it's a given that from here on in, it's just the two of them.

And then, when all is said and done . . .

It'll be just me.

There was a time when he'd have been pained at the prospect of losing his only true confidant: the one person who knows his darkest secret and understands why he did what he did.

Not anymore.

Now Garvey doesn't need anyone.

No. That's wrong. He needs his family. Marin. Caroline.

What about Annie?

How many times has his wife asked him that very question?

Always, he lies. Tells her that he needs Annie, loves Annie, too. Of course he does. Isn't he her father?

Garvey's eyes narrow.

She's your child, Garvey. That's all that matters now.

He can still hear Marin's voice; still see her tearstained face as she held out the pink swaddled bundle.

He forced himself to take it, forced himself to glance down at the baby he wished had never been born. Unlike her big sister, Annie looked nothing like a Quinn. But he could forgive her that. He thought he could forgive her— and Marin—the rest of it, too.

Maybe he could have, if she hadn't been such a demanding baby from the start. So different from Caroline. Annie was colicky. Annie had allergies and asthma. Annie kept the household up all night with her screaming.

"Difficult babies become easygoing kids later," Marin liked to say. "And vice versa."

"Where'd you hear that?" he'd ask, and Marin would shrug. She heard a lot of things.

When all was said and done, she was half right. Annie turned out to be an easygoing child. Even now, at fourteen, she tends to go with the flow.

Not Caroline. But she's certainly not *difficult*. Willful, yes. But that's a characteristic Garvey wholeheartedly admires. Caroline is a Quinn, through and through.

He can't help the way he feels about his daughters. And it's not as though he treats Annie any differently. Like Caroline, she has everything she needs, and pretty much everything she wants, from designer clothes to her own horse boarded up in Westchester—though both girls have lost interest, lately, in riding. They used to love to spend weekends on the trails at Greymeadow.

Ah, well. That's how it goes. Children grow up.

If they're lucky.

Garvey's thoughts turn to the little girl up in Glenhaven Park—somebody else's daughter.

No, he doesn't need the details.

He doesn't want to know.

He just wants—*needs*—it to be over, one way or another.

Yawning deeply, Lauren pads barefoot into the still-darkened kitchen and flips on the light.

She probably would have had a sleepless night even without Sadie in her bed, but it was impossible to doze off with her neck in a four-year-old's stranglehold for much of the night. Sadie kept saying she was scared, but she refused to say why—and frankly, Lauren didn't press her. She had other things to worry about.

Just when she thought she was starting to accept and move past the worst thing Nick could have done—having an affair and asking for a divorce—he had to go and top himself.

Lucy, honey, I got all your messages and I'm sorry I didn't make it back yesterday. I need a few extra days off to think things through. I love you. Please tell Mom I'll be in touch soon.

The moment Lauren read the text message on Lucy's phone, her momentary elation that Nick was alive and well—which had just replaced her fear that something had happened to him—gave way to sheer rage.

He needs a few days off to think *what* through?

What the hell is he talking about?

Lauren immediately called—and texted—both his phones to ask him the details, and of course he had ignored her.

Coward.

He should have discussed the change in plans directly with her in the first place, not with the kids.

Ryan called from the pool to report a similar text message on his phone. He was so relieved to have heard from his father that he, like Lucy, didn't seem to hold Nick accountable for their ruined Sunday plans or all the needless worry.

As far as the two of them are concerned, all that matters is that their father is okay. Then it was life as usual. By last night, they were both caught up in their typical exchange of phone calls and IMs with their friends.

Sadie—she's a different story. She was terribly quiet

yesterday, and skittish. She did seem relieved to hear that her father had been in touch, but something else seemed to be bothering her. She spent most of the day behind closed doors in her room.

Worried about her, Lauren called Dr. Rogel's office and left a message with his answering service.

Someone called her back—a woman named Dr. Prentiss, who's covering for the doctor while he's on vacation.

"Dr. Rogel won't be back for two weeks," she told Lauren, "but I'd be happy to see your daughter."

Lauren hesitated, wondering if she should just wait, rather than switch doctors now. But then it's not as though Sadie was attached to Dr. Rogel. She only met the man once.

"If you'd rather hold off," Dr. Prentiss said, "I can have him contact you when he gets back. Although I have to warn you that back-to-school is his busiest time of year, so it might take a few more weeks to get in."

A few more weeks? No. Lauren made an appointment with Dr. Prentiss for today.

As she fills the coffee carafe with cold tap water, she thinks again of Nick.

What makes him think it's okay to not show up for work, let alone to not see the kids when he's supposed to?

He really has gone off the deep end. And that phone call on Saturday afternoon . . . to think she'd convinced herself that it might have been a call for help when her first instinct—that he'd inadvertently pocket-dialed her in the midst of passion—had so obviously been correct.

"Are you positive that was inadvertent?" Alyssa asked, when Lauren called her yesterday to report the latest.

"What? That's . . . that's sick. You think he called me on purpose, so that I'd have to listen to that?"

"I wouldn't put anything past him. He's a jerk. He doesn't care about you and he doesn't care about the kids, either."

"I don't know if I'd go that far. I think he loves them, in his own way."

"Why are you defending him, Lauren? He doesn't care about anyone, other than himself. You know what they say . . . the apple doesn't fall far from the tree."

For a moment, she thought Alyssa was talking about the kids—Lauren's kids, fathered by a selfish man who can't be bothered with his responsibilities.

Then she realized her sister was referring to Nick's own mother having run off and abandoned her family.

"What if he never comes back?" Lauren bleakly voiced the thought that had been on her mind since she saw the text message.

Now, she jabs the coffeemaker's on button, remembering her sister's matter-of-fact response.

"Well, Nick survived it. Maybe he figures his kids will, too."

Lauren sinks into a kitchen chair, wishing she could find it impossible to believe Nick could actually think of it that way.

But who knows what Midlife Crisis Nick is capable of?

Not me. He's a total stranger now.

Lauren wonders if he even bothered to contact the office after he resurfaced yesterday—and whether HR ever managed to get in touch with Beth. Marcia Kramer never called Lauren back with any updated information, and Lauren decided it wasn't her place to call Marcia and let her know she'd heard from Nick.

Is Beth there with him as he thinks things through?

Wherever *there* is.

At first Lauren had assumed he was still at the island beach house, but maybe not. Vacation rentals on Martha's Vineyard are notoriously heavily booked at this time of year, and they tend to run weekend to weekend. Besides, Nick already mentioned—several times—that the kids' first week home from camp was the only week his vacation house was available.

Unless he had lied to her—or had planned all along to stay through this week.

"But if he did that," Alyssa said when she brought up the possibility, "then he probably would have arranged to take extra vacation time from work, wouldn't he?

"Probably. Considering that he cares about his job more than anything else."

"Even Beth?"

Lauren didn't bother to reply to that.

"Okay," Alyssa went on, "so you honestly believe that this really might be a spur-of-the-moment thing?"

"I don't know what to believe."

"Well, if he's not at the island house, where is he doing all this thinking?"

"Who knows? Maybe he's holed up in his apartment down in White Plains. Maybe he got back home over the weekend, but didn't feel like dealing with the kids, or humdrum daily routine, or real life in general."

"Yeah, well, who does? But real men suck it up and do what has to be done."

Lucky Alyssa, married to a real man. Ben is great with the baby and around the house. Of course, so is their live-in nanny, whose name is Maria, just like in *Sound of Music*. She even plays the guitar.

Alyssa really does live a charmed life.

Things were different when they were growing up, though. Lauren was one of those rare high school girls who were on top of the world, and college was even better. Then she met Nick . . .

Her older sister, meanwhile, was a bookworm who focused on academics throughout high school and college and rarely dated, even after she moved to New York to take a job in the finance industry. A late bloomer, Alyssa met Ben around the time Lauren got pregnant with Sadie, and embarked on a whirlwind courtship.

Lauren squeezed herself—six weeks postpartum, and nursing—into a matron of honor sheath for their wedding.

"You look gorgeous," Nick told her, and she knew she didn't, but she thought it was cute, the way he believed it.

That was probably a lie, like everything else.

Lauren pours a cup of coffee and sits with it at the table, brooding.

She has half a mind to get Nick's key and drive down to his apartment to see if he's there. If he is, she'll ask him what the hell he thinks he's doing. Remind him that the world doesn't revolve around him. That his three children need their father . . .

Even if their mother has no use for you whatsoever, you SOB.

Sadie woke up when Mommy got out of bed a little while ago. It was so dark she thought it was the middle of the night. She heard Mommy go downstairs, and she waited for her to come back, but she didn't.

Alone in the big bed, Sadie couldn't fall back to sleep.

After a little while, through the open windows, she started to hear the birds calling to one another outside. They don't do that in the middle of the night. She noticed that the room wasn't quite as dark, and she realized it wasn't the middle of the night after all. It was—*is*—morning.

She waits in bed until there's more light filtering through the cracks around the closed shade. Then, carefully, quietly, she gets up out of bed and tiptoes across the floor.

Peeking out into the shadowy hallway, she sees that Ryan's and Lucy's doors are closed. Sadie left her own door open when she left her room last night.

As she slowly walks toward it, she can hear her mother moving around downstairs in the kitchen, and she can smell coffee. Familiar household sounds and smells make the hallway seem a little less scary.

Sadie stops in front of her bedroom door.

Last night, she rigged the fishing line again.

In this dim light, she can't tell whether it's still intact.

She drops to her knees and feels around in the open doorway.

There it is.

Sadie breathes a sigh of relief. Good. This time, nobody's been in her room.

But that doesn't mean someone wasn't in here yesterday.

Maybe she should tell Mommy after all. She was about to run down and tell her when she first discovered the dislodged fishing line, but then Lucy came running in and made that big commotion about hearing from Daddy, and then Ryan called, and no one paid any attention to Sadie.

Or to Chauncey.

No one else seemed to care that he was still sound asleep, barely moving. He didn't stir at all when Sadie crept over and touched his paws. She knew something was wrong. She tried to tell Mommy again, but Mommy took a quick look and said he was okay.

Sadie was mad about that. She was mad about a lot of things.

So she went back up to her room and she sat on her bed and she guarded her stuff.

Mommy had said she was going to clean out the bedrooms yesterday, but she didn't.

Still, Sadie sat there all day. Until it got dark. Then Mommy made her come down and eat something for dinner. After that, Mommy came back up with her and tucked her into bed.

Lying there alone, Sadie started to wonder what might happen if the person who had been there came back in the night.

Frightened, she tried to stick it out, afraid that if she left, the burglar might come in and steal all of her things.

Finally, though, she was too scared to stay. She rigged the fishing line again and then she crawled into bed with Mommy.

She does that a lot, so Mommy didn't ask her many questions about what was bothering her. If she had, Sadie might have told her.

She didn't, and Sadie decided not to bring it up. She was afraid that if she mentioned her bedroom, Mommy would remember that she was planning to clean it out and give some of Sadie's things away to the tag sale.

She crawls under the fishing line and walks around her room, checking to make sure that everything is right where it's supposed to be.

Pausing at her bureau, she notes that it still looks a little empty. She moves her My Little Pony lamp to the left a bit, then moves her Tinker Bell music box to the right.

Now it's not so obvious that the pink dog is missing.

Satisfied, Sadie turns away.

"What are we doing today, Mom?" Lucy, wearing shorty pajamas and carrying her book and her iPod, appears in the kitchen as Lauren tosses a filter full of cold, wet coffee grounds into the trash.

Ordinarily, she pours what's left of the morning coffee into a pitcher to ice in the fridge for later, but today, she drank the entire pot herself.

And I'm still exhausted.

A warm breeze billows the curtains at the screen above the sink as Lauren runs water into the empty glass carafe, telling Lucy, "I'm not sure what we'll do."

She only knows that it's going to be another long, hard day.

Stress, anger, exhaustion—all of it due to Nick.

"Maybe we can go back to the mall," Lucy suggests hopefully.

"Maybe we can—wait, no. Sadie has a doctor appointment this afternoon."

"I hope she doesn't have to have any shots. Remember last time?"

Last time. How could she forget Sadie's annual checkup, in April? Sadie, hysterical, writhing, needing two nurses, Lauren, and Lucy all to restrain her for the needle . . .

That was not long after Nick left. Lauren was in tears, too, by the time the ordeal was over.

"It's not that kind of doctor appointment," she tells Lucy.

"Oh. It's the shrink?"

"Please don't say that in front of your sister. And please don't tell anyone outside the family about this."

"Mom, it's no big deal. Everyone has a shrink."

Everyone, who? Everyone at camp? Lauren is too tired to ask.

Lucy opens a cupboard. "We need more cereal."

"Add it to the list."

It was Nick who, years ago, pinned a magnetic "Groceries" pad to the fridge. Whenever someone notices the household has run out of something, he's supposed to write it down. No one but Lauren ever does it without prompting—though Ryan has been known to list wishful items like Pepsi and Ring Dings.

"When was the last time you went to the supermarket? Because we're actually out of a lot of stuff," Lucy announces from behind the cupboard door, where she's apparently taking inventory.

"I don't know—it's been a while."

The truth is, it's been months. All summer, she's been picking up a few grocery items here and there at the Korean market and the Rite Aid a few towns over, reluctant to visit Glenhaven's lone supermarket. She's never been able to get into and out of that store without running into several people she knows.

"I'll stop at the store today after Sadie's appointment," Lauren tells Lucy.

After all, it's August. No one's around. Plus, the A & P happens to be located in the same strip mall as Dr. Rogel's office. Pinch-hitting Dr. Prentiss said she has her own office elsewhere but that she'd meet them here so that Sadie will feel more comfortable.

"Don't forget to buy Lucky Charms. And sugar, and chocolate."

"*Chocolate?*"

"We don't have any."

"Did you write it all down?"

No answer from Lucy.

Lauren turns to see that she's just plugged in her iPod earphones and is fiddling with the volume.

With a sigh, she turns off the water, dries her hands on a dishtowel, and reaches for the magnetic pad. *Lucky Charms, sugar, chocolate . . .*

Household staples, for sure. Good thing Nick isn't around to criticize their eating habits.

She adds to the list because really, what the hell? *Pepsi. Ring Dings. Doritos. And fake yellow cheese that comes in jar.*

She can never remember what you call the stuff. Nick used to say it was toxic. Lauren considers it decadent.

She tears the list off the pad, sticks it into her purse, and waves her arms at Lucy.

"What?" Lucy unplugs one earbud.

"I'm going to go up and take a shower and get dressed now before something else pops up."

"Have fun." Lucy plugs in again.

"Oh, I will," Lauren mutters. She's been trying to get back upstairs for the last couple of hours, but there's been a barrage of interruptions: Sadie waking up and wanting breakfast, Ryan waking up and wanting breakfast, Sadie and Ryan arguing over the television, an endless phone call from her mother . . .

Lauren didn't tell her about Nick's latest misdeed, and she had asked her sister not to mention it, either. She knows her parents now loathe Nick as much as they adored him over the course of the marriage—and they aren't opposed to bad-mouthing him in front of the kids, Lauren discovered during their last visit.

The less ammunition she provides, the better.

"How's you-know-who?" her mother asked, just before

they hung up—and right after she pressed Lauren to set a date for a visit.

"Mom, you can say his name."

"I know I *can*, but I don't want to. How is he?"

Lauren sighed and told her Nick was fine.

Which is true—if "fine" entails dropping off the face of the earth for a few days to "think."

Lauren steps over Chauncey, snoozing on the rug in the foyer, and starts up the stairs.

How nice for Nick to have the luxury of undistracted "thinking." Or undistracted anything. What she wouldn't give for a little less distraction, and a little more—

The doorbell rings.

Perfect. Just perfect.

"Can someone get that?" Lauren calls, just having reached the top of the stairs.

No reply.

Oh, right. Lucy is plugged in. Ryan and Sadie are presumably behind their closed bedroom doors.

With a sigh, Lauren makes an about-face and heads back down to answer it. Through the frosted glass panel in the door, she can see the silhouette of someone standing on the porch.

Chauncey, having sprung to life, meets her at the bottom of the steps, barking and wagging his tail.

"I guess you're back to normal today, huh, boy?" Lauren rubs his head, then opens the door.

John, the pinch-hit dog walker—make that the *legitimate* pinch-hit dog walker—is standing on the porch, her house key in his outstretched hand.

"Hi. I was about to let myself in but I figured maybe I should ring first."

"Oh, well . . . thanks."

John pockets the key and reaches down to pet Chauncey. "How's it going there, pal?"

"You know, I should ask you . . . he seemed kind of under the weather yesterday. Was he low energy when you walked him, did you notice?"

"This guy? Low energy?" John shakes his head. "Nope. I wouldn't say that. Not that I know what he's usually like, but he was chasing squirrels around and all that good stuff. Maybe I just wore him out."

"Maybe."

Lauren watches him head down the street with Chauncey on the leash. The dog certainly has a spring in his step this morning. Everything seems to be okay now, thank goodness.

Sadie was so worried about him yesterday. Lauren tried to play it down for her sake, but poor Chauncey was definitely out of it.

Just one of those days, she decides. *I guess everyone has them.*

Especially me.

Spending yesterday shopping for school clothes with Annie was an absolute pleasure.

Marin wishes she could look forward to a similar experience today with Caroline, but she doubts pleasure is on the agenda.

After insisting that she wants to shop with her friends instead of her mother, Caroline grudgingly agreed to indulge Marin in their yearly tradition for a few hours.

"But I don't want to have lunch," she said, "and I don't want you to tell me what to try on."

"Don't worry, I wouldn't dream of it." Still nursing a headache, Marin hated that she, like Caroline, just wanted to get the shopping trip over with.

Now, in the backseat of a Town Car sitting in traffic on the southbound FDR, she fights the urge to tell Caroline they should have stuck to their own neighborhood, where they could walk. But her daughter has her heart set on hitting the trendy boutiques along West Broadway.

"What do you want to shop for today, Car?" Marin asks.

"I don't know. Cute stuff." Caroline is busy texting on her cell phone, as usual.

"Juniors get to have casual Fridays, don't they?"

"Mmm hmm."

Casual Friday privileges are as big a deal at the girls' private school as they were at Marin's back in the old days in Boston. Remembering the other things that were a big deal by the time she was sixteen, Marin wonders if she should have a talk with Caroline about alcohol, drugs, sex . . .

Not that she hasn't already had that talk on some level, countless times, over the years. The message, regardless of the topic: Don't Do It.

"Did you, when you were my age?" Caroline asked the last time Marin brought up underage drinking.

Marin faltered, unable to remember the latest parenting advice. Were you supposed to admit your own teenage sins, or not? She was pretty sure the jury was still out, so she chose to sidestep the question.

This morning, feeling the effects of too much wine last night, she's a prime example of what happens to people who overindulge.

And when it comes to the repercussions of premarital sex—

I could write a book, Marin thinks sadly.

But she won't, of course, because she and Garvey swore they would never tell. The news would most certainly destroy his prospects of running on the conservative ticket.

Even though, Marin thinks grimly, *it all happened more than twenty years ago. Even though we did the so-called right thing and had the baby.*

Lauren is dousing her head beneath the hot spray when someone bangs on the bathroom door. She sighs. Does it ever fail?

"Use the downstairs bathroom!" she calls, lathering her hair.

More banging. "Mom!"

It's Ryan.

Lauren parts the vinyl shower curtain—which, she notices, is dotted with mildew. "Use the downstairs, Ry! I'm in the shower."

"No, I don't have to go. The maids are here!"

Oh no—the maids!

How could she have spaced out like that? She knows they always come on Tuesdays.

"I'll be right out," she tells Ryan hurriedly. "Just tell your sisters we have to clear out of here. And . . . can you make sure your room is picked up?"

Ryan grumbles something on the other side of the door. Lauren doesn't bother to ask him to repeat it. She sticks her head under the water again, doing her best to get all the suds out and skipping the conditioner.

After swiftly toweling off, she grabs her terry bathrobe, belts it on, and reaches for the doorknob.

Before she can touch it, the door jerks open.

"Oh, sorry!" A middle-aged blond woman with a strikingly pretty face—who also happens to be a complete stranger—faces her from the opposite side of the threshold. She's wearing a Magic Maids T-shirt and carrying a bucket filled with cleaning supplies.

"It's okay. I was just . . ."

Naked. I was just naked, and you almost caught me. And this is turning into an even crappier day than I expected.

"Go ahead." Lauren steps past her and flees down the hall to her bedroom. There, she finds Olga, one of the regulars, stripping the sheets from the mattress.

"Hello, Mrs. Lauren," Olga says pleasantly—though obviously a little taken aback to see her there in her robe.

"Hi, Olga. I'm sorry—I forgot you were coming."

"Miss Rosa didn't call?"

"No, she called, I just . . . forgot. The kids and I will be out of the way in a few minutes. I need to put on my clothes."

"Of course." Olga steps out into the hall, closing the door behind her.

Lauren dives into shorts, a T-shirt, flip-flops. She runs a brush through her wet hair, grabs a pair of sunglasses, and, as an afterthought, a bathing suit.

She might as well take the kids to the pool again. Maybe she'll be able to swim some laps today, work off some of the bad energy.

Speaking of bad energy . . .

Maybe Beth will be there. And if she is, maybe I'll ask her what the hell is up with Nick.

Opening the bedroom door, Lauren finds Olga standing down the hall in front of Sadie's room—which appears to be barricaded by Sadie herself. Wearing a defiant scowl, she's standing with her arms folded across her stomach, her back against the closed door.

"What's going on?" Lauren asks brightly—though it's pretty obvious.

"Your daughter, she doesn't want me to go in there."

"Sadie, Olga just needs to clean your room."

"No!"

"Sweetie, we're going out now anyway. When we get back, you can go back into your room, okay?" Until it's time for the appointment with Dr. Prentiss, anyway.

Judging by her daughter's troubled expression and the adamant shake of her head, Lauren figures that the appointment can't come soon enough.

"No! No one can go into my room."

"I'm just going to clean it. I'm not going to touch anything, honey."

"No!" Sadie screams at poor Olga, who takes a step backward.

"Okay, you know what, Sadie? You don't talk to people that way. Ever. Apologize to Olga right now."

"I'm sorry." Sadie bows her head.

"I'm sorry, too, Olga. She can be very touchy about her things."

"It's okay. I have kids too." Olga smiles, revealing a gold tooth that matches the gold band on the fourth finger of her left hand—and tells Lauren that Olga's kids probably aren't dealing with the same problems her own kids are facing.

"Sadie." She rests a hand on her daughter's shoulder.

Sadie looks up. "What?"

The bleak look in her eyes and the defeated slump of her narrow shoulders worries Lauren.

"You want Olga to skip your room for today? How about that?"

"Yes."

"Okay." Lauren turns to Olga, who nods that she

understands, just as the other maid steps out of the bathroom to empty the waste can into a large garbage bag in the hall.

"Mary—it's Mary, right?" Olga asks.

The woman nods.

"This is Mrs. Lauren."

"We met, sort of. Hello again, Mary." Lauren smiles at the new woman, who looks as though it pains her to smile back.

"And this is her little girl. That's her room. She doesn't want us to clean it today, okay?"

Mary nods briefly, then disappears back into the bathroom.

She's either very shy, Lauren decides, or very unfriendly, or she doesn't speak much English. Probably not the latter, though you never know. At first glance, Mary struck her as the all-American type.

"I'll tell the other two ladies, too," Olga promises.

"Thank you." Lauren starts to turn toward the stairs. "Wait—there are two more women here today?"

"Four of us. Yes."

"I thought there were going to be just three." Maybe she misunderstood Rosa's message.

"Sometimes we change things," Olga explains. "Depending on who is around. The more ladies, the faster it goes."

Lauren nods. Whatever. She just needs to make sure she leaves tips for four instead of three.

"Come on, Sadie," she says, "let's get moving."

"Just a second." Her daughter crouches in front of her bedroom door as if she's looking for something.

Lauren is about to ask her what she's doing, but she gives an abrupt nod and straightens again. "Okay. Let's go, Mommy."

Lauren ushers her toward the stairs, worried. Sadie's behavior is growing stranger by the day.

Thank goodness for the child psychiatrist. Hopefully Dr. Prentiss will say that it's all totally normal, just a phase. If not . . .

We'll just have to handle it, Lauren tells herself—then she remembers. *No,* I'll *just have to handle it.*

She'd be a fool to count on Nick for anything, ever again.

Elsa pulled out of her driveway back in Groton at eight o'clock this morning, just after Brett left for work. He had no idea about her little excursion, and she wasn't about to tell him. She knew what he would say.

Don't do that to yourself. Why pour salt on an un-healed wound?

He was right, she'd thought at the time. Of course he was.

But then yesterday, when she held that orphaned puppy, and Karyn told her she'd have been a good mother, and the flower garden came back to life . . .

According to the GPS on the dashboard, Elsa should have been in Boston by ten—barring traffic complications. Ha. As always, Interstate 95 was riddled with construction zones and accidents.

The legendary Big Dig—a construction nightmare—might have wound down over the years, but the city is by no means a pleasure to navigate. It's been almost fourteen years since she negotiated the narrow network of Boston streets, yet it all comes right back to her: the endless congestion, the shortcuts and detours, the roads that unexpectedly fork off without advance signage, the streets that begin as one-way but wind up two-way, and vice versa.

Something else comes back to her, too: the countless visits into the city to take Jeremy to various doctors and experts, none of whom was really able to help him.

Oh, Jeremy. I failed you. I'm so sorry.

It's well past noon by the time she pulls into the parking garage off Hanover Street, having had plenty of time to rethink the meeting with Mike. It seemed like a good idea yesterday, when she impulsively made the call. Now, however, she has to force herself to get out of the car.

She smooths her trim black suit, pulled from the back of her closet, shrouded in clear plastic from a San Diego dry cleaner. She'd gotten rid of plenty of clothes over the year, but she kept this one. Not just because of the designer label, but because she knew, with morbid practicality, that the day might come when she might need a black suit.

Not this day. Not under these circumstances. But it's all she could find in her closet that doesn't scream small-town housewife.

Or does it? Are pencil skirts even still in style? Are sling backs? she wonders, her heels tapping briskly along the sidewalk as she makes her way past the neighborhood's tenement architecture toward the café.

Does it matter what she's wearing?

No. But cities tend to evoke faint memories of her fashionista past—a life that might as well have belonged to someone else.

Who am I now?

Why am I even here?

Pausing to wait for a pedestrian signal to change, Elsa fights the urge to turn around and run back to the car, to get the hell out of here and go back home where she belongs.

But that house isn't home—not really. She doesn't feel

as though she belongs there yet. Oh hell, she doesn't feel as though she belongs anywhere without Jeremy.

The light changes, and she makes her way across the street.

I have to touch base with Mike in person. Just to remind him that I haven't given up on finding Jeremy, and to find out whether he's made any progress on my other requests. Just to see if there's anything new at all, any shred of information . . .

Mike Fantoni knows as well as anyone that Elsa is desperate to have her son back—or at least to learn his fate. Mike would never withhold information.

No—but maybe seeing her in person will trigger something. Some forgotten detail, some new avenue to explore, perhaps just the renewed need to do whatever it takes to pick up a trail that's been cold for fourteen years.

CHAPTER THIRTEEN

Ryan really didn't want to come to the pool today.

His friends are all busy with dentists' appointments and shopping and day trips and all the other stuff parents like to squeeze in before school starts.

All except Ian, anyway. Ryan doesn't know what he's doing today, and he didn't call to find out. Ian doesn't go to the town pool since he has one in his own backyard. He'd probably invite Ryan over, but then Ryan would have to deal with Mrs. Wasserman and her nosy questions again. No thanks.

So here he is, dangling his feet in the shallow end, chewing on his pinky fingernail, and watching his little sister splash around. Lucy is off somewhere flirting with Josh, and Mom is swimming laps. Talk about a sucky way to spend a precious summer day . . .

Though, to be fair, Mom did offer to pay him to mind Sadie, and he can sure use the money. Dad always slips him a few bucks when Ryan sees him, but it's been a while, and now who knows when Dad is coming back?

At first, Ryan was so relieved to get the text message from his father that he didn't even think much about what it said. He'd been so worried something bad might have happened, and he knew Mom and Lucy and even Sadie were worried, too.

But yesterday, once it sank in that his father was okay, Ryan started to get mad.

Really mad.

Madder, even, than he was about the divorce.

Dad has time to go away on vacation for a whole week with his girlfriend, and he has time to sit around and think, but he doesn't have time to take Ryan on their annual fishing trip?

"Hey, Sadie, stay on this side," he calls to his sister, noticing she's drifting over to the opposite end of the steps, where a couple of other kids her age are bobbing around.

Sadie pointedly ignores him.

"Sadie!"

She turns to look at him, waves.

"Come back over here, near me."

"In a minute." She turns to grab a sponge ball as it floats past, and tosses it back to the little boy who let it go.

Hmm. Maybe he should just move over there so that she can play with the other kids. Sadie could probably stand to make a few friends. Maybe that would help her act more . . . normal.

He feels bad for even thinking that, but it's true. His little sister is downright weird lately. She's always worrying about her stuff, and she throws tantrums and cries at the drop of a hat. What if she gets to school and none of the other kindergarteners like her? What if she goes through life as one of those pathetic kids who have no friends?

That'll be Dad's fault, too, Ryan tells himself. Sadie was just fine before he left.

We all were.

"Is that your little sister?"

Ryan looks up to see a lady talking to him. "Yeah," he tells her, "that's Sadie. I'm watching her for my mom."

"Aren't you a sweet big brother."

"She's paying me."

The woman laughs. "Sweet, and smart, too."

Obviously a mom, she's in up to her knees, holding a little kid who looks petrified of the water. But of course Ryan would know she's a mom even without the kid attached to her, because she's wearing a one-piece black bathing suit with a little skirt. Only moms wear those—including his own.

She lowers the baby so that the bottoms of his feet skim the water. He screams.

"It's okay, little guy," his mother tells him. "See? It's fun."

The baby screams harder. He obviously does not think it's fun.

"My sister used to do that when she was a baby," Ryan offers, feeling sorry for the mom, who holds the baby up high above the water again.

"Really? Do you remember how she got over it?"

"No, but my mom probably does. She used to read all these books about stuff like that. You know—how to get kids to do stuff."

The woman smiles. "Where's your mom?"

Ryan points at the lap lanes on the far side of the pool, where his mother is gliding toward the opposite end in a rhythmic freestyle.

"I'll have to ask her for some tips, or at least some good book titles. What's her name?"

"Lauren. I'm Ryan," he adds.

"Good to meet you, Ryan. I'm Jessica Wolfe."

She's nice. Maybe she can be friends with Mom.

Oh geez. Why am I so worried about finding friends for other people?

Ryan isn't quite sure. All he knows is that his mother and sister both seem lonely, and he feels like he should probably do something about it now that . . .

Now that I'm the man of the house?

But he's only twelve. He doesn't want to be a man. He doesn't want to take care of other people. Half the time, he feels like he wants someone to take care of him.

Mom does, to be fair. Yeah. She takes good care of him.

But Dad doesn't. Not anymore. These days, Dad only takes care of himself.

Again, Ryan feels a flash of anger toward his father.

His jaw clenches and he tries to think about something else. Something happy.

He watches Jessica scoop some water over her baby's feet. More screams. Okay, that's definitely not happy.

"Shh, sweetie, you're not even in the water, see?" Jessica says. "I'm just splashing you. See the big girl? See how Sadie splashy-splashes over there?"

Hearing her name, Sadie looks up with interest. Ryan notices once again that she's drifted too far away.

"Hey, Sades, c'mere."

"No! You come here!"

Ryan sighs, hoists himself to his feet. He might as well go sit on the other side.

"It was nice meeting you," he tells Jessica.

"You too, Ryan."

As he makes his way around the stairs, he glances over toward the lap lanes again, wishing he could introduce the nice mom to his mom. She said Trilby is coming back any day now, but that doesn't mean she doesn't need someone else to hang around with.

His mother is no longer swimming in the lap lanes.

Where . . . ?

Oh. She's over there, out of the pool, and no wonder it took him a minute to recognize her. She's not wearing one of those black mom bathing suits with a little skirt today, he notices. She's wearing a red two-piece. And—Ryan's eyes widen—she's talking to some guy.

His heart sinks.

Weren't you just thinking Mom can use some new friends? Maybe she made one.

Yeah, but he's a guy. And he's not looking at Ryan's mother like he wants her to be his friend.

He's looking at her like . . .

Ryan sighs.

Yeah. Life definitely sucks.

Three hours—and well over three thousand dollars—after stepping out of the Town Car on West Broadway, Caroline is well outfitted for the fall season. In Marin's opinion, anyway.

In Caroline's opinion, they're just getting started. Funny, because she's the one who didn't want this shopping expedition in the first place.

"I still need new black boots," she declares as they walk along Prince Street, "and I want one of those long wool coats like Desdemona's. I know where she got it, and the place is right down here."

Desdemona is one of Caroline's best friends, the daughter of a famously bisexual eighties rock star and his Tony-winning actress wife. She's a good kid, even if her parents tend to cold-shoulder Marin and Garvey whenever they run into each other.

"It's because you guys are conservative Republicans," Caroline once mentioned—as if that explained it.

On some level, Marin supposes, it does. Garvey represents everything the right wing stands for, and Desdemona's parents couldn't be more left.

Marin herself privately comes down somewhere in the middle, but it's been years since she dared voice an opinion that could be construed as even vaguely liberal. It bothers her, sometimes, that people assume she shares Garvey's politics. Pro–capital punishment, anti–gay marriage, pro-gun, anti-choice . . .

Particularly that one. Anti-choice.

It isn't necessarily that she wishes she herself had done things differently years ago. She wouldn't have anyway— even if a choice wasn't absolutely out of the question, as far as Garvey was concerned. She had made up her mind to have the baby before she even told him.

Had she opted not to, though, would she eventually have made peace with her decision? Or would she be enduring a private hell all these years later?

Does it matter? She's in hell anyway.

You weren't forced to give birth, Marin. It's what you wanted. What Garvey wanted.

Yes. They even agreed on what should happen after the child was born—until the moment when Marin held her baby in her arms.

That was when she changed her mind.

But it was too late.

"Come on, that's the place." Caroline is tugging her toward yet another boutique.

Marin's head is pounding. "You don't need a wool coat for a few more months, at least. Or boots, for that matter."

"Please, Mommy. I really, really, *reeeeally* want to look."

Caroline only calls her Mommy when she really, really, *reeeeally* wants something.

Torn between the maternal desire to make her daughter happy and the selfish need to go home and take a handful of Advil, Marin relents. "One more store. But this is it."

"*ThankyouMommyIloveyou!*" Caroline is already pushing through the wide glass door.

Marin follows, and is immediately assaulted by a blast of throbbing music.

Great. This'll do wonders for my headache.

She looks around for a place to park herself while Caroline browses. No benches. No chairs. The store is modernist white from ceiling to floor, with strategically positioned track lighting and a soundtrack befitting a nightclub.

Marin wanders around glancing at impossibly hip clothes while Caroline disappears into the dressing room with an armload of coats.

"Can I help you?"

She looks up to see a male sales clerk, wearing faded, beat-up, low-slung jeans and a disinterested expression. There's something familiar about him, and her heart immediately skips a beat.

Can it be . . . ?

Marin clears her throat. "No, I'm just . . . uh . . . looking."

He nods and turns to straighten a display.

He's the right age. He's good-looking, with dark hair and eyes . . .

And I feel like I've met him.

She can't place him, but she feels as though she knows him. In all the reading she's done on this particular topic, in every firsthand account related by women who have been in her shoes, that inexplicable familiarity is the dead giveaway.

The heart knows, one mother said, *even when the brain does not.*

The quote has stuck with Marin. It resounds in her head whenever something like this happens. These encounters don't occur on a daily basis, by any means—but frequently enough to keep her in a perpetual state of what-if.

"Mom, can I get both of these?" Caroline emerges from the dressing room with two hangers. "I can't decide, and they both look great, and—hey, Jackson, what are *you* doing here?"

The young man Marin was just watching—the one her heart seems to remember—turns toward her daughter. "Hey, Caroline. How's it going?"

"Great! I didn't know you worked here!" Caroline's bright tone makes it obvious—to Marin, anyway—that her daughter did, indeed, know that. That he might even be the reason she absolutely had to have the coat Desdemona bought in this particular boutique.

"Yeah. I've been working here all summer."

"Cool. Are you still at Juilliard?"

"I graduated."

"Oh, right. I *think* I knew that."

Seeing her daughter's flirty smile, Marin is seized by a new and terrible what-if . . .

"Mom, this is Jackson," Caroline tells her. "Remember? My friend Emily's brother? He used to teach me guitar?"

Guitar. Jackson. No wonder he looks familiar.

Thank God, thank God . . .

"Do you still play?" Jackson is asking Caroline, who shakes her head.

Thank God it isn't him.

This time.

But someday, it might be.

What then?

"We meet again."

Toweling off at the side of the pool, Lauren glances up to see a stranger standing behind her.

"Playground," he prods, at her blank stare.

"Pardon? Oh—right!" She didn't recognize him without the baseball cap, and the baby, and . . . his shirt. "You're the new dad."

"New? Not exactly. My son is almost a year old."

"That's pretty new from where I sit. But what I meant was, you're the new dad in town."

"That's me. Castle Lane. Puke green shutters."

Lauren grins and tries not to notice that he's wearing only boardshorts, and that . . . well, wow. Did she actually think he was someone's chubby hubby the other day? It couldn't be farther from the truth. His tanned chest is solid muscle.

"Where's your son?" She looks around, expecting to see a baby carriage or port-a-playpen.

"He's with his mom. We share custody."

So he's not chubby *or* a hubby.

"Oh. Well that's, uh . . ."

"Difficult. Very difficult. That's what it is." He shrugs. "It was harder when I lived in the city, though. At least he's only ten minutes away now."

"So your ex-wife lives up here?"

"Actually, my ex-wife lives on the West Coast."

"And you share custody?"

"No, I never had kids with Zoe—she's my ex-wife, in L.A. But my son's mom, Kendra, lives here in Westchester, over in Yorktown Heights. Confused yet?"

"Very."

"Kendra and I were never married, thank God. That would have been more disastrous than my first marriage. We were dating, Kendra got pregnant, we had the baby together. By the way, since you now know everything about me except my name—I'm Sam Henning."

"Lauren Walsh."

They shake hands. She resists the urge to look around and make sure no one's watching them. Like her children, or Beth, or . . . people she once called friends.

It's August. There are few familiar faces here.

"So . . . is that it?" Sam asks.

"Is what it?"

"That's all you're going to tell me? Your name? When I just poured out my whole life story?"

"I—you want to hear my life story?"

"If you want to tell it."

Trying to decide whether he's a sweet, fun guy or some kind of nutcase, she smiles. "Maybe some other time."

"Sure. Personally, I like to get it out there right from the start, you know? All my baggage. That way, if someone's not interested, she's free to move on."

Interested? Lauren raises an eyebrow.

It's been a while—okay, decades—since a man flirted with her. So long that she's not even positive that's what Sam Henning is doing.

But it sure seems that way.

"You know, you were pretty chatty the other day," he observes. "Now you don't have much to say."

That might be because they're both standing here half dressed, without the buffer of kids and swings and sunglasses and anonymity.

Plus, he no longer has a wife.

He never even *had* a wife. Well, he has an ex-wife.

And the mother of his child. But there doesn't seem to be a current woman in his life, which makes him more than just some random playground dad.

It makes him . . .

Potentially . . .

Oh hell, what do you even call it these days? Dating material? A love interest?

"So you live in the big yellow Victorian house in my backyard, right?" he asks.

"Well, I'm in the only yellow Victorian on our block, so . . . I guess so."

"You should cut through the yard and say hello sometime. That is, if poison ivy doesn't bother you. My yard is full of it. And it turns into a marsh when it rains, so you'd need waders, but otherwise . . ."

"Sounds inviting."

"Oh, it is."

She laughs.

So does he, but he says, "I'm serious. Pop over. I get lonely, living alone."

So do I, she wants to say.

But she doesn't live alone, and she doesn't want him to think she's flirting.

Is she?

She's pretty sure he is. Or maybe that's just his personality.

After all, what makes you think he'd even be interested in a worn-out mother of three with just as much baggage as he has—if not more?

Sure, he's acting interested . . .

But maybe he wants something else from her.

Like what? Your riches? Your body? Your three kids, dog, and rattletrap house?

Puh-leeze.

"I should go check on my daughter," she tells him, wrapping the towel around her hips like a sarong.

"Sadie? Or Lucy?"

She looks up, startled. "How do you know their names?"

"Yesterday . . . on the playground. Remember?"

She does remember meeting him. But she doesn't remember telling him the girls' names. Maybe she did.

Does it even matter?

"It was good seeing you again," she tells Sam, not quite sure she means it.

"Interesting" might be a better word. "Unsettling" would be even more accurate.

"You too, Lauren."

She definitely told him her own name. Yet there's something about hearing him say it that makes her vaguely . . . Once again, "unsettled" is the right word.

Most people don't address others by name in conversation unless they know each other quite well. She doesn't know Sam Henning at all.

But maybe I'd like to, she admits to herself as she walks away.

That, perhaps, is the most unsettling thought of all.

Was Mike Fantoni always this good-looking? Elsa wonders, sitting across the round café table from him, nursing a cup of tea.

Probably. She just never noticed before, too devastated by her loss to pay attention.

Today, despite her coffee-fueled jitters, she can't help but admire his square jaw peppered with a manly five o'clock shadow; his muscular build; his full head of dark, wavy hair worn a little longer than she recalls.

She can't help but note that he isn't wearing a wedding ring. Did he ever?

I don't remember. It's all a blur. It didn't matter then.

It doesn't matter now, either, she reminds herself.

But it's strange that the details of their meetings in the past are all so fuzzy. For all she knows, this little Italian café was once an upscale trattoria. Maybe she and Mike sat here rubbing shoulders with Boston's elite, sipping lattes and eating cannoli on china plates.

Not likely, though. She suspects the place always appeared just as it is now. These booths, with white cotton batting peering through cracked red vinyl seats, couldn't possibly have been installed in this century. The same goes for the individual jukeboxes that haven't been updated since the soundtrack from *Footloose*—the original movie—was on top of the charts. And the thick cups faintly stained with lipstick in shades Elsa would never wear, and glass cases with congealed, rotating wedges of pie . . .

"So what brings you into Boston?" Mike stirs a third packet of sugar into his second cup of black coffee—having ordered two at once, downing the first in the amount of time it took him and Elsa to exchange perfunctory pleasantries.

"I wanted to see you," she says simply.

Mike raises an eyebrow, and she realizes he might have the wrong idea.

"About Jeremy," she clarifies. "I wanted to see you about Jeremy."

Is that a flicker of disappointment in his dark eyes?

It's gone before she can be sure.

"And I wanted to ask you," she goes on, "whether you'd found a way past those sealed records yet."

"I'm working on it." He looks down at his coffee, stirring it even though the sugar has long dissolved.

Elsa's heart pounds.

Pointedly, she asks, "Do you have new information, Mike?"

"I wish I did." He sets down the spoon and meets her gaze head-on. Now there's no sign of the look that made her wonder if he'd been withholding something from her.

She must have imagined it.

"But I don't want to go!" Sadie complains, bobbing in the pool on a purple foam noodle as Lauren, standing above her on the concrete deck, holds out a dry towel.

"We can come back tomorrow."

Sadie shakes her head and leans over to examine a waterlogged dead bug in the slotted drain that runs along the pool's edge.

Lauren sighs and darts yet another glance toward the lap lanes, where Sam Henning is still swimming back and forth. No wonder he's so muscular. He's been at it for almost an hour.

Yes, she's been keeping track.

No, she can't figure out why on earth he seems interested in her, but he does. Every once in a while, he takes a short break at the end of the pool to adjust his goggles, and she's caught him looking at her.

She turns her attention back to her daughter. "Sades, we have to be somewhere in twenty minutes."

"Where?"

Conscious of a cluster of moms—and their perfect, obedient children—observing the exchange from their usual encampment by the stairs, Lauren keeps her voice at a reasonable level. "Just come *on*."

"Where do we have to be?"

Lauren lowers her voice even more. "You have . . . an appointment."

"What?"

"An appointment. You have an appointment."

"Where?"

"At the doctor."

"I'm not sick."

"Just . . . come on!"

"Not yet."

Lauren sighs and shakes her head in exasperation.

"I know what you're thinking."

She turns to see a woman in sunglasses and a black bathing suit sitting at the edge of the pool, dunking her feet into the water.

"You're thinking, 'What did I ever do to deserve this,' right?"

Lauren laughs. "How'd you guess?"

"Because I was thinking the same thing myself a little while ago, before he fell asleep." She indicates the sleeping baby on her lap. "I'm sure you heard him screaming at the top of his lungs. He hates the water."

"Right now I wish my daughter did." Lauren watches Sadie splash her way along the edge.

"She's your youngest, right?"

"Is it that obvious?"

The woman laughs. "No—your son told me. Ryan, right? He's such a sweet kid."

"Are we talking about the same Ryan?"

"Over there—the one who's on the diving board ladder?"

Lauren turns her head. "That's my Ryan. But . . . sweet?"

"Really, he was."

"No, I'm just kidding. He can be sweet. But he's going through a phase. Kind of like her." Again, she focuses her attention on Sadie. "You have two minutes, Sadie Walsh. Do you hear me?"

"Can I have five?"

"You can have three."

"Four."

"God help me," Lauren mutters, shaking her head.

"What about Lucy and Ryan?"

"They're staying here. We'll pick them up later."

"That's no fair, Mommy!"

"Sadie . . . you're down to two minutes." She folds her arms.

"It's too bad you have to leave on such a beautiful day," the woman with the baby tells her. "I was hoping I could pick your brain a little."

"You were?"

"Your son told me your daughter used to be deathly afraid of the water, too. How'd you get her over it?"

"Well, she was older at the time. I mean, I don't think you have to worry. It's not like your son needs to learn to swim anytime soon, so . . ."

"No, it's not just that. He's terrified of water. All water. Even the bathtub. That's why I haven't been coming to the pool all summer, as much as I love it myself. I'm Jessica Wolfe, by the way."

"I'm Lauren."

She smiles. "Lauren Walsh. I know. Your son told me."

Wow, Ryan certainly was chatty. What else did he tell her?

Remembering her conversation with him about losing friends and making new ones, Lauren wonders if her son was trying to network on her behalf. If that's the case, it's pretty sweet—and a welcome effort, because Jessica seems a lot more down-to-earth than some of the other moms around here.

"Are you new in town?" Lauren asks.

"Not that new. But I haven't been out much. First I was pregnant for, like, a year—that's what it felt like, anyway—and I was sick as a dog with morning sickness 24–7, the whole pregnancy. Then I had him, and trying to get used to being a mom was so insane. I couldn't get my act together. So I've kind of been, you know—hibernating."

Do I ever know.

"It's hard when the kids are little," Lauren agrees. *And even harder when they're older, and your husband dumps you for another woman.*

"So where do you live?" Jessica asks her.

"We're over on Elm."

"Oh, I love the big old houses there. I was hoping we could buy one of those, but we wound up in a development."

"Which one?"

"Glenhaven Crossing."

"Want to trade?" Lauren asks wryly.

Jessica laughs, and her son stirs in her arms.

"Uh-oh—he's so overtired," she whispers, stroking his head. "I should probably just take him home for a regular nap but I hate to be stuck in the house on a beautiful day, and it's supposed to rain later and tomorrow."

"You can always put him on a blanket in the shade. I used to do that when my kids were little. A lot of people do." Lauren gestures at the smattering of sleeping babies and toddlers on the grassy area beneath the trees.

"Good idea. Next time I will. I'll be around here a lot. The pediatrician told me the best thing I can do is keep exposing him to water and eventually, he'll get used to it.

So I guess that's my only plan for now. Come here every day until he stops screaming—or someone kicks us out."

"Trust me, that won't happen. They're pretty laid back here, in case you haven't noticed."

"Not the lifeguards, I hope."

"No, but—"

"Mom!"

She turns to see Lucy, holding her pink phone. "What's wrong?"

"I texted Daddy last night and asked him where he is—you know, home or still on vacation. I just checked my phone and he answered."

"Just now?"

"No . . . a while ago, but—"

"What did he say?"

"It was kind of weird."

"Weird, how? Here, let's see."

Lucy gives her the phone. The sun glares on the screen no matter which way Lauren turns it.

"I have to go over there into the shade." She hands over the towel. "Can you please get your sister out of the pool for me?"

"Sure."

Lauren starts away, then remembers Jessica. "Oh . . . it was nice meeting you."

"You too." The woman smiles and waves.

"Sadie," Lucy is calling, "come on."

Hurrying over to the shade beneath several towering oaks, Lauren examines Lucy's phone.

I'm still on vacation with Elizabeth. I will be back soon.

What's so weird about that?

Other than the fact that it's completely selfish and callous . . .

She looks around to see that Sadie is out of the pool and wrapped in a towel, little stinker.

"Lucy, come here for a minute," she calls.

Lucy hurries over. "Did you see it?"

"I did. Why is it weird?"

"Because her name is Beth. Not Elizabeth."

"Beth is a nickname for Elizabeth."

"No, I know that, but . . . I mean, Dad never calls her that. Ever."

"Oh, well . . ." Uncomfortable, she shrugs. "Maybe he does sometimes, and you've just never heard him."

"No. I'm worried that maybe . . . you know."

"What?"

Lucy takes a deep breath. "I'm worried that maybe Dad's trying to tell us something—you know, like maybe he's trapped somewhere or someone's holding him hostage and he's sending a signal."

"Oh, Lucy . . . are you still reading that Robert Ludlum spy book?"

"That's not why, Mom. I seriously feel like something's wrong with Dad."

Lauren looks at her, then, again, at the phone.

Just yesterday, she herself was consumed with the same feeling. But then they heard from Nick, and she felt better.

Now she wonders uneasily why he's so cagey, avoiding the kids, and his job . . .

Maybe something really is wrong. Maybe he's in some kind of trouble.

"Mom? You're worried about him, too, aren't you?"

Slowly, Lauren nods.

"What are we going to do?" All at once, Lucy sounds—and looks—like a frightened little girl.

This, Lauren tells herself, *is why you can't admit to her that Nick might be in some kind of trouble. You're the mother. You have to be the optimistic one.*

Lauren hugs her. "Oh, sweetie, try not to worry. Daddy's a grown man. He knows how to take care of himself. He'll be okay."

Lucy nods bleakly, clearly not buying that any more than Lauren does.

Elsa's instinct was—*is*—to trust Mike, just as she always has, and yet . . .

She could have sworn she'd seen something in his eyes there, just for a moment.

But she's probably mistaken.

That's why you need to forget it and move on.

"Let's go over what we know," Mike suggests, and opens the folder he brought with him.

There never were many details. One minute, Jeremy was there. The next, he was gone.

Someone must have taken him, unless . . .

"Maybe he ran away," Brett suggested on that awful long-ago day when, hysterical, Elsa reached him at work.

"How could he run away? He's seven."

"How many times has he told us he was going to leave, Elsa?"

"He didn't mean it."

"How do you know? He says a lot of things he claims he didn't mean to say. He does a lot of things he says he didn't mean to do."

Brett was jaded. After what they'd been through with Jeremy, who could blame him?

I could. I did.

They've come a long way in fourteen years.

But we still have a long, long way to go.

Before they leave the restaurant, Elsa asks Mike if he remembers what he said to her the first time they'd met—back when Jeremy was newly missing and she hired Mike because she was getting nowhere with the authorities.

"What did I say?"

"You said that in cases like these, there's always someone who saw something, or knows something. You told me the trick is to figure out who that person is, and find him."

Mike nods.

"Have you given up on that? Or do you still think someone is out there?"

"I'll never give up. On anything. I'm always searching for new leads, Elsa."

She believes that.

She tells him to keep trying, and he promises that he will.

"Thank you, Mike. Because I need . . ."

Once, a long time ago, she would have ended that sentence . . . *my son back.*

Now, older and wiser and realistic, she seeks something else.

"Closure, Mike. I need closure."

No traffic to speak of; wooded parks; tree-lined, brick-paved streets; old-fashioned gingerbread houses instead of skyscraper apartments . . .

I bet I could get used to this lifestyle.

Here in Glenhaven Park, anyway. Unlike most cookie-cutter suburbs, the town has its share of charm. So does the Walsh family.

What a shame to have discovered both under such unfortunate circumstances.

What a shame it would be if something were to happen to Lauren Walsh, or worse yet, to one of her precious children.

Or to all of them—Lauren included. An entire family, wiped out due to nothing more than incredible bad luck.

Dammit. Where is that pink stuffed animal?

A search of the house turned up nothing. And it was a thorough search, once the pooch had enjoyed his special treat and drifted into a dead sleep.

Dead, indeed.

Some watchdog. Maybe the dosage was a little too high. But a sedative overdose beats killing the kids' pet, right?

No unnecessary canine casualties. Garvey will be pleased.

So what happened to the damned toy? Maybe it was never even in the house.

No. It was. Nick Walsh said it was.

So where is it now?

There's only one way to find out.

Make that two.

You can either ask the Walshes nicely—and subtly— and be on your way. Or you can force it out of them, and leave no witnesses behind.

The first option is infinitely more appealing, of course. But the clock is ticking, and Garvey Quinn isn't exactly known for his infinite patience.

A little more time. That's all I need. I've already blended into their lives here. No one's giving me a second glance. If I can find it on my own, no one will ever be the wiser. No casualties, like Garvey said.

Just a couple more days. Then, if the stuffed animal—

and the file—still haven't turned up, there will be no alternative.

The nice little suburban family will, regrettably, have to be destroyed.

Oh well.

Better the Walshes than the Quinns.

It would have been nice, Mike thinks as he heads up Hanover Street, if Elsa Cavalon had wanted to see him about something other than her missing son, or the woman she had more recently asked him to track down.

He turns to catch a last glimpse of her walking in the opposite direction. Damn, she's hot. Even after all these years, and a one-way trip to hell, there's something about her that turns him on.

Better not to get involved with her on an emotional level, though.

What the hell are you talking about? You've always been emotionally involved, from the moment she showed up with that picture of her missing kid.

Physically. That's what he meant. He can't get physically involved . . . much as he'd like to. Even though his policy is to mix business with pleasure whenever possible.

But for him, Elsa Cavalon is off limits. She's married, she's classy, and—most importantly—Mike suspects she's hanging on to her sanity by a mere thread.

She's better now, though, than she was. She told him she's been keeping busy—doing some volunteer work, taking care of her new house . . .

She looks a lot better, too, than she used to. She was always a beautiful woman—anyone could see that—but there was a ravaged look to her back then.

Her gorgeous face has some color to it now. She's

wearing makeup today, and all dressed up. She's still skin and bones, but her kind of figure has always appealed to Mike, who grew up surrounded by voluptuous women—and married one.

Yeah. Elsa Cavalon gets to him. And he's not going to do a damned thing about it.

Mike waits for a delivery truck to rattle past, then crosses the street in mid-block.

"Hey, Mik*ey*," the Sicilian butcher calls, emphasis on the second syllable.

"Hey, Joe. Whatsa matter, you got nothin' to do today? No dead cows to chop up?"

"I got plenty of dead cows. And I got some nice capicolla just for you." Cigarette in hand and wearing his red-stained apron, Joe lounges against a globe-topped lamppost. "You want a sang-wich, Mikey?"

"Later, Joe. Maybe later." Mike unlocks the door tucked between Joe's shop and the neighboring pharmacy storefront.

Inside, he doesn't bother to stop at the row of postboxes and check mail. Nothing that matters comes to this address. He rents a box down at the main branch for that.

Up he goes, taking three narrow flights of stairs with practiced ease. On the top floor, he unlocks his door and thinks again of Elsa.

She's on her way home now, to her husband and their new house down by the Connecticut shore. What's she going to tell him when she gets there? That this was a wasted trip? That they might as well give up on Mike, because he's given up on them?

"I wish I had something new that I could tell you," he said to Elsa earlier—and it was true. He did wish he could tell her . . . something.

But he can't. Not unless . . .

Time to make a call.

Tossing his keys on the table, he notes that the cordless phone isn't sitting in the charger base. Not unusual. He looks around but doesn't see it, and that's not just because the shades are drawn. There's crap everywhere. Papers, files, magazines. Beer bottles—a lot of those. Piles of dirty laundry and even a few stacks of clean clothes.

No freaking phone.

Mike pulls out his cell, dials the apartment number, and waits.

Ah—the ringing is coming from a pillow on the futon. He lifts it up, and there's the cordless.

He hangs up the cell and tosses it aside, not wanting to dial this particular number from that particular phone. Better that it comes from the landline, which will register his name. Maybe this time, for a change, the call will be answered. He's been trying for a couple of days now.

He dials the number.

The line rings once . . . twice . . . three, four, five times.

Then the voice mail picks up, as it has been lately.

"Hey, this is Byron. You know what to do. Do it at the beep."

CHAPTER
FOURTEEN

Dr. Rogel's office is unusual, as medical offices go. It's a two-room deal. There's no receptionist, and not much of a waiting area—just two chairs and a table with a few magazines: *Highlights*, *Woman's Day*, *Sports Illustrated Kids*.

There's a white noise machine, too, right next to the closed door leading to the inner office. The pleasant rhythm of ocean waves makes it impossible to hear what's being said on the other side of the door.

Her thoughts consumed with questions about Nick, Lauren goes through the motions of flipping through a magazine as she and Sadie sit waiting.

One thing at a time. First the doctor, with Sadie . . .

Then she'll go home and see if she can get in touch with Nick. Even if it means calling Beth.

"Is it almost time, Mommy?" Sadie asks.

"Almost. Are you sure you don't want to look at *Highlights* or play Brickbreaker on my phone or something?"

Sadie just shakes her head, green eyes haunted.

Lauren would give anything to erase that expression.

It'll happen. That's why you're here. One thing at a

time. Sadie comes first, no matter what might be going on with Nick.

She hears the faint sound of a door closing somewhere out in the hall, meaning the current patient has left. Patients exit the office through a second door that leads right into the stairwell. It's all very private.

Lauren appreciates that. She doesn't particularly want anyone to know that her four-year-old is seeing a psychiatrist. And she doesn't particularly care who else's kid is a patient here—even if, according to Lucy, *Everyone has a shrink.*

"Sadie, it's almost our turn. Are you ready?"

"I guess."

The door opens and a woman appears. Dr. Prentiss looks nothing like Lauren expected. Which was . . . what? A female version of Sigmund Freud? Maybe. Dr. Rogel has round glasses, white beard and mustache, and a distinguished air.

This woman, an attractive brunette, is about Lauren's age and wearing the same sleeveless top and summer skirt Lauren admired on a mannequin at Ann Taylor at the mall the other day.

I love your outfit, she's about to say—but Dr. Prentiss is entirely focused on her daughter.

"Well, hello there, my friend," she addresses Sadie warmly. "How have you been?"

"She's been well," Lauren answers, when Sadie fails to—and instantly regrets it. She wonders if the psychiatrist has pegged her as a pushy parent who won't let her child speak for herself.

Dr. Prentiss doesn't seem fazed, though, as she says, "Hello to you, too, Mom. Are you having a nice summer?"

Hardly. But Lauren nods.

"How about you, Sadie? Are you having a nice summer, too?"

Sadie looks down at her shoes.

"I'll tell you what—why don't you come in and have a nice chat about it?" Dr. Prentiss asks.

Still no reply from Sadie.

"Sadie?" Lauren nudges.

Her daughter looks questioningly at her.

"It's rude not to answer when someone asks you a question, sweetie. Dr. Prentiss wanted to know if—"

"It's all right, Mrs. Walsh. We'll do just fine. Why don't you wait here for a little while so that Sadie and I can get to know each other? I'll call you in shortly."

"Sure. That's fine."

But is it?

Lauren sits back down in the guest chair as Dr. Prentiss holds open the door to the office and motions for Sadie to go inside.

Just before the door closes after them, Sadie shoots a worried look over her shoulder at Lauren.

Lauren gives her a reassuring smile and picks up her magazine again. But she doesn't even bother turning the pages this time. And instead of allowing her thoughts to wind back to Nick, she finds herself straining to hear what's going on in the office. It's impossible, of course, with the white noise machine, but still . . .

She doesn't know anything about Dr. Prentiss, really, other than that she's filling in for Dr. Rogel.

Yet you just entrusted your little girl into her care, behind closed doors. What are you thinking?

Lauren shifts in her chair, staring at the closed door, and tells herself she's just paranoid. Because she thinks

something might have happened to Nick. Now she thinks
something might happen to Sadie . . . even here.

Bad things happen everywhere.

Lauren goes over to the other door, the one leading to
the corridor and stairwell. The second door to Dr. Rogel's
interior office—the one patients use to exit—is closed.
She sneaks toward it and stands there, listening.

From here, away from the canned ocean waves, she
can hear the murmur of voices. Dr. Prentiss is talking.

Then Lauren hears Sadie, too. Not just talking—
laughing.

She can't make out what they're talking about, but it
doesn't matter.

It's the first time she's heard Sadie laugh in ages.

See? she tells herself as she slips back into the waiting room. *There's nothing to worry about. Dr. Prentiss
is here to help.*

"Marin? What's going on?"

She opens her eyes to find Garvey standing over the
bed. He's wearing a suit, and the room is brighter than
it should be; sun shining in from the window facing the
western terrace.

"What time is it?" she asks.

"Almost four. I just got back from a meeting. What are
you doing in bed?"

"Taking a nap."

"Are you sick?"

"Maybe." Marin sits up, rubbing her eyes. "I had a
headache."

"Caroline told me. She said you promised to take
her shopping, but you cut it short to come home and lie
down."

"I *did* take her shopping, Garvey. All morning, and into the afternoon. I bought her everything she wanted."

"She said you wouldn't get her a coat."

Oh please. Daddy's girl strikes again.

"It's August," Marin points out. "I really think it could have waited another day."

"Caroline was worried it would be gone. They only had one in her size."

She sighs. "Look, I wasn't feeling well in that store. I had to get out of there. I told her we'll go back, and—"

"Shh, it's okay." He pats her shoulder, then steps away from the bed, loosening his tie. "No big deal. I told Caroline to call the store and arrange to have the coat sent over."

"Yeah? I bet I know who's going to bring it."

"What do you mean?"

"She has a crush on one of the guys who works there."

Garvey's eyes narrow. "She has a crush on a store clerk?"

"Turns out he's her friend's brother, but at first I thought . . ."

"What?" he prompts when she trails off.

"You *know* what I thought. I saw him, and he had dark hair and dark eyes and he was in his early twenties, and—"

"Stop." Garvey strides over to the bedroom door, closes it, and turns to face her. "Are you going to spend the rest of our lives doing this to yourself?"

Doing this to me, is what he should have said, because that's really what he's worried about. Garvey has always taken pride in his ability to compartmentalize his life.

"I can't help it," she tells him now. "I can't just pretend he never existed. How can you?"

"Keep your voice down, please." He casts a glance at the closed door. "Do you really think I'm that cold-hearted, Marin? Of course he existed. He still exists, somewhere."

"You don't know that. You couldn't find him fourteen years ago, when you tried."

"That doesn't mean he isn't out there. And wherever he is, I'm sure he's thankful to us."

"For abandoning him?"

"We did what we had to do—for his sake."

"No, Garvey. For our own sakes," she hisses, and turns away.

For your sake, really.

She would never have given up her child, if not for Garvey. He talked her into it in the first place—and he made her follow through in the end, when she wavered, holding the baby in her arms.

Garvey never did. Never even touched him.

Maybe that's why Marin's the one who can't forget.

And maybe that's why Garvey was able to put the whole trauma behind him years ago, as effectively as if he had packed their son into a trunk and buried him somewhere.

"Your daughter is very bright, Mrs. Walsh, and very imaginative. I'm sure you don't need me to tell you that."

"It's always nice to hear," Lauren tells Dr. Prentiss. She keeps her voice down, conscious of the open door to the waiting room, where Sadie's now settled in a chair with *Highlights* and a grape lollipop.

"Sadie is experiencing some anxiety, as you and Dr. Rogel have discussed." Dr. Prentiss indicates the manila file folder on the desk between them.

"Is it directly related to the divorce?"

"It's hard to say, but possibly. She seems reluctant to speak about her father at all."

Should she tell Dr. Prentiss about Nick?

What if Dr. Prentiss decides she, Lauren, is making mountains out of molehills—or worse? What if she blames Sadie's problems on her?

But wouldn't it be negligent for Lauren not to mention that Nick is—or at least *was*—more or less missing in action?

She forces herself to look up at the woman, who seems to be waiting for her to elaborate.

"My ex-husband hasn't been around much lately, and . . ." *Tread carefully, Lauren.* "Um, did Sadie mention what happened this past weekend?"

Dr. Prentiss skirts the question with one of her own. "Why don't you tell me?"

"Nick had been on vacation for a week and he was supposed to be back Sunday to have a visitation with the kids. He never showed up. We didn't hear from him until yesterday, and he wasn't very . . . apologetic, I guess, is the word. In fact, he didn't bother to call—and that's out of character, so . . . I mean, he just sent a text message."

Dr. Prentiss nods.

"So Sadie didn't say anything about that?" Lauren asks.

"Not specifically, no."

"What *did* she say, then?"

The doctor glances at her notes as though she doesn't remember, though she just saw Sadie a few minutes ago. "She's shown an excessive attachment to certain belongings."

"Right. Dr. Rogel said that's common in . . ." *Just go ahead and say it.* " . . . in children of divorce."

"Your daughter feels quite vulnerable and threatened at home."

"Threatened?"

"She's convinced that you or her sister are going to come into her room and take away her toys."

"What? I mean, we have been getting rid of old things—clutter—for a tag sale, but nothing of Sadie's. I wouldn't take away anything of hers. Especially lately, with the way she's been acting. I didn't even let the cleaning ladies go into her room today. Didn't she tell you that?" Aware that she sounds defensive, Lauren can't seem to help herself.

"Sadie told me that someone was there, though, while she was gone. You might want to talk to your cleaning ladies again," Dr. Prentiss suggests, "to make sure they understand how important it is not to violate your daughter's private space. A few dust bunnies won't kill her."

"I know that," Lauren murmurs, deciding she doesn't like Dr. Prentiss, who seems to have her pegged as one of those fussy women who need everything perfect—which couldn't be farther from the truth.

"Really," she says, "the cleaning ladies weren't in Sadie's room while we were gone today. Or if they were, Sadie would have no way of knowing about it. We haven't even been home since this morning."

"No, it happened yesterday. Not today."

"The cleaning ladies weren't there yesterday. They were there today. They come on Tuesdays."

"Someone was there yesterday, Mommy."

Lauren turns to see Sadie in the doorway.

"Oh, sweetie . . ." She gets up and hurries toward her daughter.

"Someone was there! In my room! I set a trap so I would know."

A trap. Lauren remembers how Sadie examined an invisible something—a trap?—in the doorway of her room before she was willing to leave this morning.

She has an active imagination, but still . . .

"Maybe it was your brother or sister or even me," she tells Sadie, her thoughts whirling. "I go into your room all the time, to put away your laundry and open your blinds and—"

"It wasn't you or Lucy or Ryan! It was when we were all out. I set the trap before we left, and I checked it when we got back. Someone was there."

What if she's right? What if someone really was there? *Come on . . . this is crazy. You're overreacting.*

"What kind of trap was it, Sadie?"

"It was an invisible piece of fishing wire. I taped it across the doorway. And when I looked, it was all unstuck. That means someone walked through the door."

Lauren and Dr. Prentiss exchange a glance.

She wants me to say something, Lauren realizes. But what am I supposed to say? That Sadie's on to something? That someone really might have been there?

Absolutely not, she decides, remembering Lucy's frightened reaction back at the pool, when Lauren admitted her own vulnerability.

"That's a really smart idea for a trap," Lauren says gently, "but I think maybe the tape fell off the door, because really, no one was in the house while we were gone yesterday."

Obviously, that was the wrong thing to say, because her daughter immediately opens her mouth—to protest, cry, scream.

Dr. Prentiss cuts her off. "How about if when you get home, you and your mom can check everything out and make sure it's all just the way you left it?"

It will be, Lauren tells herself. Of course it will.

But it's all so creepily coincidental. What if something strange is going on at home . . . all around them? Something to do with Nick?

"I have an idea, Sadie," Dr. Prentiss goes on. "Maybe you can get your crayons and color some signs to put on your door and Mom will help you hang them up."

"What kind of signs?"

"You know—'Sadie's Room. Keep Out.' "

"I don't know how to spell that."

"I bet your mom will help you, right, Mom?"

"Sure, Sadie." Lauren pushes stray strands of hair back from her daughter's worried face. "We'll go home and make some signs, okay?"

Sadie shrugs grudgingly. "You don't believe me."

Lauren glances at Dr. Prentiss, who nods slightly.

"I believe you, Sadie," Lauren tells her daughter.

"You do?"

She nods. *Who knows? Maybe I do.*

Elsa's cell phone rings just as she passes the Rhode Island border into Connecticut, creeping along at about ten miles an hour.

That's got to be Brett, looking for her. Thanks to rush hour traffic, the reverse trip is taking twice as long as this morning's drive to Boston.

She grabs the phone from the passenger's seat and glances at the caller ID window. Sure enough, her husband is at home. He's wondering why she's not.

Should she answer the call?

No. She'll be there soon enough. Let him worry for another fifteen minutes. That'll give her a chance to figure out what she's going to tell him.

It isn't as if she hasn't had a few hours to come up

with something. But she's spent the time going over every detail of the meeting with Mike, analyzing everything they said, trying to figure out whether . . .

It seems crazy, but . . .

Was he hiding something when he told her there's been nothing new?

It doesn't make sense that he'd lie, yet something didn't ring true.

Maybe it wasn't about Jeremy—not directly, anyway. What if he has, as Elsa requested, broken past the barrier of sealed records? What if he's picked up the trail of the shadowy woman who wanted to put the past behind her?

By the time she reaches her driveway, Elsa is no closer to knowing what to tell Brett. She takes her time getting out of the car, and pauses in front of the flowerbeds to check on the impatiens. Today, the plants are standing straight and tall, with bright red blossoms.

Again, Elsa wonders if that's a sign.

But how many times over the past fourteen years has she looked for signs—and found them?

A cardinal sitting in a branch outside the window for days on end, a phone ringing with no one on the other end of the line, a chance meeting with someone also named Jeremy . . .

With fleeting hope, she's interpreted all those incidents, and countless others, to mean her son is still alive.

This is no different, she tells herself. As she told Mike, she needs closure. And that's all she can expect.

Reluctantly, Elsa goes inside to face her husband.

"Lauren! Long time no see!"

She turns to see Janet Wasserman pushing a grocery cart around the aisle, and her heart sinks.

"Hi, Janet." She should have known better than to shop at the A & P, convenient or not. But after what happened in the doctor's office, she was in no hurry to go back to the empty—hopefully empty, anyway—house, and deal, too, with Nick's disappearance. She just needed to prolong it all a little longer. To lose herself in something mundane.

"And Sadie, Sadie, little lady . . . look at what a big girl you've turned into!" Janet leans over to give her a hug.

Sadie stiffens and takes a step closer to Lauren.

"She's shy," Lauren feels obligated to explain. Shy, and still a little traumatized from her appointment with Dr. Prentiss.

"Well, I don't blame her. It's been ages since she's seen me. She probably doesn't even know who I am. I'm Ian's mommy, sweetheart. He's your brother Ryan's friend."

No response from Sadie.

"Oh, thanks for having Ryan stay for dinner the other night," Lauren tells Janet.

"Anytime—he's never any trouble, and he was so appreciative. You should have seen him gobble down the steak and shrimp."

"I can just imagine," Lauren murmurs.

"We enjoy having him around. You know how much I love to cook, and I'm always glad to help out."

Maybe it's just me, Lauren thinks. But something about Janet's tone—and her words—is rubbing Lauren the wrong way.

It's as if she assumes she's providing Ryan with something his own mother can't give him: an expensive, home-cooked, sit-down family dinner.

I can do that for him, too, Lauren wants to tell her.

But the truth is, she can't. She just checked out the prices on steaks and seafood, and wound up throwing chicken into the cart instead. Which she'll be lucky to get onto the grill before it goes bad since she, unlike Janet Wasserman, doesn't particularly love to cook. And there's no getting around the fact that there's an empty chair at family dinners in the Walsh home these days.

So . . . you win, Janet.

"I hear you dropped off a carload for the tag sale yesterday."

"Oh—Ryan told you?"

"No, Alana Fleming did. I'm on the committee."

Of course you are.

"Well . . ." Lauren checks her watch. "I've got to get moving. I need to pick up Ryan and Lucy at the pool before it rains and get home to make dinner."

"Why don't you all come over to our house for dinner? We can catch up . . . would you like that, Sadie? We have our very own swimming pool. Wouldn't that be fun?"

Sadie shakes her head no.

"That's really nice of you, Janet," Lauren says quickly, "but not tonight. It's supposed to rain, and it's been a long day so . . . maybe some other time."

"Definitely. I'll give you a call. And again, if there's anything I can do to help out with Ryan—or the other children—you know I'm always here for you."

"Thank you. I appreciate it. And you know I'm always here for you, too," Lauren can't resist adding.

"Er—of course."

Mercifully, Janet makes small talk for only another minute or two, then pushes her cart on past.

As much as she'd suddenly love to get out of here, Lauren lingers on the aisle, not wanting to catch up to her again.

"You know what, Sadie? I think you're a big enough girl to try some new foods, don't you?"

"I don't like them."

"What don't you like?"

"New foods."

Lauren sighs inwardly. She can't help but remember the time she and Nick had discovered a stash of rancid meat and spoiled dairy in the hidden compartment in Sadie's closet. She should probably check it again, just to make sure.

"You know, Ryan and Lucy like to try new foods. Don't you want to be a big girl like they are?"

"Ryan isn't a big girl."

Despite everything, Lauren can't help but laugh. And it feels good. So good—so normal—that she wonders, for a moment, if everything is okay after all.

"Oooh, SpongeBob!" Sadie picks up a box of fruit snacks and points to the cartoon character. "Can we get them?"

"No"—Lauren takes them out of her hands and puts them back on the shelf—"but we can get these." She picks up the store brand.

"I don't want those."

"They have seven fruit juices," Lauren informs her—wondering if that's even true.

Once he got on his health kick, Nick wasn't a big fan of these gummy fruity treats, telling Lauren they're probably full of chemicals.

"Or," she tells Sadie, "how about if we get some watermelon and peaches on the produce aisle instead?"

"I want SpongeBob."

About to remind her daughter that it's silly to pay a dollar extra for a cartoon image—which is what she said in the previous aisle, where Sadie begged for Shrek toothpaste—Lauren thinks better of it. Whose fault is it that Sadie's watched too much television this summer?

Poor kid—she has enough problems. Why not indulge her in SpongeBob, just this once?

Too bad you already said no.

Changing a no to a yes is something that Lauren and Nick vowed never to do as parents.

Then again, Nick's not even here. And why is he the only one who gets to break vows?

Everything must be okay, Lauren tells herself, *because I'm back to feeling annoyed with Nick, instead of worried about him.*

Somehow, that thought seems rational enough to hold on to for the time being.

"Okay," she decides, "we'll get SpongeBob."

"Thank you, Mommy!" Sadie rushes back to grab the box.

"You're quite the pushover, aren't you, Mommy?"

Hearing the male voice behind her, Lauren turns to see Sam Henning.

"Oh . . . hi!" She wants to ask him what he's doing there, but that's a silly question, considering that he's holding a plastic shopping basket.

"How are you?" she asks instead—which also sounds like a silly question, considering she just saw him at the pool.

"I'm great. How are you?" Somehow, the question is less silly coming from him.

"I'm . . . you know. Wondering why I ended up with a cartful of groceries when I just came in to get a couple of things."

"And I'm wondering," he says in return, "what it means that we keep running into each other."

"It means there's only one supermarket and one public pool in town. Unless you're following me around?"

Oh Lord, why did I have to say such a stupid thing?

Does he know I was just kidding? Please let him know I was just kidding.

Lauren is relieved when he grins.

"Who knows? Maybe I am following you around. I can think of worse ways to spend a summer day."

"Mommy, can I get these, too?" Sadie pops up again, carrying a bag of Chips Ahoy! "They're irresistibly delicious."

"You have quite the vocabulary there, Miss Sadie," Sam comments.

"I'm pretty sure she's quoting the commercial," Lauren tells him. "Not that she isn't brilliant, of course."

"Of course. My son is also brilliant, mind you. Although he's not quoting commercials yet. But he did find his feet."

"Ah, the first sign of extraordinary intelligence."

"So they say. Oops, there's my cell." Sam pulls his vibrating phone from his pocket and looks at it. "Excuse me for a second."

"Sure." Lauren fights the urge to smooth her hair as he steps away. Chlorine-stiff and air-dried after her swim, it hasn't seen a brush in a few hours. She wishes she was wearing something other than a pair of shorts and T-shirt that have seen better days.

"Mommy, can we go?" Sadie asks impatiently.

"In a minute."

Lauren sneaks a peek at Sam's basket. It holds a loaf of white bread, a six-pack of beer, a box of Entenmann's donuts. Bachelor food.

She hears him say, "I'm in a store, can I call you back? . . . Yeah, give me two minutes."

He hangs up and covers the short distance back to her. "Sorry—that was work."

"What do you do?"

"I'm a consultant. I'll tell you more next time I see you. Gotta take off now."

"Sure. Take care."

"You too. Hey, why don't you give me your number so I can call you sometime?"

"Sure." Her stomach flutters. "Um, do you have something to write with?"

"No. Do you?"

She searches through her bag, conscious that her hands are shaking. She can't help it. It's been years since a man asked her for her phone number.

That Sam Henning even requested it is an unexpected pleasure. That she finds herself wanting him to have it—and use it—is shocking.

"Sorry—I don't have a pen," she tells him.

"No worries. Just call me."

"I . . . I don't have your number."

He grins. "No, I mean my cell. Right now. I'll tell you the number and you dial it, and then you'll have it in your phone and I'll have yours in mine."

"Mommy, can we buy these?" Sadie again, with a box of Cheez-Its.

"Hang on a second, sweetie. Okay, what's the number?"

Lauren dials it in as Sam tells her, then hits send. His phone rings promptly.

He answers it—standing two feet away from her and smiling into her eyes. "Hello?"

"Hi, is Sam there, please?"

"Speaking."

"Sam, it's Lauren Walsh."

"Lauren! It's good to hear from you. I've been wondering how you are."

"Pretty good, Sam, pretty good. And you?"

"Mommy! He's right there!"

Lauren looks down at Sadie, sees the exasperated expression on her daughter's face. Clearly, she's not thrilled by the flirtation.

The spell is broken.

"Bye, Sam," Lauren says abruptly into the phone.

"Bye, Lauren."

They hang up.

"Mommy, can I have these?"

"Hmm?" Lauren gives a little wave at Sam. He waves back and walks away.

"Mommy!"

Lauren turns to Sadie and the box of crackers, but out of the corner of her eye, she watches Sam until he disappears around the end of the aisle.

"Elsa! There you are." Brett puts aside his newspaper and rises from his leather recliner. He's changed out of his suit into a pink polo shirt, madras shorts, and loafers. A martini glass sits on the table beside him.

Ordinarily, Elsa mixes his drink for him, and pours a glass of wine for herself—an evening tradition begun long before Jeremy came along.

For a few years after their son went missing, Elsa didn't drink at all—and Brett drank too much. At some point, though, they settled back into the civilized nightly routine.

"I tried to call you," Brett tells her, crossing the room to place a perfunctory kiss on her cheek.

"I'm sorry . . . I heard it ring but I couldn't get to it in time." And so the lies begin.

Hadn't she just been thinking of telling him the truth?

But it's so much harder, now that they're face-to-face.

Brett Cavalon is an imposing man—tall, handsome, distinguished, accomplished, brilliant. At twenty-one, she met him in New York and fell in love with him at first sight. Miraculously, he was equally smitten, and Elsa began to fantasize about something she'd never imagined for herself: marriage and children in a world far from the glamorous runways, showrooms, and avenues of Manhattan's fashion industry.

She'd never dreamed about a domestic happily-ever-after because she'd never seen it, thus never believed in it. Raised by a single mother who'd been an industry icon in her own right, Elsa had inherited her mother's incredible beauty—and, until she met Brett, her single-minded ambition.

"It'll never last," her mother warned her when she got engaged.

"How can you say that?"

"Because nothing worthwhile ever does."

At the time, Elsa hated her mother for that, certain she was wrong.

She hates her still—because she might have been right.

"Where were you? Shopping?" Settling back into his chair, Brett inadvertently provides Elsa with a viable alibi, and she's fully prepared to take it.

But then she hears herself say, "No. Not shopping."

"No? Where were you, then?"

Should she or shouldn't she?

She probably shouldn't, but she does.

"I went to Boston."

About to sip his drink, he looks up sharply.

"I saw Mike Fantoni."

Brett hesitates a moment longer, then raises the glass to his lips. Elsa perches on the edge of the sofa, waiting.

"Why?" he asks at last, setting down the martini, now half empty.

Or half full, as the cliché goes, depending on one's philosophy.

Before Jeremy, Elsa was a glass-full kind of woman. And now . . .

"I want closure, Brett, if nothing else. Don't you?"

He's silent for a minute.

Then he asks, "Why now?"

"It's not just now. I've always wanted—"

"No, I know, but why all of a sudden are you getting in touch with Mike Fantoni again, going to see him? What's changed?"

"Being back here, in New England—it's brought back so many memories. It's like we've come full circle, but we're no closer to knowing what happened to him than we were when we left."

"Chances are we're never going to know. Why can't you accept that, Elsa?"

"Why can you?" she returns. "I feel like you've given up. I feel like you gave up years ago."

"You know that's not true. You know I've done everything in my power to get him back, from day one."

Yes, Brett was just as involved, initially. But somewhere along the line, he drifted back to the real world, the world without Jeremy, leaving Elsa behind.

Or was it the other way around? Was it Elsa who drifted away, Elsa who left Brett behind?

"What did Mike say?" Brett asks, after a long moment of silence.

"He said he's still looking."

"He should be. We're still paying him. We've been paying him for years."

"We can afford it."

Brett shrugs. "That's not the point."

"What is the point?"

"Never mind."

She wants to tell him the private investigator's fee is a hell of a lot cheaper than fourteen years' worth of food and clothing and baseball equipment and college tuition and all the things they'd expected to provide for Jeremy.

But he knows all that. She's said it before—and so has he. Just . . . not in a long time. Years.

"Why didn't you tell me you were going, Elsa?"

"Because I knew you wouldn't approve."

"You just don't get it, do you? It's not that I don't approve. It's that I'm trying to protect you. Going down this road again . . ." He shakes his head, drinks from his martini. "I don't want to lose you, too."

"You won't. You won't lose me, Brett, if you let me do what I have to do."

He looks at her. Shrugs. "The same is true for me."

For a long time, they just look at each other.

Then Brett sets down the glass, leans toward her, and holds out his hand.

She hesitates only for a moment. Then she takes it.

At last alone behind the closed door of the bedroom she shared with Nick, the kids safely tucked in down the hall, Lauren clutches the phone in one hand, a piece of paper containing a scribbled phone number in the other.

She can't put it off any longer.

She dials.

The phone rings. Rings. Rings.

"Hi, it's Beth, I'm out, leave a message."

Beep.

"Beth, hi, it's Lauren Walsh. The kids have been

trying to get in touch with Nick, and I'm wondering if you can have him call them back. Thanks."

After uttering the speech she memorized word for word over the course of the last few hours, she hangs up, feeling shaken.

There.

Done.

She exhales through puffed cheeks and goes over to the open window, where a cool breeze stirs the curtains.

What if Beth calls her back?

She might, now that Lauren has made an overture. Never mind that she only did it because she's been backed into a corner. Beth might decide the two of them should talk.

But that's not what I want. Not in a million years.

All I want is to know where Nick is, and that he's okay. For the kids' sake.

Hearing a telltale rustling in the boughs beyond the screen, she wonders if the rain that's been threatening all evening is about to roll in at last.

Flipping off the lamp, she peers outside. Most of the neighboring houses have darkened windows. In a bucolic town like Glenhaven Park, no one bothers to leave lights on timers when they go on vacation.

Elm Street is deserted in the glow of the streetlamps. No strange shadows or Peeping Toms tonight.

Lauren tries not to think about what happened to her in the kitchen, when she thought she saw someone out there in the yard. No reason to get spooked by that now. It was her imagination, right?

Right.

And it was Sadie's imagination that someone was prowling around her room, too, she tells herself firmly.

But if it wasn't . . .

A chill slithers down Lauren's back.

She's done her best to make as light of Sadie's suspicion as she has of her own. Lauren helped her make several "Keep Out" signs before bed and taped them up outside her room. That seems to have helped, because Sadie has actually stayed in her own room so far tonight. She's probably worn out from all that swimming—not to mention all the worry, and the visit to the psychiatrist.

Thunder rumbles in the distance.

Nick always loved to fall asleep listening to the rain, Lauren finds herself remembering—and then wondering, like a teenage girl with a crush, about Sam Henning.

Does he like the rain?

She wonders what he's doing now, just a block away over on Castle Lane. If she were Lucy's age, she might find an excuse to call him, or even walk by his house. But he lives on a dead end street, and she's not Lucy's age; she's a grown woman with more baggage than a 747, and there is no way she's going to get into another relationship—even if someone was interested in her.

Which Sam seems to be, though God only knows why.

Pushing Sam—and, for that matter, Nick and Beth—from her mind, she turns away from the window and flips the light on again.

There. That's better. She climbs into bed with the new issue of *People* magazine she'd thrown into her cart at the checkout line earlier. She figured some fluffy reading might help to take her mind off her problems, but now she finds herself absently flipping pages, listening to the rain and thinking about Sam Henning.

When she hears her cell phone buzz with an incoming text, the first thought that pops into her head is, *It's him! Sam!*

Who else would it be? Not Beth. She wouldn't text . . .

would she? No, and besides, she wouldn't have Lauren's
cell number . . . would she?

No. No way.

God, I hope not.

Lucy and Ryan occasionally text her, but they're both
home tonight.

Lauren leans over the bedside table, where the phone
is plugged into the charger.

We need to talk. Meet me at my place tomorrow at noon.

Whoa! Talk about forward. Does Sam Henning actually think she—

Oh.

It's not from Sam at all.

It's from Nick.

"This is absolutely insane," Garvey hisses into the phone,
having snatched it up on the first ring. "Where the hell
have you been?"

"What do you mean where have I been? In Glenhaven
Park, looking for the file."

"And the reason I haven't heard from you in two days
is because you haven't found it yet."

"Right."

He slams his elbow down onto his desk and plunks his
forehead into his hand, kneading his temples. It's late,
and he's exhausted. Coming home from a charity benefit
a half hour ago, he'd been tempted to go down the hall to
his bedroom and climb into bed beside Marin.

Instead, he forced himself to settle into his home
office to go over some paperwork—and it's a good
thing. This is one phone call he needs to be wide-awake
to handle.

"I thought you said you knew where it was," he says succinctly into the phone.

"I thought I did. I mean, I think I do. I just need a little more time to pinpoint it. You'd be proud of me, Garvey. I've managed to work myself right in like a chameleon. They have no idea that I don't belong there. Sooner or later, I'm going to get close enough to—"

"Sooner or later?" Garvey cuts in. "There *is* no later—there's only too late. And *sooner* can't come soon enough. Stop playing charades, do you hear me? I need that file and I need it now."

"Now? But—"

"You have until tomorrow. That's it. Twenty-four hours, and then . . ."

There's a long moment of silence on the other end of the line.

Then Garvey hears a heavy sigh, followed by a re-signed "Okay."

With a crisp nod to himself, he hangs up.

"Damn, damn, damn," he whispers, pounding his hand softly on the polished mahogany desktop with each utterance.

He should have known better.

He *did* know better.

The only way to get something done right is to do it yourself. Don't you ever forget that, Garvey.

Why, *why* hadn't he listened to his grandmother? To his own conscience?

Because you were afraid. Admit it. You were afraid that if you got involved directly, you'd get caught. You thought it was much safer to keep your distance, to rely on someone else to do the dirty work . . . just like before. With Jeremy.

That turned out fine.

This will, too.

It *has* to.

Sitting on her bed, Lauren holds the cell phone with Nick's text message in one hand and the cordless phone to her ear with her other.

On the other end of the line, her sister says, "I think he's up to something, texting you out of the blue after pulling a disappearing act like that—and right after you leave a message for his girlfriend."

"What could he possibly be up to?"

"He obviously has something big to tell you. Something so serious that he blew off work—not to mention the kids—just to do some soul-searching about it."

"Right. Something that warrants a face-to-face meeting—at his place, no less."

"So are you going?"

"No way."

"I think that's a mistake, Laur."

"Why? He's probably going to tell me he's getting married again. I don't need to hear that in person. He can send me a lovely announcement in the mail. Who knows, maybe I'll even be invited to the wedding." She tries to come off as glib, but she's feeling far from it.

"I doubt it's going to be that," Alyssa tells her. "Maybe it's something serious about his job or his health or something."

"Well, unless they fired him for not showing up on Monday, his job is fine. You're not thinking he's dying of cancer or something, are you?"

"His father did."

"I know." Lauren exhales through puffed cheeks. The thought of her children losing their father is sobering. Then again, they already did their share of mourning when he moved out. Nothing is the same. And for as much as they've seen him lately, their day-to-day lives wouldn't be drastically different if something were to happen to Nick.

Still . . .

"I honestly hope he's not sick," she tells Alyssa.

"I really doubt it. I bet I know what it is."

"What?"

"Bet you anything he wants to come home again."

Lauren is silent for a minute. Then she forces a laugh. "That's about as appealing as cancer."

"Seriously?"

"I don't want him back, Alyssa. And I doubt he wants me back, so . . ."

"I think you're wrong."

"Really?"

"He wants you back, Lauren. Trust me."

It figures.

Just when she's gotten used to being on her own . . .

Just when she's met someone she might actually want to date . . .

Nick barges back into her life, demanding her attention.

"What if he tells her he made a mistake when he left?" Alyssa asks.

"He won't. Are you kidding?"

"So what are you going to do?"

"Ignore him," Lauren informs her sister.

They chat for a few more minutes. Then Alyssa tells her, "I've got to get going. Ben just got out of the shower and we were going to watch *CSI.*"

"That's on?"

"DVD. I got him a box set for our anniversary. We've been working our way through it all summer. I'll call you tomorrow."

"Okay. 'Night, Alyssa."

Lauren hangs up, envying her sister a cozy evening at home with her husband. It's been so long since she and Nick were that happy that she can't even remember what it was like.

And I don't want to. What's the use now?

Picking up her magazine again, she turns a couple of pages, still unable to focus. This time, it's not because she's daydreaming about Sam.

Nick probably wants to tell her that he's marrying Beth.

But if not . . .

After all he's put us through—the kids and me—he's out of his mind if he thinks he's going to walk back in here and pick up where we left off.

If that's what he wants, she'll say no. She's ready to move on. He should know that. She should tell him. In person.

She snatches up the phone and thumb-types a return message.

I'll be there.

She hesitates, looking at it. What if she's not strong enough to tell him he can't come home? What if she says yes when she means no?

It wouldn't be the first time.

But she's different now. Stronger.

Why? Because some good-looking guy paid attention to you?

Sam did ask for her phone number.

Yeah—so what? He's a flirt. You don't know anything about him. You don't know if you're ready to go out on a date. You don't know if he'll actually even call. Look at the way you got your hopes up just now, thinking it was him.

This is crazy.

Lauren might not know what she wants, exactly, but she knows what she *doesn't* want. A cheating ex-husband tops the list.

If Nick tells me he wants to come home, I'll say no. Gladly.

Jaw set, she hits send.

Lying wide-awake in her bed, listening to thunder, Sadie thinks back over the day. Mostly, she thinks about one thing that happened. It's been bothering her, and she's not sure why.

Well, maybe she is.

Mommy has always told her not to talk to strangers. Once, she even read Sadie a library book about that very thing. About how strangers don't always look like bad guys—they could be disguised as nice guys, or even nice women. Sometimes, they try to make friends with children by giving them candy or asking for directions or saying that Mommy said to get a ride home with them.

But what if the person doesn't do any of those things?

What if the person is someone Mommy herself has talked to?

What if the person even knows Sadie's name?

Does the person still count as a stranger then?

Sadie didn't think so at the time.

It was broad daylight, and her mother was nearby, so there was no need to worry.

So when asked, "It's a beautiful day today, isn't it?"

Sadie agreed that it was. Like Mommy said, it was rude to ignore someone's question.

"What's your favorite thing to do on a beautiful day, Sadie?"

"Swim in the pool," she answered, "or swing on the swings."

"How about on a rainy day?"

She shrugged.

"I like to read books on rainy days. How about you, Sadie?"

"I can't really read yet."

"Well, I bet you like to color in your coloring books, right?"

"Yes."

"And play with your toys? What toys do you like to play with?"

"My Little Pony. And puzzles. And . . . lots of stuff."

"Stuffed animals?"

"No, I said lots of *stuff*," Sadie repeated.

"*Stuff* like *stuffed* animals?"

Sadie couldn't help but grin. "Sometimes."

She was enjoying the conversation.

Adults usually don't really bother to talk to kids, and when they do, they seem like they're only pretending to be interested.

This was different.

For a change, someone was interested.

She talked about her favorite stuffed animals. She talked about Fred. She told how Daddy promised to get him back from the lost and found, but didn't. She even mentioned the stupid pink dog.

"And where is the pink dog now?"

For the first time since the conversation started, Sadie

hesitated. Should she tell? Even Mommy doesn't know the truth.

If she didn't tell Mommy, she probably shouldn't tell someone else, she decided.

No matter how nice the person is.

"Sadie? Where's the pink dog?"

"I don't know," Sadie lied.

That's something she hardly ever does. Whenever she lies to Mommy, Mommy seems to know.

Mommy isn't the only one.

She could tell the stranger—and it really was a stranger, she decides now, no matter what she thought at first—didn't believe her about the dog.

"Sure you do, Sadie. You know. Come on. Think about it. You'll remember."

"I didn't forget. I just don't know."

"I'll bet you do." There wasn't any anger, or anything like that.

Yet now, thinking back on the conversation, Sadie feels scared. She doesn't know why.

Maybe she should tell Mommy about it.

But then she might get into trouble.

I won't tell, Sadie decides. *I'll just make sure I never, ever,* ever *talk to strangers again.*

It's when kids get involved—that's when it's hard.

It was true fourteen years ago, and it's true now.

Hard, but not impossible. There's no question that the little girl knows what happened to that pink stuffed dog. The lie was blatant in those big green eyes of hers. But for whatever reason, she's not talking.

Not to me, anyway.

Not yet.

Could it be that Sadie Walsh found the memory stick

hidden inside the toy? If she did, it's only a matter of time before she turns it over to her mother. Maybe she already has.

If that's the case, then Garvey's a sitting duck. And he's not the only one.

There was a time when self-sacrifice would have been an automatic, even willing, move to make.

But Garvey was a different man back then. A man worth dying for.

Or was he?

Is anyone?

What makes one human life more valuable than another?

Mine . . . Caroline's . . . Jeremy's . . .

Garvey's . . .

Maybe I was such an idealist that I didn't want to see him for who—for what—*he really was all along . . .*

A cold-blooded murderer.

And now . . . he's not the only one with blood on his hands.

You do what has to be done, and then you wash your hands and you move on.

Or so Garvey likes to say.

But there is no moving on just yet. The worst is yet to come. The plan is in motion. By this time tomorrow, it will be over, one way or another.

You don't even have kids, Garvey said—as though it's any easier for a childless person to obliterate the life of a child.

Or children.

A mother, for that matter, or a father.

All for the sake of . . . what? Ambition? Justice?

Garvey Quinn was wronged—no doubt about that. Byron Gregson got what he had coming.

This is different.

The Walsh family didn't blackmail Garvey. Do they really deserve to die?

Did Jeremy Cavalon?

To Garvey, they're all disposable players in a game he's been waiting all his life to win.

What makes you think you'll be spared if he ever finds out you defied his orders to do whatever has to be done?

Only a fool with a death wish would take that risk.

It'll all be worth it when this is over and Garvey is sitting in the governor's mansion.

When that day comes, I'll put all of this behind me; make a fresh start somewhere . . .

If I survive.

CHAPTER FIFTEEN

Ryan opens his eyes to a dreary morning, rain pattering on the gabled roof above his bed.

The clock on his nightstand tells him it's past ten, but he might as well roll over and go back to sleep.

No pool today. Nothing else to do. Most of his friends are busy, other than Ian, who texted last night and invited Ryan to come over and play a new Xbox game. Ryan lied that he had other plans.

Maybe he shouldn't have. Maybe he should go after all.

But then he'll have to deal with nosy Mrs. Wasserman again, and he's afraid he might snap and tell her to mind her own business. She probably deserves it, but he has a feeling Mom won't see it that way. She told Ryan he has to be polite, no matter what.

He stares at the sloping ceiling, lined with taped-up magazine posters of his favorite baseball players. He hasn't even been to a game at Yankee Stadium this season. Dad takes him every year; he gets great box seats from someone at work. Ryan asked him about it a few months ago, and he said he'd look into it.

Now the summer's almost over.

Actually, Ryan's kind of glad about that.

Other years, he couldn't get enough of summer, on nice days and rainy ones, too—the weather didn't matter. There always seemed to be something to do. Even lying around with nothing to do held a certain appeal.

Back then, he never worried that too much thinking might make him feel depressed. Not like now.

Ryan rolls over and punches his pillow beneath his cheek.

It's not just the Yankee game. He really thought his father was going to be able to squeeze in their annual fishing trip. That was the one thing Ryan was worried about missing when his parents told him he was going to sleepaway camp.

"Don't worry, Ry," Dad told him. "There will be plenty of fishing up at camp."

"But I like to go with you."

"We will, when you get back in August. That's when the fish do all their biting."

Yeah, right.

Whatever.

He'll be glad to get back to school, and sports, and having something to do every second so that he doesn't have to dwell on how his great old life somehow turned into this totally miserable new one.

Ryan rolls over again, trying to get comfortable. It isn't working.

Might as well get up.

He slips out of bed and heads out into the hall. Lucy's door is closed. Mom's is open, bed made, shades up. Sadie's door is also open, but surrounded by the "Keep Out" signs she and Mom made last night.

Seeing them, Ryan shakes his head. His little sister is acting pretty kooky lately. Mom told him and Lucy just to go along with Sadie's crazy story about someone prowling around her room. As if anyone would actually be interested in stealing a four-year-old's stuff.

Downstairs, Ryan finds Chauncey perched expectantly beside the front door.

"What's the matter, boy, you need to be walked?" Ryan pats the dog's head and is rewarded with a wagging tail.

Mom sticks her head in from the kitchen. She's wearing makeup and earrings, and her hair is pulled back in a barrette. She looks pretty. Much too nice for this time of day.

"Morning, Ry. John took Chauncey out earlier, but if you want to take him out to play for a while . . ."

"No, thanks."

His mother looks disappointed. "You always loved to romp around with Chauncey. Are you too old for that now?"

"Nah, I've just got some other stuff to do."

"What kind of stuff?"

He shrugs.

"Well, I need you to stay here with Sadie today while I go out and take care of some things."

"What things?"

"You know . . . errands." Mom bends over to finger-comb the fringe on the edge of the rug. Ryan is surprised to see that she's wearing a skirt and blouse, and sandals with heels.

"Geez, Mom, why didn't you tell me yesterday that you needed me to babysit?"

"Because I didn't know I had to go someplace until late last night."

"Well, where do you have to go?"

"Does it matter?"

Seeing the dangerous gleam in her eye, Ryan wonders what's going on. He nibbles a hangnail from his thumb.

Maybe Mom's going on a date with that guy she was talking to at the pool yesterday.

He considers asking her about it. Then he decides he'd rather not know.

"What do I get?" he asks instead.

"What do you mean?"

"For watching Sadie. If I do it, will I get paid?"

"Yes. Fine. You'll get paid."

"How long will you be gone?"

"I have no idea."

"So you're going somewhere, but you won't tell me where, and you don't know when you'll be back? You would never let me get away with that."

"That's because you're the kid. I'm the mother."

Yeah, Ryan decides, she's up to something for sure. And if it has to do with some guy, he really, really doesn't want to know. He scowls.

Mom gives him a sharp look. "What's the problem, Ryan?"

"There's no problem."

"Are you sure? Because Sadie has been having a hard time lately, and she could use some support. It won't kill you to entertain her while I go out."

"Entertain her? Like what, do a tap dance for her?"

Mom cracks a smile.

Ryan, in the mood to be difficult, does not. "Why can't Lucy watch her? Why do I have to do it?"

"You both have to watch her." Mom is no longer smiling. "And I don't want to hear another word about it. Got it?"

Ryan rolls his eyes.

"*Got it?*" Mom repeats.

"Got it," Ryan grumbles, hating her—and hating himself even more.

From the shelter of a vine-covered trellis in a neighboring yard, the Walsh home is in full view. Under surveillance since sunup, the Victorian appears as deserted as the conveniently vacated house beside the trellis, but it isn't. They're in there—all four of them. Lauren, Lucy, Ryan, and Sadie.

Only Chauncey left the house this morning, on his daily outing. He pranced along jauntily on his leash—no visible sign of any lingering effects from Monday's sedative.

The rest of the family has remained at home, going about their morning business—or perhaps still asleep, as the drawn shades on the girls' bedrooms would seem to indicate.

Sometime in the next fifteen minutes or so, Lauren Walsh is going to get into her car and drive away, and then . . .

Such a shame.

But Garvey is out of patience. It's time to make a move. Today.

Enjoy those sweet dreams, Lucy and Sadie.

They might be your last.

Marin moodily dumps the remains of her morning coffee into the sink, wishing she had time to drink it.

"Look on the bright side," Caroline tells her, perched at the breakfast bar eating mango and papaya from a gourmet deli container. "At least it's raining."

"That's the bright side?"

"You wouldn't want to go to some stupid campaign thing on a gorgeous day, would you?"

Marin offers her a tight smile, rinses her mug, and puts it into the dishwasher.

The truth is, she wouldn't mind never having to go to another stupid campaign thing again.

But that's not going to happen. The next best thing would be skipping today's required appearance with Garvey at a particularly troubling event.

Marin rubs her temples.

"Another headache?" her daughter asks.

"Yes."

"Are you sick, do you think?"

"No, it's just stress. Why?"

Caroline shrugs.

"What's up, Car?"

"Nothing."

"Something."

Caroline looks at her for a long moment, as if weighing something. Then she shrugs. "Okay. Whatever. I just—I saw those forms you filled out for me to give to the school nurse next week."

"The forms I put into your backpack?"

"Why didn't you want me to look at them?"

"I never said that."

"You sealed them in an envelope."

"I just didn't want you to lose them, and anyway . . . you opened a sealed envelope?"

"I thought it was something else."

"No, you didn't. The school nurse's name was on the envelope."

"Okay. Whatever. I was curious."

"About . . . ?"

"You said I had to have an operation when I was little. I was just wondering what was wrong with me."

"I told you—you were very sick."

"You never told me I had some rare genetic disease and I almost died."

"I never told that to the school nurse on those medical forms, either, Caroline." Marin levels a look at her.

Caroline returns the gaze, her chin held stubbornly high. "I must have seen it somewhere else."

She's been snooping, Marin realizes. Does she know about Annie, then?

Driving down 684 toward White Plains, the wipers beating a soggy staccato against the windshield, Lauren wonders what her ex-husband is about to tell her, trying to prepare herself . . .

For what?

For Nick marrying Beth.

For Nick wanting to come home.

For Nick telling her he's suing for full custody of the kids, or that he's moving across the country, or . . .

God only knows what's coming.

But whatever it is, she can handle it.

If you're so sure of that, then why didn't you tell the kids you were on your way to see him?

Well, the girls didn't exactly ask. Lucy was barely awake by the time Lauren left, and Sadie was busy picking out board games for her siblings to play with her.

Only Ryan wanted to know where Lauren was going. She probably could have told him the truth, or at least have been more sensitive, but his attitude got to her.

Maybe he suspects that Lauren's outing today has to do with Nick.

A boy needs his father. All three kids do, but especially Ryan. Especially at his age.

If Nick really does ask her to take him back . . .

He won't. There's no way.

But if he does . . .

"Arriving . . . at . . . destination . . . on . . . left," the robotic voice of the GPS announces, and Lauren spots a tall apartment building just ahead.

This is it.

Can she really tell him no if he wants a second chance? Is that the right thing to do?

The right thing, she reminds herself, is to put her children's needs before her own. She just has to decide whether they're better off with him, or without him.

That's *if* he called her here to ask for a second chance.

As she pulls into the covered parking garage, she tells herself she's ready for absolutely anything that can possibly happen.

A scant five minutes later, she finds out that she's wrong.

Dead wrong.

Before Mommy left, she promised Sadie that Ryan and Lucy would play a game with her.

"Right, guys?" Mommy asked them pointedly from the bottom of the stairs, just before she walked out the door.

"Right," they said together.

Then Mommy drove away, and Lucy got on the phone with someone, and Ryan went into his room and shut the door.

That was a while ago. When Sadie knocked, her brother told her he was busy and to come back later.

Having decided this is later enough, she knocks again.

"Now what?" Ryan calls through the door.

"You're supposed to play with me."

"Geez, Sades, I *said* I will. But in a little bit, okay? I'm in the middle of something."

"What?"

"Cleaning my room."

Sadie turns away quickly, wondering if he's finding stuff to give away for the tag sale. Nobody's mentioned that today, and the fishing line has been strung across her doorway without any problems now, but Sadie's still worried.

She goes down the hall to Lucy's room. She can hear her sister in there on the phone, giggling and talking in a low voice.

Sadie knocks.

"Oh God, hang on a minute," she hears Lucy say. Then she calls, "What's up, Sadie?"

"How did you know it's me?"

"Because it's been you the last three times. What do you want?"

"You have to play Chutes and Ladders with me. Mommy said."

"Yeah, I know. As soon as I get off the phone."

"When?"

"When I'm done talking, okay?" Lucy lowers her voice and Sadie hears her say, "God, she's such a pain."

Feeling like she's going to cry, Sadie walks down the hall toward her room. Lucy and Ryan don't even care about her. And Mommy had to go somewhere, and Daddy . . . Daddy's been gone for so long Sadie sometimes can't remember what he looks like, exactly, or what his voice sounds like, or what it was like when he lived here with them.

If Daddy were around, no one would have snuck into Sadie's room.

If Daddy were around, she would have Fred back, too.

She thinks of the pink dog as she walks into her room, and glances at the empty spot on her dresser.

She knew as soon as she put him into the tag sale box that it would be wrong to give him away, but—

Uh-oh.

Belatedly, Sadie remembers the fishing line. She'd forgotten all about it when she crossed the threshold just now. Sure enough, one end has become unfastened from the doorframe.

She tries to put it up again, but the tape isn't sticky enough. Maybe she can just take it down now that she has the signs.

But the signs probably aren't going to stop anyone. Even Sadie knows that. No matter what Mommy and Dr. Prentiss said.

The fishing wire trap won't stop anyone, either, but at least she'll know if someone has been in her room.

Opening her desk drawer, she looks for the roll of tape she keeps with her art supplies. It's gone.

She's positive she didn't hide it. There wasn't enough room for everything.

Did someone steal it? Was someone else in here? Was the fishing line already down before she herself crossed the threshold just now?

Sadie nervously rummages through the drawer. No tape. Someone must have—

Suddenly, she remembers that she and Mommy used up almost the whole roll last night when they hung the signs. Thank goodness. Thank goodness no one stole it.

Heading downstairs to borrow some tape from the kitchen drawer, she sees Chauncey at the foot of the steps, facing the front door. His tail is sticking straight up, and his ears are perked like he's listening for something.

"What are you doing, boy?" Sadie opens the doggy gate and goes over to him.

Poised, silent, Chauncey seems to be on high alert.

Sadie looks toward the door just as the bell rings.

She can see someone standing on the other side of the frosted glass.

The security guard in the lobby of Nick's building barely glances up from his newspaper as Lauren walks past his kiosk. Things are different here than they are in the city, that's for sure. At Alyssa's building, you need ID and a signature to get past the doorman—and even then, you can't get onto an elevator until the tenant has been buzzed and notified.

Around here, apparently, if you don't look like a threat, you're not considered a threat. Maybe Lauren should discuss that with Nick—and question whether the kids are safe in a building with such lax security.

Then again, anyone who really wanted to could easily get into their own house. No security guard, no alarm system, windows covered only by flimsy screens, locks to which strangers have the keys . . .

Again, Lauren remembers what Sadie said about someone prowling around her room.

What if she was right? What if someone really did get into the house at some point while they were gone?

But nothing is missing. The electronics, Lauren's jewelry . . .

When she got dressed a little while ago, she opened the chest on her dresser and saw her diamond engagement ring and gold wedding band right there on top. Anyone who was looking for something of value to steal wouldn't have to look very hard—and probably wouldn't waste any time in a four-year-old's room.

Lauren steps into the elevator and pushes the button for the fourteenth floor.

The doors close, and she leans toward one of the mirrored walls to check her teeth for lipstick, then turns her back to the mirror and looks over her shoulder to make sure she doesn't have any panty lines. She does, a little. She tugs the band into place, hoping there's no security camera broadcasting her actions back to the lobby. Not that the guard is likely to be paying attention.

Why do you care what you look like, anyway? It's just Nick.

He's certainly seen her at her worst: sick with the flu, giving birth—and in a sobbing, crumpled, devastated heap when he told her he was leaving.

Maybe that's why she wants to look her best now. To show him that she's doing very well, thank you, without him.

The attractive woman in the mirror radiates self-assurance—regardless of how insecure she might be feeling inside.

On the fourteenth floor, Lauren steps into a wide, carpeted corridor.

She pictures her kids here. Nick probably tells them to keep their voices down.

She imagines Beth here, too. Maybe she has her own key so that she can come and go the way Lauren used to at Nick's Manhattan apartment years ago, when they were newly dating.

No. Don't think about that. Don't think about any of the good times with him. You don't want to go into this with your emotions all worked up.

Hell, she doesn't want to go into this at all. She wants to turn around and walk out of Nick's new life, the way he walked out of her old one.

But she can't. She won't.
So just take a deep breath and get it over with.

"Ryan! Lucy! Someone's at the door!" Sadie calls.

No reply from the second floor. Her sister and brother are supposed to be in charge, but they're still busy in their own little worlds, ignoring her.

As far as Sadie's concerned, that means she's in charge.

Chauncey is on all fours, still focused on the door.

She looks again at the silhouette in the window. She can't tell if it's a man or a woman.

The bell rings again.

Sadie reaches for the knob, hesitates, turns it. Opening the door, she's surprised to see a familiar face.

"Hello, Sadie. How are you?"

"I'm good," she replies tentatively. "How are you?"

"Not very well, I'm afraid," is the response.

Then Sadie sees the gun.

CHAPTER SIXTEEN

H ey, this is Byron. You know what to do. Do it at the
beep."

"Yo, it's Fantoni again. What the hell, man? Where
are you? Call me back. I need to know what's up with
that . . . *thing.*"

Mike hangs up the phone with a curse and paces across
the room, rubbing yesterday's five o'clock shadow.

He's known Byron Gregson since they collided on a
case twenty years ago—he a fledgling private eye, Byron
a cub reporter for the *Providence Journal.* They shared a
couple of tips, cartons of cigarettes, and a burning need
to uncover the truth.

They found it.

Byron landed a major scoop, broke a huge political
corruption story in the *Pro-Jo*, and became an investigative journalist—one of the best. Mike opened his own PI
firm in Boston and at first spent his days—well, mostly,
his nights—tailing cheating spouses and deadbeat dads.
As time went on, he branched out into background
checks, employee investigations, missing persons . . .

Like Jeremy Cavalon.

Dammit—he really needs to talk to Byron, and the

guy chooses now to pull one of his famous disappearing acts? Mike would be more aggravated than worried if his friend hadn't alluded to the fact that he had stumbled across something big.

As in dangerous big.

That happened a while back. Before the holidays. Last fall, maybe. It happened because Byron was digging around, as a favor to Mike, in Jeremy Cavalon's past.

"I think I found the kid's birth parents," he told Mike in a late night phone call—the only kind Byron ever placed. "And if I'm right, you're not going to believe who they are."

"Who?"

"I'll tell you if I'm right. I've got some more digging to do."

And that was that.

Mike more or less back-burnered the case until last month, when he received a voice mail from Byron.

"Dude, I was right. It's bigger than I thought. I need some help. I'll be in touch."

He hasn't been. The silence is as ominous as Byron's admission that he needed help. It's always been the other way around. Byron in control, coming to Mike's aid, bailing him out—sometimes, quite literally.

Now Mike is wondering if maybe Byron got in over his head.

It wouldn't be the first time.

Mike just hopes it wasn't the last.

About to knock on the door marked 14D, Lauren realizes it's slightly ajar.

"Nick?" she calls, suddenly nervous.

It's been such a long time since she's seen him.

What if Nick tells her he wants to come home?

What if the moment she lays eyes on him all the old feelings come rushing back to her and she forgets to stay strong?

Or what if Nick tells her he's marrying Beth, and she falls apart crying, begging him not to?

God, I hate what-ifs. Why do I do this to myself?

She pushes the door open farther. "Nick?"

The apartment feels empty even before she steps over the threshold to find it silent and dim. The shades are drawn across the wide windows at the far end of the living room.

"Nick?"

He's not here.

Maybe he had to step out for something, and he'll be right back.

But even as that theory enters her mind, she discards it. If he was here, the air-conditioning would be on. The place is stuffy, as though it's been sealed up for a while.

Maybe Nick had planned to come back from his trip this morning and meet her here, but got hung up in traffic.

No. There's his luggage. It's sitting just inside the door, as though he walked in and dropped it right there.

But clearly, he wasn't alone. Beside the familiar black Samsonite rolling bag and nylon duffel are a Louis Vuitton suitcase and matching tote.

Obviously Beth's luggage.

Okay . . . so they're back, the two of them. Where are they now?

Lauren's cell phone rings in her pocket, startling her.

Pulling it out, she looks at the caller ID window. The call is coming from home. She flips open the phone, wondering if the kids are fighting, or hungry, or bored, or all of the above.

"Hello?"

"Mommy?"

"Sadie?"

"No."

It's Lucy, she realizes. Why does she sound so young, and why is she calling Lauren Mommy?

"What's up, sweetie?"

"You have to help us . . ."

Lauren's heart stops. "Lucy, are you crying?"

"Please, Mommy—"

She hears a scratching, rustling sound, as if someone—Ryan?—is scuffling the phone out of Lucy's hand.

But it isn't her son who comes on the line. The voice is guttural and unfamiliar.

"I'm here with your kids, Lauren. One of them has something I want. And I'll do whatever it takes to get it back. Do you understand?"

"I'm home!"

The apartment door slams behind Molly Cameron and her heels tap across the parquet floor of the entry hall, accompanied by the rattling wheels of her rolling suitcase trundling along behind her.

"Mrs. Cameron!" Sharon appears in the corridor leading to the bedrooms. "I thought you weren't coming home until late tonight!"

"There was an earlier flight to La Guardia so I got on it standby. What's the matter? Aren't you thrilled to see me, Sharon?" she teases the nanny.

"Oh no, I am . . ." She toys with a strand of her long, blond hair. "I mean, I was just putting Avery down for his nap, and when I heard the door, it scared me. I thought maybe it was Mr. Cameron."

"I know you've only been working here a month, darling, but haven't you figured out yet that Mr. Cameron never, ever shows up at home while the stock market's open?"

Sharon smiles faintly. To her credit, she doesn't mention that Mr. Cameron doesn't exactly rush home at the closing bell, either.

After a long day on the trading floor, Andrew likes to stop off at the Battery Park Ritz-Carlton bar for a couple of scotches.

"I might as well," he tells Molly, if she ever dares to criticize the habit. "You never get home until late anyway."

True—and that's *if* she gets home at all. Now that Avery is almost a year old, Molly's been traveling on business again. Not as much as she did before she was pregnant, but enough that she feels more maternal jealousy for the new nanny than she did for the Jamaican baby nurse they'd had for the first six months. Back then, Molly was working from home a lot, and glad for every opportunity to hand her son over to someone else's capable hands.

She had her doubts about hiring Sharon, who's younger and a lot more inexperienced with babies than Molly would have liked. Yet she did have a certain aesthetic appeal—an attractive, all-American blonde who had been raised in New England. And though Sharon's child care references were slim, they were most impressive.

"Are you crazy, hiring a gorgeous young nanny and leaving her alone in the house with your husband?" one of Molly's friends had asked, the first time she saw Sharon.

"Not at all. For one thing, Andrew is hardly ever in the house. For another thing, she's not the brightest bulb on the tree. Andrew has no patience for idiots."

"So you hired an idiot to care for your child? Even better."

"She's very sweet, and kind, and Avery loves her," Molly replied. "And let's face it, it's not like I'm going to find a nanny with Mensa on her résumé. Which, by the way, is impressive. Did I tell you who her last employer was?"

So far, Sharon seems to be working out okay. Time will tell.

"I want to see Avery before he falls asleep." Molly leaves the suitcase and heads for the nursery.

"Oh, are you sure? I mean, he's so tired, and—"

"I want to see my son." Molly tosses Sharon a look over her shoulder—her withering look of death, Andrew calls it—that quite effectively cuts her off.

Sharon's got to be kidding. After three days away, Molly is going to wait until Avery wakes up to see him? Sharon was undoubtedly counting on some free time while the baby sleeps. She's probably afraid that if Molly disturbs him, he'll be fussy and refuse to settle back down.

Too bad. Sharon's job is to take care of him.

Molly opens the door to the nursery. "Mama's home, baby!"

To her surprise, the shades are open. Avery is in his crib, but he's not tucked in with the mobile tinkling above. He's sitting there clad in just his diaper, wide-awake and whimpering.

Molly takes one look at him and screams.

Swamped in a churning tide of panic, Lauren clings to the phone like a life buoy.

Do something! Say something!

She can't move, can't seem to find her voice.

"Here's what I'm going to do," the caller tells her. "Are you listening?"

She nods mutely.

"Lauren?"

This can't be happening.

"Yes. Yes, I'm . . . I'm listening."

"I'm going take the kids someplace safe. Okay?"

No! Not okay! You can't take my children!

"Here's what you're *not* going to do," the strange voice goes on. "You're not going to call the police. Do you want to know why not? Tell Mommy what I'm holding in my hand, Ryan."

Her son's voice is hoarse; barely recognizable. "A gun."

No. God, no.

"And where is it pointed, Ryan? Tell Mommy."

"At me."

Ryan. Her baby boy.

Please, no, no, no . . .

"That's right, Lauren. I'm pointing a gun at your son's head, and I will pull the trigger if I hear a siren, if I spot a police car, anywhere near this house. Do you understand?"

"Yes," she whispers.

"What?"

"*Yes!* Yes, I understand."

"Good. I've told you what you're *not* going to do. Do you want to know what I would like you to do?"

Lauren forces the word. "Yes."

"Drive back here and wait by the phone. I'm going to call you in a half hour, and you'd better be here, because if you're not . . ."

The threat is ominously left unspoken.

There's a click, and the line goes dead.

* * *

"What did you do to my baby?" Molly shrieks at Sharon, rushing to the crib and snatching her son from it.

Avery screams.

"I'm so sorry, Avery. Mama's so sorry . . ." The physical contact against his skin must be excruciating; his little body scorched in a red, blistering burn.

"I didn't—it's just—it's a sunburn, Mrs. Cameron."

"*Just* a sunburn?"

"I'm so sorry. I had him out in the stroller yesterday, and—"

"You had him out where?" Molly demands over Avery's miserable wails. "On the beach for hours without sunscreen? Where?"

"No, just around the neighborhood."

"Where does a baby get a sunburn like this in the middle of Manhattan, in a stroller with an awning?"

"It was hot and sunny and—"

"And was he naked? Because his stomach is burned, and his legs—oh, Avery. Oh, my poor baby."

"I'm so sorry, Mrs. Cameron."

"You dim-witted, idiotic . . . Get out!"

"You mean . . ."

"I mean get out. You're done here. Fired."

Sharon stares for a long moment, then hangs her head and leaves.

Why, oh why did I hire her? Molly berates herself as her son screams in pain.

But she knows the answer to that question.

She hired Sharon because she was impressed by her last position: caring for the daughters of a high-profile congressman, whose office had graciously provided a glowing reference.

Sharon was good enough for the Camerons, Molly figured, if she was good enough for Garvey Quinn.

* * *

Barring traffic, it takes almost half an hour to get from White Plains to Glenhaven Park.

Thoughts careening wildly, Lauren races to the elevator and punches the down button repeatedly.

"Hurry, hurry, hurry . . ."

She needs help. Desperately, immediately. Help from someone other than the police. She has no intention of risking her son's life.

Dear God, why did she leave the kids? She hardly ever goes anywhere. Why, on the rare occasion the kids are home alone, did someone come into the house to harm them?

"Oh, Nick, why? Where are you? I need you."

But Nick isn't here for her. He hasn't been here for her in ages . . . and he won't be, ever again. She's on her own. With this. This . . .

The thought drifting at the back of her mind barges forward. *This is no accident.*

Unless . . .

Is it some kind of hoax?

No. Remembering the strangled fear in Ryan's voice, Lauren knows the danger is real.

Were they being watched all along? Was someone waiting to pounce the moment she left the house?

She couldn't even tell if the voice belonged to a man or a woman. Someone was working hard to disguise it. Why?

Was the caller someone she knows?

If the children are being taken away—*oh God, someone's taking them away!*—there must be a car.

I need a description, a license plate, something . . .

Still clutching her cell phone, she looks down at it in frustration. If only there were someone—a friend, a neighbor—who could look out a window and see what's going on at her house without drawing any attention.

But they're all gone. Trilby, the Hilberts, the Levines, O'Neals . . .

There's no one around, she realizes in despair. No one at all.

Or is there?

It's a crazy thought, but she's desperate.

Flipping open her phone, she presses the call log button. There it is—the number is right at the top.

And Sam Henning answers on the first ring.

At first, Ryan thought it was a joke. Something his sisters cooked up, fake gun, very funny, ha ha.

How he wishes that was the case.

But this is real. He, Lucy, and Sadie are really being held at gunpoint by a lunatic who's obsessed with some stuffed animal of his sister's.

"But I don't know where it is," Sadie said—a few times now.

Ryan can tell that she's lying. He only hopes their captor cannot.

"Sadie," he says softly, keeping one eye on the gun as the three of them sit lined up on the couch, "you can hand over the toy. Seriously. Mom will get you a new one."

"She didn't give it to me. Daddy did."

"Then Daddy will get you a new one."

"Daddy moved away."

"He's not that far away," Lucy assures Sadie, sitting between the two of them. "Right, Ryan?"

"Yeah, he's just on vacation."

"Mommy said they're having a divorce and he's never coming back."

"Not to live with us," Lucy whispers, "but we'll see him."

"When?"

"Soon."

"What if he's gone forever?"

"He won't be," Ryan tells Sadie.

"But Fred is."

Ryan and Lucy exchange a glance.

Lucy clears her throat. "He's not, sweetie. Daddy will find him, and he'll get you a new toy. But right now, we really need you to go get the pink—"

"No!" Sadie bellows. "No, no, no! It's mine and you can't have it!"

"Shut up! Shut up now!"

Ryan sees that the gun is dangerously close, and pointed right at his little sister.

Lucy puts a protective arm around Sadie, and her hand comes to rest on Ryan's shoulder. He feels a lump rise in his throat.

"Please," Lucy says in a small voice, "don't hurt us."

"Believe me, I don't want to. And I won't, if you just tell me where it is."

Ryan closes his eyes and tilts his head back, willing Sadie to give in before she gets them all killed.

"Sam, this is Lauren Walsh," she says in a rush. "Do you remember me?"

"Lauren! Good to hear from—"

"Are you at home?"

"Yes. What—"

"Please just listen to me. I need your help. My kids are at my house, and someone is there with them. Someone who's armed with a gun and taking them away."

"*What?*"

"Whoever it is wants something from me, and he's going to hurt my kids if he doesn't get it, or if I call the police."

The elevator arrives. The doors slide open. Still talking to Sam, Lauren steps in.

"They were still in the house a minute ago." She repeatedly jabs the lobby and door close buttons. "Can you see if you can tell through the yard what's going on? Don't let them know you're there—he's got a gun pointed at my son's head, and he'll shoot. But if you can get a description of the person and the car and a license plate—"

"Are you sure there's only one?"

"Car?"

"Person."

"No."

"But you know that it's a man, and—"

"I'm not sure of that, either."

"I'll check it out. Where are you, Lauren?"

"White Plains, but I'm on my way home. Call me when—"

The elevator descends abruptly, cutting off the connection.

Knees wobbling, head spinning, Lauren catches a glimpse of herself in the mirrored wall. Deer in headlights—a stark contrast to the self-assured reflection she saw upon her ascent.

It's going to be all right, she tells herself.

If only there was someone here with her; someone who could say the words aloud and make her believe them. She's never felt more alone in her life.

But you're not.

Thank God, she thinks. *Thank God for Sam.*

* * *

Brooding, Garvey sits in his office, one eye on the clock, the other on his silent cell phone, clutched in his hand. All morning, he's been waiting for word.

Today. It has to be today.

Don't let me down. If you do, you'll be sorry.

And I'll be sorrier, he thinks grimly.

"Garvey."

He looks up to see Marin standing in the doorway. Her hair is pulled back in a prim chignon and she has on a navy blue suit with pumps.

"I'm ready to go." She tucks a compact into her clutch purse and snaps it closed. "Do you have an umbrella?"

"The driver will. That's what you're wearing?"

"No. I'm wearing jeans and sneakers. I was about to change."

He forces a smile at the quip.

"Trust me," she tells him, "I didn't pick it out."

Of course she didn't. She rarely chooses her own clothes for public appearances these days. His campaign staff has taken over his wife's wardrobe, along with everything else. They organize Marin's clothing well in advance, according to what's on the calendar.

Garvey looks her up and down. "It's not bad. Just kind of . . . boring, and buttoned up. But it matches your eyes."

"Beverly said the same thing."

Beverly. He keeps his expression carefully neutral.

Funny—his longtime campaign aide didn't mention that she's dressing his wife these days, going around telling Marin that her blue suit matches her blue eyes.

Once, a long time ago, Garvey told Beverly that her own eyes were the color of the summer sun—and just as warm and welcoming.

He honestly believed that, then.

"Beverly thought this outfit presented the right image

for this event," Marin tells him. "So where's it being held, in a nunnery?"

"Close. It's—"

"I *know* where it is," Marin interrupts, giving him a look. "And I know *what* it is."

Yes. Of course she does.

"Okay. So let's go." Garvey pushes back his chair and stands. He's been dreading it all morning: a luncheon with religious leaders opposed to stem cell research.

The bitter irony doesn't escape him—nor does it escape Marin. He can see the tightness in her expression; can sense the tension in her posture as they walk, side by side, to the door.

He knows what she's thinking; he's thinking the same thing.

Just another hypocritical incident in the lives of the wholesome, conservative Quinns.

"It's fine. We're the only ones who know, Marin," he reminds her in a low tone as they ride down to the lobby in the elevator.

"Sometimes, I'm not so sure," is her cryptic reply.

Startled, Garvey looks up to find her with her arms folded, staring at the doors. They glide open before he can ask her what she meant by that comment. Marin and Garvey are immediately overtaken by the security detail accompanying them to the luncheon.

The question will have to wait.

Barreling north on I–684, Lauren is careful to keep the speedometer less than ten miles over the limit. This road is notorious for speed traps, and getting stopped by the cops will cost precious time.

Please, please, please . . . Please, God, don't let anything happen to my babies.

Fighting off hysteria, she drives with her cell phone in hand, dialing Sam every couple of minutes.

His phone keeps going straight to voice mail. The outgoing message is automated.

"The person you are trying to reach is not available. Please leave a message."

What if she has the wrong number? But it can't be. She reached him the first time, and she's been hitting redial.

The first few times, she left frantic messages.

Now she doesn't bother, just hangs up, waits as long as she can stand to wait, and tries again.

Why isn't he answering?

What if . . . ?

No. She can't bear the thought and so she pushes it away, focusing on the road ahead. The landmarks are familiar. Just a few more miles.

She's going to make it on time.

She tries Sam again.

"The person you are trying to reach—"

Where, where, *where* is Sam?

Please, please, please . . .

Her mantra beats in time with the windshield wipers.

What does this person want from her?

Ransom?

It makes no sense. Why her? Anyone who's seen the Queen Anne Victorian on Elm Street would know that it doesn't hold a candle to many of the other homes in town. There are mansions right around the corner; vast estates a stone's throw away. Why would anyone target the Walshes for financial gain?

Dear God. What if they want a million bucks in exchange for the kids? Two million?

Lauren can't get her hands on that kind of money. Can Nick?

Nick.

Anyone could have sent her that text message asking her to meet him at his apartment. Anyone with access to his phone.

Why didn't I realize that before now?

I'm such a fool.

Maybe he lost his phone. Maybe he was mugged. Or his apartment was robbed.

But who would steal a cell phone and leave Louis Vuitton luggage behind?

Someone who wanted to use it to trick me.

Where are Nick and Beth, though? Clearly, they're not still on Martha's Vineyard.

If Nick was robbed and his phone stolen, he'd have canceled the service immediately.

If he was aware of it.

Having reached the exit for Glenhaven Park, Lauren forces herself to decelerate along the ramp when her instinct is to pick up speed and barrel toward home.

Stay calm. Almost there.

This—today—was a setup. Someone used Nick's phone to get Lauren out of the way.

Tears stream down her face, her body quakes with sobs.

Did something happen to Nick?

On the heels of that unwanted thought, the other one—the darkest thought of all—barges into her brain at last:

Are my children dead?

Bile rises in Lauren's throat.

Lucy.

Ryan.

Sadie.

Please, please, please . . .

CHAPTER **SEVENTEEN**

Sadie wore a blindfold once before, when she played piñata at someone's birthday party. She didn't like it then, even though there was candy involved.

She really doesn't like it now. Her hair is pinched in the fabric knot at the back of her head. But when she fussed, Ryan and Lucy told her to be quiet and wear it. They all have them on.

The three of them are crouched down in back of a car that's been driving for a long, long time. It was a smooth, fast ride at first, and Sadie could hear other trucks and cars around them. But then they started making turns, and the drive got slower, and a lot bumpier.

Every so often, she hears a harsh "Keep your head down" from the front seat, and she wonders if Lucy or Ryan is trying to peek out and see where they're going.

They're both crying. Not loudly, but Sadie can hear them sniffling, and she can feel their bodies shaking. She's seen Lucy cry before, a few times, but not Ryan. It scares her.

"I want Mommy," she says in a small voice.

Someone—she's not sure who—pats her shoulder and shushes her. It makes her feel better. She can't see them, but at least she's not alone. Her big brother and sister won't let anything bad happen to her.

Finally, the car comes to a stop. The engine cuts, and it's quiet. The driver's door opens.

There are birds singing, Sadie realizes. She can smell the rain and hear it dripping, like it does from the trees after a storm.

The back door opens. "Come on. Get out. You first."

"Please, no . . . please, we want to stay together," Lucy protests. Her voice sounds funny. High-pitched.

"You will be together, trust me. And Ryan and Sadie, if you two try to escape while we're gone, I'll shoot your sister in the head."

Sadie gasps. "No! Please don't shoot her!"

"You know I'm not afraid to use this gun."

They know. Sadie shudders. This is scarier than the Wicked Witch of the West, by far.

"Stay put." The car door slams shut.

She feels a hand groping for hers. It's Ryan. His grasp makes her feel a little better. But not entirely.

"Are we going to die?"

Ryan doesn't answer right away, and when he says no, she doesn't believe him.

"I'm afraid."

"So am I. You've got to tell, Sadie. I know you know where that stuffed animal is."

Sadie bites her lip. "I can't tell."

"Don't you get it?" her brother explodes, and jerks his hand away from hers. "This is life or death."

She gets it. She does.

But there has to be some other way.

The children are gone.

Lauren had known they would be.

Still, somehow, it's shocking to step over the threshold into the empty house. Sobbing, she calls out for them. Chauncey is there, barking wildly, following her from room to room in a futile search.

From the first floor to the second, everything is in its place; the entire house just as Lauren left it. No sign of a break-in, no sign of a struggle.

In the doorway to Sadie's room, Lauren runs her fingertips over the waxy crayon lettering she herself had done just last night.

"Keep Out."

Oh, Sadie. You were so afraid. And I didn't believe you. No one did.

Someone really was here before, and came back today.

Was the intruder someone the kids willingly let into the house?

Again, she remembers the caller's effort to disguise his—or her—voice.

Again, she thinks of Sam.

What if . . . ?

No. He was going to help her.

But he hasn't called back.

How well does she know him, really?

Not at all.

He came out of nowhere. Single. Handsome. Interested in her.

If something seems too good to be true, it probably is.

"Oh my God."

Lauren sinks onto the bed in Sadie's room as the terrible truth washes over her.

Sadie is the last to be taken from the car.

It was scary to wait alone after Ryan was dragged

away. But it's even scarier to be blindly led to some un-
known fate.

"Careful. Don't fall."

She's on some kind of rocky path that winds through
some high, wet grass that feels slimy against her bare
legs. Birds are singing all around her. If only they could
fly away for help. But they don't know that she's in
danger.

"This is it." The firm hands on Sadie's shoulders jerk
her to a stop. She hears a creaking sound: a door being
opened.

"Step up."

Sadie fumbles around with her sneaker.

"No, here."

A hand grasps her leg and places her foot, then gives
her a little nudge forward, up, and in. A door closes
behind her and she's no longer outside. There's a musty
smell, like the basement back home.

"Sadie?"

"Ryan!" Relieved to hear his voice, she asks, "Is
Lucy—?"

"I'm here, sweetie."

"So am I, sweetie," a mocking voice announces, and
Sadie shudders.

She can feel her blindfold being untied.

She blinks as it's lifted away. There's nothing to see
but a tiny room of some sort, with wooden plank walls
and no windows. The only light is from a flashlight, and
it beams into Sadie's face, blinding her.

"Okay. Here we are, all cozy."

"I'm not cozy!" Sadie protests. "I want to go home!"

"Then I'm going to ask you one more time. Where is
it?"

Sadie chews her lower lip. If she tells, she'll lose the

one thing her father gave her. Well, maybe he gave her other stuff, but she doesn't remember it. Not like this.

The funny thing is, she hated the dog when Daddy brought it to her. But that was mostly because it wasn't Fred.

She sort of got used to Fred being gone. And then she sort of got used to the pink dog in her room. But she didn't even know it until she tried to give it away.

"I'm waiting for an answer, Sadie."

She makes up her mind. "The tag sale. I put it into the box for the tag sale."

"Where is the box?"

"I don't know."

"I do," Ryan speaks up. "Mom and I brought everything to the basement of Glenhaven Episcopal."

Sam.

Incredible.

Sam Henning is behind this—if that's his real name.

Of course. That day she saw the Peeping Tom in the backyard . . . it was he. It must have been. Why didn't she trust her instincts? Why was it so easy to chalk it up to a trick of the light, or paranoia, or stress, or whatever the hell excuse she used to decide there was nobody there?

He was there. Watching her. Waiting.

But why the charade? What does he want from her? From her kids?

Is he keeping them at the house on Castle Street?

There's one way to find out. She can sneak through the yard and peek through the windows.

But there are so many things wrong with that plan. He might be watching for her and see her coming. And even if he's not, he isn't going to have the kids out in full view of anyone who happens to glance into the house.

The dumpy white Cape with the puke green shutters.

How does she even know he really lives there, though? How does she even know such a house exists?

Lauren's mind is spinning.

Maybe she should call the police.

But what if he's watching her? He said he would be. If he's living in her backyard, that wouldn't be difficult.

As Lauren wrestles with the decision, the ringing telephone shatters the silence. The house phone, not her cell.

When she looks at it, she sees Sam's number in the caller ID window.

Maybe she was wrong about him.

Maybe he's calling her back because she asked him to.

Maybe . . .

"Hello?" she says breathlessly.

"Ah, you made it home," the strange, guttural voice tells her—still disguised, but now she knows, and her heart sinks.

She was right. Sam. He's the one. And to think she'd been hoping he might ask her out.

The thought of it makes her sick.

"Listen carefully, Lauren. Your daughter has a pink stuffed dog your husband took from the lost and found a few weeks ago. Do you know what I'm talking about?"

"Yes." Lauren's eyes go automatically to Sadie's dresser, where she keeps the dog. Bewildered, she wonders what it has to do with anything.

"It's mine, and I need it back."

"You can have—" Stunned, Lauren sees that the dog is no longer there.

"Thank you for being here. I can't tell you how much we appreciate your support, Congressman Quinn."

"It's a pleasure, Father." Garvey smiles, shaking hands with the priest. "And this is my wife, Marin."

"So nice to meet you, Mrs. Quinn."

"I'm glad to be here, Father." Marin is the model of decorum, a modern-day Jackie Kennedy to Garvey's charismatic JFK.

We can do this, he reminds himself as they take their seats at the banquet table. *We can do anything, as long as we hold it together and protect our secret.*

What did Marin mean, back there in the elevator? The cryptic statement has his stomach in knots.

Who can possibly know what they did?

Hell, even Marin doesn't know the worst of it. Not by a long shot.

Maybe he should come clean with her.

After all, Garvey wasn't the only one willing to do whatever it took to spare their child's life.

Caroline needed a hematopoietic stem cell transplant. The chance of finding a nonrelated donor was next to nothing; the waiting list was impossibly long. Caroline didn't have that kind of time.

But she did have a brother out there somewhere.

The adoption records had been sealed at Garvey and Marin's request. A court order could potentially open them—but that would risk making public the fact that they had borne a baby out of wedlock. It could also take months—and there were no guarantees.

Garvey had promised Marin he would begin the process, even at the risk of destroying his political career.

"But in the meantime," he told her, "we have to consider other options."

She knew what he was talking about, of course.

A savior sibling was Caroline's only chance. What parent wouldn't seize it?

Together, Garvey and Marin made the decision to conceive another child, regardless of the heated moral and religious controversy surrounding the issue. They were planning to add on to their family anyway . . . someday.

No one would ever have to know they had accelerated the plan . . . or why they had done it.

And so they conceived Annie.

She was meant to save her dying sister. Doctors and geneticists assured the Quinns that the odds were in their favor.

But in utero testing showed that the baby wasn't a donor match.

Garvey was beside himself. He wanted Marin to terminate the pregnancy.

"I've already lost one child and I might be about to lose another," she told him. "I'm not going to destroy a third."

"But we can try again, right away. The next baby might be a match."

"What about this one? Are we just going to discard it like some science experiment gone wrong?"

"It isn't like that, Marin. I'm talking about saving our child's life."

"So am I," Marin told him, arms wrapped protectively around her still-flat stomach.

She did what she had to do.

So did Garvey.

Lauren Walsh is out of her mind, frantic.

It's so very easy to picture her pale, terrified face on the other end of the phone line. It would be easy, too, to feel sorry for her—and, of course, for her children.

But that would be a terrible mistake.

Sympathy got the best of you once, fourteen years ago.

You don't dare let it happen again. This time, Garvey would find out for sure, and if that happens . . .

No. That can't happen.

His instructions were clear. Do what has to be done; no outside help this time. No hiring a professional, like the one who so efficiently disposed of Byron Gregson and that Rodriguez kid.

Pop and pay . . . such an easy, uncomplicated way of doing business compared to what came afterward.

But I did it. I took care of the husband and girlfriend all by myself. And it wasn't even as upsetting as I expected it to be, once we got rolling.

The first order of business that day was to get into the White Plains apartment building and wait for Nick Walsh to come home. Such a shame that it was impossible to get into his apartment without a key to the deadbolt, or bloodshed might have been completely unnecessary.

That's what I thought at the time, anyway . . . when I figured that the stuffed animal was conveniently located on the other side of that locked door.

Of course, it wasn't. And so there were complications. Too bad. It should have been so easy.

The wait there in the corridor was endless, and when Nick finally arrived midday, he wasn't alone. A beautiful woman accompanied him. They were both tanned, relaxed, weighed down with luggage; obviously returning from a vacation.

That was surprising. One would expect a man who'd picked up a stuffed animal from a lost and found to be accompanied by a child, and probably a wife. But it was obvious this woman wasn't his wife—they were too playful and affectionate with each other, pausing for a long kiss as he unlocked the door.

They didn't even notice they were being watched from the shadows at the end of the hall. They stepped into the apartment, dropped their luggage, and kissed again. Nick Walsh was reaching to pull the door closed when he realized that someone was about to step over the threshold after them.

He paled beneath his summer tan when he saw the gun. The woman opened her mouth to scream, but was effectively silenced with a curt "Make one sound, and I will pull the trigger."

They assumed it was a robbery. It might have been that simple, were the pink stuffed dog in the apartment.

No.

It would have been a robbery-murder, because Garvey wanted no witnesses. They never had a chance.

Nick claimed that the toy wasn't there, and it didn't take long to search the place, thanks to the minimalist decor and obvious bachelor pad setup.

"Where is it?"

Nick, oh so heroic at that point, wasn't willing to talk. He had probably realized that it would be messy—and loud—for two people to be gunned down in the middle of the day in an apartment building. Not to mention that he had something his adversary wanted—his only bargaining chip if he wanted to stay alive.

"You need to come with me, then. Both of you."

"Why me?" the woman whimpered. "I don't even know what you're talking about."

"Not my problem. Let's go."

They took the elevator down to the basement and exited onto the side street, where the car was waiting. An SUV, rented, tinted windows.

The drive up to Greymeadow took almost an hour.

What came next took five minutes—unless you counted the time it took to drag the bodies over to the pond, weigh them, sink them.

And now I'm going to have to do it all again . . . with four of them.

At least the kids are smaller. They'll be easier to move when the time comes.

"Do you remember the boxes you donated for a tag sale, Lauren?"

"Yes . . ." On the other end of the phone line, she's barely audible.

"In one of them—the one marked with black letters, your daughter tells me—is the pink stuffed dog. She put it there. Drive over to the church basement, get the dog, and bring it back to your house. Don't talk to anyone."

"But . . . what if someone is there? I can't just barge in and—"

"Tell them your daughter wants her toy back. Nothing else. It's very simple."

It is, almost laughably simple—but it's doubtful Lauren finds anything remotely humorous about her children being held for ransom.

"What about my kids?"

"When I get what I want, you get what you want."

"How do I know?" Her voice is trembling, poor thing.

"We'll just have to trust each other, won't we?"

Listening to an endless speech about the evils of stem cell research, Garvey pretends to be riveted. He's gotten quite good at feigning rapt attention.

But his thoughts are on his elder daughter. On the bitter irony that one day, stem cell research might result in a cure for her disease.

But Caroline is going to be all right regardless.

Thanks to me.

After the failed effort to conceive a savior sibling, Garvey knew he had to take matters into his own hands. If he didn't do something to stop the death march through his little girl's bloodstream, Caroline was going to die.

And so he made the decision that would come back to haunt him years later.

Yet, looking back, he knows he wouldn't have done anything differently.

As a lawyer, he was well aware that the legal process to open sealed records was incredibly complicated—and hardly private.

He was on the verge of a congressional career built on family values. If the truth got out, his life would be destroyed.

But he told himself that wasn't the main reason he opted not to go the legal route. No, it wasn't about him. It was about Caroline. There was no time to waste.

For a man with Garvey's connections, sidestepping legality was ridiculously easy.

It didn't take him long to find out that the infant he and Marin had given up for adoption seven years earlier had been originally placed with a Rhode Island couple who already had four daughters and wanted a son.

But they changed their minds not long after accepting the baby and gave him back.

A real shame. Garvey was glad Marin didn't know their son had wound up in the foster care system.

A few years later, he was adopted at last—and Garvey knew exactly where to find him.

Few cars are parked on the street in front of Glenhaven Episcopal Church today. Lauren easily finds a double space right out front, but it takes her several tries to pull in correctly.

How can she drive when she can barely breathe? She's lucky she managed to maneuver the couple of blocks over from her house without crashing into anything.

The instructions were clear.

She hurries toward the door, remembering the last time she was here, with Ryan.

Now Ryan is out there somewhere with a gun to his head.

Please, please, please . . .

The church vestibule is dark and quiet. Lauren grasps her keys in a shaky hand as she descends the steps. What if he's waiting for her here?

The basement is empty—or so she believes.

"Lauren!"

She jumps, startled by the voice.

"Oh, I'm sorry. I didn't mean to scare you!"

She whirls around and spots Janet Wasserman in the far corner, waving, calling, "What are you doing here?"

Never mind me, Lauren thinks, *what are* you *doing here?*

Janet appears to be sorting through a box of clothing. Oh, that's right. Janet's in the Junior League.

Oh Lord. Why here? Why now? Why her?

Clenching her keys so hard they dig painfully into her palm, Lauren struggles to keep her cool. "I . . . you'll never believe it, Janet, but I accidentally gave away something that I need back."

"What is it?"

"One of Sadie's stuffed animals."

"What does it look like?"

"It's a pink dog."

"All the stuffed animals are over there." Janet points at a table. "Let's check it out."

"Oh, I can do it. I don't want to bother you."

"It's no bother."

Yes it is, dammit. It's a bother to me. Just let me do this. Please. My children's lives are at stake.

Forced to swallow her fear, Lauren follows Janet over to a table piled with teddy bears, Beanie Babies, and enormous carnival prizes.

"Adorable, aren't they?"

"Adorable. Yes."

It doesn't take long for Lauren to realize that the pink stuffed dog she seeks isn't among them.

Sadie put it into one of the tag sale boxes, though.

Or so she claimed.

"Lauren?" Janet is asking.

Ignoring her, Lauren wonders if Sadie could have been lying.

It's hard to imagine her parting with anything, given her attachment to her possessions.

Then again, she never wanted the dog. She said so just the other night, when Lauren was tucking her in.

Still, it doesn't make sense. If she gave it away in a tag sale box, why isn't it here?

"Earth to Lauren. Come in, Lauren."

She looks up at Janet, wanting to kill her.

"I *said*," Janet overenunciates, "I really don't think it's here."

"Are you sure this is everything?"

"Positive."

"But . . . maybe it got mixed in with something else."

"I'll keep an eye out for it, and I'll call you if—"

"No, you don't understand! I need it now!" Lauren cuts in shrilly.

Janet gapes at her, for once stunned to silence.

"I'm sorry, it's just . . . you know how kids are when they're attached to something. Sadie has been beside herself, and . . . I have to find it. Right now. Today. Or else . . ."

Or else my children will die.

Sitting in her living room with a cup of tea and the stack of photo albums, Elsa decides to begin today at the very beginning: Jeremy at four.

The first photo is one the foster agency sent.

She remembers her first thought upon seeing it: *That little boy has the saddest eyes I've ever seen.*

She knew, in that moment, that he was the one.

Brett wasn't so sure—not after reading the file that came with the photo.

"This kid has serious problems, Elsa."

"They all do."

"Not like this."

"He needs us, Brett. Please."

To this day, she marvels that her husband agreed to try foster parenting in the first place, after years of infertility and failed adoption efforts. That he was willing to reach out to a troubled kid like Jeremy is even more surprising.

"I'm game if you are," he said, and she made the call immediately, before he could change his mind.

The rest of the photos in the first album were taken after Jeremy came to live with them.

There he is in his new bedroom, outfitted with bunk beds for future sleepovers with friends he would never make. There he is on his swing set, with the teeter-totter that only Elsa ever shared with him. There he is as a Cub

Scout, and a Little Leaguer—always standing away from the other children, never a part of the group.

There he is dressed as a Pilgrim for the Thanksgiving pageant and as a monster for Halloween.

He was supposed to be a clown that year, Elsa recalls. She sewed him an adorable ruffled costume out of bright gingham patchwork fabric. He hated it.

"I want to be a bad guy!"

Jeremy threw a violent tantrum, and she gave in.

That was the usual pattern.

She spoiled him. She knows it now. Knew it then, really. But she kept trying to make up for the suffering he'd endured before he came to live with them. The doctors kept telling her that his problems weren't her fault. That his severe mood swings and frightening behavior were a combined result of genetics and the abuse he'd suffered before he came to live with the Cavalons. Elsa and Brett were told that the right combination of medication and therapy could turn Jeremy's life around.

They never had a chance to find it.

As they comb through piles of discarded toys and clothes and household items, Lauren manages to hold up her end of the endless conversation Janet forces on her.

Yes, the kids loved camp.

No, she doesn't know where the summer went.

Yes, the weather is lousy today.

No, she hasn't heard the forecast.

"I'm thinking of throwing a little dinner party next weekend," Janet tells her, "if you're available. We have some new neighbors in Glenhaven Crossing and I thought it would be nice to introduce them around. Can you make it?"

This is positively surreal.

"Lauren? Are you free next weekend?"

"Maybe—I'm not sure." She rifles through a pile of hats and mittens, looking for a sign of pink fur.

"You really should try to make it. It would be nice for you and Jennifer to become friends, since you both have young children."

"Jessica," Lauren corrects her. "And actually, we already met."

"You met Jennifer? Where?"

"Jessica," Lauren says again. "Her last name is Wolfe. I met her at the pool. She has a baby, right?"

"He's not exactly a baby. Bobby is four. Sadie's age. And their last name is Seaver."

"I must be thinking of someone else."

"Who?" Janet presses.

"I don't know, there was a woman named Jessica who said she lives in Glenhaven Crossing."

"But the Seavers are the only ones who have moved in lately."

"It was a while ago. At least a year, maybe two."

"I don't know anyone in the neighborhood named Jessica."

Wanting to scream, Lauren says, "You'll meet her, I guess."

"No. Trust me, I know what goes on in every house in the Crossing."

Yes, I'm sure you do.

This is a nightmare. A living—

"Oh my goodness, look!" Janet is triumphant, pointing to several boxes tucked under a long table. "These haven't even been opened yet!"

They're Lauren's. She can tell by looking at them.

Alana was obviously in no hurry to sort through the Walsh donations.

Lauren dives under the table and looks for the one marked "FRAGILE."

No . . . no . . . no . . . Yes! There it is.

Anxiously, she rips open the flaps.

No stuffed animal.

She goes through the whole box, just in case. Nothing.

Frantic, she tears into the others, tossing the contents into a pile on the floor.

"Whoa there, take it easy," Janet protests mildly.

"It's not here!" Her eyes are flooded.

"Relax, I'm sure it'll turn up. Is there any chance it's still at home? Maybe you were mistaken about giving it away."

Lauren shakes her head. It definitely wasn't in Sadie's room.

She closes her eyes, picturing the barren dresser top. Unless it was someplace else in the room?

Suddenly, she realizes something.

She hadn't seen Sadie's Dora the Explorer pillow, either. Or her favorite Barbies on the nightstand.

Granted, she'd been distracted, but . . .

I don't think they were there.

Sadie would never give away any of those precious possessions. So where are they?

"Lauren?"

"Hmm?"

"Are you okay?"

She looks up at Janet. "I have to go."

"But—"

Lauren is already on her way out the door.

CHAPTER EIGHTEEN

Walking into the house again, Lauren can feel the presence as palpably as she could feel the earlier emptiness.

He's here.

She doesn't let on, treading cautiously across the floor.

"Chauncey?" she calls, unsettled.

Silence.

Her instinct is to go straight upstairs to Sadie's room, to see if her hunch is correct. She fights it, though. She can't do that.

The stuffed toy is her only bargaining chip. Once Sam has it, there will be no reason for him to return the children.

She makes her way to the kitchen, her eyes peeled for any sign of an intruder. She sees nothing, but knows he's lurking.

Goosebumps prickle the skin on the back of her neck.

What if he already has the toy? Maybe he beat her to it.

But he couldn't possibly know where to find it. Not unless someone told him.

Sadie had already lied about the toy being in the tag

sale boxes. Would she suddenly decide to reveal the truth now?

If it is, indeed, really the truth.

What if Lauren is wrong?

I can't be. If I don't find that toy, he'll kill them.

She realizes she's standing idly in the kitchen.

I have to do something. Anything.

She goes to the sink and runs water into a glass. Glancing out the window, she wonders if the bucolic backyard really does shield a predator. Does Sam Henning really live back there, on Castle Lane? Are her children being held there, a stone's throw away?

Lauren turns off the tap and raises the glass to her lips, forcing herself to drink.

Then something catches her eye in the trees at the edge of the property line, and she nearly chokes on it.

Before she can react, a floorboard creaks behind her.

"Hello, Lauren."

"It's a slippery slope, my friends. If we allow human life to be devalued in this manner, what will be next?"

The speaker pounds the podium to make his point, temporarily startling Garvey from his reverie.

He glances at Marin.

She meets his gaze with a level one of her own, and as always, he can read her mind.

Such controversy over methods meant to save lives.

Stem cell research . . .

Savior siblings . . .

Medical tourism . . .

Garvey is well aware of the ethical implications that come with traveling abroad for surgical procedures and treatments difficult to come by in the States. These days, it's a hot button topic.

Fourteen years ago, it wasn't even on his radar—until he realized it was the perfect solution.

Only two people knew of his plan. He trusted both women implicitly—one with a truth so damaging that she could have destroyed him with it. He knew she never would.

Meanwhile, all he told Marin was that an overseas donor had been found for Caroline.

His wife rejoiced. She didn't ask many questions. In the final trimester of pregnancy, she was not only preoccupied, but of course she couldn't accompany her husband and daughter to India for the surgery. He was counting on that.

It was so long ago. Another lifetime, really. Caroline was a toddler. Annie wasn't born yet. Nor was the city of Mumbai. Back then it was still called Bombay, and elephants walked the streets amid the filth and chaos.

He remembers Caroline's wide eyes when she spotted one as they pulled up in front of their hotel on that first day.

"Doggy!" she trilled, clapping her hands together. "Big, big doggy!"

"No, sweetheart, that's an elephant. When we get back home, Daddy will take you to the Bronx Zoo and show you lots of elephants."

He remembers brushing tears from his eyes, praying he'd be able to keep that promise. Praying that the next round of lab tests would prove that the donor was compatible.

Traveling under fake passports, Beverly arrived in Bombay two days later with Jeremy.

Ryan would give anything for a flashlight.

That, or at least some fingernails. Too bad he's chewed them all away.

Without them, it's nearly impossible to claw at the wobbly board. He discovered it while feeling along the wall in the darkness of his wooden prison, looking for a way to escape before the lunatic comes back to kill them.

Ryan has no doubt that it will happen, thanks to Sadie.

When she realized what she'd done, she was filled with regret. But it was too late to change anything. They were already left alone, their captor off on a mission that wasn't going to end well.

"It's all right," Lucy told Sadie, even though it wasn't. "You didn't mean it."

Ryan couldn't say anything at all. Partly because he was furious with his little sister, and partly because there wasn't a minute to waste on talking.

There has to be a way out of here. It's their only hope.

Sadie eventually cried herself to sleep on the dusty floor. Ryan can't see her, but he can hear her even breathing in the darkness. He's starting to feel bad about being angry with her. She's just a little kid. No match for a crazy person with a gun.

Meanwhile, he's doing his best to pry the plank loose, with Lucy's help. There still isn't much slack, but it's getting a little better.

"I think we should try the door again, Ry. Maybe if we both throw all our weight against it . . ."

"We've tried that," he reminds his sister. "There's no way. It's solid. But this wall isn't. Here, feel this? I think it's starting to give."

"I think you're right."

"What do we do if we escape?"

"Are you kidding? Run like hell."

"We don't even know where we are." Lucy's voice is hollow. "We might be in the middle of nowhere."

"It doesn't matter. Anyplace is better than stuck in here, waiting to die."

Ryan's fingertips burn as he goes back to work on the board.

"How do you take your coffee, Congressman?" the waitress asks quietly, filling his cup.

"Just a little cream, thank you," he whispers back, and focuses on the new speaker, a physician who is—surprise, surprise—opposed to stem cell research.

Garvey leans back in his chair, watching the speaker, but in his mind's eye he's seeing another doctor he once knew. A surgeon.

Dr. Pujari understood Jeremy to be Caroline's sibling. That, of course, was the truth.

What he didn't know was that the boy had been abducted from the home of his adoptive parents.

Garvey was fluent in Hindi. Of course, Caroline, Beverly, and Jeremy spoke not a word of it. The language barrier was a necessary measure of protection.

No one at the hospital thought it odd that Jeremy was frightened and crying for his mother. And no one had any reason to question that Garvey was his father—both Jeremy and Caroline looked just like him. Nor did anyone seem to suspect that Beverly, with her unusual golden eyes and fair hair, was not the children's mother.

The tests had confirmed that Jeremy was Caroline's blood relative and a capable donor. That was all anyone seemed to care about—and all they needed to know.

The surgery was a success.

Days later, Garvey and Caroline were on their way home.

When he bid farewell to Beverly at the hotel, he saw a glimmer of misgiving in her amber-colored eyes.

"You're stronger than you think," he assured her, as Jeremy played on the floor at her feet. "I believe in you."

"I know."

"You do what has to be done, and then you wash your hands and you move on. Right?"

Beverly nodded.

"Good. I'll see you back in New York."

Garvey kissed her on the cheek and walked away with his daughter in his arms, not allowing himself even a last glance at Jeremy, afraid he might change his mind.

The boy simply could not live to tell what had happened to him.

Lauren whirls at the sound of the voice behind her.

Stunned not to see Sam there, she fails to recognize the vaguely familiar face for a moment. Then she does, and she sees the gun, and the water glass slips from her hand, shattering on the floor.

Her visitor clucks her tongue and shakes her head.

"Who are you?" Lauren asks.

"Does it matter?"

"Your name isn't Jessica."

"Very clever of you. No, it isn't."

No wonder. No wonder Janet Wasserman didn't know a new neighbor named Jessica.

"You don't have what I asked you to get for me, Lauren."

"How do you know?" Stalling for time, she glances down at the broken glass at her feet.

"You were supposed to bring it back from the church for me. You didn't come in with it. I was watching you."

"How do you know I didn't stash it somewhere along the way?"

Jessica's strange, amber-colored eyes narrow dangerously. The other day, sunglasses hid them. She looked for all the world like any other mom at the pool.

If Lauren had been able to see her eyes then, would she have been suspicious?

Possibly. But this isn't about a delusional person fixated on a child's toy. The woman's expression is sharply focused; she's completely sane and she means business.

So it isn't just a toy. It's something disguised as a toy, or something hidden inside a toy . . .

And she's willing to kill for it.

"Where is it, Lauren?"

"Where are my children?" she returns, fighting to keep her voice from quaking. She can't afford to lose her composure now. If she can stay focused, she might just have a chance . . .

"You'll see your children when I get what I need."

"What about Nick? Where is he?"

"Do you really care, Lauren?"

She says nothing.

"Nick and his friend won't be making your life miserable anymore. You have me to thank for that."

A chill slithers down Lauren's spine. "What . . . what do you mean?"

"I took care of them. I met them at his apartment and I showed them this"—she brandishes the gun—"and then we went for a little ride. A one-way trip for the two of them."

"Oh my God." Lauren clasps a hand across her mouth.

"I wouldn't be so upset if I were you. He sold you out, Lauren. You and the kids. And his girlfriend, too. I put a gun to her head and I asked him where the stuffed animal was, and he wouldn't say anything. Not a word. Then I pulled the trigger, and wouldn't you know, he started talking. He told me where to find what I needed. I guess he thought he had nothing to lose. Too bad he was wrong."

"You killed him." Trembling in disbelief, Lauren can't seem to wrap her mind around it.

"Don't tell me you didn't know. He called you, at the end. Isn't that interesting? I didn't even realize he had his phone in his hand until it was over."

Dear Lord, the phone call. He really was calling for help.

And I couldn't help him. It was already too late.

Nick . . . oh, Nick. I'm so sorry.

Nick is dead. She can't seem to absorb it, and yet . . .

Beth . . . Beth is dead, too.

And the body Lauren glimpsed out the window just now, lying on the ground amid the backyard trees . . .

It's not one of the children. That was immediately, blessedly obvious from the size, and the clothes, and the hair . . .

Sam Henning.

He must have been sneaking over here, and Jessica saw him and shot him . . .

Oh God. Oh my God.

This woman is a cold-blooded killer. Lauren doesn't stand a chance against her. Telling her what she wants to know didn't save Nick; it won't save Lauren and the children, either.

There's only one way out of this . . . and no time to waste.

Fired.
   Again.
   Now what?

Sharon makes her way along Park Avenue amid the usual pedestrian horde: executives on cell phones, roaming groups of teenagers, nannies pushing their charges along in strollers.

Sharon was among them just this morning, pushing Avery over to the park and back for their daily stroll. He screamed the whole time, miserably sunburned.

"I'm so sorry, little guy," Sharon told him over and over, brushing tears from her own eyes. "What have I done to you?"

But no—it wasn't her fault. She wasn't the one who had hauled him up to the suburbs and failed to sunscreen him before he spent hours in the sun and water.

You were *the one who loaned him out for the day, though.*

A favor in return for a favor.

"I helped you land the nanny job in the first place, Sharon, remember? I gave you a great reference when you needed it, and you asked me how you could ever repay me. Now you can."

Yeah, right. She'd been a damned fool to go along with it. It had cost her a job that was even cushier than her last one: "babysitting" Congressman Quinn's two teenage daughters—another job her cousin had managed to land for her.

So when her cousin called in the favor, accepting the offer had been a no-brainer. It seemed like a win-win situation—Avery would get to spend the day as a baby extra on a movie shoot; Sharon would receive a thousand dollars for letting him go.

Not bad for a day's work—rather, a day off, lounging around the Camerons' apartment watching the soaps.

The only hitch: Sharon couldn't tell a soul. Not even Avery's parents.

That was fine with her. She had a feeling Molly and Andrew Cameron wouldn't approve. And it wasn't as if they'd ever find out. Their son would be onscreen for only a few seconds, Sharon was told. Plus, he looks like a thousand other babies. What were the chances that Molly and Andrew would even see that movie or recognize him?

Anyway, Molly was away on business, and Andrew was never home during his son's waking hours on weekdays. Sharon was promised that Avery would be safely delivered back home again by five-thirty—and he was. No harm, no foul.

A few hours later, though, he fussed as she undressed him for his bath. That was when she saw the sunburn. He screamed bloody murder when she put him into the tub, and the water wasn't even that hot.

By the time Mr. Cameron came home, the baby had cried himself to sleep. His father didn't bother to look in on him. He never does.

Sharon tried to reach her cousin that night, to tell her what had happened and ask her what to do. But she didn't pick up her phone, and she didn't call back last night or today, and that isn't like her.

Sharon has no idea where Beverly is, but she has a bad feeling.

"Sadie . . . Sadie!"

She opens her eyes.

Or does she?

All she can see is pitch black.

She blinks, and it's the same. But then she turns her head, and there's a sliver of light.

"Sadie, wake up." Lucy's voice is hushed.

"Is she okay?" Sadie hears Ryan ask.

And then it all comes rushing back to her.

That scary woman at the front door . . .

The way she threatened them, and herded them all to the car . . .

And then the gun went off outside, and Sadie knew she had shot someone, and she prayed it wasn't Mommy . . .

But Ryan told her that it wasn't. It was some man, sneaking around the back of the property, maybe another bad guy . . .

Then the car ride, and being locked in this tiny room in the dark . . .

"Sadie?"

"I'm awake," she tells Lucy.

"We need you, Sades." Ryan sounds hoarse. "We got this board loose enough to make an opening. But you're the only one who's going to fit through it."

"I'm scared."

"It'll be okay," he tells her.

"I don't want to go alone!"

Lucy says, "Ryan, maybe—"

"Sadie, listen to me. You have to do this. Please. No one else can save us. If you don't go for help, we're going to die."

Sadie swallows hard.

Then she nods and says, in a small voice, "I'll do it."

Staring into Lauren Walsh's terrified eyes, Beverly knows the time has come to make up for her own past shortcomings.

This time, unlike last, she'll follow through on what Garvey asked her to do.

This time, there's no way around it. Not like before.

Fourteen years ago, Beverly had honestly believed she would do anything for Garvey. Anything at all.

She had boldly abducted a little boy from his own

suburban backyard. She had traveled overseas with him under false identification. She had gone along with Garvey's scheme, pretending to be Jeremy's mother at the foreign hospital, assuring him he was going to be just fine when, sobbing in terror, he was wheeled into surgery.

She had done it all for Garvey, because she loved him, had loved him from the moment they met. It was a bitter cliché—the dashing, married politician and the naïve campaign aide. Stories like theirs had been played out in bedrooms and headlines all over the world.

He was a family man; he told her he'd never leave his wife.

"But I'll be there for you," he promised Beverly. Because of him, she had a job, a place to live, someone to love.

She'd had a lousy childhood, a lonely life. Her father abandoned her mother; her mother killed herself. The only person who ever took care of Beverly was her older cousin Joanne. She's been dead for years, though. Now Beverly looks out for Joanne's daughter, Sharon, keeping her deathbed promise.

And Garvey looks out for Beverly. She vowed never to ask more from him than he was willing to give; in return, she would give him anything he wanted.

Almost anything.

When the time came to prove her loyalty, she crumbled.

She couldn't bring herself to kill the little boy who had been terrified of her at first, and now clung to her hand on the crowded streets of Bombay.

"All you have to do is triple up on his pain meds tonight," Garvey told her. "Maybe quadruple, just to be sure. Then tuck him into bed and go straight to the airport. Your flight leaves at eleven. By the time the hotel maid finds him, you'll be safe in New York. No one there will have any way of tracing you."

He'd made sure of that. No one she'd encountered in India knew her real name. She'd never get caught.

But that wouldn't change the fact that she'd have killed an innocent child in the process of saving another.

How could Garvey live with himself?

How could she?

That was the first time she'd ever toyed with the idea of taking her own life, as her mother had.

Mom had put a gun into her mouth and pulled the trigger. Beverly found her, and the note that read simply, *Suicide is painless.*

But it didn't have to be that violent. Maybe she could just swallow a handful of pills along with Jeremy.

Suicide is painless . . .

The idea was much more appealing than killing him and living with her conscience afterward.

Or not killing him and being abandoned by Garvey as a result. She couldn't live without Garvey.

But in the end, she realized there might be an alternative to both those grim scenarios.

She tucked some money into Jeremy's pocket and took him for a long walk. With his dark hair and eyes, he blended in with the hordes of children on the teeming streets of Bombay—so many of them orphans or beggars.

When he turned his head to watch an elephant plod slowly by, Beverly slipped away.

She caught her flight back to the States. Garvey called her right after she landed.

"Did you take care of it?"

She hesitated only briefly. "Yes," she told him. "I took care of it."

Maybe not in the way he'd asked, but for all intents and purposes, Jeremy Cavalon had vanished forever.

And Beverly still had Garvey in her life.

Lauren pointedly shifts her eyes to a point just beyond the right shoulder of the woman she knew as Jessica. She focuses hard on the empty doorway behind her, as if someone is standing there.

She can tell Jessica is unnerved, but she doesn't turn around. "Now, Lauren, do you want to do this the easy way, or the hard way?"

"What do you mean?"

"I mean, do you want to tell me what I need to know, or do I have to force it out of you? Because the children aren't alone. All I have to do is give the word that you refuse to cooperate, and one of them will be shot."

A wave of nausea swishes through Lauren's gut, but she manages to stay strong. She keeps her eyes on the empty doorway.

"I will," she says. "I'll cooperate."

Jessica frowns, watching Lauren closely.

This is it. I have her.

Still focused on the doorway, Lauren gives a slight nod, as if signaling someone.

Sure enough, Jessica darts a glance over her shoulder.

In one swift movement Lauren lunges for the floor, snatches a large, dagger-shaped shard of glass, and plunges it into the woman's right arm—the one holding the gun.

With a howl, Jessica drops the weapon. Lauren grabs it and scrambles backward across the floor with it, slicing her bare legs on the broken glass.

Aiming the gun in both outstretched hands, Lauren sees that the woman's right arm is bleeding badly.

Clutching it with her left hand, blood pouring over her fingers, she looks up at Lauren in fury.

"Tell me where my children are, or I'll kill you." Lauren fights to keep the gun steady in her hands.

"No, you won't," Jessica says calmly. "You can't. Because without me, you'll never find them."

Lauren wants to cry out in frustration. She's right. There's no way Lauren is going to pull the trigger now.

But . . . there might just be another way to get control of the situation.

"How do I even know they're still alive?" she asks.

"You don't. But they are. And you'll see them again when you give me the stuffed animal."

Lauren weighs her options.

It's a huge gamble.

Yes, and it might pay off.

But if it doesn't . . .

What choice do you have?

"I can't give it to you, Jessica. I wish I could . . . but I can't."

"You mean you *won't* and you're a fool."

"No, I mean I *can't* . . . because I already gave it to the police."

Jessica doesn't utter a word, but she pales.

Now who's the fool?

It's working. Lauren can sense the wheels turning.

"Come on," she says, "did you think I was stupid enough not to realize what I had in my possession?"

"But how . . . ?"

Careful, Lauren. Don't let on. Careful what you say.

"Seriously . . . who's going to kill anyone over a plain old stuffed animal? I knew there was something more to it. I figured it out, and I turned it over to the police. They *know*."

It's working. She can see the stark fear in those odd yellow eyes.

"They know everything, Jessica. Right now, they're surrounding the house. They can hear us. Any second now, they're going to storm in here and arrest you."

"Nooooooo!" Jessica lunges for her, grabs for the gun.

They tumble to the floor, rolling over broken glass.

Lauren struggles to hang on to the weapon, but the woman wrestles it away. She heaves herself to her feet and stands over Lauren, breathing hard.

And Lauren watches in horror as she takes aim and pulls the trigger.

A splinter rips into Sadie's hand as she pulls herself through the narrow crack created by the loose board, and she cries out in pain.

"What happened?"

"Are you all right?"

Hearing her brother and sister calling to her from the other side of the wall, Sadie longs to go back to them. But she can't. Not now.

"I'm okay," she tells them, and gets to her feet.

She looks around. She's standing in front of a small wooden storage shed, and it appears to be entirely surrounded by trees and brush.

"What do you see, Sades?" Ryan asks.

"The woods. That's it. We're in the middle of the woods."

"Is there a road or something?"

"No," she tells Lucy. Then—"Wait, maybe."

Not a road . . . a path. And a faint one at that, overgrown with vines and grass. It disappears into the shadows among the trees.

But it looks like the only way out. Sadie has no choice but to take it.

Shaken, Lauren greets the police officers at the door. They'd arrived almost immediately; she had dialed 911 moments after Jessica put the gun into her mouth and killed herself just minutes ago.

"Ma'am, are you all right? We have a report of—"

"She's in there!" Lauren points toward the kitchen, fighting to keep the hysteria out of her voice. "I don't know who she is. She took my children. And—oh my God, Sam. There's a body out in my backyard. Please . . ."

With dizzying speed, the scene transforms. Suddenly, there are uniforms swarming everywhere, squawking radios, yellow tape. Through it all, Lauren struggles to remain coherent.

An ambulance wails up. She learns that Sam was indeed shot, but he's clinging to life.

"Is he going to make it?" Lauren asks in dread.

"Hard to tell. We need to get him stabilized."

A detective wants a statement, searching for a motive.

"Did she ask for ransom?"

"No . . . a toy. A pink stuffed dog that belonged to my daughter," she tells him, dazed. "My ex-husband mistakenly picked it up from the lost and found in Grand Central, and—"

Her throat closes as she remembers. Nick. Beth.

"She killed them, too. Oh God, my children . . . please, you have to find my children."

"Ma'am, we'll do everything we can. Do you have any idea where this toy is?"

"Yes." Her head snaps up. "I think I know."

She's already on her feet, heading for the stairs.

* * *

Having followed the path until it came to an end at a narrow, tree-lined dirt lane, Sadie isn't sure where to turn.

Either way, the road winds its way into deep, dark woods.

In one direction are only muddy ruts.

In the other, fresh tire marks.

The crazy lady must have driven away in that direction. If Sadie follows the tire marks, they'll lead right to her.

Sadie shudders.

I never want to see her again.

Mind made up, she turns in the opposite direction.

Trailed by the detective and a uniformed officer, Lauren makes her way to Sadie's room.

Sure enough, the shelves, bed, tabletop, and dresser are far less cluttered than usual. There's no sign of the Dora pillow, the Barbie dolls . . . or the dog.

Lauren walks over to the closet and opens the door.

Her heart is pounding.

"Do you have a flashlight?" she asks the men, and one is quickly produced for her.

She crouches and shines the beam along the wall at the back of the closet, beyond the hanging clothes. Her fingertips find the hidden latch on what looks like a panel of molding.

It's actually a door, built into the house more than a century ago.

Opening it, Lauren shines the light inside the secret cubby.

There, sure enough, is the Dora pillow. She pulls it out.

A couple of Barbie dolls tumble to the floor.

"Oh, Sadie. Oh, my little girl."

"Steady there, Mrs. Walsh." The detective lays a gentle hand on her shoulder. "You okay?"

Okay? Is she okay? Her children are missing, their father has been murdered, her friend is clinging to life, and a woman blew her brains out before Lauren's eyes.

Lauren doesn't bother to speak. There's nothing to say.

She sniffles, wipes the stream of tears from her eyes, and again directs the flashlight's beam into the space behind the closet wall.

This time, she sees it.

Pink fur.

"Congressman Quinn?"

About to step into his limousine after Marin, Garvey turns to see a stranger in a dark suit coat.

The man flashes a badge.

More security. Good. Garvey can use it. The street is filled with press, and cops, and stem cell research supporters, chanting wildly and waving signs of protest.

But this security guard isn't looking at the crowd; he's looking at Garvey. And his eyes are cold.

"I need you to come with me, Congressman."

Garvey stares at him. And in that instant, he knows.

It's all over.

"What's going on?" Marin asks from inside the car. "Garvey?"

He can't bring himself to look back at her as the detective leads him away.

It's been over an hour since the police back in Glenhaven Park examined the stuffed toy and found a memory stick hidden in the stuffing.

On it was evidence of some sort of scandal involving

Congressman Garvey Quinn. The woman who lay dead on Lauren's kitchen floor was Beverly Madsen, a long-time campaign aide of Quinn's.

The congressman was questioned and claimed not to know where the children are, but guessed that Madsen might have taken them to a place called Greymeadow. Beverly Madsen once resided in the guesthouse of his family's long-unused country estate, about twenty miles north of Glenhaven Park.

That's as much as Lauren was told before she was hustled into a police cruiser that now barrels up the Taconic Parkway, sirens wailing.

She doesn't really care about the rest of the details surrounding the case, as long as her children are safe.

Please, she prays as the car slows. Gray stone pillars mark a rutted, tree-shaded country lane, and there's an enormous wrought-iron gate with elaborate grillwork etched with the word "GREYMEADOW."

Please let them be alive . . .

Sitting shoulder to shoulder with Lucy in the darkness, Ryan thinks bleakly about all the things he never got to do.

The fishing trip . . .

A Yankee game . . .

Xbox with Ian . . .

A double summersault off the high dive . . .

A sound reaches his ears.

He frowns, listening.

It's the distant hum of a helicopter.

"Lucy?"

"Yeah," she whispers. "I hear it."

They listen for a long time, and the helicopter fades away.

But now there are voices. And a dog is barking.

Someone is out there.

This is it.

Either Sadie managed to go for help . . .

Or their kidnapper is back and they're about to die.

"Lucy! Ryan! Sadie!" a voice calls.

A male voice. Not *hers*.

"Lucy! Ry—"

"In here!" Ryan bellows, and his sister starts to sob.

He hears scrambling outside, and now the dog is barking excitedly, and there are other voices, and walkie-talkies.

"Stand back from the door!" a man calls. "Do you hear me, kids? Get back as far as you can!"

Ryan grabs his sister's hand and the two of them move to the wall opposite the door—only a few feet away.

There's a loud, whacking sound. Axe on wood.

Then the door splinters and is gone. Light streams in.

Daylight. So strange, after what felt like endless hours of imprisonment. Ryan could have sworn it would be the middle of the night. Maybe it's tomorrow.

There are police officers, about a million of them.

"Everyone all right?" the closest one asks, helping Ryan outside.

He blinks against the glare.

"I'm okay," he hears Lucy say. "You have to call my mother. Please . . ."

"Where's the little one?" somebody asks. "Where's Sadie?"

His eyes accustomed to the light at last, Ryan sees the cops looking at each other and shrugging.

"Isn't Sadie the one who told you where to find us? We sent her for help."

Ryan can tell the answer by their expressions, and his heart sinks.

"We got 'em!"

Hearing the message squawk over the police radio, Lauren bolts from the cruiser parked at the foot of the overgrown path into the woods.

"Wait, Mrs. Walsh . . ." Behind her, the nice young officer hurries to get out of the car.

Lauren has no intention of waiting.

Vines twine around her legs as she runs up the uneven path; twice she falls and picks herself up again, hurtling forward. Her knees rip open against the rocks, her palms, too, are torn and bleeding. She can still feel the agonizing cuts all over her body from the ground glass on her kitchen floor, but the physical pain means nothing. Nothing at all. She can bear anything but the loss of her children.

At last she emerges in a tiny clearing.

There's a small wooden shack, and there are cops, and dogs, and . . .

"Lucy! Ryan!"

"Mom!" they scream in unison, and Lauren dives toward them.

Thank God, thank God, thank God . . .

She hugs them hard, and she kisses their hair, and she looks around for Sadie, too . . .

A chill shoots through her.

Uniformed officers are gathered in small, concerned knots, looking off into the trees, searching the ground.

"Where is Sadie?" Lauren asks frantically. "Oh God, where is she?"

"She went for help, Mom," Lucy tells her.

"She was so brave." Tears are streaming down Ryan's face. "She didn't want to go, but we made her."

"Sadie!" Lauren shouts, and renewed dread creeps over her. "Sadie!"

Thirsty, exhausted, bug-bitten, bleeding from where she scraped the splinter out of her hand, Sadie sits with her back against a big tree, worried about her brother and sister.

Lucy and Ryan are counting on her to save them, but how?

She's been walking in circles, and the woods are getting darker and darker, and she keeps hearing rustling in the branches surrounding her.

Lions? Tigers? Bears?

If night comes, they're going to get her.

Mommy said they won't . . .

But that was back at home, in her room, where it was safe. Now she's lost in the middle of the jungle, all alone.

Ryan was right. She should have told the bad lady the truth—that she had snuck back down the stairs that day and taken the pink stuffed dog out of the tag sale box. That she couldn't bear to part with it, because even though it wasn't Fred, her father had given it to her.

But now look what's happened, all because she told a lie.

Sadie wipes tears from her eyes, and the salt stings the cut on her hand.

She has to keep moving, but in which direction?

She forces herself back to her feet, brushes off her shorts, and looks around.

Nothing but trees.

This is it.

She's had enough.

She wants to go home.

Opening her mouth, she screams out the one word that's been on her mind since she ventured out on her own.

"Mommmmmmyyyyy!"

Staring at a rare, smiling picture of her son standing between her and Brett, Elsa recalls that it was taken on the day the adoption became official.

Even now, she's amazed to note how much Jeremy resembles her, with his dark hair and eyes. No one ever questioned that she'd given birth to him.

Somewhere out there, the woman who did must have the same questions that cross Elsa's mind every day.

Where is Jeremy?

What does he look like now?

Is he happy?

Is he alive?

His birth mother has no real reason to wonder about that last one, though.

Elsa had briefly toyed with the idea of trying to find her after Jeremy disappeared, to let her know what had happened. But she opted not to.

She's not sure why. Maybe she resented the woman whose gene pool might have contributed to Jeremy's problems. Maybe she didn't want to meet someone who had willingly given away the child Elsa would give anything to hold in her arms. Maybe she was worried that if she let Jeremy's birth mother into their lives, she'd have to share him when he came back home.

It wasn't until last winter, facing the prospect of returning to New England, that Elsa changed her mind.

She called Mike.

"Can you find her?"

"I can sure as hell try."

The records were sealed. But there are ways of getting around any obstacles, Mike told her, if you're not hung up on legalities.

Mike isn't.

But if he did manage to find out the birth mother's identity, he's chosen not to share it with Elsa.

It's probably just as well. What good would it do now?

Staring off into space, Elsa remembers how she'd considered the born-again impatiens as some kind of sign about Jeremy.

Wrong again, she thinks, closing the photo album and wiping tears from her eyes.

"*Mommmmmmyyyyy!*"

Of course there's no reply.

The only sounds are the birds calling to one another overhead, the crickets and frogs chirping; a breeze rustling the leaves; and the lions and tigers and bears prowling around in the shadows beyond the trees, waiting for the sun to go down so that they can attack Sadie.

"*Mommmmmmyyyyy! Help me!*"

But it's no use. Mommy is a million miles away.

Sadie is never going to see her again.

Or Daddy.

Or Ryan, or Lucy. She tried to save them, but she couldn't. The bad lady is going to come back and shoot them. Maybe she has already. Maybe she's killed Mommy, too, and Daddy . . .

Maybe I'm alone forever.

A tear plops onto Sadie's scraped and dirty leg. And then another. And then . . .

Suddenly, she hears something.

A shrill, high-pitched whistle.

For a moment, she thinks it came from a bird.

But then she hears a far-off shout.

Did someone hear her calling for her mother?

Is someone out there?

Is it the lady with the gun?

Sadie dives into the brush and lies flat on her stomach, as still as she can be.

After a long time, she hears movement in the brush. If it's animals, there are a lot of them. And a dog is barking, and then she hears a shout.

"Sadie!"

Someone knows her name!

"Sadie Walsh! Where are you?"

That isn't Mommy's voice, but it isn't the crazy lady's, either.

"I'm here!" she cries out, and the next thing she knows, there are policemen.

And, at last, her mother comes running toward her, arms outstretched.

"Sadie," Mommy sobs, "Sadie, are you okay?"

"Not really. I got a splinter, and my legs are bleeding, and I have to pee really bad."

Mommy laughs for some reason, laughs and cries and hugs her close, and Sadie knows everything is going to be okay.

Two days later, Lauren tentatively walks down the hospital corridor toward Sam Henning's room, a bouquet of flowers in her hand. She had thought of cutting some from her yard, but that didn't seem like a great idea, under the circumstances. So she'd stopped off at the florist in the strip mall on the way over. Naturally, she ran into countless people she knows, and they all stared.

The news coverage has been nonstop for forty-eight hours now, given Congressman Garvey Quinn's involvement. As his career crashes and burns around him, bits and pieces of a shocking truth—a mistress, an illegitimate son, a blackmail plot—have emerged. The puzzle is far from complete, but it has, predictably, consumed the scandal-loving New York press.

Alyssa came this morning and picked up Lucy, Ryan, and Sadie and drove them upstate to their grandparents' house to keep them away from the media firestorm. Lauren, who is also headed up there later, can't bear for them to see their father's picture plastered all over the media. Right now, Nick and Beth are missing persons connected with the case.

Dogs picked up their scent at Greymeadow, and the police are searching the vast property for their bodies.

Lauren doesn't know how, or when, she's going to tell her children that their father is gone. Without evidence, it seems pointless—though she knows in her heart that Beverly spoke the truth about the double murder.

She's going to have to find Nick's mother, too. Wherever she is, she deserves to know she's lost a child.

As for Lucy, Ryan, and Sadie . . . they're going to have a rough road ahead. But they're strong—so much stronger than Lauren ever imagined. Her babies . . .

Every time Lauren thinks about what they've been through . . .

But it could have been so much worse.

A nurse steps out of Sam's room, sees Lauren, and raises her eyebrows. "You're the woman from TV. The brave mom with the three kids who were kidnapped."

"That's me." Lauren offers a tight smile.

"And you're here to see Sam, right?"

"Yes."

"We're only supposed to allow family, but I know he'll be glad to see you." The nurse offers a conspiratorial wink. "Go on in."

"Thank you."

Lauren walks into the room. Sam is lying in bed, heavily bandaged and hooked up to an IV. He turns his head, sees her.

"Oh man, do you ever owe me one." His voice is weak, but there's a gleam in his eye.

Lauren crosses to the bed. "I'm so sorry this happened to you."

"Yeah, you're not the only one," he says ruefully. "There I was, trying to impress you and rescue your kids, and . . . guess I pretty much suck as a superhero, huh?"

Lauren can't help but smile. "Practice makes perfect."

"Perfect is overrated," he returns. Then he asks, "How about you? Are *you* okay?"

"Not really," she tells him. "But I will be."

She honestly believes that.

Sam must, too, because the smile is back in his eyes. "In that case, how about dinner some night, when we're both okay?"

Lauren hesitates. She wants to say yes, but who in their right mind starts dating someone under circumstances like this? Talk about being jinxed from the start . . .

"I took a bullet for you," Sam points out. "The least you can do is go out with me."

"I bet you say that to all the girls."

"Is that a yes?"

"Yes."

"Good."

Lauren stays at his bedside until the nurse pokes her head in again, with a gentle reminder that the patient needs his rest.

"Come back and see me again, Lauren, will you?"

"Sure. Bye, Sam."

She takes the elevator back downstairs. Waiting in line to buy a token for the parking booth, she glances over at the gift shop across the lobby—and can't believe her eyes.

There, in the window, is a pink plush rabbit.

Of course. A visitor brought the original stuffed toy, festooned with a Mylar "It's a Girl" balloon, to Lauren's bedside when Sadie was born here four years ago. Whoever it was must have picked it up in the gift shop, which obviously doesn't change inventory very often.

Forgetting the parking token, Lauren hurries over to the shop.

The woman behind the counter looks up. "Yes? Can I help you?"

"Absolutely," Lauren tells her with a bittersweet smile.

A few minutes later, she steps out into the summer sunshine with a pink stuffed bunny in her arms.

"Come on, Fred. Let's go home."

Sitting with the photo album open on her lap, a cup of tea on the table beside her, Elsa studies the picture of her husband and son. They're dressed almost alike: polo shirts, khaki slacks. Behind them, against a rolling green backdrop, is a sign that reads "Harbor Hills Golf." Brett's hand is resting on Jeremy's shoulder, and he's smiling.

At a glance, Jeremy appears to be smiling as well.

But now, looking closer, Elsa can see that it's more of a smirk. Why didn't she notice that before now?

At the time, she remembers, she was simply relieved that they'd made it to the golf course at all, after the usual morning drama. That he actually agreed to pose with Brett—and cracked a grin at her "Say cheese"—had seemed too good to be true.

Jeremy didn't want golf lessons.

"Do it for me," she begged him, and, when that didn't work, "Do it for Daddy."

That didn't work, either. He went, kicking and screaming—literally. It wasn't unusual. It was the way Elsa got him to school some mornings, and to whatever doctor he was seeing at the time.

When they got to the golf course, Brett was waiting. Jeremy underwent one of his miraculous temporary transformations.

But it didn't last for long. God, no.

Elsa shudders, remembering.

That was the day she realized Jeremy needed more help than they'd been giving him. Serious help.

She'll never forget the sight of him marching off onto the green with the madras-clad instructor and a quartet of eager junior golfers, one an adorable little girl with blond braids swinging behind her.

Nor will Elsa ever forget the bloodcurdling screams that reached her ears a half hour later, as she and Brett sat waiting, sipping gin and tonics with the other parents.

One of the kids, ashen-faced, came dashing down to the clubhouse bellowing, "Call 911! Hurry!"

All hell broke loose.

Elsa remembers tearing across the plush grass in heels, her heart in her mouth, fearing that something had happened to Jeremy.

Brett beat her to the scene. By the time she made it there, people were hovering around a crumpled figure on the ground—the little girl with blond braids, now streaked with red.

Anguished screams from the child's mother, chaotic voices all around.

"What happened to her?"

"Is she breathing?"

"Does anyone know CPR?"

Brett turned to look at Elsa, and the moment she saw his face, she knew. Knew even before she spotted Jeremy, standing there with the bloody seven-iron still in his hand.

"What did you do?" Brett hollered at him, as medics carried away the unconscious child.

"I didn't mean it. She laughed at me, and I got mad."

The child survived, thank God.

And so, somehow, did Elsa and Brett.

But Jeremy . . .

Less than six months later, Jeremy was gone.

Elsa closes the book and sits, for a long time, looking back.

Maybe it's time she stopped doing that.

Maybe it's time she started looking ahead after all. Maybe it's time she gave serious thought to the question that's been floating around for a while now, in the back of her mind, where Jeremy lives.

Have you ever considered another child, Elsa?

And hope, like the dangling ribbons of a helium balloon on a soft summer breeze, drifts back within her grasp at last.

Epilogue

Dallas, Texas

The sun is blistering hot today as he steps out of the air-conditioned pickup truck in front of the barbecue joint out on North Stemmons.

His boots kick up a cloud of dust from the parking lot to the front door, and sweat breaks out on his forehead beneath the brim of his Stetson. He's never been big on hats, but when in Rome . . .

Stepping over the threshold, he's greeted by a welcome blast of air-conditioning and a decidedly unwelcome blast of honky-tonk music.

Damned Texans.

"Hello there, sugar." The hostess is teased and dyed and primped to death, with a pair of double Ds sticking halfway out of her denim shirt. "All by your lonesome?"

He shrugs. He's been alone for just about as long as he can remember, but never lonesome.

There are women. They always come into his life willingly—and some leave that way as well, never knowing his secret, but perhaps sensing that something is off.

The ones who don't . . . well, they leave, too. He gets rid of most the easy way—"It's not you, it's me . . . I'm not ready for a serious relationship . . . I think we both need to see other people . . ."

Some women are more tenacious than others, though. Stubborn. Nosy. Asking too many questions. He takes care of them the hard way . . .

Then again, is it really so hard at all, anymore?

You do what has to be done, and then you wash your hands and you move on.

He heard that somewhere, a very long time ago. It stuck with him. It's served him well.

The hostess consults her clipboard. "Gonna be about a ten-minute wait. You wanna step over there into the bar and have a cold one till I call you?"

"Why not?"

"You sure you're twenty-one?"

"Hay-ell, yes." Tossing her a look, he walks toward the bar.

"Wait, sugar?"

He turns to see the hostess with a pen poised over the clipboard.

"I need your name."

"It's Jeremy."

Turn the page for a preview of

SCARED TO DEATH,

the next suspenseful page-turner
from *New York Times* bestselling author

Wendy Corsi Staub

Coming Soon
From Avon Books

Dallas, Texas
September

Mind if I turn on the TV?"

Hell, yes, Jeremy minds.

Minds the disruption of television and minds suddenly having a roommate.

Until an hour ago, when an orderly pushed a wheelchair through the doorway, Jeremy had the double hospital room all to himself. He should have known that was too good to be true.

Most good things are.

An image flashes into his head, and he winces.

Funny how, even after all these years, that same face—a beautiful, female face—pops in and out of his consciousness. He doesn't know whose face it is, or whether she even exists.

"Hey, are you in pain?" the stranger in the next bed asks, interrupting Jeremy's speculation about the face: *Is she a figment of my imagination—or an actual memory?*

He almost welcomes the question whose answer is readily at hand.

Am I in pain?

Hell, yes. He feels as though every bone in his face has been broken—and that's pretty damned near the truth.

"I can ring the nurse for you," the man offers, waving his good hand. The other hand—like Jeremy's face—is swathed in gauze. Some kind of finger surgery, he mentioned when he first rolled into the room, as if Jeremy might care.

Reaching for the bedrail buzzer, he adds, in his lazy twang, "That Demerol's good stuff, ain't it?"

Yeah, and I wish you'd take some and knock yourself out.

Aloud, Jeremy only says, "No, thanks," and shakes his head.

Bad idea. The slightest movement above the neck rockets pain through his skull. He fights the instinct to scream; that would be even more torturous.

"You sure you're okay, pal? You looked like you were hurting for a minute there. Before. I saw you wince."

Jeremy's jaw tightens—more agony. Dammit. Why won't this fool leave him alone? Doesn't he realize it's a bad idea to stick your nose where it doesn't belong?

"You don't have to be a hero, you know. If you're in pain, all you need to do is—"

"I'm fine," Jeremy manages to interrupt, in an almost civil tone. "Really. Just—go ahead, turn on the TV."

"You sure? Because if it'll bother you I don't want to—"

"I'm positive. Watch TV."

"Yeah? Thanks." Working the remote with his unbandaged hand, his roommate channel surfs.

Face throbbing, Jeremy gazes absently at the barrage of images on the changing screen, half-hearing the snippets of sound from the speaker above his bed. Audience applause, country music, gunfire, a sitcom laugh track, meaningless words.

"... *ladies and gentlemen, please welcome ...*"

"... *be mostly sunny with a high of ...*"

"... *and the Emmy-nominated drama will return on ...*"

His roommate pauses to ask, "Anything in particular you feel like watching?"

"Nope."

"You a sports fan?"

"Sometimes."

"Rangers?"

"Sure," Jeremy lies.

"News should be on. Let's see if we can get us some scores."

More channel surfing.

More fleeting images.

More meaningless sound, then . . .

" . . . *in Manhattan today indicted Congressman Garvey Quinn for . . .*"

"Here's the news." The clicking stops. "I'll leave it. Sports should be coming up soon."

"Great." As if Jeremy gives a damn about sports, or the news, or—unlike the rest of the world, it seems—television in general.

"You don't know what you're missing," someone—Lisa?—once said to him.

She was right. And when you grow up deprived of something, you can't miss it.

Or can you?

" . . . *kidnapping the seven-year-old son of Elsa and Brett Cavalon. In an incredible twist, the child . . .*"

A close-up flashes on the screen: a photograph of a striking couple. The woman . . .

Jeremy gasps, his body involuntarily jerking to sit up.

"What?" Glancing over, his roommate immediately mutes the volume. "What's wrong? It's the pain, right? I knew it!"

Jeremy can't speak, can't move, can only stare at the face on TV. It's as if the pain exploding inside Jeremy's head has catapulted a fragment of his imagination onto the screen. Of course, that's impossible.

But so is this, unless . . .

As suddenly as she appeared on the screen, she's gone, and the camera shifts back to the anchorman.

Unless . . .

Unless she's real.

She was there. On TV.

She does exist. She has a name—one he's heard before in another place, another time . . .

Now, the name—*her* name—echoes back at him from the darkest recesses of his mind.

Elsa.

Groton, Connecticut
June

"Mommy . . ."

Elsa Cavalon stirs in her sleep.

Jeremy.

Jeremy is calling me.

"Mommy!"

No. Jeremy is gone, remember?

There was a time when that renewed awareness would have jarred her fully awake. But it's been fifteen years since her son disappeared, and almost a year since Elsa learned that he'd been murdered shortly afterward.

The terrible truth came as no surprise. Throughout the dark era of worrying and wondering, she'd struggled to keep hope alive, while knowing in her heart that Jeremy was never coming home again. All those years she'd longed for closure.

When it came last August, she had braced herself, expecting her already fragile emotions to hit bottom.

Instead, somehow, she found peace.

"It's because you've already done your grieving," her therapist, Joan, told her. "You're in the final stage now. Acceptance."

Yes. She accepts that Jeremy is no longer alive, accepts that she is, and—

"Mommy!"

Jeremy isn't calling you. It's just a dream. Go back to sleep . . .

"What's wrong?" Brett's voice, not imagined, plucks Elsa from the drowsy descent toward slumber. Her eyelids pop open.

The light is dim; her husband is stirring beside her in bed, calling out to a child who isn't Jeremy, "What is it? Are you okay?"

"I need Mommy."

"She's sleeping. What's wrong?"

"No, Brett, I'm awake," she murmurs, sitting up, and calls, "Renny, I'm awake."

"Mommy, I need you!"

Elsa gets up and feels her way across the room as Brett mumbles something and settles back into the pillows. With a prickle of envy-tinged resentment, she hears him snoring again by the time she reaches the hallway.

It was always this way, back when Jeremy was here to disrupt their wee-hour rest—and when his palpable, tragic absence disrupted it even more. All those sleepless nights . . .

Brett would make some halfhearted attempt to respond to whatever was going on, then fall immediately back to sleep, leaving Elsa wide awake to cope alone with the matter at hand: a needy child, parental doubt, haunting memories, her own demons.

"Mommy!"

"I'm coming, I'm coming." Shivering, she makes her way down the hall toward Renny's bedroom.

The house is chilly. Before bed, Elsa had gone from room to room closing windows that had been open all day, with eighty-degree sunshine falling through the screens. Late spring in coastal New England can be so unpredictable.

And yet Elsa wouldn't trade it for the more temperate climates where Brett's work as a nautical engineer transported them in recent years. It's good to be settled back in the northeast. This is home.

Especially now that we have Renny.

Her bedroom door is ajar, as always. Plagued by claustrophobia, she can't sleep unless it's open. That's understandable, considering what she's been through.

Whenever Elsa allows herself to think of Renny's past, she feels as though a tremendous fist has clenched her gut. It's the same sickening dread that used to seize her whenever she imagined what Jeremy had endured—both before he came into their lives, and after he was kidnapped.

But Renny isn't Jeremy. Everything about her, other than the route she traveled through the foster system and into Elsa's life, is different.

Well—almost everything. With her black hair and eyes, Renny resembles Elsa as much as Jeremy did. No one would ever doubt a biological connection between mother and child based on looks alone. But their bond goes much deeper than that. From the moment she saw the little girl, Elsa felt a connection.

And yet . . . had she felt the same thing when she first met Jeremy? There was a time, not so long ago, when her memory of her son was more vivid than the landscape beyond the window. Now it's as if the glass has warped, distorting the view.

Now.

Now . . . what?

Now that I know Jeremy is dead?

Now that there's Renny?

Elsa pushes aside a twinge of guilt.

Her daughter's arrival didn't erase the memories of her son. Of course not. She'll never forget Jeremy. But it's time to move on. Everyone says so: her husband, her therapist, even Mike Fantoni, the private eye who had finally brought the truth to light by identifying Jeremy's birth mother.

"Why would you want to meet her now?" he'd asked Elsa the last time they'd seen each other over the winter.

"I didn't say I want to . . . I said I feel like I should."

"Has she been in touch with you?"

"No."

"Then let it go," Mike advised, and for the most part Elsa has.

She finds Renny sitting up in bed, knees to chest, her worried face illuminated by the Tinkerbell nightlight plugged into the baseboard outlet.

"What's wrong, honey? Are you feeling sick?" Elsa is well aware that her daughter had eaten an entire box of Sno-caps at the new Disney princess movie Brett had taken her to see after dinner.

"Why would you let her have all that candy?" Elsa asked in dismay when he filled her in on the father-daughter evening.

"Because it's fun to spoil her."

"I know, Brett . . . but she's going to have an awful stomachache. She'll never get to sleep now."

Renny proved her wrong, drifting off within five minutes of hitting the pillow. And right now, she doesn't look sick at all . . .

She looks terrified. Her black eyes are enormous and her wiry little body quivers beneath the quilt clutched to her chin.

"I'm not sick, Mommy."

"Did you have a nightmare?" Elsa asks. It wouldn't be the first time.

"No. It was *real*."

"Well, sometimes nightmares *feel* real."

And sometimes, they *are* real. Renny knows that as well as she does. But things are different now. She's safe here with Elsa and Brett and nothing will ever hurt her again.

Elsa sits beside her daughter and folds her into an embrace. "Do you want to tell me about it?"

"It wasn't a nightmare. It was real," Renny insists, trembling. "A monster was here, in my room . . . I woke up and I saw him standing over my bed."

"It was just a bad dream, honey. There's no monster."

"Yes, there is. And when I saw him, he went out the window."

Elsa turns to follow her daughter's gaze, saying, "No, Renny, see? The window isn't even—"

Open.

But Elsa's throat constricts around the word as she stares in numb horror.

The window she'd closed and locked earlier is now, indeed, wide open—and so is the screen, creating a gaping portal to the inky night beyond.

Not a creature is stirring, not even a mouse . . .
What nursery rhyme was that?
Not that it matters.
Really, right now, the only thing that matters is getting away from the Cavalon house without being spotted. Good thing the streets are deserted at this hour; there's no one around to glimpse the dark figure stealing through the shadows.
Not a creature is stirring . . .
Damn, it's frustrating when you can't remember something that seems to be right there, teasing your brain.
Not a creature was stirring . . .

Leaning on the terrace railing, gazing at the smattering of lit windows on the Queens skyline across the East River, Marin Hartwell Quinn finds herself wishing the sun would never come up.
When it does, she'll be launched headlong into another exhausting, lonely day of single motherhood, a role she never imagined for herself.
At this time last year, the storybook Quinn family was all over the press: Marin, Garvey, and their two beautiful daughters destined to live happily-ever-after on the Upper East Side—and then, if the expected nomination came through and the election turned out predictably, in the governor's mansion . . . and someday, the White House.
But in a flash—a flash, yes, like those from the ever-present paparazzi cameras—Garvey was transported from Park Avenue to Park Row, the lower Manhattan

street that houses the notorious Metropolitan Correctional Center.

Naturally, the photographers who had dogged Congressman Quinn along the campaign trail were there to capture the moment he was hauled away in handcuffs on a public street. And when the detectives had driven off with their prisoner, sirens wailing, the press turned their cameras on Marin, still sitting, stunned, in the back seat of the limousine.

Later, she forced herself to look at the photos, to read the captions. One referred to her as "the humiliated would-be first lady," another as "a blond, blue-eyed Jackie Kennedy, shell-shocked at witnessing her husband's sudden demise on a city street."

That wasn't the first time the press had drawn a Kennedy-Quinn comparison. But while the slain JFK had remained a hero and his wife lauded as a heartbroken, dignified widow, the fallen Garvey Quinn had been exposed as a coldhearted villain—and his wife drew nothing but scorn from his disillusioned constituents.

No one seemed to grasp—or care—that Marin herself had been blindsided, that the man she loved had betrayed her—and their children—with his unspeakable crime.

She has to force herself to get up every morning—if she manages to stay in bed that long—and face the wreckage of her life.

Public contempt is nothing compared to the rest of it: grieving her firstborn; helping her surviving children cope with the realization that their father is a criminal; looking Garvey in the eye through protective prison visitor's room glass and telling him that she'll never forgive him.

With a sigh, Marin turns away from the railing. Still no hint of sunrise on the eastern horizon, but it will appear any moment now, and the day will be underway.

In the master bedroom she once shared with Garvey, Marin smooths the coverlet on her side, arranges the European throw pillows, strips out of her nightgown, and hangs it on a hook in her walk-in closet.

Beside it, Garvey's closet door remains closed, as it has been for months now. His expensive suits and shirts, shrouded in dry cleaners plastic, are presumably still inside, along with dozens of pairs of Italian leather shoes and French silk ties.

What is she supposed to do with any of it? Burn it? Give it away? Save it? For what? For whom?

She has no idea, and so his clothes hang on in a dark limbo.

Sort of like I do.

In the bathroom, Marin showers, brushes her teeth, and blow-dries her hair.

Same routine every morning, and yet, today will be different. Still a living hell, but June has arrived. Finals are over, as are the latest round of lessons and extra-curricular activities that consumed the weekends. The school year that began in the immediate aftermath of Garvey's downfall has come to an end.

This morning, instead of heading over to their private school off Fifth Avenue, Caroline and Annie will be here at home with Marin.

That means she'll have to hold herself together from dawn until long after dark. No crying. No ranting. No swallowing a couple of prescription pills and crawling into bed in the middle of the day to capture the sleep that evades her in the night.

Maybe it's better that way.

When she sleeps, she dreams.

Dreams of a little boy with big black eyes, and he's calling for her.

"Mommy . . . Mommy, please help me . . ."

Not dreams—nightmares. Because she can never help him. Nobody can.

It's too late to save Jeremy.

And maybe, Marin thinks, staring at her haggard reflection in the bathroom mirror, too late to save herself as well.

Brett yawns audibly, promptly evoking a dark glance from his wife. He belatedly covers his mouth and resumes a riveted expression. Too late.

"You're not even listening to me." Elsa's tone is more weary than irritated, and she reaches for her mug of coffee.

"I'm listening. I'm just tired. It's five in the morning, and we didn't even have to be up for another—"

"There's no way I can sleep now."

Maybe not, but *he* certainly could. In fact, after he'd dutifully gone through the entire house clutching a baseball bat, checking closets and under the beds for prowlers, he'd had every intention of climbing right back under the covers. He saw no reason to lose another moment's sleep. Even Renny had gone from frantic to drowsy, allowing Brett to tuck her back in with reassurances that there were no monsters.

Not in this house, anyway.

And the man—the monster—responsible for Jeremy's death is behind bars.

"It was just a nightmare," Brett had told Renny—and he tells Elsa the same thing now.

"But the window was open."

"Maybe you just thought you'd closed it."

She gives him a *look*. One that says, *I'm not crazy.*

He knows that, though there was a time when he'd thought . . .

No, he'd never thought Elsa was actually crazy.

But back when Jeremy was newly missing, he'd sensed that she was so distraught she might harm herself. He'd done his best to keep it from happening, and when it did—when she nearly died—he'd blamed himself.

From that moment on, he'd vowed to save his wife. From therapy to medication, from rehashing the tragedy to sidestepping the topic, from avoiding children to considering parenthood again—he'd do whatever was necessary to help Elsa recover.

Now, after a decade and a half of torture, she's finally healing—or perhaps, healed.

Renny's arrival in their lives has given her a sense of purpose again.

And yet, watching his wife with their soon-to-be-adopted child, Brett worries. She's so protective of Renny, almost . . . paranoid.

Who can blame her? Their first child was kidnapped. Murdered.

But that doesn't mean it's going to happen again.

It doesn't mean there really was someone in Renny's room in the dead of night.

"I think we should call the police," Elsa announces and Brett looks up, startled.

"You're not serious."

"I am."

"Elsa, the press is finally off our backs. Do you really want to stir it all up again?"

"The press doesn't have to be involved. I'm just talking about calling the police and—"

"And you don't think it's going to get out somehow that the mother of Jeremy Cavalon thinks someone is prowling around her new kid's bedroom?"

"New kid? Brett, how can you—"

"I'm sorry, I didn't mean it that way."

New kid. As in replacement for old kid.

God. Brett rakes a hand through his hair. That's not what he meant at all.

"If you honestly want to call the police," he tells his wife, "go ahead. You know I would never take a chance with Renata."

He sees Elsa's nose wrinkle slightly, and he knows why. Neither of them is very fond of their daughter's given name—probably because it was bestowed by her abusive parents. They shortened it, with Renny's blessing, soon after she came to live with them last fall. But sometimes, when Brett means business, he refers to her as Renata.

"Don't make yourself nuts with this, Elsa." Brett reaches out and pats her thin shoulder. "Everything is fine. Renny is fine. There's nothing to worry about."

"There's always something to worry about when you have a child."

"Yes, but not . . . not like that. Not what you're thinking."

Elsa just looks at him. She can be stubborn.

So can he. "Look, there's no reason to call the police because a window was open."

"How did it get open?"

"Maybe Renny sleepwalked and did it herself."

Elsa tilts her head. Clearly, she hadn't thought of that.

Brett hadn't either, until it popped out, but who knows? Maybe it's true. And if it's not, there are countless other explanations for the open window. Explanations that don't involve a prowler creeping around their daughter's bedroom.

Brett presses on. "Elsa, think about it. The adoption isn't even finalized. You don't want to risk it, do you? A police report is going to go on the records."

Something else she hadn't thought of.

Brett glimpses a spark of uncertainty in her dark eyes. He's winning her over. Good. And yet, what if . . . ?

No, he tells himself firmly. *Just like you told Elsa— and Renny, too—there's nothing to worry about. Nothing at all.*

The car is parked on a quiet waterside street several blocks from the Cavalon home—a perfect spot, near the marina. Fishermen, rising in the wee hours to pursue the day's catch, often leave their cars here.

It would have probably been a good idea to have some poles and a tackle box in the back seat, just in case some-one came along.

Oh, well. Next time.

The engine turns over with a quiet rumble and the tires make a faint crunching sound on the gravelly road.

Mission accomplished.

Almost.

Not a creature was stirring, not even a mouse . . .

What the heck is the rest of it?

Not even a mouse . . .

Not even a mouse . . .

Oh, the next line is, *The children are nestled all snug in their beds . . .*

Ha. Isn't that fitting? Renny Cavalon certainly was nestled all snug in her bed just a short time ago.

Then she opened her eyes, took one look, and screamed.

No wonder.

That hideous rubber mask—now tucked safely into the glove compartment—would scare anyone to death, loom-ing over them in the dead of night.

Night . . .

Night . . .

'Twas the Night Before Christmas . . .

That's it!

It wasn't a nursery rhyme after all; it was a storybook.

Is Elsa planning to read it to Renny when the holidays roll around?

Ha. Come December, Renny will be long gone.

Just like Jeremy.